PRAISE FOR THE WORK OF
JAMES ALEXANDER THOM

SAINT PATRICK'S BATTALION

"A hell of a book... a world-class writer." – *Kurt Vonnegut*

"Not only a striking (and often horrific) account of pre–Civil War army life, Quinn's narrative beautifully conveys the boy's coming of age against a backdrop of eerily familiar war and rebellion. ...a stirring tale that does everything that smart historical fiction ought to do: illuminating the past while throwing new light on the present."
– *Starred Review, Publishers Weekly*

"Noted historical novelist Thom takes a painful period in American history and treats it with great imagination and verve..., this fine novel makes for gripping reading." – *Joanne Wilkinson, Booklist*

FROM SEA TO SHINING SEA

"Splendid...Thom tells the story with humor and eloquence, and a thumping good tale it is, too." – *The Washington Post*

THE RED HEART

"A spellbinding journey into America's past." – *Sharyn McCrumb*, author of *King's Mountain* and *The Devil Amongst the Lawyers*

PANTHER IN THE SKY

"What particularly distinguishes this splendidly vigorous and imaginative recreation of the life of the great Shawnee chief Tecumseh (1768-1813) is its bid to capture the spirit of Midwestern Indian culture from within." – *Publishers Weekly*

"...Thom states he "was looking especially for insights into the culture, morality, ceremony, and psychic condition of the Shawnee people in the time of their greatest crisis." He seems to have found them, as the characters are alive and believable."
– *Andrea Lee Shuey, Dallas P.L., Library Journal*

"In all, then: popular historical fiction at its best." – *Kirkus Reviews*

"Thom shows how, in honest, capable hands, fictionalized biography can add verisimilitude to the life and times of this extraordinary American... . The dialogue has the ring of reality about it... . Thom is able to get into the thoughts and emotions of his characters..."
– *Dee Brown, Los Angeles Times*

Follow the River

"It takes a rare individual not only to see that history can live, but also to make it live for others. James Thom has that gift."
– *The Indianapolis News*

Warrior Woman (Co-Authored with Dark Rain Thom)

"Collaborating for the first time on fiction with his Shawnee wife, Thom adds to his gallery of Native American heroes a woman whose character transcends her culture, but whose culture gives her incomparable skills, strengths, beauty and insights. Stirring, often bitter, but ultimately uplifting." – *Kirkus Reviews*

"...impressive research and well-rounded characters give the novel force and breadth." – *Publishers Weekly*

"...the Thoms have vibrantly enriched the chief's story, keeping alive a remarkable figure from a painful period in American history."
– *Deborah Donovan, Booklist*

Sign-Talker

"Very readable, fresh, original, and vivid." – *Larry McMurtry*

"The majesty of the scenery, the wonder of the stately tribes who greet, and menace, the expedition and the expedition's mix of soldiers, ne'er-do-wells, and French traders all combine to produce a strong novel about the days when Missouri was at the edge of the map."
– *The Kansas City Star*

"Authentically detailed and populated with a cast of celebrated real-life characters, this stirring tale of tragedy and triumph will captivate fans of epic historical fiction." – *Margaret Flanagan, Booklist*

"James Alexander Thom . . . make[s] the story of North America come alive. He puts flesh and blood on forgotten names, and he breathes life into the stale past. He is probably the most important author of American historic novels writing today because he helps to interpret the distant past for the mind and interest of the modern reader."
– *Jack Weatherford,* author of *Indian Givers*

FIRE IN THE WATER

"James Alexander Thom, author of such classics as *Panther in the Sky* and *The Red Heart*, is one of our finest and most entertaining historical novelists. His new *Fire in the Water* is a powerful recreation of the days after the death of Lincoln, and two men's commitment to go through fire and water to honor their fallen hero."
– *Dan Wakefield,* author of *Under the Apple Tree: A World War II Home Front Novel* and editor of *Kurt Vonnegut: Letters*

"If Mark Twain could have imagined that the curse of slavery would still be tearing our nation apart a century and a half after the end of the Civil War, he might have written a book such as *Fire in the Water*. As in all of his masterful novels, James Alexander Thom evokes the past by making it present. He carries us into bars and back alleys, frontier outposts and swarming cities, steamboats and military prisons. He plunges us into the Mississippi River and draws us into the funeral cortège of Abraham Lincoln, bringing history to life. One emerges from this riveting narrative more convinced of the ugliness of racism and the folly of war." – *Scott Russell Sanders,* author of *Divine Animal*

"The intensity of Thom's story grows through the full-blown appeal to every sense, every emotion. Though wrung out by book's end each page turned is a gift toward understanding was and its aftermath, greed and generosity, love and loss, loyalty and friendship. Particularly loyalty and friendship." – *Rita Kohn, Nuvo* writer

Fire in the Water

a novel by

James Alexander Thom

Fire in the Water

Published by Blue River Press
Indianapolis, Indiana
www.brpressbooks.com

Distributed by Cardinal Publishers Group
2402 N. Shadeland Avenue, Suite A
Indianapolis, IN 46219
317-352-8200 phone
317-352-8202 fax
www.cardinalpub.com

ISBN: 978-1-935628-56-9

Cover Design: David Miles
Editor: Morgan Sears
Illustrations: James Alexander Thom
Book Design: Dave Reed

Printed in the United States of America

For Dick Cady,
fellow Sagamore and Stargeezer

Fire in the Water

PADRAIC QUINN
HIS DIARY

A pristine new book, Post War. No more battlefields!

This wedding gift from your loving mother, who brought you into this world and made you literate. Given on occasion of your marriage to Felice Beaulieu, in New Orleans, 17th April 1865.

Live long, write much, make me grandchildren.

MOIRA COLLEEN QUINN

A New Diary Book

On "Hornymoon" in New Orleans April 19th 1865

12:30 a.m.

So, then. Will this diary, like all my others, be written at night?

What war has made me dread more than anything else is sleep.

*

A purring bride, not a snorer, thank the Lord.

I myself neither purr nor snore, as I don't sleep.

Curse of the writing man: Creative insomnia.

I envy the illiterate; they must be well rested.

*

Lecture preambles for my postwar career flit like bats through my insomnolent belfry:

"Ladies and Gentlemen, all wars are 'holy' wars: Holy causes, wholly insane. (And they make holes in people.) Holy, wholly, holey..."

"Ladies & Gentlemen, I speak with authority on the subject of Nothingness, as all my ancestors were stillborn..."

"Ladies & Gentlemen, please excuse my self-defecating sense of humor." (Sure and if an Irishman doesn't defecate on himself, someone else will.}

*

This is being writ next to a covert candle, so as not to wake my bride Felice. For if I waken her, we'll "pursue glory" again. Can't help myself. In Nomen Patrie et Spiritu Sancti, just thinking of it makes me want to wake her for another sweet debauch!

No, let her rest. I should too; would if I could.

How much pleasure can a man bear? Sure and I've been seeking that limit! Skin & scent of a naked woman! What's the magic in nipples & dimples? Maybe a poet could say well enough, but can an old war correspondent?

Felice might prove the poet of this family. Reads Latin! Good God but I'm outclassed!

*

So this most wholly holey of holy wars is ending at last. Some Reb generals too mulish to quit, but Gen. Lee gave up his sword to Sam Grant ten days ago. PAX VOBISCUM

*

Will Peace be too boring ? Who knows? Whenever has there been a peace long enough in the world for us to know how boring it might be? A war correspondent should always be able to find employment somewhere, if history is any indication. But in the event of Peace, go on the lecture circuit, before name and fame fade away. Make a living between Yesterwar and Tomorrwar.

*

3 o'clock a.m.

Up again. Goddamned war is over; why can't a body sleep? I envy the dead; surely they're resting well!

Why this dread? Am I just a superstitious Irishman?

Maybe another dram, god damn.

Faith, I don't mind if I do.

CHAPTER ONE

The Shamrock Hotel

New Orleans Waterfront

April 19,1865

"President Lincoln's been murdered!"

That shout, in a man's voice from outside the hotel, a deep voice over a drone of voices, yanks Paddy Quinn up out of his old recurring nightmare: searching the blood-soaked Buena Vista battleground for his lost left hand. His heart is slamming.

A bell clangs three times, so close by it hurts his head. Machinery is rumbling and chuffing. His mouth and tongue feel parched. Felice is moving in the bedding beside him, shaking his shoulder. In the moment before he opens his eyes, he envisions Mister Lincoln's craggy visage, smiling and winking as he did that one time they'd met in Washington. Sees those even white teeth, feels the President's handshake, like warm iron. In memory, an echo of that cackling chuckle.

What Paddy sees when he opens his eyes is the mildewed tan wallpaper on the ceiling of their room in his mother's hotel, then he sees the tousled dark hair of his bride, sees her eyes wide with alarm and confusion. She is up on an elbow, looking down on him. The love musk of her body wafts in the stirring of the bed linens, and all that comes back to him, too, but also coalsmoke and the stench of the fish markets on the levee. But here amid the waking smells and sensations lingers the echo of that stunning cry that has woken him:

"President Lincoln's been murdered!"

Many other voices are yelling outdoors in the street below. "Bull puckey! You're jokin', huh? Goddamn Rebel wishful thinking, is it?"

Now that first stentorian voice again: "No! It's true! Shot in the head with a pistol!"

And a shrill one: "Assassin got away!"

"When?" someone cries.

"Shot last Friday night. Dead by Saturday morning!"

Paddy Quinn in his insomnia had sipped whiskey almost until dawn and has not yet quite slept it off, though it is plainly full daylight now. But he's been a war correspondent these last four years, is a veteran of three wars, man and boy, the Seminole, the Mexican and this one Between the States, so he's used to waking up in tumults and quickly assembling thoughts, facts and action out of his crapulent confusions.

This day he knows to be Wednesday. If the President was dead Saturday, why in blue hell wasn't such awful news telegraphed to New Orleans *then,* instead of five days later? Good God Almighty, this would mean that the President was already dead when Paddy Quinn and Felice Beaulieu were having their wedding! And all New Orleans oblivious until now? There must be some explanation.

Paddy and Felice crawl out of their rumpled wedding bed and grope around for their discarded garments. Dressing with only one hand is awkward, but second nature to him after eighteen years of it. Noise from the street and from the steam machinery outside is so loud he doesn't hear her question: "Could that be true?" She looks like a pretty little girl about to cry in the playground, this bride he has been wantonly rutting with two days and nights.

He draws aside the mosquito gauze that curtains the French doors, and they stumble out onto the balcony to see a gigantic structure looming above them, as big as three hotels, eclipsing the usual sunbright expanse of the Mississippi. It is a steamboat, a high, long, rakish sidewheeler, her name, *Sultana,* in letters taller than a man, in glossy black paint on her wheel housing. The noise is her engines and paddlewheels still churning to hold her prow to the levee as the gangway is being swung ashore and mooring hawsers are coiled onto the bollards. Coal smoke from her stacks, acrid and gritty, envelops everything as the breeze comes off the river. Paddy is astonished how high the steamer rides; the river must have risen more than a fathom during the night. The balcony he stands on is ten feet above the cobbles of Gravier Street, but the river is now nearly to the levee top, raising the *Sultana's* maindeck up to a level with his eyes. The agitated, yelling passengers who crowd the rails of the boat's promenade deck stand a full storey height above Paddy and his bride, and the vessel's smokestacks jut into the sky as high as church steeples. Below, crowds mill on the levee among mountains of coal, stacks of cotton bales, and wagonloads of sugar barrels. Farther along down the street is a roped corral of horses and mules, and from somewhere out of sight nearby come the squeals of swine and the reek of their dung. Felice at once goes pale and has to sit down on a rattan porch chair and fan herself. Paddy, now like an old warhorse at the sound of a bugle, desperate to know the news, feels a rush of impatience toward his bride, but then a twinge of shame for it. He instinctively seeks in the confused crowd that face a correspondent always looks for: whoever seems to know something.

He hears again from high above that same big voice that woke him up. It's now yelling for another turn on the windlass, and Paddy sees up on the pilot deck a man in the black coat and cap of a First Mate, leaning out over the rail supervising the deckhands. Cupping his mouth, Paddy gives a whistle shrill as a bo's'n's pipe and bellows at the officer in his loudest battlefield voice:

"You! Mate! How d'you know it's true, about Mister Lincoln?"

The officer's gaze comes searching down to Paddy, then shifts a moment to Felice, who in her white negligee must look like a fallen angel, and now reaches into a coat pocket and holds up a folded newspaper.

"This! The Cairo *War Eagle,*" the officer calls down. "Printed the day we sailed from Illinois!"

Now from inside the hotel, Paddy hears his mother's muffled voice, calling his name. She must be in the hall outside the door of their room, pounding it with her fist. "Paddy!" she's bellowing. "Wake up! There's awful news from up North!"

"We heard!" He darts into the room, past the desk where his diary lies shut and tied, beside his half-empty whiskey bottle. He pivots around the tumbled bed and draws the bolt of the door to let her in.

Moira Quinn at half a century of age is imposing, nearly six feet tall, full-bosomed, her thick mane of red hair gone white at the temples and the rest beginning to turn the same, piled in a loose chignon. Her face is squarish, handsome still, but with a right eyebrow permanently gnarled from a longago beating by Paddy's father, that act of violence which was Paddy's first memory in a lifetime of violence. She has never told Paddy what she did to provoke that beating, or to retaliate for it, but the man had been so totally banished from Paddy's childhood that he can't even remember his face. Moira Quinn had kept her maiden name, and Paddy kept it too. She has always refused to speak the man's name, so Paddy Quinn has never known who his sire was. *NEMO ME LACESSIT IMPUNE* was on the only sampler she had ever embroidered. Though she was born Irish, it was that motto of Scotland that she claimed as her credo: that no man could ever put a hand on her except with her permission. In her rough past as an Army camp seamstress, laundress and sometime bootlegger, though, she apparently had given some such permissions over the years, gaining a reputation she works diligently now to expunge. Paddy conspires as well as he can in the restoration of her respectability, as would any good son, especially one with his own national reputation coming to fruition, and also as one newly married into a notable St. Louis family he has yet to meet. Felice's parents, already indignant about not being consulted on the wedding, will be stunned enough to find that their new son-in-law, the famous *Harper's* war correspondent, is actually a raffish one-armed jugsucking Irish quillpusher who needs to drink himself to sleep; his mother's *demimondaine* past would overload their dismay, if it ever got to them. Therefore, even Felice herself has needed to be misled a bit about her new mother-in-law's biography. Paddy sweats dread whenever he and his bride go out in public in Moira Quinn's company, lest they meet some Mexican War veteran who'll recognize her as the notorious "Harney's Whore," mistress of that fiery cavalry officer in Mexico seventeen years ago. Unfortunately, nearly every senior officer of note, Union or Rebel, is a veteran of that conflict in Mexico, and the city of New Orleans is now infested with them since the occupation, so Moira Quinn is hard to hide.

All that notwithstanding, Paddy Quinn admires his mother as much as anyone he's ever known. There isn't a soldier anywhere more courageous or principled than the notorious Moira Quinn. She made him a man of words and protected him as a child from every danger that bullies or molesters could put in his path, once even threatening to kick a deviant priest "in your organ, whatever it might be." She is the one person he knows who thinks of everyone else's needs before her own. And there surely isn't an American citizen anywhere who honors and admires President Lincoln more than Moira Quinn does. So Paddy is not surprised to see her nose red and her eyes stricken as she barges into the room with her fingers twisted together over her bosom.

"Please, tell me they didn't murder Father Abraham!" That's what she always calls Mister Lincoln, even though she's just about his age.

"Sounds like it. But I won't believe it until I learn it from somebody I trust for the truth." She clutches at his hand and squeezes it in her washerwoman's grip until he winces. It is, as she proudly knows, this hand of his that once shook Lincoln's.

Paddy says, "Ma, tend to Felice, would you now, she's gone woozy on me, while I run over to the *Picayune* office and find out how it could be true and not a word of it known in New Orleans."

"We'll go with you."

"No! Felice is faint," he protests quickly. "Please, stay here with her." Some of the editors at the *Picayune* know his mother's reputation, and he doesn't want the two women to go into the office with him together. Paddy himself is a correspondent well esteemed in the eyes of the *Picayune*'s editors, his reputation independent of his mother's. But if she goes there with him, there will be those knowing smirks. And if Felice is with him too, she might perceive or overhear something that could make her start wondering about her mother-in-law.

It's not that Paddy's bride is some frail or squeamish thing. When he first saw Felice Beaulieu, she was a blood-spattered nurse helper aboard the Army hospital steamboat *Red Rover* on the Mississippi, as ghastly and grisly a job as any young woman ever worked. She's no bit of fluff, even though born of the St. Louis gentry. Felice knows more Mississippi River lore than most men know. Her innate sense of merciful duty had been inspired by the Sisters of Charity. When Paddy had boarded the *Red Rover* to write and illustrate an article for *Harper's* about hospital ships, this deceptively delicate-looking lass told him that well over two hundred souls had expired with her hand on their pillows. She had nursed men so mangled, delimbed and scorched that he could hardly bear to look at them. So her swoony spell on the balcony just now is the result of no weakness. It's from their honeymoon excesses, Paddy supposes.

Now he simply wants to hurry over to the newspaper office, see the editors, get some explanation for the delay of the assassination news, and check the telegraph for any other news pertinent to it, or to General Sherman's campaign against Johnston in the Carolinas, without having an office full of cigar-reeking newspapermen smirking at his mother or leering at his bride.

Besides, if Paddy goes by himself, he can dodge in someplace for a surreptitious swig of something to settle his morning-after queasiness. He needs that, but doesn't want his bride to see him drink in the morning. His mother well knows how he is with the spirits, but Felice has no real idea yet. It is a matter that will have to be dealt with in their marriage eventually, one way or another, but not just now.

*

He has to press through a tide of debarking passengers and cargo from the *Sultana* as he leaves the hotel, and the vessel looms huge. Something clutches him like a cold hand and compels him to pause and look up at it. Paddy doesn't deem himself a particularly superstitious Irishman, but he has had to develop an intuition for danger. Now he goes cold and hears in his head: *Tub of Doom.*

Trim and stately as she is, filigreed, fresh-painted, not an aging vessel at all, maybe two years in use. A beauty, in fact. In the war along the rivers Paddy has seen steamboats as squat and grim as old turtles, plated with sheet iron gray as death, their last lines of nautical comeliness obscured by riveted armor, clanking, seething, gasping behemoths of ugliness all abristle with cannon and mortars, but even those gunboats never gave him the chill he now feels looking at this elegant thing.

Maybe it's just from the dire message she brings, he thinks.

At head height the quoin stones of his mother's Shamrock Hotel bear a deep and ragged scar, which is a point of historical interest. It looks like a pulverized dent such as a cannonball might have made. Visitors often presume it to have been from a stray shot in the recent war, or even from the War of 1812. Of course neither of those wars had bombarded this part of the old city, but tourists do like to imagine interesting things, and the natives don't bother to disillusion them. The damage had actually been done in 1849 when the steamboat *Louisiana* blew up right here, killing one hundred and fifty persons. Flying metal from her boiler wrecked two adjacent vessels and divided a mule into two equal parts before killing a drayman and his horse far up a side street. When Mrs. Moira Quinn explains the damage, she always says truthfully that it was an explosion, not a cannonade. But in telling of it, she does let her paying guests presume that she had owned the hotel that long ago; she lets people presume that she had been established here as a landlady as long ago as the Mexican War years. Such vagueness helps fog up the real chronology of her life, and eventually the neighborhood might forget that she wasn't one of the old establishment. Actually, she had not bought the old inn until five years ago, when Paddy's writings had earned enough to help her meet the price. Though he calls it her hotel, he's half owner.

The scar on the building is, to Paddy, a reminder of the awful power of steam, that every engine is a potential explosion. In the wars, he has seen and felt enough explosions for any man. He knows the facts of shipping competition, of steamboat builders constantly improving their vessels for speed and power, always experimenting, testing and racing. Before the war he had written several articles on steam engine innovations, about overtaxed vessels that blow to pieces like bombshells. In one article he had dubbed them "swimming volcanoes," a coinage since grown popular. He knows of course that one can't predict a vessel's fate by just a glance. But this one somehow chills his soul. He'll be relieved when it's no longer moored next to the Quinns' Shamrock Hotel.

Pushing through the excited, noisome crowd in New Orleans' oppressive heat, Paddy again turns his thoughts to President Lincoln, and he remembers their one meeting at the White House. Mister Lincoln had sent an officer to summon Paddy so he could praise him for a battlefield story and pictures in *Harper's*. Observing Paddy's empty left sleeve, the President had said, "The Union is grateful they didn't take your pencil hand." Mister Lincoln had naturally assumed that he'd lost the hand in this, his own war.. When Paddy had explained then that he was actually maimed in Mexico, as an Army camp errand boy, Mister Lincoln recalled his own condemnation of that war when he was a young Congressman, how he had censured President Polk for starting it and wasting so many lives in it.

"I remember that, Mister President. I read about you in the newspapers. I knew about you when I was twelve, and even then thought you were right." It was then that the President had smiled that bright smile at him and given him that strong, gentle handshake whose feeling Paddy can still relish in every bone and tendon of his writing hand. Someday, Paddy imagines, he might use this very hand to write about that very handshake. You could make a good tribute to a man by writing about his handshake, if you wrote it right.

But now Mister Lincoln's own war has wrought carnage on a much grander scale than Polk's little war. Polk's had been to seize Mexican land and open the West to slavery. Lincoln's was to preserve the Union, abolishing slavery in doing so. Somehow Father Abraham had kept believing that saving the Union was worth any cost.

Paddy doesn't judge whether it was worth it or not. All those thousands of dead soldiers he's seen, eventually they would have died anyway, of course, perhaps for no worthy cause at all. The mortality rate is, he likes to say, one hundred per cent, a factor seldom calculated into the balance of ends and means. Paddy has always been told that life is sacred, but always instead he's seen how cheap it is. Such paradoxes will be the substance of his lectures when he makes the transition from war journalism into public oratory. He hopes to make audiences scratch their heads, smile wistfully, laugh aloud, even weep. They'll go home from his lectures and try to absorb what amazing and absurd truths he's told them. These ideas that fill his insomnia.

All he's seen and recorded of war and suffering so far have just been preparation for his impending new career. He doesn't know yet just what he'll say. He just knows from experience that when he begins to talk, it all comes to him. The gift of blarney. Flattering the ear of the listener. Inspirited by the sweet ether arising off of liquid spirits, he can express anything. Or so he hopes.

We're bards by blood, we Irish.

This New Orleans waterfront is old ground to Paddy Quinn. He remembers waiting weeks here in the summer of 1845 while the American Army built up its supplies to sail off and invade Mexico. He had been on his own in those times, an urchin following the Army, no mother to tell him what he could or couldn't do. Moira Quinn then was at some Army garrison up in Michigan, from which he'd run off to follow a unit that was headed down to whip the Seminoles. The Army never did whip them, finally just gave up, and soon after that was headed for Mexico. New Orleans was at that time the biggest city he'd ever been in, and in its noisy, mouldering, smelly streets he had heard every language and accent and song in the world, it had seemed. People drank day or night, there was every kind of food to try, if you could get a little money to buy some. There was a place where Negro slaves were put up on a kind of stage and sold to bidders. Sometimes they were stripped and exhibited naked.. Paddy had drawn sketches at the slave market, to learn how to draw Negroes and Negresses. By then he had already learned to draw the faces of Indians, at least the Seminole kind.

Here in New Orleans the boy Paddy Quinn had taught himself to sketch quickly, to show how people looked when they moved and worked and idled. Rich, fancy people got on and off of steamboats, and he had once written in his diary, *You can't quite tell the whores from the other ladies.* In those days he was practicing different kinds of writing, sometimes imitating the kinds of serial stories that he read in periodicals. He'd earned pennies now and then by writing letters home for soldiers who didn't know how to write. Most of his time, though, he had spent his days tucked away in some corner or under a tarpaulin, reading every newspaper and magazine he could buy, salvage or steal, and occasionally even a book. There had been more and stranger things to read in this city than the boy Paddy Quinn had ever dreamed there could be. If not for the time he had spent here waiting for the Army to go to Mexico, he surely wouldn't have become the field artist and war correspondent that he is now. Here he had contracted the malady he calls *kakoethes scribendi* – the irrepressible urge to write. And it has made him famous. This is the city that started making him the man he is, so long ago, and now at war's end it has made him a married man with responsibilities, able to plan beyond the next bomb burst. He means to provide a very good life for this exquisite woman who for some reason has chosen him as mate, and his experience in life has taught him that any success comes from knowing all one can know, and then telling it, like a bard. He has to know about this assassination. Somehow it will involve him. Events always have involved him. They have never gone by in the distance.

Moored at the next wharf is another new arrival, a trim vessel named *Olive Branch.* A timely and promising name, he thinks. Must have come in about the same time as the *Sultana,* and is being unloaded now. He wends through her disembarking passengers, who are also buzzing with the terrible news, then he turns up the next street toward the newspaper office.

Paddy has known of the New Orleans *Picayune* most of his life. He had begun reading it as a boy in the Army camps in Florida, then in the Mexican War. He had always cadged newspapers from the officers when he couldn't afford to buy one himself. The *Picayune* in particular had been the funnel for most of that war's news into the States. War reports had reached New Orleans from Mexico by fast ships. There had been no telegraph in the South yet during that war, but express riders had sped out from the *Picayune* and war news eventually spread to the rest of the country. And for the Army serving in Mexico, that paper had been the best source of news from the States. Paddy usually approaches the *Picayune* office with a feeling almost of reverence, but today he is wildly exasperated as he pushes into the messy editorial room, which reeks of cigar smoke and sweaty clothing. He heads for the editor, who sits with his elbows in a drift of handwritten sheets on a low table and his forehead in his hands. "Blackie," Paddy hisses, leaning close, "I hate to wake you, dear sir, but momentous events are falling upon you with the weight of mountains!" The man peeks out at him between his fingers.

"Hello, Saint Patrick. I am quite awake, thank you, and aware of all momentous events."

"Are ye now? Might I read some of them in your worthy sheet, then? Such as, oh, say, the violent death of a famous Illinois railsplitter in a faraway city?"

"Spare me your sarcasm, Paddy. We know of it."

"From the *Sultana*, I'll bet."

The editor sighs and stands up. "Right."

"It's five days, Blackie. With a telegraph, what's your excuse? God damn!"

"It wasn't telegraphed to the South. Orders of the Secretary of War." The editor glowers at Paddy and nibbles his lower lip with an eyetooth. "For strategic reasons."

"What strategic reasons?"

"That General Johnston hasn't surrendered to Sherman yet. And other Reb commanders still not admitting they're whipped. Stanton fears the news might delay the peace."

"How would it make a difference?" Paddy asks. "Am I missing something?"

Blackie explains, "Mister Lincoln called for a benign and forgiving peace. His vice-president wants all Rebs hanged as traitors. The war might linger on if the South knows that Andrew Johnson's now the President."

That makes sense all at once, and Paddy suddenly feels tired. Annoyed with himself for caring so little about the world outside of battlefields. With this slump comes the familiar morning-after yearning. "Blackie? Anything to drink here? Surely you've got something?"

Being a newspaperman, Blackie has spirits on the premises, sets Paddy down with a glass of rum and a copy of the Cairo newspaper, with its great black headline: NATIONAL CALAMITY! , and tells him, "It won't stay bottled up any longer, now that it's known in New Orleans. You know news. Even if they think it's false rumor, it'll spread through the South like a hot fart in a cold room. Well, read and weep, Paddy me laddie. It's a sad day. They say the assassin's an actor, named Booth. If that's so, I've seen the man that killed the President. Saw him in a play once. We'll, I'll be in the print shop if you need me."

Paddy sips the rum and reads. The images form. The print blurs. At the thought of Lincoln unconscious, gasping for breath through the long night and bleeding slowly to death from a bullet wound in his brain, Paddy is sniffling. He has seen so many men bleed to death from bullet wounds in their brains, many because that particular man was so determined to preserve the Union. Paddy's own bride Felice deems Mister Lincoln guilty of all those deaths she saw in the hospital ship, equally guilty with the Secessionist leaders who challenged him to turn to force. She is neutral; she holds no killer innocent.

In a theater. Watching a play with Mrs. Lincoln and some friends around him. The pistol shot scarcely heard because of the audience's laughter. Father Abraham probably celebrating that his war was almost over, probably himself laughing when the ball went into his head. That high cackle of a laugh that Paddy can still hear in the ear of memory. These details will be so hard to relate to his mother.

Now he begins reading about the national funereal schedules. "By God," he murmurs.

He swallows rum, reads on, then jumps up from the chair.

He finds Blackie in the composing room in rolled shirtsleeves, hunched over a type tray with a begrimed pressman, and interrupts him to ask: "May I have permission to use your telegraph?"

Blackie straightens up and sighs. "I'm not supposed to do that."

"But you could. You know I'm an operator."

"You're not *our* operator."

"Blackie, I learned Morse's Code as soon as he invented it. I'm better than your operator."

"What is it you want to send? I have the Secretary of War to worry about."

"Nothing 'strategic.' About funerals. The President's funeral in Washington is today. Right now. Just imagine that: right now!"

"I know, Paddy. I know. How much of my liquor did you take, by the way?"

"Don't worry, I left some. Look, Blackie: The President's body won't be buried in Washington. It's going on tour."

"I know."

"See this: 'After lying in state in the Capitol, the President's body will be put on a funeral train, to stop at all major cities to allow the citizens to pay their respects. Will reach his Illinois home in Springfield, for burial in early May.' That's what it says. I pray to the sweet mercy of Saint Patrick they mean to have that funeral car iced down. A body after two weeks...Well, if y've smelled a battlefield after that long..."

"So what you want my telegraph for is to advise them to preserve him proper? Paddy, laddie, I'm sure they've already thought that out. Embalmed and packed like a Northern Pike, probably." The editor glances at the printer who stands waiting and rolls his eyes, which Paddy notices.

"No, Blackie, what I want your precious telegraph for is to telegraph *Harper's* and get myself assigned to his funeral in Illinois, since you must know my business. I can get on a boat here and be in Springfield before that train gets there."

Blackie raises his eyebrows and purses his lips. "Oh? You want to use our telegraph, to get yourself a paying assignment, do you? With our competition up North? Talk about brazen ballocks!" Paddy can see in Blackie's eyes that he's thinking about this.

"*Harper's* isn't your competition, Blackie. It's a magazine, not a newspaper. Let me ask this, then: Might the *Picayune* pay to send me up to Illinois? Just think: Funeral of the Century, story and illustrations by the celebrated Padraic Quinn, a *Picayune* exclusive."

"Can't afford you. Anyway, aren't you on honeymoon? I seem to remember we covered very recently the wedding of the celebrated Padraic Quinn. A *Picayune* exclusive, as you say. Pray tell the honeymoon's not over already?" He's considering the offer, Paddy thinks, and replies:

"No, not over. A honeymoon cruise up the Mississippi!" He's already thought of that.

Felice's family in St. Louis would be precisely en route to the funeral and they could meet their new son-in-law . He wants to get Felice away from his mother anyway, and a story assignment could pay for the trip. Felice is homesick for that homeland she knows so well, where her Beaulieu family are old and prominent, and she has already said she'd like to get out of Louisiana before malaria season.

"If I can't afford you for an assignment," the editor says, " I sure as the devil can't afford to buy you a honeymoon cruise. But here's a thought for your crafty Irish mind, Mister Quinn: Persuade your *Harper's* man to pay for your passage. Do your funeral masterpiece for him. Then send me down another text of it, and one drawing at least, and I'll pay you our *Picayune* rate for them. Which is picayune indeed, as the name implies. You ought to book passage right away, if you intend to get to Illinois before Father Abraham does. There are two boats scheduled to start up tomorrow afternoon, the *Olive Branch* and the *Sultana*."

"Ah, Blackie! Couldn't have come up with a better plan meself! And that means I can use your telegraph key, eh?"

"Damn it all, don't brogue me, you boozy Irishman, or I'll change my mind. Come on. I'll take you down to Telegraph."

"I know where it is, Blackie. You've let me use it before, despite your rules."

"Did I? Must've been drunk."

"Yes, ye were, Blackie. Every time."

"You're a bad influence. It'll be good to have you gone."

"Faith, and I'll drink to that!"

*

"It's ages since anyone brushed my hair for me," says Felice. "I'd forgotten what luxury it is!" It is that, but it hurts, too.

"Likewise, I've had no such crownin' glory to brush," Mrs. Quinn replies with a powerful tug. "Your own Mum loved to do this, I bet?"

Felice has to tense her neck and suppress a groan. Mrs. Quinn's hands are unbelievably strong, and occasionally Felice thinks her hair will be unrooted. But it feels too good, tingly and flushing, for her to beg "quit, please!" This is good for her scalp, she knows.

"Strange to say, Mama just hardly ever did. A servant did all the pampering I got."

"A servant, ye say! My!" In the mirror Mrs. Quinn's face shows a momentary scowl.

"Her name's Faith. She raised me from a baby."

"Faith, eh? An Irish servant?" There's an edge on Mrs. Quinn's voice as she asks this, and she gives a harder pull.

"No, Ma'am. A Negress."

"Ay, well, a Negress. Hm. Now! Shall we braid this? How d'ye want to look in the picture?" A midday appointment at a portrait photographer's loft for a portrait of the newlyweds had been in today's schedule, but Felice had presumed that the assassination news would have blown that, or any other trifle, from her mother-in-law's mind. And certainly from Paddy's.

"Oh, Mrs. Quinn, we needn't go on with that; it's not that impor..."

"You may call me 'Mother,' or 'Mum,' or whatever ye like, but please not 'Mrs. Quinn,' for you're me daughter now."

"Yes, mum. I'm sorry. But really, we needn't go for the portraits. Not with that grief on your mind. And Paddy might miss the appointment, going after the news he wants."

"Dear, I make it a habit to keep appointments I've made, however I might feel. It's good business. And I want to send a photograph up to your parents right away, since they couldn't come for the wedding. They *must* see how comely a couple you make."

"They've seen Paddy's picture in the magazines. They know how handsome he is."

"Those are just engravings. They need t' see him as he is. And you beside him. Instead o' braids, let me put you up in a chignon. With maybe a curly tendril at either temple? And I have a stunning big hat that'll look like a halo on ye. About your Negress: You had a slave, then?"

"She wasn't a slave. Papa wouldn't have slaves, even if we were Southerns. In fact, he used to write ferocious letters to the President for stalling on manumission." In the mirror Felice catches a glimpse of Paddy's whiskey bottle, nearly full last night, half empty this morning. She frowns.

"*Ferocious* letters? He know Mister Lincoln personal enough to scold 'im?"

"Only knew him through law. Lack of it, rather; Mister Lincoln always talked him out of litigating."

"That sounds like a fine sort o' lawyer t' me."

Felice's eye returns to that diminished whiskey bottle over there, and she feels a twinge of concern about it. But the delightful sensations of the brush and fingers in her hair race through the length of her body, and mingle with the lingering, tingling, seeping, aching tiredness down in her pelvis, the superflux of all those flexings and strainings and cascading climaxes that she and Paddy have wrought together. Paddy makes love the way his mother brushes hair, Felice thinks.

And ah the awe in his eyes as he urges me over the verge!

She has astonished herself that she can rut so wantonly, past the point of frenzy, to those moments when she seems to collapse within like a concertina, yielding a gushing chord of tumult. How, after such exertions, could Paddy not fall into oblivious slumber, as she does, but instead sit awake writing and drinking whiskey the rest of the night, but still awaken her to yet another vibrant cockstand? Where do these Quinns get such strength?

Surely not from the whiskey, God forbid!

I'm sure I look too tired to show well in a photograph today, she thinks.

Felice has been photographed only once in her life: when she was working in the hospital ship. She doesn't like photographs, or the obtrusive pests who take them. They mostly exhibit an overweening sense of privilege and importance, their work being in such demand.

How they had vexed her sometimes, traipsing into the wards with written authorizations to photograph the most grotesquely maimed soldiers or leprous-looking syphilitics. Felice now remembers a corporal whose whole left leg and hip and genitalia had been carried off by a cannonball, his lower torso a gnarled mass of stitched-up scar tissue, being propped up naked against a whitewashed wall so the photographer could record the marvel of his survival. Felice had cried over that until she was cold and dry clear to her heart. And photographers also callously made those panoramic pictures of hundreds of bloated corpses strewn over the battlefields. Why had such horrors needed to be shown? Who needed to see such carnage? By and large Felice had considered the hordes of photographers like buzzards fattening on the carrion of war.

And then too, so many soldiers carried lewd photographs, single or stereoptic, of every perverse and disgusting sort: blowsy nudes, spraddled whores with lifted skirts, gray studio tableaus of bestiality and sodomy – *pornographos*, the Greeks had called it, the writing of harlots. She had seen evidence of so much traffic of the new photographic kind that she imagined there must be at least one camera in every brothel in the world. Often some dying soldier had begged her, in abject shame, to take and destroy such rubbish lest it be sent home with his other personal effects. Her impression of photography is so unfavorable that she has no desire to be photographed, even in a wedding picture, for surely, she imagines, any lens and its black-hooded operator in this land must be tainted by having aimed up some gaping vulva not long before.

God knows I'm no prude, Felice muses. I've looked every obscenity straight in the face during this war, be it a chancrous penis or a careless amputation or an exploded skull. Thank heaven my husband corresponded war by pen and pencil, not by a camera lens. Though photographers were in every theatre of war, their film plates were too slow to record anything in motion, and thus it was still the sketch artist who portrayed the clashing regiments, the charging cavalry, the shellbursts, the crawling casualties. Her Paddy is a wordsmith and a deft illustrator, not a voyeur behind a lens shutter, and she can take pride in his fame, even though his subject, war, is in her mind the greatest obscenity of any. Paddy has soldiered in the field everywhere but never killed or maimed a fellow man – one of the reasons why she fell in love with him rather than with some pedigreed West Pointer with a sword at his side.

Mama Quinn, you've given me a humane and literate man, she thinks.

And a desperate lover.

When she really fell in love with him was when he tried so hard to make her laugh, after she had thought she never would again.

"A cockstand," he had said once, "is proof of faith."

And he had declared:

"Cleanliness is next to Godliness - especially in *cunnilingus*."

God forbid my mother should ever hear his boudoir adages!

Why, admit it, sometimes he's as lewd as those camera people!

"What's funny, dear?" says Mrs. Quinn, whose fingers are shaping her hair, and Felice realizes she's been quaking with a voiceless laugh.

"Your son."

"True. For instance?"

Thinking it unseemly to quote such bawdy sayings, she replies, "He said if he scratches my back and I won't scratch his, I'm *selfitch*."

"Ah yes. Paddy and his puns."

"As he gets into public lecturing, humor will help him."

"It will. But he 's got serious stories to tell. He's been right in the middle of everything all his life. Humor's just the sauce, for my lad."

"I know, Mrs....Mum. I look forward to hearing all those stories. I've never known a dull moment with him."

"You never will. Did he tell you he was known in Mexico as the boy who eats rattlesnakes?"

"Oh, heavens, no! What..."

"Never told you? Afraid you wouldn't kiss 'im, I guess. But ask him about it. Now, dear, let's dress up lovely and go find him. I want to know about the murder of Father Abraham. And we've pictures to sit for."

*

By early afternoon Paddy has had three shots of Blackie's liquor and half an hour at the telegraph key, where he talks with his right index fingertip eloquently enough to persuade Alfred Guernsey, his editor at *HARPER'S,* to send him to Springfield, Illinois for the President's final funeral and his burial. *HARPER'S* was not one of the few periodicals assigned a reporter's berth on the funeral train, and the editor had decided against sending a reporter all the way out to Illinois. But when Paddy assures him of a thorough, solemn, heart-moving account of the funeral and burial, with panoramic sketches of his usual excellent battlefield quality, for a fee less than half the cost of sending a man to Springfield and back , the editor sees it as a Godsend – *if* Paddy can promise to have his account written, drawings finished for the engraver and hand- delivered in New York five days after the funeral. Mister Guernsey has known Paddy Quinn to miss a deadline now and then, and gives no slack. But he likes this offer.

It's a Godsend for Paddy, too. He slumps back in the chair for a moment with his eyes closed and gives up a prayer of thanks. The combined fees promised by *Harper's* and the *Picayune* might well be the equivalent of a fourth of his whole year's expected income as he makes the transition from war correspondent into the uncertainties of living by one's wits. This might be his last project as a war correspondent, and he is thankful to have it. He now has responsibility for a life in addition to his own, one he loves desperately and dares not fail. His fame must not diminish; it must become different. The first half of Paddy Quinn's life he was an utter nobody and he won't go back to that. Felice Beaulieu did not mean to marry a failure, and he will see that she hasn't.

Must go and tell her, he thinks. And get us passage on a boat up that river, or I've no job at all.

I doubt Ma's going to be happy we're leaving so soon, but it's for the best.

Not going to be happy hearing how Father Abraham died, either. Going to be sad telling her that story.

"Blackie, thanks, friend. Honored to be writing for the *Picayune*!"

"Make it good, Paddy. I've stuck my neck out so far for you my rectum's between my shoulder blades. Do give my fond regards to your bride and your mama. And I suppose you'll tell 'em I forced liquor into you so early in the day."

"Thank you! Couldn't have invented a better excuse meself!"

The mention of his bride and his mother reminds Paddy of something they meant to do today, but he can't remember what it was. No matter what, it's not as important as getting passage on a steamer going up to Illinois.

*

The crowd in the streets is even bigger and more agitated than it was this morning. In every knot of bystanders Paddy overhears, the name is "Lincoln" and the word is "murdered." Women and Negroes move along as if in shock, tears glistening on their faces, some moving voiceless lips, some rubbing their cheeks with the heels of their hands, others narrow-eyed and smug. Clusters of well-dressed gents are posturing and declaiming. Where the topic yesterday would have been the ebbtide of warmaking, the liberation of prisoners of war, the disbanding of armies, today it is as if war is forgotten, as if one man's death by pistol ball weighs more than thousands by musketball and bayonet. Not everyone here in the South is sad about the assassination, but almost all are shocked. An intriguing lecture could be made about these reactions here in the occupied city of New Orleans. Paddy would be pausing to listen and make notes if he had brought his portfolio, but he didn't, and anyway he's in too much of a hurry. He squeezes through a knot of loud talkers outside a saloon, men waving their cigars and beer schooners, and sees above their heads the upper decks and smokestacks of the steamer *Olive Branch* trembling in the hot air. He decides he'd better book passage before going back to the hotel, or they might not get a cabin at all.

But first, a quick whiskey.

The scents from inside the dim saloon insinuate themselves in his nostrils like the ring in a hog's nose and lead him in. No time to sit, nor any place, either, as the place is packed with excited drinkers and ranters. Paddy without placing his order is served his usual shotglass full, slaps a coin on the bar, douses his tonsils and shakes his head, signals for another, and while waiting for it eavesdrops on a table of white-haired, hard-eyed gentrymen who are quietly celebrating the death of "the chief national nigra-lover." Paddy tosses down the second shot and starts for the sunbright rectangle of the front door. As he passes the old men he feigns more inebriation than he actually enjoys, and lurches over against their table, spilling all their glasses and beer pitchers on their laps. They curse and clamber up from their chairs, grabbing onto Paddy and shoving him about. He retreats with feigned apologies, leaving them glowering at him and mopping their laps, and he staggers laughing out into the bright street. By now he has attained that level of stimulation most pleasing to him, that which for years has enabled him to overcome his innate fear, fatigue and shyness, and perform with elan and poise on battlefields and in other intimidating circumstances. In this state, he feels tireless and sure; he can ride like a cavalryman, fight like a pugilist, charm like a courtier, draw like daVinci, write like Addison and Steele. Or so it seems to Paddy as long as he maintains this ideal degree of elation. He doesn't like being really drunk; he has been that, too often; he has trained himself, under the most trying conditions, not to yield to sottishness. These are lessons he learned from Gen. Grant, who believed that a man is at his best not sober, but not drunk either. But it is an equilibrium difficult to sustain, for full sobriety is perhaps even worse. Paddy has a theory, and has notes on it in his portfolio, about the peculiar chemical humors of Irish blood which need adjustment by way of the careful mixing of liquid spirits. Someday he will lecture upon that theorem, among many others. And there will be a little glass of something there on the lectern, just a *little* glass.

At his ticket table on the wharf, at the foot of the gangplank, the fat little clerk of the *Olive Branch* appraises Paddy's clothes, visage, and general condition with a darting eye and says, "I've just this minute booked the last cabin, sir."

"Damn me!" All because of that detour into the tavern, he thinks. "You're absolutely certain?" He draws his wallet and strokes it with his thumb, the common cue to the bribeworthy.

"Absolutely. Nothing but deck passage, sir."

"Can't do the deck. My wife's traveling with me, and she's quite above that."

"Very sorry then, sir. Er, ah, if she'd be comfortable with a *chaise longue* in the Ladies' Parlor and you on deck just as far as Vicksburg, I do have a family vacating their cabin there. I could, well, obtain that cabin for you and your lady, from Vicksburg on to...?"

"St. Louis. But that won't do. We're, ahm, newly wed, you see."

"Really! My congratulations! I'm so sorry about the cabin, though. And you're..." He glances down at Paddy's empty left cuff. "...a veteran, I take it?"

"Aren't we all. And you?"

"Only as far as Murfreesboro, in Sixty-two. Got hurt there too bad to serve any longer."

"Dreadful sorry. Which side?"

The clerk moves a hand down instinctively to indicate something in the vicinity of his left buttock, but Paddy laughs and says, "No, I mean which army?"

"Why, sir, sorry to say this if you're a Southerner, but I was 38th Indiana."

"Ooh, you faced Bragg, then!"

"We gave him a rough time, by God!"

"Had it coming," Paddy says. "Sure and he was one of the nastiest popinjays I ever met."

The clerk suddenly gets a cautious tilt to his head. "You knew him...personal?" The man obviously is wondering if Paddy was a Reb, maybe a high-ranking one at that.

"Known him since Mexico. I was once a powder monkey for him. At Matamoros."

"Begging your pardon, then, sir, I wasn't thinking Mexico; you look too young, if I may say so. Not doubting, mind you..."

"I was eleven then. But I did know Bragg in this war, too."

The clerk's face hints at a confusion of feelings. "Then you were, ah, Southern?"

"Neutral, if that makes it easier for you. I've never been in any army, just *with* a few of them." The clerk is glancing at the loose cuff again, and Paddy raises the other arm and tells him, "I've only this one paw left me, sir, but what tales it could tell you, if we were destined to sail together. This hand has shaken Bragg's, and Lee's, Jeff Davis's, General Rosecrans's, Lew Wallace's, of your own home state... It's raised many a bottle with Hooker and with my dear friend Sam Grant, who was my drinking mentor. And speaking of drinking with Hooker, this poor limb could tell you such a story as you've never heard, and probably shouldn't. But never mind that." He sighs, aware that he's jawing too much, giving away free the kind of yarns, true ones, that lecture hall audiences will pay to hear, if only he can find a berth on a boat going up North where people might actually have some money to spend for lectures. He looks into the eyes of the boat clerk, eyes showing a mixture of awe and incredulity, and adds, "But what makes this hand sacred, sir, is that President Lincoln, rest his great soul, once summoned me to the White House and shook this hand, he did, with a wink and a smile, and thanked me for using it well to serve the cause of preserving the Union!' *By th' sweet brow of Saint Patrick that's a good line!* he thinks, and he adds, "I'm on my way to Mister Lincoln's funeral, you see. That's why I really do need a berth, and now."

"Well, Mister, if I could do it, I'd trade you a cabin on the *Olive Branch* just for the honor of shaking that sacred hand of yours. But as I said, I've no cabin open before Vicksburg, I truly haven't. So if you've just got to get to that funeral, my advice is, run down to the Gravier Street wharf as quick as those legs'll carry you, and see if there's still a vacancy on the *Sultana*. She's our competition, but she's a good Lodwick vessel like this'n, and I can vouch too for Captain Mason, as I've run this river with him."

Paddy's spirit, which has been aloft on the sunny wings of whiskeyed self-satisfaction, drops into a shadow of dread at the sound of the name *Sultana*. He remembers that ominous feeling he'd had on seeing her. *Tub of Doom.*

Other people are crowding up the gangplank, demanding the clerk's attention, and he calls, "Ladies and gents, only deck passage remains available on the sailing of the *Olive Branch* tomorrow ! Those needing cabin class, try the *Sultana* at the next wharf. She leaves same time! That means you, young fellow." He seizes and squeezes Paddy's hand. "If you get there for the funeral, give my fond regards to Father Abraham, will ye? Pete Tickler, 38th Indiana. Godspeed!" As Paddy walks away, he begins chuckling. He imagines standing beside the President's casket and saying: "I bring you fond greeting from an Indiana Peter Tickler." Wouldn't that put a smile and a wink on his face!

When he gets to the Gravier Street wharf he finds a queue already at the gangplank. An annoyance, but he decides he'd best get in line. "Still any cabins available to St. Louis?" he calls up the line to the clerk, who glances up from his ticket-selling and nods at him.

"Paddy!" comes his mother's plangent voice piercing the street din. He glances across the levee and there she stands on the second-floor balcony of her Shamrock Hotel, waving at him, with a stunningly beautiful young woman at her side. The beauty is of course his own bride, Felice. She's waving at him too, dressed all in white and wearing one of his mother's wide-brimmed straw hats such as he's never seen her in, and now he remembers what was on their schedule this afternoon: a photograph sitting. Paddy makes a summoning wave to them and yells, "Come over! Come here!"

He waits in the creeping line while the *Sultana*'s clerk meticulously books passengers, one by one, writing down names and giving out boarding passes, while on the gangplank moves a steady two-way parade of porters, longshoremen and Negroes, pushing wheelbarrows of coal and of sugar sacks, pulling baggage carts, manhandling trunks and chests and bales of hay and straw. Below, between hull and levee, runs a vile soup of human waste, as the steamboat's spittoons and chamberpots are emptied and rinsed in readiness for the boat's return upriver tomorrow. From the street side of the levee rises a stink familiar to most soldiers who have foraged through the countryside with empty bellies: pig dung. Down there awaits a pen full of them, fated to be steamboat cargo going up the Mississippi. Paddy in his whiskey-enhanced daydream imagines how a God of Swine might design such an uncommon adventure for those earth-rooting stinkers and squealers: a boat trip. A boat trip to where? In the case of pigs, of course, to certain death; all pigs are destined for the smokehouse and the table, any strange detours notwithstanding. Just as any shipload of men, by their God's mysterious system of lading, will end as a banquet for worms, some soon, some later. In the years just past, Paddy Quinn has seen whole herds of men -- battalions and regiments, as such human consignments are known -- shipped on steamboats and railroads all over this vast land, and unloaded at roads leading straight to slaughter pens, which are euphemized as battlegrounds...

But now, he muses, at last some soldiers will be riding trains and boats not to battlegrounds, but homeward. Among dispatches on Blackie's desk he had read of armies disbanding, volunteers going home to muster out. Going home *alive.* One story in particular had struck him deep in the heart: that the terrible death camp in Andersonville in Georgia had been liberated, the legendary Lower Bowel of Confederate Prisons, where twenty thousand Union prisoners had died, starved, sick, or shot by guards. Survivors had called it a giant pigsty, and its overseer would face trial for their inhumane treatment. Its few living survivors were being processed at Camp Fisk near Vicksburg and would board steamboats, up the Mississippi toward home. What Paddy had heard of that prison had depressed him more than reading "The Inferno."

It had made him feel he should be damned just for being a member of this human race that creates worse Hells than Dante did in his imagination. It was said that a hundred prisoners a day died there, that their burials were so hasty and shallow that wild pigs rooted them up. Pigs eating human cadavers before the worms could! Isn't it supposed to be in God's plan that people eat pigs?

I should be writing down these figments, he thinks; memorable lectures can be made of them. But this morning he left the hotel without his portfolio, or even a notebook, so unsettled was he by the news brought downriver by this very boat.

Tub of Doom was the term he'd thought of when he saw the *Sultana* this morning, and he feels he should erase that from his thoughts. *Absit nomen absit omen.*

Damn this waiting in lines, he thinks. The last cabin might be gone before I get up there! If that be the case, I'll just have to take deck passage by myself to go up and fulfill the assignment, and book Felice to go up by a later boat to St. Louis. She'd not like that, nor would I. We should have this honeymoon journey together. First voyage in peacetime. The husband her family has yet to meet should bring her home in person.

That in itself is a daunting prospect. Her parents live in a mansion on the bluff above St. Louis, and are important in the city's society. Her father is apparently a learned man, who has taught his daughter a great deal about such things as sons, not daughters, usually know. Paddy can talk with her about such matters as engineering, geology and mining, history and biology without having to pause and explain anything. She isn't even afraid to discuss labor, capital, politics and war, those subjects he's most familiar with as a journalist. Her father, then, is surely an enlightened gentleman, and doubtless a good conversationalist, all of which would dispose Paddy to enjoy his company and benefit from it. His dread of meeting the man, though, stems from his expectation that Mister Beaulieu will dislike Paddy himself from the first meeting, on the grounds that an Irish pen-pusher of common social origin could not be good enough for his darling daughter. Especially so, since the wedding was such an impromptu event that the Beaulieus had been left out of it. They would have wanted it held on their estate or in their church, after a proper time for evaluating their prospective son-in-law, and then with all the elegant protocol and folderol that go with marrying in the lofty strata. But Felice didn't give them the chance to manage it that way. It was she who wanted to avoid all that, not from disregard of her parents, but because of the woman she had become while tending to hundreds of mangled, burned, battleworn, dying soldiers on the hospital ships. She nurtured a disdain now for the elegance and pretense of her own class. She had expressed it to Paddy one evening in a way that tickled his bardic soul: "I guess I've gone from the *hoity-toity* to the *hoi polloi*. And you know, Mister Quinn, it feels like a step up." That statement alone would have made him want to marry her.

He stands in line in the stinking heat and waits, turning often and impatiently to watch for her to come out from the hotel. He is beginning to wilt, and the comfort of the whiskey is evanescing. He should have brought a flask. Should never get caught so unprepared, he thinks. Was always ready for anything during the war.

Now here come his mother and his bride out of the hotel and across the street, the full-bodied old Irish redhead and the slender brunette with her delicate French features and deep,dark eyes, both graceful and eye-catching as they wend through the crowd toward him. Felice is shaded by the big hat, while his mother is bareheaded in the sunlight but carrying her customary rolled parasol; Paddy knows that her parasol is a weapon in disguise with a sharpened tip, used now and then over the years to fend off unwanted advances and prevent purse-grabbings. She is a woman who has always navigated among rude and dangerous men. The two women climb the steps to the top of the levee and come toward him, and just now the *Sultana*'s clerk says from his little booth, "You're next, sir. You were asking for a cabin to St. Louis?" Paddy turns and sees that the man is glancing at his empty sleeve cuff.

"Yes. For me and my wife. Here she comes. Please say you have one open. Very important."

"I do have, Mister Quinn, happy to say so."

"I...beg your pardon. You know me?"

"Mister O'Hara there told me who you are, sir," says the clerk, nodding toward an pear-shaped bystander in a tight, dingy linen suit, cheeks aflame with gin blossoms. The stranger salutes Paddy by touching a forefinger to the brim of his straw hat, then completes the greetings by turning, bowing and doffing the hat to the two arriving women. Moira Quinn answers his salute with a wary squint, then tilts her head.in apparent recognition and comes on, looking intently to her son's face.

"I'm Bill Gambrel, First Clerk," says the man in the booth. "Welcome to the *Sultana*, Mister Quinn."

"And what's this, son?" Moira Quinn asks. "Why are you here? We're due at the photography studio."

"A big change of plan, Ma. We...Felice and I...we'll be going up on this boat tomorrow. I'm assigned to Mister Lincoln's funeral. I'll explain later..."

At the mention of the President and his funeral, her face seems to melt and droop; she puts a hand over her mouth and her eyes go wet and glimmer with sudden tears. He glances at Felice and nods. Her eyes are wide as she seems to consider this vicissitude and what it'll mean. More men are lining up behind the Quinns, and a couple with a small son and daughter. The clerk touches Paddy's elbow and urges him toward the booth, pencil in hand, to reserve his cabin and get on with the business.

The portly man has stood patiently by, puffing on a dudeen pipe, slyly appreciating the beauty of both women, and when Mister Gambrel has issued a boarding voucher to Paddy, he crowds close in, extending a fat hand, and begins in a rich brogue:

"Mister Quinn, permit me to introduce meself, I'm an appreciative reader of yours, and me name is Jamie O'Hara. Me partner Tom McGinty and me keep the boat's bar, well forward in the grand saloon and far from the livestock and pigpens. Nicest place on the *Sultana* it is sure, fretwork most pleasing to the eye, and as extensive a variety of spirits as any afloat upon the bosom of the great river, every lovely amber hue of liquor a distiller can make. We'll be honored t'serve ye, and the first round will be on the house. By that I mean the first round each and every evenin' you're aboard, sir."

"Why, how generous," Paddy says in a tone barely masking the somersault his heart has just performed at that lucky invitation. "So glad I've pleased you.."

"McGinty and me were in Mexico with John Riley, lad. We want to thank ye fer writing that he was no such villain as they all said."

"Riley? *Riley!* You were with Riley and didn't get hanged? Congratulations!" Paddy is flooding with heart-twisting memories. But his mother and wife stand vibrant with impatience, needing to know more about this voyage he's planning. "Mister O'Hara, I'm honored to know you, eager to talk with you and, of course, to try your lovely saloon. I have to ask: do you know if Mister Riley's still alive? I've tried to find out, but the Army pretends he never existed..."

In his researches he found that a John Riley had died a drunk in Vera Cruz, but Paddy believes that must have been a different John Riley, for rumors have it that the great rogue went back to Ireland.

"We've reason to think he lives on, Mister Quinn. We'll tell ye why. Come and talk."

"Tomorrow, then!" He wishes they could start now, `just sip enough whiskey to maintain the feeling. But can't now.

"San Patricios!" he exclaims to his mother as the three go down the levee and head for the studio. "Riley men! I never thought I'd ever see a one of them again walking and breathing!"

His mother, holding his good arm, nods. She had been in Mexico with her son in that war and she saw the Irish deserters hanging in a row on that long, long gallows. In fact it had been her own paramour Col. Harney who strung them up. Moira Quinn had at that moment turned her back on Harney and never spoke to him again.

"Son, I'll let you board that boat and go North," she says with a long sigh, "if y' promise not to get hurt, or caught up with dangerous folks. It's worryin' after you that gave me all these white hairs!" He's thinking now, and surely she is too, that it would be better if she said nothing about that longago execution of the notorious San Patricios. There's no seemly way to explain why she was in Mexico without piquing Felice's curiosity.

It is Felice now, clinging on his lesser arm, who tries to set her at ease. "You needn't worry about him any more, Mum," she says. "I've got the ring in his nose."

Paddy feels his mother's fingers dig into his right forearm and he winces, thinking:

Damn it, Felice, don't say that! Ma might hope you do have the ring in my nose, but y' can't let her hear you say it! You're too new in the family!

But he squeezes Felice's fingers inside his elbow and looks down at her flawless pale skin in the shade of the straw hat, at that mouth with its tiny dimples in its lip corners, that mouth worthy of a thousand Ruskin essays on beauty, and he smiles down at her and winks at her glinting dark eyes.

He tells her, just above a whisper: "We'll have one more night here in our spacious hotel room. Then we'll be cramped down in a steamboat cabin, so close that one must exhale so the other can take a breath."

"The closer to you the better," she murmurs.

"But I love it when you can open your luminous limbs."

"O, Paddy, hush, dear!"

PADRAIC QUINN'S DIARY

New Orleans

April 20 1865

Finagled a plum assignment to President's funeral in Illinois, for Harper's & also New Orleans Picayune. Booked passage to St. Louis on the sidewheeler SULTANA. (Dread of this boat irrational, unfounded I do pray.)

Went to have photograph made for Felice's parents. But as we'll see them in person before the picture's processed, it's more for Ma than for them.

Ma morose because she can't leave hotel to go up to Father Abraham's funeral with us. (Better this way.)

She tried to cheer herself by inviting all the Shamrock guests down for a farewell dinner for us. Many eloquent toasts to the Martyr, as she's now calling him. Felice in her turn proposed a toast to the thousands of martyrs who died for the President's cause. She's not for letting him off.

Night so still, for New Orleans. Mournful singing voices outside on the levee, as loaders coal up the SULTANA. Any sensible person must be mourning. Except such as that gathering of slaver coots I deluged with beer today. Almost bragged about it to the guests, but caught myself before letting it slip I was in that saloon. (Felice mentioned to me my whiskey breath; first time she's said such a thing.)

To lighten the pall, I related the time I met the President, described him as he was then with the wink and the bright smile. That cheered Ma up a bit. She remembered the pencil sketch I drew of him after that meeting, and went to her room and brought it out to show around, that sketch I titled "Abraham Winkin'."

So the dinner party ended in a brighter mood. Which I like to imagine the President would appreciate, wherever he is just now, in his casket up there in the North.

(The spirit part of him, though, it's surely gone on beyond. If he was a Catholic, he might hang around expecting to be sainted.)

*

1 o'clock a.m.

Did our packing after the party. I watched F. bathe to come to bed. Tried to capture that God-given grace of her that's beyond my power to describe in words. About a minute to sketch her in pencil, behind her back. What would she think of me for doing this! Maybe show it to her sometime , maybe not, though. She might not see it so beautiful as I do.

Anyway, whatever that soap is that Ma gave her makes her delicious. Everywhere, down to the littlest cran and nooky.

Oughtn't write such thoughts down anywhere. It's the whiskey makes me do it.

(Irishman's excuse for anything. Of course Saint Peter will swallow that when I get there! Surely Sts. Pete & Pat have an understanding.)

*

2:30 a.m.

Can't sleep for thinking of those Riley men, the barkeeps. Love thinking John Riley might be still alive. Can hear his laughter twenty years later as clear as if I heard it today!

Just remembering that Mexican war gives me a thirst.

Abraham
Winkin'
Drawn in pencil
by P. Quinn
at Washington

CHAPTER TWO

Camp Fisk Prisoner Exchange Post

Near Vicksburg, Mississippi

Friday, April 21, 1865

Robbie Macombie and his hundreds of fellow wretches, the final human effluvia of Andersonville prison, raise their heads every time they hear one of those distant steamboat whistles. The next one might be the one that will load them on and take them up the river toward home.

They had thought of those steamboat whistles as a sort of hopeful music.

But then the other day, that one boat had come down from Illinois with the news that President Lincoln was shot to death.

That had made Robbie Macombie want to just go ahead and die. Mister Lincoln was like Robbie's personal saint. Just like him, grew up in Southern Indiana a woodcutter, hardscrabble farmer, one of the settler families. Most of the war, Robbie Macombie had felt he was going through it all for Mister Lincoln, rather than for some vague big thing called the Union.

Robbie has been sure for several months that he's dying himself. Guts and lungs went bad in the prison. He'd made a bet with the last living man from his company that he'd never get out of that prison gate except in the Dead Wagon. Lost that bet. Then the man he'd made the bet with just slumped down and died right there outside the gate. Guess that was as far ahead as he'd planned: getting outside the gate.

Robbie of course hadn't even planned that far. But he hasn't died yet. Lately he's been thinking he might live long enough to get up to Saluda, there on that high bluff over the Ohio River, where the beautiful graveyard is, where his Grandpa Joseph Macombie lies. That's where Robbie wants to go to his rest, there at his birthplace.

Robbie can remember helping plane and join the wood for Grandpa's coffin, can remember helping shovel dirt to dig his grave, and can remember Grandpa's headstone, which noted that he'd been a soldier in the Revolution. That was why Robbie had joined the Army in '46 to go fight in the Mexican War, because he'd imagined Grandpa would be proud of him. And he'd thought of Grandpa when he joined the Pennsylvania Volunteers for this war, in '62, but mostly because Abraham Lincoln called for soldiers. That, and the fact that Robbie and his wife made each other so miserable that he was glad to go away. In their fifteen years married, they'd had so many babies sicken and die that they didn't even like to talk to each other.

Robbie had enlisted with his brother, Jim Alexander Macombie, and they'd stayed together until Fredericksburg, where Jim Alex got hit and died with his bloody head on Robbie's arm.

Robbie had never been much of a dreamer, not in any sentimental way. His dreams had been more practical, like designing and building a whole mill himself, a waterwheel mill engineered to convert between gristmill and sawmill. Robbie had been a first rate millwright carpenter.

Then he'd got in the Army where there never was a day of doing anything useful, just destroying things and trying to kill people so they couldn't kill you.

Only thing he'd ever built in the Army was a gallows. There in the prison. Didn't want to, but was the only good carpenter not too sick to do it. Then they'd nicknamed him Hangman, and he hated that.

One day, he thinks sometimes, every son of a bitch who remembers that nickname will be dead, and I'll be rid of it. Most of them died back there in the prison, but a few still say it.

It's not much to dream for, that everybody will forget your

nickname, he thinks.

He doesn't dream of going back to his wife Tildie, or to his two sons who lived. They probably all believe he's dead by now anyway.

One thing Robbie had liked to imagine during the war was that somehow he might meet Mister Lincoln face to face. Not that he'd ever thought it very likely.

But Mister Lincoln's dead now, so that hope's gone the way of all the others he ever had.

While they wait for their homebound boats to toot in the distance, this place is tolerable, as anything after Andersonville would be. They're under the Stars and Stripes now, not the Stars and Bars; there are no Reb guards. There's plenty of blessed clean water, firewood to cook with and food to cook: dried beef to boil for broth, for those who can't handle solid food yet, beef with pickled cabbage for those who can, unlimited hardtack to chew if your teeth are good enough, or to mumble and gum if not. As much coffee as you can drink, but if your stomach can't take coffee, soak and soften the tack in water. Even some fresh vegetables come in now and then, early produce brought out from Vicksburg by the Sisters of Charity, radishes and lettuce. Indian women sometimes come to the camp with cattail tubers and shoots and pollen, with burdock roots, with armloads of fresh field greens, lamb's-quarter, milkweed flowerbuds, dried squash, maple sugar, sassafras bark for a tonic tea. The Indians were supposed to have been driven out of here twenty years ago, but some just hid. And here they come out of the Big Black River canebrake with bags and baskets of surprisingly tasty forage, stuff that soothes the stomach and makes the skin sores and itchy gums go away, and then they leave without saying a word in English, their ragged calico disappearing into the swamp shadows, leaving the pale, scabby veterans to gawk, mystified. But they remind Robbie of something, something he'd read before the war, a story he's never quite forgotten, and though Robbie seldom talks, he says now to his shantymates:

"When the Indians down in these parts were all, ye know, rounded up, driven out West? Well, those Indians heard that people in

Ireland were starving to death, 'cause all their potato crops got blighted. Ye know what? Those poor homeless savages took up a collection, most of the coin they had amongst them. Came to a bit more than two hundred dollars, if I recall. And sent it over to Ireland, can you imagine that? Later on the Irish over there put up some kind of a little, uhm, monument thing to those poor Indians. For their kindness. Think of that, boys! We white folks been killing and tormenting our own countrymen here for four years, but some poor savages can do like that for some faraway white folks they didn't even know!"

There's not much one can say about meanness and misery that will surprise these veterans, after Andersonville, but hearing some decent thing like that moves them to sit quiet for a spell with a thoughtful look on their faces, and a few will even turn away and thumb off a tear.

Now somebody says, "Good story, Hangman."

"Kindly stop calling me that."

Robbie's mind has been roiled by three years of battles and captivity, but he remembers when he first read the story. It was one day at McClelland's headquarters in Virginia, when he was a courier. Young war correspondent, man with just one hand, came over to the campfire.

Gave Robbie a copy of *Harper's Weekly*, said, "Here, soldier. Why should the officers get all the good reading?" Something like that. Robbie's pretty sure he didn't just dream that.

The Indian story was in that magazine. Robbie had carried the magazine in his kit for months.

He was robbed of it, of his whole kit, by a gang of ruffians among the inmates at the prison.

Over time, that gang cut, robbed, beat up, even killed, some of the other prisoners. So a vigilante company was formed. It raided the thugs, assembled a court, sentenced the ringleaders, and hanged six of them. Yankee soldiers hanging Yankee soldiers, and all done by enlisted men who'd organized themselves sort of like a government of their own. No officers. All Robbie had to do with it was making the gallows.

Sometimes he wonders what might happen if the official Army finds out that enlisted men did that.

It's one reason why he doesn't like his nickname.

Camp Fisk here, established long ago as a prisoner exchange station, is now just a holding pen full of sick, skinny, half-addled survivors, one or two giving up the ghost about every day or so, but they believe they'll be going home. They have few tents, but their handmade cane shelters are adequate, now that Spring is here. Every time those steamboat whistles reverberate through the bottomland, announcing another vessel coming up to Vicksburg, hopes rise up. Then after that boat goes on up the river taking a thousand more freed prisoners, the ones left here slump back into waiting.

Robbie spends much of his time trying to clean the filth of Andersonville off his body.

Most everybody here is gray with baked-on soot from the pine campfires in the prison, where there was no way to wash off. Here at Camp Fisk, Robbie heats water to bathe himself two or three times a day, using strong soap brought by the Sisters of Charity. You'd think they ran a soap factory, judging by the amounts of it they bring. He grooms himself obsessively for lice, using a nit comb also provided by the Sisters. He sits naked in sunlight, still incredulous at the knobby fleshlessness of his limbs, and combs and picks and pinches, even over and under his scrotum, chasing down every itch real or imagined. His comrades gibe at him for his diligent louse-hunting, saying how easy it must be to root out lice if every hair on you is white and your skin's so pale that even a nit can't find shade to hide in. Well, with all that soap and water, day by day the scabies and skin sores do heal and go to scurf and at last slough off.

It's not that he expects to live much longer. But if he gets to Saluda, it'll be a clean and presentable corpse they bury beside Grandpa Joseph.

PADRAIC QUINN'S DIARY

Saturday April 22

On steamer Sultana

Departure from New Orleans delayed a day by loading. Capt Mason making up lost time, steaming hard, no stop at Baton Rouge, barely nosed into Natchez for a quick load.

River in broad flood, running high and fast. Cabin pretty but cramped. Several families aboard with children. Dining good, so far.

Passed two southbound boats in daytime, looking like wedding cakes. Passed three at night all aglitter like floating hotels. Could hear music of their entertainments coming across river, even over engines. A far cry from gunboats, tinclads & hospital ships. PAX VOBISCUM.

Mr Gambrel, clerk & part owner of Sultana, very friendly; seems infatuated with Felice. Not the only gent who seems so. He is aglow with avarice, as postwar steamboat business promises to be like the Old Days. Discussed Elder-made boilers at some length, advantages & dangers. This boat has them. Trying not to worry thereon.

Been to the Irishmen's bar for the gratis guzzle they promised, most congenial and generous but no chance to talk of John Riley; bar too crowded. But these gents have bruited my reputation , and I receive nods from many passengers. Have been engaged in banter by several self-prestigious passengers who would like to talk to me about the extreme importance of their postwar enterprises. For humility's sake, I remind myself that they see not Paddy Quinn before them, but Harper's Weekly.

Had to restrain my mouth and fist when an overstuffed Natchez lawyer expressed an unseemly lack of remorse over the assassination.

Shared my flask with a major on deck who remembered me from Gen. Hooker's headquarters. (Needless to say, I didn't remember him.) Hope he doesn't recall too much.

Honeymoon still on. Viva!

Oh, have I married up!

CHAPTER THREE

Aboard the Sidewheeler SULTANA

Saturday, April 22, 1865

Paddy and Felice Quinn have found the place on the boat where the breeze and the view are best, on the port side forward, Texas deck, and they are privileged to have chairs set there for them, because O'Hara the saloonkeeper told Captain Mason that Mister Quinn is a famous war correspondent. Captain Mason himself eagerly shook the hand that the late President once had shaken, and he apologized for the tardy departure from New Orleans, which was due to a delay in loading of cargo. Instead of sailing on Thursday afternoon as advertised, the *Sultana* had lain at the Gravier Street wharf another day, until yesterday. The captain has assured Paddy that he will be able to get to the President's funeral in good time despite the late start, thanks to *Sultana*'s speed and power. "Don't be surprised," the dapper captain said with a chuckle, "if I overtake and pass the *Olive Branch*, well before St. Louis." The *Olive Branch* had departed New Orleans on Thursday true to schedule, leaving Paddy to fret and damn himself for missing that boat by pausing in a saloon a few minutes too long.

Now, even with the captain's deferential treatment of the honeymooners, the generosity of the boat's bartenders, the cleanliness and elegance of the vessel, and the palatability of its cuisine, Paddy remains ill at ease. He lays his right hand over on Felice's left, on the arm of her deck chair, and glances at her breeze-ruffled tresses, her delicate profile, and asks, "How does this boat feel to you, my sweet?" She has long been a river traveler, with her St. Louis family and then her tours of duty on the hospital boats, so he expects her to have a feel for a vessel, like his own. If she's comfortable on this one, it might settle his own apprehension.

She says, "I worry, the river being so high. And what the engineer told you about running so hard on these new boilers. I'll be glad when we get there and get off. But what good is it to worry?" She puts on that serene smile, and shrugs.

The high water is indeed worrisome. In spring flood times like these, a steamboat pilot usually edges along the riverbanks where the current is slower. Floating trees speed down the fast water. But the *Sultana* is now being run at full steam in the swift midriver current to make up lost time. On some stretches of the river, the bottomlands are so flooded that the Mississippi looks like a muddy sea instead of a muddy river. As for the new boilers, Paddy and Felice are probably the only passengers on this boat who know enough to discuss them. Her father had taught her about steam engines when she was a girl, and she has read Paddy's magazine article on the recent development of more efficient boilers, particularly the fire-tube boiler invented in 1862 by the Scots engineer named Elder. Felice, much to Paddy's pride and delight, can discuss such subjects. The *Sultana*'s boilers are of the Elder design, with tubes built into the water tanks, allowing heat from the firebox to pass through the tanks instead of just heating them from beneath. Paddy knows what Mississippi River engineers don't like about the Scotsman's design: river sediment can clog the spaces between the fire tubes, creating a danger of dry pockets and hot spots, which in turn can lead to leaks and ruptures. And water of the lower Mississippi is notoriously dense with sediment. Any steamboat travel has the underlying danger of boiler explosion, as all passengers are vaguely aware. Most are familiar with Paddy's famous coinage, "swimming volcanoes." But few passengers have ever heard of the volatile new fire-tube boiler. For their peace of mind, that's just as well. As Felice just said, what's the use of worrying? The boiler room engineers know what they're dealing with, and the boat inspectors have to sign certification. So there is a tacit trust in such transportation, beyond that tacit trust all sojourners put in their Lord Protector. Paddy and Felice both understand, after the war just past, that there are no full assurances of safety in this world. Both of them have seen more sudden and undeserved death than most civilians ever imagined. In this new marriage, that's one of the crucial understandings they have in common, and he is thinking just that, as he sits here beside her on the Texas deck basking in the mild spring sunlight and a gentle breeze coming off the river faint with the scents of spring's greening. And he is thinking of all the thousands of poor, exhausted veterans, Union and Rebel both, who must be afoot on every road in America just now, trudging home from the war to whatever might remain of homes and families. There are a few veterans on this boat, some taking cheap deck passage and sitting inscrutable, patient, with their muskets and haversacks and in the faded remnants of their uniforms. In the cabins there are officers, some in uniform, some not.

Paddy knows that this vast, weary exodus from war is only just begun and will go on for weeks, maybe months. Father Abraham isn't the only one going home slowly. His brains are scrambled like eggs by an assassin's derringer bullet that killed his body. Many of these other myriad homeward-bound are still alive in body but their brains too are scrambled. And as the axiom says, you can't unscramble an egg. Many soldiers, Yankee or Reb, will return into their families as strangers, having endured in a terrible reality their home folks can't imagine.

A dark line of oaks, willows and cottonwoods a mile to the west shows where the western riverbank is, but the flood stretches far beyond that line. Paddy points at a distant angularity. "That's the roof of a house. Aren't you glad we don't live there?" She turns her hand palm up and squeezes his wrist. He sighs and turns his face to the breeze, wistful, remembering sad and terrible things, thankful for the unfamiliar comfort of a mere hand on his wrist. Yearning for a drink, but only a faint yearning as yet. So many things he hopes she will come to know and understand! His mind strays ahead into vague plans. He will want her to learn all about the Irish Battalion in the Mexican War and his longago involvement in it. That conflict had shaped his whole life. Keeping a war diary and sketchbook had made him grow up to be a war correspondent as surely as being born Irish had made him grow up to be a drinking man. Remembering all that makes him think again of John Riley's old veterans, O'Hara and McGinty the barkeeps. Paddy yearns to go down and drink and talk with them. But he is also thinking ahead toward Vicksburg, the next city stop on the *Sultana*'s schedule, probably late tomorrow.

There's so much he wants to tell Felice about the campaign for Vicksburg, so fraught with memories for him, the "Gibraltar of the Mississippi" on the high bluff with its terrible big defensive guns and its dugouts and tunnels where the city's people lived like groundhogs and had to hunt rats for meat during the long siege. He will tell her how it was being under sniper fire as a correspondent, about learning the art of "sketch and duck;" he'll tell how it was to be one of the few journalists favored by General Grant, he whose dogged strategic wisdom had eventually conquered that place and opened the Mississippi for the Union forces. Paddy will practice for her ear the telling of those stories, and eventually he will polish them into narratives fit for lecture hall audiences. He wonders whether she can possibly imagine the affinity he had with Grant during that long, dismal campaign, those sly empathies they had as they sneaked a little whiskey together. They had first shared bottles nearly twenty years ago, in Mexico, when the boy Paddy was a bootlegger's apprentice and Grant was a fresh-faced lieutenant just out of West Point. Probably he won't tell her about that, though. The less he tells her about drinking, the better. A spy had been sent to Vicksburg to monitor Grant's drinking and to tattle to the President if it got too bad. That had become an odd game, and Paddy had of course got involved in it; he believed that Grant thought better when he drank than when he didn't, as Paddy believes he does himself.

Someday, he thinks, I can show her all she needs to understand about me, including tendencies that might look like weaknesses but aren't necessarily, not in my occupation. Then we'll be at ease, and this will be everything that a marriage ever was meant to be in God's scheme of things. This Felice, he believes, is God's greatest gift to him, bestowed just when he most desperately needed her.

Yes, even his own doting mother had condescended to tell him so, just as she saw them onto the boat. Moira Quinn had made her assessment of Felice by then, and told him, "Lose her, and *you're* lost, son. Hear me? In that diary I gave you, she should be mentioned as often as you are yourself." And saying it, she had rapped a hard knuckle against the portfolio in which he carries the diary.

On his lap now rests that piece of portable furniture that has become a part of him, his wooden portfolio that contains his writing and drawing paraphernalia, his notebooks, sketchbook and the diary. It has been scuffed and dented by rough usage before and during the war, but he keeps it agleam with wax. Long ago he devised a leather harness rig that allows him to fix it securely on the stump of his left forearm so that he can write or draw upon it in any posture or under any conditions afield. Along one edge is carved in deep Roman capital letters, by his own penknife, P. QUINN. Its tight, hinged lid and all its seams he has sealed with glue and strips of caoutchouc rubber, a measure taken after rain and seepage too frequently ruined or stained the desk's contents. This portfolio he sometimes refers to as "my left hand." He was known by it everywhere during the war, where he campaigned among that horde of battlefield artists like Fred Waud and Theodore Davis, photographers like Sullivan and Brady and Gardner, all those writers and image-makers jokingly known as the "Bohemian Brigade." Paddy Quinn's fame was created almost entirely by his work in and upon this battered rosewood box. It had been originally a Mexican Army officer's tiny field desk. When he found it in on a Mexican battlefield it had two broken legs, and he cut off all the legs to make it small and portable. By now he usually feels incomplete if it's not with him, slung under his arm for carrying, or strapped on for use. He sometimes rubs it and manipulates it unconsciously, as some crack their knuckles or drum fingertips on tabletops. Some amputees wear a hook where a hand used to be; he has a writing box.

The river here between Natchez and Vicksburg is a series of long loops and bends, confusing in normal conditions, bewildering now with the bottomlands covered with muddy water. From this high deck Paddy can see miles across the flooded Louisiana lowlands, sometimes squinting at the sunlight reflecting off the muddy water. As the trembling vessel swings through the great turns, sometimes the shadow of the superstructure glides over Paddy and Felice, cooling their sunwarmed faces and bodies, causing them to shiver in the breeze.

The great paddlewheels slosh and churn, and the steam engines throb far below the decks. High in the sky above the billowing coalsmoke from the stacks, an eagle hovers, riding on the wind. The *Sultana,* two hundred and sixty feet long and forty-two abeam, is pressing against the spring flood as fast as she can be driven. The boat's engineer, a grim-faced, heavy-browed fellow named Wintreger, has already been heard complaining that the *Sultana*'s machinery is being overtaxed. In the saloon last evening, just when Paddy sat down to quiz the bartender McGinty about their old hero John Riley, the engineer had wedged his way in to order a shot of rye and complain loudly about the pressure that's being put on the boilers, the coalheavers, the whole machine, just because the Captain thinks he has to pass up the *Olive Branch.* "You got to coddle them fire-tube boilers," the engineer declaimed several times, and he was still grousing on the subject when Paddy left the bar to rejoin his bride in their tiny cabin.

Paddy sighs and turns in his chair, adjusting for a chronic twinge of pain in the back of his waist, a result of years in cold bivouacs. He fiddles with the latch of his portfolio, unfastens it, reaches in to finger the edge of a sketchbook. Hand and mind restless, wanting to put something on paper, word or image, he says, "My sweet, I need to move around a little. Thought I might go see that alligator, draw a sketch of it. I've never once drawn an alligator, even though I saw them in the swamps, in the Seminole War." Amid the odd items of cargo on the *Sultana* is a wooden crate containing an alligator, which a crewman is taking North to sell to a circus or a raree-show. It is already an attraction for the passengers on this boat, especially the families with children. The crate is constantly surrounded by gawkers. Paddy anticipates a quick sketch of the reptile, then a visit to the saloon, a bit of whiskey and some talk with O'Hara and McGinty about John Riley and the Irish Battalion. Felice of course won't sit with him in the bar, so she'll probably go to the cabin for a nap, or back to the Ladies' Parlor, which, with more than three hundred passengers on board, is the least crowded room on the vessel, and the most pleasant. He is already anticipating the bracing effect of a whiskey, thumbing the sketchbook absent-mindedly, when Felice exclaims:

"What...is...*that?*"

"What..." He follows her shocked gaze, down to the raised lid of his portfolio, the open cover of his sketchbook. Feeling his face flush, he laughs, "Why, it's you, sweet..."

"Me? *Me?* That's the backside of a naked woman! What do you mean, that's *me*?"

"I just sketched you bathing the other evening...Such beauty..."

"How dare you draw such filth! How could you *peek* on me?"

"Felice! This is anything *but* filth. This is *grace*! I drew this in...in... *tribute*." But it does dawn on him how salacious this might seem to her, how shocked she might well be. He protests, "I meant to show you this, as soon as...as soon as..."

She's looking at the picture now, not glaring at him. "*This* is how I look?"

"Of course, beloved."

"And how would I know? I've never seen myself from back there. And what am I supposed to be doing, for heaven's sake? It looks like, like I'm, well...*douching*. You didn't see me do any such thing."

"My dear, I didn't watch what you did. Just how you looked. I'd guess you were cleaning your *toenails*, by the looks of this..."

She shakes her head and after a while she says:

"Lord in heaven! What kind of war correspondent were you? What could people tell from your reports, if..." she begins tittering "...you can't tell a douche from a pedicure?"

It's a while before they can stop laughing. They're red-faced, leaning onto each other's shoulders. Eventually, Paddy is able to say:

"Sure and there was no such a doubt, m'love. Soldiers never did either one, that I ever saw."

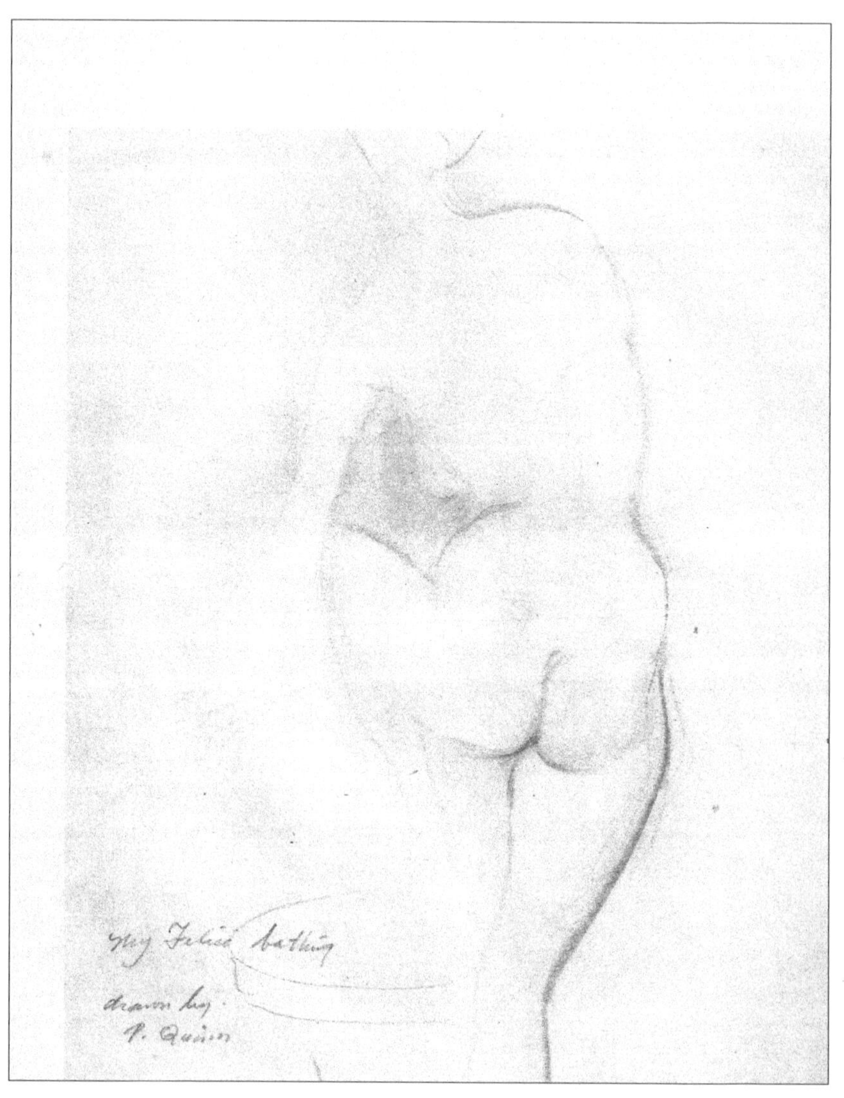
my Felice bathing
drawn by
P. Quinn

PADRAIC QUINN'S DIARY

Aboard steamer Sultana

Sunday April 23, 1865

12:30 o'clock a.m.

Just in from O'Hara & McGinty's bar. Learned much. Felice miffed I was there so late.

Bed now, write later.

*

6 o'clock a.m.

O'H. & McG. about Riley I'll write later; first ,this before I forget:

A new theory, my adjunct to "Creative Insomnia":

Few nocturnal revelations and meaningful dreams survive the light of day. The best of them flow in the gutters & sewers & streams, having been emptied out of chamberpots, flushed from waterclosets. Here's why: we wake up because we need to piss. Our minds are at that time richest with vivid dreams & novel notions. We rise and relieve ourselves. By the time we get to pen and paper, those ideas & visions have faded beyond recall. Whither? Gone with the urine. Down the sluice, into the latrine, dispersed in the sewage, flushed by Lethe, the River of Forgetting. Thus, proving that the bladder, not the brain, is the seat of Intellect. (Subject for an eyebrow-raising lecture, spoof of scientific theorising?}

I captured this revelatory theory by the expedient of coming straight to write in this diary upon awakening, instead of chamberpot first. Now that it's written down I can go pee.

Then perhaps get another hour of sleep, another great insight.

*

7 o'clock a.m. Lay awake, afraid of losing this thought: A genius should *arise before daybreak to write,& enrich his inkwell with his urine! Goethe, Poe, Descartes, Voltaire, Hume, Dante, da Vinci, might have sold theirs by the pint, had they understood this. Too late for them. I could offer mine at $10.00 a quart --more, as my fame grows. "Ladies & Gentlemen, bottles available in the Lobby!"*

Could charge a premium for the vintage years. Must entertain Felice with this when she wakes. (Or maybe shouldn't) Writ in piss. Notes on Riley when I'm not so tired.

*

11:30 o'clock a.m. Sunday cont'd

Distressing news --

A boiler leak.

First announced during chapel service in the Grand Salon, followed by a reminder to keep our cork life-savers where we can find them; gave the Protestant passengers something specific to pray about, I imagine. Felice & I had already guessed, hearing the engines slow down. We had been worrying about these fire-tube boilers.

At breakfast we heard controversy at Capt. Mason's table. He would like it repaired on the move, but 1st Engr. Mr. Wintreger is adamant, it must be repaired at dock, with fire pulled and steel cooled. That means laying over at Vicksburg a day at least -- if the boat can make it that far -- about 50 miles yet -- without exploding.

So now we run at half steam in slow water at starboard bank (as we should have been doing anyway in this flood). At this rate we mightn't outrun the President's funeral train after all. Damnation!

To more pleasant news. The good bartenders treated me as promised, and gave me evidence John Riley still lives -- or did as lately as '63. They heard by way of Agustin Juvero of Mexico City who went to Ireland for the Mex. gov't on mission to memorialize Col. Riley for his valor in their war against us, &c. Senor Juvero traced him to his native Galway County, living on his family plot with his son. Not prospering (it being Ireland) but surviving with help of Mex. Army mustering out stipend. Intemperate (aren't we all!), virtually a hermit due to stigma of the branding scars on cheeks; otherwise robust health but gone fully whiteheaded. So glad the good Sr. Juvero provided enough description to help me envision him after so many years. What a fraught reunion that must have been for both of them, Col. Riley having been like father to Juvero after the war! By St Padraic's holy snakeprod I must find a means to get to Ireland while he survives, for he was likewise fatherly to me, before he swam the Rio Grande to join the Mexicans.

Irony: here I daydream of crossing to Ireland on a seagoing ship, while this luckless tub mightn't even get us alive to Vicksburg! But O to see John Riley again, Viva Riley!

As for now, Felice and I auscultate the throb of this vessel like doctors with a stethoscope.

*

My efforts to sketch alligator always thwarted by too much crowd around its crate. Looks to be about 8 feet long.

*

Observing Capt. Mason I'd say he works harder reassuring and cheering passengers about the ailing boiler than nursing the vessel itself. Chirky fellow with fine posture and handsome sandy mustache, somehow avoided war service but knows how to look like an Admiral. I personally wouldn't trade that glum engineer Wintreger for a dozen such captains, as I prefer a useful man over a pretty one.

A general observation of P. Quinn, orator and sage: The unsmiling know something the smiling don't.

Another observation of same sage, different circumstances: Those who are smiling know something the unsmiling don't.

Reminding me of what Walpole said: This world is a comedy to those that think, a tragedy to those that feel. (I can hope that others might someday quote something memorable I've said or written.)

*

Afternoon and still chugging. I pointed out to Felice where I rode with Grant, how he made strategy out of adverse riverscapes, where he crossed Mississippi to come up at Vicksburg from below. Where I sat under a shot-scarred oak and drew a skirmish scene while musketballs rattled through the foliage. Is there a place in this country where I haven't done the like, these last four years?

Why am I even still alive?

Not complaining, Lord. Keep up me luck for a boiler holding together till we make Vicksburg!

Should be there before dusk. Want to see how the city's rebuilding from all that battering in the siege. Much, much to remember here.

Reckon I'd have to go overseas to find a place where I haven't tracked blood!

CHAPTER FOUR

Camp Fisk

Near Vicksburg, Mississippi

Sunday, April 23, 1865

Robbie Macombie is eating pickled cabbage off a tin plate, hoping it won't torture his poor innards the way beef does, when he hears another steamboat's whistle in the distance: Three toots, meaning it's coming in to dock at Vicksburg. If it's coming up from New Orleans, it could be *his* transportation. He's moved that far up on the roster.

But it might be a boat going south instead. This camp is out of sight of the Mississippi, three or four miles from Vicksburg, so the soldiers here can't see which way a boat is going even though they hear it. It's been four or five days since the one called *Sultana* went downriver carrying the news that President Lincoln had been assassinated. Since that day such a morose air has prevailed that it doesn't feel much better here than back at the prison. Robbie has sat much of the time since then bent down over his burning gut, forehead on his knees, sometimes groaning with grief, envisioning that gaunt and homely face of Lincoln that seems personally familiar though he's really seen it only in newspaper engravings and on pasteboard cards. Last time he'd felt hit so hard personally was when his brother Jim Alex died on him at Fredericksburg.

The *Sultana* is a name he doubts he'll ever be able to forget. It's a rather pretty name, but it is now so linked in his soul with the abominable tidings it had brought that he hates the sound of it.

Yesterday, 700 men, most of them from Wisconsin units, got on flatcars of the Jackson & Vicksburg Railroad train into Vicksburg, and by late afternoon had been loaded onto a boat called the *Olive Branch* and are now headed up the Mississippi on their way home. Its departure whistles had been heard way out here in the camp. Then the rest of the evening and night, no more boat whistles, just the restless murmur of the camp and its remaining sixteen hundred waiting wretches. Robbie had tried to shake off his dark feelings and had passed the evening in his usual obsessions: trying to get clean, and trying to keep food down. So far, not much luck at either one. There is always a slump in morale in the camp after other soldiers leave. Everyone here thinks he should be on the river homeward bound by now. It's been more than a month since they were liberated from Andersonville. Robbie still worries that the Army might come while they're still gathered here and start investigating the hanging executions they did back there in the prison.

Now it's Sunday afternoon, and by the sound of it, another boat has come. Capt. Frederick Speed, Camp Fisk's commandant, gets dispatches from Vicksburg every day about northbound steamboats scheduled to arrive there. Capt. Speed has already put together a roster of those for the next boatload: about 400 soldiers from Ohio, then another list of about twelve hundred mixed names from Indiana and other places. Robbie Macombie is near the top of the second list, so he has a chance to board the boat now coming in.

An hour later Robbie sits among hundreds who have gathered on the trampled ground in front of the camp office, sits with all his belongings in his pockets or bundled in a handkerchief, and waits to be summoned to the shuttle train. He stuffs cut tobacco into his pipe, strikes a wooden match, puffs up a pungent cloud, sucks in a chestful of smoke that would have made him cough to death as little as a month ago, gets that pleasant little buzzing sensation between his ears. There had been so little tobacco to be gotten at Andersonville that he'd become used to doing without, so now its effect is strong, now that he has it again. His smoke rises and curls and dissolves into that of scores of other smokers in the late afternoon sunshine. In the drone of voices Robbie hears now and then *Lincoln,* or *Abe,* or *Father Abraham.*

Now a tall, knobby-jointed sergeant, whom they've nicknamed Big Noise, comes out of Capt. Speed's office, holding a slip of paper, and bellows:

"Here's the word! Boat that came in today is called the *Sultana*. You on the new roster will board 'er, but not yet awhile. She has to lay over and get a leaky boiler fixed. Won't be done till tomorrow at the soonest." Groans rise from the crowd of wretches, and a few oaths and obscenities.

Sultana! Robbie thinks. Of all the damn steamboats, that bad news boat?

The sergeant raises his voice over the crowd's murmur. "Go on back to your hutches, people. We'll muster you when the boat's fixed, or when others come up. You all ain't that eager to leave good old Camp Purgatory, are ye?"

After a general jeer, they begin rising, stiff and groaning, to disperse. Most, like Robbie, shuffle and limp barefoot. Most have been issued shoes here, but new shoes hurt on bone-sore feet. More waiting, he thinks. Still more waiting. Well, he's good at waiting. And every day he waits here he can pick among the varied foods available, figure out what he can keep down, get a little strength maybe to keep him alive until he's on his way home to that pretty graveyard in Saluda. Here he vomits more food in one day than he got to eat in a month at Andersonville. The Army doctor here has dosed him with "starters" and "stoppers," but whether he's clogged up or spewing, his gut still feels like the passageway to Hell. A little more time here, a little more food, more soap, some of those Indian salves and sunshine healing his itchy, scurfy places...and then he'll show up dead or alive looking clean and respectable enough for his own funeral, and his Uncle Alexander will give him a nice burial there next to Grandpa Joseph.

He doesn't give a thought to anything beyond that graveyard anymore. *Saluda*. He thinks the name of that town on the bluff, and he starts seeing it again. Those great oaks and maples on the steep bluff. That tall waterfall beside the road with ferns and moss all the way up. His wife Tildie in Pennsylvania is too far beyond that for him even to think of. She's dead to him, and no doubt thinks he's already dead. Now, if she'd ever considered leaving her Pennsylvania folks and moving to Indiana, she might still be alive to him. But, hell, he hadn't expected to be coming home alive from Andersonville anyway. So waiting and being delayed again and again aren't anything he can't bear another day or so, or a week, or whatever it turns out to be. When they take him they'll take him.

Now Robbie sits outside his shebang heating water over a fire of sticks, thinking about that broken steamboat *Sultana* at Vicksburg dock four miles away, and about boiler mechanics fixing it so that he can get on it in a day of two to continue home. Good to know they're fixing whatever it is. He has lived near the rivers long enough that he knows steamboats explode. Fix it before we get on, he thinks. We all been through enough blowin' up troubles.

At nightfall he takes one more bath, scrubbing off a little more of the pine soot and filth of that prison, then sits by the fire, talking to no one, and fills and lights his pipe. He could get up and wander a bit, go find Romulus Tolbert, his old Saluda neighbor, and talk to him. He knows Tolbert's still here. Still on the roster. But Tolbert is so conscious of his shot-off chin and mangled jaw, it's uncomfortable to talk with him. He seems to think every eye in the world is on his chin, and he tries to twist away or down, and that makes people frown and squint at him, and he thinks they're concentrating on his wound, or repelled by it. It's easier to be alone than with someone so squirmy. Maybe Tolbert wouldn't be that way about it if he hadn't grown up such a handsome boy and always fussed over for his looks. A homely man marred that way wouldn't think he'd lost so much, and would stop thinking about it after a while. Take that Abe Lincoln. His face could take a real beating and not look much worse. Robbie remembers reading once long ago that a political rival accused Mister Lincoln of being two-faced, and he answered, "If I had two faces, would I be wearing this one?" Robbie smiles almost every time he thinks of him, thinks of that hard-working Southern Indiana fellow, who grew up so much like himself. But no matter how good it's always been to consider him, the fact is, he's dead now.

Would've been an honor to make *his* casket, Robbie thinks..

Black walnut. With inlays of wild cherry and something pale like sycamore.

Wish I could've built that instead of the gallows.

He gazes into the fire and in his thoughts he designs and makes it, starting with the rough walnut tree itself, remembers again what it was like to use all those tools on the dark walnut wood: the saws and froes, adzes and slicks, the curved gouges, the rasps, the augers and rabbeting planes and drawknives -- he remembers the feel of them in his hands, remembers how one has to modify the angle or force of a tool in different kinds of wood, how easily walnut splits if you're too forceful on certain cuts. His nose remembers the specific musky smell of walnut, when you saw it and when it burns.

It is a rich remembering and makes him yearn to work again with his hands and mind. Soldiering, he hadn't felt useful one day out of a year. Now in his daydream he leaves the walnut casket and is busy cutting and joining hard maple to make gears and wheels for a grain mill; he remembers a rachet he was inventing before the war started, and spends a long while in his mind improving on it, wishing he had a pencil and some paper to draw these modifications he's thinking up. Robbie has never designed and built a whole mill, always worked in crews of journeymen, but now he tilts his head and runs the tip of his tongue through the space where molars fell out back in Andersonville, and wishes he could have built even one good mill all by himself before he died. Just one whole mill to be remembered by. A watermill.

They're running some mills on steam engines nowadays, he muses. Wasteful and dirty.

Think of the cost of the coal. Falling water's free. Clean, not dirty like coal engines.

Had enough dirty in Andersonville to last me for good.

He remembers the high waterfall, the one called Clifty Falls, on the road out from Madison to Saluda. Used to stop and bathe in it on hot days, and would just hide under the bridge when he'd hear a wagon or hooves coming. Never felt so clean ever since.

Then his mind and hands are remembering woodworking again. Compares beech with maple for making a particular rack and pinion that would last near as long as any iron one could.

He remembers locking a hickory stave into a shaving-horse and shaping a perfect axe handle out with his drawknife in less than ten minutes. Remembers making toy tops and dancing puppets out of sycamore. He'd made his wife's spinning wheel, of rock maple. Chiseled out big dough-mixing bowls of wild cherry wood, sold them at fairs.

Bet there's a real dearth of skilled wood crafters in Indiana now, he thinks. Or the whole country, for that matter. Killed off God knows how many.

Going to need some of those freed Negroes to do work all the dead soldiers used to do.

Robbie raises both bony white hands up, turns them, palm to back, back to palm in the firelight, remembering what good work they did with tools instead of weapons.

If I could've made Mister Lincoln's casket for him, he thinks, I'd die happy.

*

Vicksburg Mississippi

Aboard SULTANA

Sunday 23 April 1865

My dear Mother,

Taking advantage of an unplanned lay- over in this place for repair of a leak (the boat, not me, ha ha), I pen this to be sent down to you via the next vessel. Your loving daughter-in-law asks to add a few words also.

An uneventful trip otherwise. The boiler trouble requires the fires be pulled now, to allow some smithy to come aboard with a sheet of boiler plate, tools, &c. and fix it. Captain Cass Mason, who regales the famous correspondent & bride most solicitously, insists he need not terminate the voyage here for a full replacement of the offending boiler, that the leak can be made perfectly safe to serve until reaching St. Louis, where the replacement can be made without having delayed any of us passengers. This being particularly important as you know, to your son the journalist. Capt.Mason assures we'll be one day at most here which will allow me time to reach Springfield before the late President. (The later the President the better in this instance, excuse the feeble joke.)

The voyage hereto has been a pleasant continuation of the honeymoon begun so happily there in your care, tho the stateroom is very small compared to our suite at ye Shamrock. Indeed, Father Abraham's on his Funeral Train is probably near as roomy, at least it is when they open the lid to exhibit him.

Poor old Vicksburg still shows scars of war, some of the diggings, bunkers, &c, when the populace were obliged to live like groundhogs. Scaffolds up as repairs are made of bombshell damage. Felice of course is appalled as is her wont by the destruction, and has expressed her empathy for the womenfolk and their families who lay under the siege here. I'm in awe of her natural compassion & humaneness. Rest easy, I shall never lay any but the gentlest hand on her.

We intend to go ashore and walk in the town tomorrow while the boat is being fixed. I'm teaching her the history of the siege as only an eyewitness can teach it. Before I conclude this letter, two matters that might interest you, first, that the barkeeps of this vessel give me to believe that Col. John Riley really is still alive in Ireland, living in his native Galway County, the thought of which warms my heart, & second, that all big boats stopping at this place are obliged by the authorities to board & carry as far as Cairo Illinois as many freed prisoners of war as they can carry, from a prisoner exchange camp nearby. Two vessels that preceded this one, the Henry Ames & the Olive Branch, already gone on upriver overloaded with wretches barely still alive. "Official Rumor" is that 400 Ohioans will come aboard this *vessel & encamp on the decks as far as Cairo. This will of course cramp our honeymoon cruise a bit, but Capt. Mason & his First Clerk can scarcely mask their avarice, as the Army is paying $5 a head for their transport. Much better a rate than for the other livestock -- swine & mules -- already aboard! Just the aforesaid Ohioans will add $2000 to the profit of this voyage; may alleviate the costs of delay & repairs. War, alas, is a profitable business, as we all know.*

Any inconvenience suffered by your honeymooners, meantime, is overweighed by our opportunity to help these poor fellows get closer to home. They have been in the notorious death pens at Andersonville Georgia & Cahaba & from what the dockmaster says, only the homegoing keeps them alive.

In fact, I find in their homeward passage a story at least as poignant as the President's! And to my knowledge there's no other correspondent aboard any of these transports, so I have fallen perhaps onto an "Exclusive" story. I'll get to a telegraph tomorrow in town & try to sell this to Mr Guernsey at HARPER'S. Even journalists, I must admit, profit by War. I certainly have.

And speaking of HARPER'S, a recent issue, January's, came into our hands on the boat. I had missed it. This one contains an account of the Siege of Vicksburg, by John S.C. Abbott, the second in his series "Heroic Deeds of Heroic Men." How timely that it fell into our hands just as we approached the said city itself! I've met Mister Abbott in years past & consider him a fairly good writer, but must say that his account of the siege is a bit different from mine. But I was with Sam Grant through the duration of it, which gave me a different & unique viewpoint. History is, as Napoleon's said to have said, "a set of lies generally agreed upon," & I suppose that we who lived it will never be satisfied with the way it's told. I expect that these personal views of much of the war will intrigue audiences when I begin lecturing.

My dear Felice sits near me on a deck chair deck outside our cabin, writing her own missive to you, which will be enclosed with this one of mine. Remember, dear Mother, as you wade through my prolixity, that it was yourself who made me literate & infected me with this diarrhea of ink. I am, your loving & devoted son & humble servant, PADDY

*

SULTANA steamboat

Sunday, at Vicksburg dock

My dear Mrs. Quinn,

Nay: Dear Mother,

I take my pen in hand to greet you, and to express anew my heartfelt thanks for your many kindnesses in the wedding, the honeymoon suite, the feasts, and especially for so graciously accepting me into your affections. I regretted leaving you so soon.

This voyage has been an idyll so far, with good weather and amiable passengers. Our dear Paddy is a noted personage, known to the captain and several of the crew, also to other passengers, among them some officers aboard who met him in campaigns of the war. Even some of the private soldiers camping on the decks with their guns and haversacks stand to shake his hand! I can't deny that I bask in his celebrity. But it gives me joy to say that I would be honored to be Mrs. Padraic Quinn even if no one knew him. For he is the epitome of kindness and charm, a fountain of originality, and as you surely take pride in noting, a delight to the feminine eye. And – rara avis – uses no tobacco!

Paddy said he's explaining in his letter the reason for our delay here, so I needn't bore you by repeating it. The problem is a peculiar new kind of boiler. You'll remember he wrote of it in one of the magazine essays you have there in your "Paddy Scrapbook."

Novelties of this voyage are the spring flood, bottomlands overflown to make the river seem wide as a sea. And that I saw an alligator for the first time -- not in the river, though, but in a box! Some entrepreneur is taking it up to put in a circus or zoo. Perhaps the last time any such beast ever rode a boat was when a pair of them were on the Ark. Apparently Noah would accept anything, however ugly!

I'll make this letter brief so as not to be tedious. Paddy still scratches away, faster than I ever saw anyone write. Also he kindly makes little card-size portrait sketches of the soldiers, in a few minutes each but very good likenesses, and gives them to them to take home to their mothers or sweethearts. He jokes to each soldier, "This is already too valuable to lose. When you pass it on to your children, I'll be so famous, it'll be worth a fortune." Then he laughs and says it's his "self-defecating sense of humor." I imagine you've heard him use that crude phrase a time or two!

Dear Mother Quinn, let us thank God that the war is over and that dear Padraic came through it unhurt and full of the Old Nick. I expect his way with words and pictures will always bring pleasure to many. My parents will be enamored of him, I'm sure, but it might be a while before they become attuned to his playfulness. They're rather staid, as I have told you. I expect they will love to receive the studio portrait of us, when you can send it to them. I am glad you insisted we go ahead and have it taken.

I've thought, on this voyage, how fortunate we are that your New Orleans and my St. Louis, though distant in miles, are linked by the river, and only a few days apart by these fast boats. It will therefore be no great matter for dear Paddy and me to bring our respective in-laws together in the near future. I want them to know and admire you as I do, and you them.

I am, with much affection, your FELICE.

CHAPTER FIVE

Vicksburg, Mississippi

Monday, April 24, 1865

It is midmorning when Paddy and Felice finish breakfast and are dressed to leave the steamboat for their walk up into town. The day is mild and fresh, but they aren't feeling well.

They've had a fitful night: overindulged in diningroom wine; writhing half-clad and cramped in too small a lower bunk; then frantic copulation in the bestial position, which is the only way there's really room for in the tiny, cluttered cabin. She was embarrassed and reluctant at first, then ecstatic, and a second mounting soon followed. An exhausted sleep ensued, he in the upper bunk, she below, with intermittent awakenings caused by their own discomforts and dreams, and by disturbances from outside. The use of a chamberpot is not as loud as the work of a boiler mechanic, but is closer by and can't be so easily ignored. Sounds of a fisticuff brawl and a police whistle out on the wharf later had raised Felice out of her lower bunk to peek out around the window curtain, while Paddy slept through that. Then a dream of an incoming mortar shell convulsed Paddy in his upper bunk with a waking gasp and he bruised his elbow on the molding. To calm his pounding heart and trembling limbs, he had descended from his bunk to sit naked on a trunk in the dark and swig at his flask. By then he yearned to get dressed and go to the saloon, but decided that her displeasure would be too great if she woke to find him gone yet another night. He'd gotten cold sitting there naked, and eventually had to climb back up to his bunk and stupefy himself with the dregs of the flask while wrapped in a scratchy wool blanket. Back to sleep eventually, he had been awakened by another sort of dream, one he's had before, of a memory he's tried to keep buried deep:

Gen. Hooker's gathering-place in the Willard Hotel near his headquarters in Washington, one of those orgies so common there and then. Paddy that night had been too grogged even to raise a cockstand, and therefore the featured performer -- a buxom, wet-lipped whore, as he remembers, stunningly attractive -- got into a spectacularly lewd squat and ensheathed his entire left forearm stump, up to his elbow, pleasuring herself on it and then proclaiming it the most repleting ride she'd ever had, short of a Shetland pony. The way she said it had made Paddy laugh so hard he nearly choked, but soon the herring stink on his arm had turned his choking to retching. When he'd recovered enough to have conscious thought, he'd wondered how a harlot of that ilk should have command of such a word as *repleting.* But before he could get the question out through his puky gullet, she was being mounted astern by someone else, a drunken dragoon colonel who'd not even bothered to remove his jacket or scabbard. Not the only orgy Paddy ever attended there in that infamous headquarters, but the one he most wished had been only a nightmare. That such a slut had a vocabulary was perhaps no more astonishing than that prominent officers, tycoons and journalists wallowed in bacchanalia while soldiers were dying in distant fields.

Not just violence and terror, but shame, too, trouble Paddy's sleep. Wholly holey unholy war has fermented a seething, toxic brew down inside him, like a heartburn to awaken him to displeasure. If not for his lark-flights of wordplay and imagination, and this novelty of connubial love, he feels he might fall into a flood of cynic despond as deep and roiled as the Mississippi itself.

"I've had nights more restful on the battlefield than last night," he complains to Felice, wagging his head as they trudge down the gangplank to the Vicksburg dock, passing a knot of Union officers and civilians who seem to be having an argument about some sort of cargo. From the boiler deck still comes the reverberant *clonk, clonk* of a mechanic's hammer on hollow metal.

There is no wifely sympathy in the look Felice gives him from red-rimmed eyes. "About your...your restlessness...Will it get better, do you suppose? Have you always been so awfully wakeful?"

It's almost a relief that she's finally mentioning this, but unsettling, too. She might well be repelled by the undercurrents of his soul if she got a real notion of them. Thank merciful God a wife cannot see her husband's memories, Paddy thinks, and answers:

"No...yes... Well, nightmares... Shot and shell. Snipers, that constant dread; I'm just one great *flinch,* you might say. Then once I'm awake, well, I guess I just have to lie in the dark and entertain myself with my mind...But really, me darlin'...You expect a man could be sleepy, in a room alone with you?" He tries to laugh.

"No blarney just now, please."

"I mean that. You can't imagine..."

"Can you sleep without whiskey?"

He blinks and shakes his head. "My, that's blunt!"

"Can you?"

"Well, if...when I'm tired enough..."

"We *shall* have to deal with this, Paddy. It'll help if I know your..."

It is at this moment that they round the corner of a flaking whitewashed waterfront shed and run almost straight into a horde of dingy skeletons shambling down upon them from the railroad siding. She recoils, pressing back against him, raising a hand to her mouth. Paddy himself gasps audibly as if meeting ghosts.

Seeing hundreds of dead men up close is not new to Paddy Quinn; he has climbed over and waded through corpses. But those strewn on battlefields are fleshy, usually bloated near to bursting their filthy uniforms, aswarm with flies and maggots, dark with dried blood -- not desiccated, ashen, gaunt, not bones and skulls -- and not walking toward him with eyes glittering in those deep sockets, wild and hungry eyes turning to look at him and his bride, then back down toward the steamboat at the dock. He hears a low, muttering groan coming from the hundreds of them as they totter eagerly down toward the *Sultana,* many on crutches.

"It's the prisoners!" he breathes into her ear, just now understanding, just now able to get words out. "From those death camps, Andersonville, Cahaba... Good God, they're even worse than I imagined!" He feels Felice trembling against him, and believes he hears a soft moan coming from her, although the shuffling feet and the voices of the passing wretches grows louder around them. Some are laughing -- an astonishing sound to hear coming from such a ghostly mob as this. Most of them limp by, or lurch along on their crutches, their full attention on the big steamboat, but a few pause, nod, politely raise a hand to a nonexistent hatbrim, and murmur greetings:

"Mornin', sir, ma'am."

"G'day, ma'am."

"Lordy! I never saw so perty a lady as you!"

"Thank you," she manages to say in a voice half-strangled by pity, and Paddy feels a rush of tenderness toward her for saying that to someone who hardly looks human.

But most hardly see the couple, so intent are they on getting down to the *Sultana.*

"Mine eyes have seen the glory of the coming of my boat," some fine tenor is singing, "She'll return me to O-HI-O just as fast as she can float!"

"O-HI-O!" other voices cry all around.

Some of the spectral figures are going by in pairs, one supporting another. Up at the rail siding, some are still helping others down off the flatcars. *Vicksburg & Jackson Railroad.* Paddy remembers when Sam Grant cut off rail supply to Vicksburg two years ago by taking the town of Jackson, making a successful siege of Vicksburg possible. Another triumph to remember, and Paddy intends to tell Felice about it soon, but it is just a passing thought in the face of all this stark misery. The faces go by, all reduced to the basic similarity of skulls, varied only by the shades and colors of their tufts and mops of hair and beards and sideburns, the peculiar expressions in their sunken eyes, the fierce blotches and sores on their soot-stained skin. Some wear new Union blue coats, but mostly their clothes are tatters, so faded they might have begun as either Union blue or Reb butternut; every man is a spindleshanks; the shirtless are corrugations of ribs.

"Holy Mary Mother of God," she whispers. "The ones who *died* on me didn't look this bad!" He understands that she's speaking of those on the hospital ship during the war. "How can men be so cruel to each other?"

"Not so much cruelty as negligence," he answers, hoping to mitigate her horror. "The Rebs could hardly feed their own army, never mind all their prisoners."

"I know, but..." Maybe she doesn't know how to finish. Or maybe it isn't worth trying. Paddy knows her sentiments. It's not this side or that side, it's any and all who make wars.

It appears to be four or five hundred of these scarecrows climbing off the flatcars and straggling toward the steamboat. The boat already had more than three hundred persons aboard, passengers and crew, and Paddy knows it isn't supposed to carry more than three hundred seventy or so.

And he can still hear the boiler mechanic's hammer.

Tub of Doom, he remembers.

*

When they return to the *Sultana* in the afternoon, Felice has been joined by a dozen Sisters of Charity from Southern Indiana. These ladies, varying from plain to homely in visage but lovely as angels within, had been sent down by the Christian Commission weeks ago to tend to sick Yankee prisoners in the limbo known as Camp Fisk down by the Big Black River. Now that those prisoners are heading home, the Sisters' mission is done and they too will be boarding the *Sultana* to go back up North. They have been supervised and chaperoned by a pious old gent named Safford from the Indiana town of Madison, and his equally pious son.

Felice has also gathered a carpetbag full of jars containing ointments and salves, home remedies as well as those from the apothecary store, even a pot of bear oil laced with goldenseal which had been donated by an Indian woman to the Sisters. Paddy is carrying the bag for her, and it is so heavy that he must switch it now and then from his right hand into the crook of his left arm. He's glad that he left his portfolio on the boat and brought along only a notebook in his coat pocket, for the bag itself is a full load for a one-handed man.

While Felice was gathering these treatments, Paddy had found a telegraph office and a newspaper publisher, and gathered information. The Presidential Funeral Train is still far up in the East, having left Philadelphia after midnight and due in New York City this afternoon. At all major cities it will be stopped and the casket will be taken off so the President's body can be viewed by thousands of mourners in such stately venues as courthouses and capitol buildings. It is scheduled to arrive in Springfield, Illinois, on the morning of May 3rd. Nine days from now. Even with this layover for repairs, that allows plenty of time for the *Sultana* to reach St. Louis with time to spare for a meeting and visit with Paddy's new in-laws, the Beaulieus, before he and Felice board a train to Springfield. Felice believes that her parents will almost certainly attend the funeral as well, so the four of them could ride that train together. That will be a time sure to test Paddy's capacity for good behavior. He hopes that the Beaulieus will be impressed enough by his long-ago acquaintance with the President and his "sacred hand," if not his fame as a war correspondent, that Felice won't have to be too ashamed of her new husband. And he will be on his best behavior. Her parents will have to understand that he will be busy taking notes and making sketches on the funeral day.

Other news he's gathered here in Vicksburg: A manhunt for the President's assassin has rounded up accomplices in Maryland. The assassin being pursued is apparently the very man that Blackie at the *Picayune* had presumed: an actor named John Wilkes Booth, brother of the famed Shakespearean Edwin Booth. The drama is growing into the form of some maudlin theatrical tragedy of national scope, with a foul murder overshadowing a victory and stealing the scene from history, with famous actors playing famous actors..It's all such a mad dream that it caused Paddy a passionate thirst. So, after telegraphing *Harper's* about the freed prisoners, he had crossed the street into a tavern for two quick shots of whiskey before rejoining Felice and the Sisters of Charity. Surely she can smell it on his breath, but she has said nothing to him about it -- perhaps because of the presence of the Sisters. Two of them have read Paddy's dispatches throughout the war, and are agog, meeting him under these circumstances. Descending the brick streets of riverside Vicksburg now, the Sisters stoutly aver that the fiend Ulysses Grant is directly responsible for the extreme suffering of those poor Yankee captives, as it was he who put a halt to the routine exchanging of prisoners of war. Grant indeed had done that, two years ago, contending that any Reb prisoner turned loose would break parole and would just have to be fought again in subsequent battles. Though always proud of his long personal acquaintance with Gen. Grant, Paddy knows this is no time to mention the friendship or defend him. He does whisper in Felice's ear, "How charitable are these Sisters, calling someone they never met a 'fiend?'" At once he regrets that close whisper, for if she hadn't smelled the whiskey on his breath before, surely she has now.

The train of the *Vicksburg & Jackson* railroad isn't on the siding when they return. At the wharf lies the gleaming white *Sultana,* now aswarm with hundreds of shabby ex-prisoners who have already been taken aboard. Lining the deck rails in their dingy rags they look like bedraggled birds perched along telegraph wires.

These wretches represent yet another journalistic opportunity for Paddy Quinn. While at the telegraph office he sent to his editor at *Harper's* a proposal for another poignant story: gaunt survivors of the notorious Andersonville prison, desperately homeward bound on a luxury steamboat, their personal ordeals to be recorded by the able correspondent Padraic Quinn, from interviews and sketches done in his inimitable style aboard the steamboat en route to the President's final funeral in Illinois, a *Harper's* exclusive -- exclusive because to his knowledge he is the only journalist afloat upon the great river with these piteous veterans.

Maybe a country at peace won't be so boring as he had feared.

*

Camp Fisk

Monday afternoon

A bugle blows Assembly, and Robbie Macombie rises painfully to his feet, slinging the coffee dregs out of his tin cup, then ties the cup to his kerchief bundle and heads up toward the headquarters building, one among hundreds moving that way.

He has no high expectations of what this is about. The train took away some 400 Ohioans this morning. The roster was cut off before it got to him, so he's resigned to having missed still another steamboat. The train has returned from town to the Four Mile bridge; he heard it come back.

Now he hears Sgt. Big Noise bellowing, up by Capt. Speed's office. His voice seems louder than a bugle, but he's unintelligible at a distance, just a maker of deep echoes. One must get closer to understand him. Soon, most of the inmates are merging toward the building, and hundreds are gathered in front of the sergeant, listening.

"All you people get ready to move out, hear me? This camp's shutting down. By dark you're gone."

The multitude stand waiting, begin glancing at each other, frowning, mouths slack or agape, some looking afraid.

A voice finally shouts from somewhere:

"Gone where?"

"Well, on the damn boat, 'less you mean to *swim* home, sonny!"

Somebody else yells, "Thought that boat left already! With the Ohio boys? Heh?"

The door opens behind Sgt. Big Noise, and Capt. Speed, adjutant of the Department of Mississippi, steps out beside him. Seldom seen here at the camp because of his other wide-ranging duties, he is a brusque and fiery-eyed young man, and when he comes out, the tall sergeant just fades back. The captain puts his hands on his hips, nibbles his upper lip under his mustache while passing his eyes over the whole wretched mob. Robbie instinctively admires him, a stalwart like his own grandfather Joseph.

"Gentlemen," the captain begins, "I've done what I could to give you the comforts you need, and to arrange for your transportation home as fast as I could. I've had to butt my head up against some stubborn posteriors, to help you get on home. Well, I won. The rosters are as good as we can make them. You on the first list will go right now up to that train and get on it. Those it won't hold, you'll form up in companies and *walk* to Vicksburg. I mean for every last man of you to be on board that steamboat down there and going up the river before this day is out. I honor you for what you've endured -- don't know how you did it. Now you listen to the sergeant and form up, and get out of this place. Godspeed." He sniffs and steps back and clasps his hands behind his back. For a moment it is quiet. Some things take a moment to sink in. Robbie takes a long, deep breath. He feels a tear trickling a cool track down beside his nose, and envisions a bluff above the Ohio River, the excavation for the coffin of his grandfather. Up the Mississippi is the way to go to the Ohio and to that Saluda cemetery, where he most wants to go.

And just now the thousand bedraggled veterans standing in the field at Camp Fisk seem to inhale at the same time, and their craggy, wary faces are transformed as if in a revival. The scraps of their belongings are flung upward and hang there on the updraft of their cheering voices. *"LET'S GO HOME!"*

*

The *Sultana*'s fancy saloon is crowded. Both bartenders are busy. McGinty, taller and more somber than his partner, does most of the work, while O'Hara sweats, guffaws and dispenses blarney, extolling the greatness of thirst.

Never in any drinking establishment has Paddy Quinn stood among such a desperate, sickly, ragged clientele. A few well-fed civilians are here, but most of the drinkers are in remnants of military clothing. They look like cadavers standing, and smell strongly of the grave, and of the pyre, too. They are, however, happy cadavers, as if they'd passed through the Pearly Gates into a paradise of gleaming bottles, not into the Heaven of Eternal

Temperance they'd been warned to expect. These are some of the horde from the prisoner exchange camp whom Paddy had seen spilling off the railroad cars this morning. They and their comrades have been assigned up topside to the open texas deck, but seem to feel no obligation to stay where put. It's their understanding that they aren't prisoners anymore, so those not too enervated to move have wandered off to explore this vast and elegant vessel. Those who have somehow managed to obtain pocket money, and pockets to carry it, have quickly found their way to the saloon, even bringing comrades to share with, while some without money have implored civilians to "treat a hero of Antietam to his first liquid spirit since that awful day," and other such ploys.

Paddy is free to visit the bar because Felice is busy with the Sisters of Charity now, helping them distribute their sundries, remedies and homilies to the hundreds of scarecrows packed up on the texas deck. He is immediately hailed by Jamie O'Hara and summoned with a wave to come and get his complimentary first dram. The experience of pushing through the crowd to the bar is a troubling mix of pity, awe and revulsion. The men he jostles feel like bundles of broomsticks and doorknobs, reek of campfire and gunsmoke, dirty drawers, piss and old sweat, their exhalations are miasmas of gum rot and vomit, and every threadbare garment, every scurfy scalp and beard, is likely crawling with fleas and lice – "bodyguards," as soldiers call them – yet Paddy's heart swells with *agape* for every man of them, and he would like to clasp every man's hand with this one that their commander-in-chief had once gripped, to transfer Lincoln's warm strength into these frail ruins and bless their homegoing.

Jamie O'Hara greets him at the bar not with a handshake but with a glass of whiskey and a yellow-toothed grin. "Something here I thought ye'd like to have, m'lad. It's a gift. And I've a message: there's a soldier askin' to see you. An officer. A Cap'n Brown. Left you a note. Here."

Paddy takes the glass and tosses the whiskey to his tonsils, sets it on the bar to be refilled, and unfolds a heavy little packet. Inside a slip of paper is a gold medallion, embossed with the

Mexican national symbol -- an eagle with a rattlesnake in its beak -- perched atop a Celtic cross, and around it the words AL HEROICO BATALLON DE SAN PATRICIO 1847. He looks up as O'Hara sets the refilled glass down. Through a tight throat he says, "You're *giving* me this?" He knows that these were awarded, by a grateful Mexico, only to members of John Riley's illustrious unit of gunners.

McGinty has paused beside O'Hara, and says, "To us, you're one of ours."

"I...I don't know how to thank you enough!" It's real Mexican gold, but that is not its value.

"Pay for that drink, lad. Just the first one's on us, y'know." They laugh, then turn away to serve other drinkers. Paddy rubs the medallion lovingly between thumb and fingers, remembering that longago war, blinking. This is a keepsake beyond value, but not one to show to generals of either the Union or Confederacy, whose young West Point classmates Riley's gunners had mowed down in windrows in every battle of that war. By the end of that war the *San Patricios* had all been killed in battle or hanged, all but a few of them who'd escaped into Mexico, like these two barkeeps.

Now Paddy looks at the folded paper, a note written in pencil, a shaky handwriting.

> *24 Apr.*
>
> *My dear Mr Quinn,*
>
> *I was sure I recognized you this morning. Mr O'Hara confirms it is you.*
>
> *Am pleased to see how well you look.*
>
> *Last I saw of you was battle of Chickamauga. We got whipped badly & I've been a prisoner since. I am in hopes of greeting you & having a few words.*
>
> *Yr Humble Svt, A.C. BROWN*
>
> *Cmdr Co. I , 2nd Ohio Inf.*

"Brown?" he murmurs, trying to remember. How many Captain Browns did he meet in that damned war? Chickamauga was, what, a year and a half ago? Ohio 2nd Infantry. He thinks back to the second day of that chaos and remembers: Federal line broke, retreat toward Chattanooga...Right. Ohio regiment cut off...A young captain with red nose and freckles, long conversation about something or other, and drew a sketch of him, didn't I?

Can always pretend I remember him, if I don't.

He sips this second whiskey, sets it on the bar, folds the note, takes his notebook from his pocket and slips the paper into it, pockets the notebook, fondles the San Patricio medallion again, picks up the glass, sips again. One hand, one awkwardness at a time. O'Hara is in front of him again, commenting now, "Such as 'tis, the boiler repair's been done."

"Good. Sure and I'm eager to get on to Illinois. Getting nervous about lost time."

"Lad, y'might well get nervous about that cussed boiler, by what Wintreger says t'me."

"I already am. And just what is it Mister Wintreger says?"

"That the mechanic from the foundry only made a small patch, the ruptured part. Put it on over a bulged-out plate. Mechanic says it will suffice 'til St. Louis. Cap'n Mason wants to believe that, so he *does* believe it." Despite the thirsty urgency of the drinkers, O'Hara leans elbows on the bar close to Paddy and says, "Yer a valuable man, Mister Pat Quinn, with a heavenly bride. Y' could get yourselves onto the next boat. The foundryman *is* a Southerner, y'know. What's he care about a tubful o' Yankees? Just a thing to consider, eh?"

Paddy stares at him. "Well, Mister O'Hara, *you* don't seem to be closing up shop."

"What's that again?"

"If I were to see an old *San Patricio* like yourself scared enough to hop off a boat, maybe I'd abandon ship meself." He holds up the medallion. "You said I'm one of you. Now when did John Riley or any of his gunners ever run off and leave the others?"

O'Hara turns and tells McGinty: "One more on th' house for this Irishman here."

*

Paddy stands at the rail of the promenade deck with Felice, mouth dry and heart sinking, slowly shaking his head in dismay, watching the endless line of tatterdemalions that has been coming up the *Sultana's* gangplank since late afternoon. Their voices deep and high combine in a susurrant din. They have been coming down from the railroad cars and tottering down through Vicksburg's streets for hours, milling in a staging area on the wharf, and starting up the gangplank when their names are read off rosters by loud-voiced officers and clerks.

The Texas deck above is creaking and visibly sagging under the weight of the hundreds of men on it. Supported by scantlings, it was designed as a roof for the promenade deck, not as a floor for such weights. A crew with saws and hammers, supervised by the chief mate, is moving aft, cutting and erecting temporary support posts along the rails to reinforce it. Another crew astern is building a great privy, of board seats over barrels that can be emptied over the taffrail into the river.This frantic work is hindered by the inflow of shabby soldiers who are being led onto the promenade deck now that the texas deck is too packed to hold any more. Paddy points a finger down at Captain Mason at the end of the gangplank.

"The man's crazed by greed," he tells her."I thought he was just a preening fool. But he's lost his reason over five dollars a head."

What has happened, say the rumors, is that Captain Speed or his superiors decided to shut down Camp Fisk once and for all today, get every last parolee out, and down to the Vicksburg wharf tonight. Someone, somehow, had assured them that the *Sultana* has room for everybody - not just the 400 Ohioans who came down this morning, but the rest of them on all the rosters - another thousand men or more.

During this daylong loading frenzy, two more northbound

steamboats have docked at Vicksburg – the *Lady Gay* and the *Pauline Carroll* – and their captains have offered to make room for hundreds still milling on the wharf. They seem like a Godsent answer to the problem. But for some mysterious reason the stream of soldiers is not being diverted to those boats from the *Sultana*'s staging area, and keeps filing aboard like an army of ants. Paddy can see and hear arguments going on down there, military officers, boat officers, dock officials, arguments even working up to stomping, shouting and the shaking of fists. Paddy had heard a rumor that bribery is suspected but presumed it arose from natural human cynicism. With an Army transportation contract worth $5,000 or more in play, the steamboat companies in competition with each other, with officers and agents free to make deals on the spur of the moment, some corruption is to be expected.

But as the cabin passengers are summoned down to the dining tables in the Grand Salon for supper, Felice says softly into Paddy's ear, "If they keep herding people onto this boat, it's not going to be fit passage."

He understands her concern, and agrees. "But I'm willing to sacrifice a bit of comfort, even some elbow room, if it'll help these poor bloody beggars get home."

"I'm not complaining about comfort, Paddy. I mean a boat can only carry so much!"

*

The Grand Salon in normal circumstances is crowded and bustling, table service glinting in the flamelight of sconces and chandeliers, waiters and stewards moving gracefully among the tables, diners of either gender furtively inspecting their elegant selves or catching others' glances in the big, beveled mirrors along the paneled walls, scores of persons talking and laughing, their dinnerware clinking and clattering.

These are not normal circumstances. The tables have been crowded in toward the center, and the walls are being lined with dozens of cots. "For the officers," the steward explains. "After supper, these will be their, well, quarters. No more cabins vacant.

But officers can't sleep out on the decks, of course."

Paddy, already into his third glass of claret, swallows and presses his lips tight to refrain from saying, "I don't know why in hell they can't if the enlisted men can." Instead, he replies, "Of course." Though as a correspondent he has bivouacked and interviewed and imbibed with generals and colonels, his sentiments on that matter go back to the previous war when he was a shabby Irish errand boy living on the ground with the soldiers while polishing the boots and buckles and buttons and hauling the laundry of Army officers who were used to being served. . Despite his own powerful ambition to rise above his origins, Paddy is a plebeian at his core, borne by a washerwoman and seamstress who is in his esteem as noble as any queen ever was. And the greatest man he ever knew, the fabled Irish rogue John Riley, was the issue of poverty, a mere private in the American Army. Paddy reaches into his side pocket and strokes the *San Patricio* medallion. Then he has another notion, one that he knows probably would warm his mother's heart:

There was another lowborn struggler, dear to Moira Quinn and to multitudes more just now, and Paddy, with a rush of affectionate memory and a sudden glow of admiration in his breast, now rings his spoon against a glass tumbler, pushes his chair back far enough to stand, raises his wineglass to the well-dressed diners at his table and all about the salon, and announces in his battlefield voice that can be heard over any dining-room din:

"Ladies and Gentlemen: If I may claim your attention! Permit me to propose a toast! I raise my glass to a magnificent soul... who cannot be here with us this evening due to unforeseen difficulties..." He glances down at Felice, who has a wary eye tilted up at him, and he continues with a pounding heart and a hurricane roaring in his head:

"This toast is to a man who deplored military glory as 'that attractive rainbow that rises in showers of blood,' but who yet had to precipitate the greatest shower of blood we've ever known, in order to preserve the nation! I raise my glass with this hand -- the only hand I have, this hand which, I am both humbled and proud to declare, he once clasped in his own -- I drink this blood-red claret in honor of that wise and tormented soul, whose remains I go to see, as on a pilgrimage; I toast our late and lamented President, may God rest his soul -- *Abraham Lincoln!"*

The response is heartening, an uproar of voices, handclaps and whistles, diners everywhere standing and lifting their glasses. As he expected, a few Southerns remain seated and look down at their plates, refusing to do the tribute, but very few.

By God, he thinks, sitting down with his face flushed, feeling Felice's hand reach to squeeze his fingers in hers, by God, if I can stir them like this in the lecture halls, we will go far! But forgive me, Father Abraham, he thinks then. This is not for my ambition, this is foremost and most sincerely in your honor.

In his memory he sees a winking dark eye, remembers "Abraham Winkin'."

In such a crowd at such a time, no toast goes unanswered, and immediately there follows a series of them, mostly made by Army officers in honor of Ulysses Grant and General Sherman, working their way up to Secretary of War Stanton and down to the brave private soldiers, and then one startling toast given to the Rebel leader Robert E. Lee. This one causes an embarrassed stillness, until the crowd realizes that it comes not from a Southerner but from a solid, thickly-bewhiskered Union Army officer in recognition of a worthy enemy. The officer bellows, "Our own great hero, Winfield Scott himself, called Mister Lee the best soldier he ever saw in the field. Our victory is that much the greater, being measured against such an adversary!"

The applause for that is shrill and thunderous. Paddy, now having swallowed toast after toast, again rises with his glass held high and cries, "I bring these tributes back around, full circle: To President Lincoln, God rest his merciful soul, who called for amnesty and forgiveness of all such brave soldiers on the other side!" He sits down amidst another tumult of cheers, and sees in Felice's face that she has been truly pleased with him this time.

A hand on his shoulder. Still flushed with self-consciousness, he looks up to see another one of those cadaverous faces such as he's seen coming and coming all day, this one pale as wallplaster, freckled, its only color a ruddy beak of a nose. This spectre, wearing a faded blue wool tunic and the shoulderbars of an infantry captain and smelling of turpentine, that common homemade lice remedy, leans down over him and grips his hand with fingers that feel like a *fasces* of twigs in a paper sack.

"Mister Quinn, from the bottom of my heart, thank you for those words. Forgive me for intruding. I left you a note with the barkeeps? I'm Alexander Brown, 2nd Ohio? From Chickamauga?" Every statement sounds like a query. Paddy rises, still holding the brittle hand.

"Yes, Captain! I got the note...I remember that day at Chickamauga, I do... Permit me to introduce my wife, Felice..." The man is like a skeleton, tall but surely no more than a hundred pounds of bone in skin. A foot length of his leather belt hangs loose beyond its buckle, like a measure of his reduction.

The gaunt officer touches Felice's hand, and says, "Friends up home, when they heard I was out of Andersonville, took up a subscription to pay for a cabin berth on this boat and telegraphed the money to me at Vicksburg. So I'm more comfortable than my Ohio boys up on the texas deck, I daresay...Yes, hello, hello, pleased to meet you," he says to other civilians at the table who come around or reach for his skinny hand. "What I should like to do, Mister Quinn, if there's no objection, is take that tray of pastries, there on the sideboard, to my lads up on the top deck? God knows how long since they've had anything like those!" Paddy has no authority over anything in the dining room, but he says:

"Captain, I'd be honored to escort you up, and carry the tray for you, in fact. Felice, dear, would you be able to handle that big pudding over there, and come up with us? Lead on, Captain Brown."

*

The whole roofless texas deck is dimly lit by a hanging lantern behind the pilot house, and another on a pole far astern, and by the faint glow of the lights up in Vicksburg. Under the early evening stars there stand, sit and lie raggedy men, elbow to elbow, back to knee, covering every square foot of the vast deck, like a herd of livestock in a pen. Their voices drone, mutter and chuckle. Matches flare and the smell of tobacco smoke drifts about. Along the rail, they stand watching the rest of their herd trudge up the gangplank onto the *Sultana*. Overhead, coalsmoke is piling out of the smokestacks into the sky; the fire has been relaid and relit under the patched boiler. Capt. Brown and Felice have vanished into the gloomy mob with the pastries and pudding, but Paddy suddenly finds a gaunt figure standing right in his way. . In the flare of a pipesmoker's match, a pale skull with sunken eyes, with hair and whiskers pale as wheat straw, glows like a ghost in Paddy's view, and the intensity in the blue eyes makes him shudder. Paddy thinks, with a sinking sensation:

The suffering of any one of these poor bastards is surely beyond my power to describe. But I must start talking to them if I'm to write their story.

The pale skull says, "'Scuse me, sir. You're the war reporter, I think?" The man has that weak, gurgly voice of one with bad lungs.

"Paddy Quinn, at your service. Afraid I don't recognize you..."

"You wouldn't. Hell, my own wife wouldn't. But *you've* not changed. Yes. Quinn. I'd forgot the name but not your face. We met one day at General McClellan's headquarters. Talked a while, and you gave me a copy of your magazine, which was so kind of you. My name's Robbie Macombie. No reason why you'd remember it."

"And I'm afraid I don't...Sorry..." It has been two years or more. McClellan lost his command in '62, to be succeeded by Burnside. For an instant Paddy feels dizzied by the scope of the war just past, as if there had never been a place in the land undamaged by it, or a family anywhere not aggrieved by it, or a time of peace before it. This Macombie fellow could be any age, his condition is so poor, but his white hair and whiskers, with just a vestige of blond still in them, indicate that he's much older than most enlisted men. "We've brought up pastries and pudding," Paddy says. "Did you get any?"

"No, sir. But the crew broke open a sugar barrel for us. We got sweets. What I wanted to ask, sir, if you c'd refresh my memory:

that magazine you gave me, was that where I read about the poor refugee Indians giving their pocket money for the starving Irish?"

"Why, yes, it was! I wrote that story. Damn near forgotten it!"

"Well, sir, thank you for that story. I told it ever' now and then to the fellows in the prison camps, like when they got too sour about everything? Told 'em about the monument in, where was it, Dublin? To the, what were they, Choctaw Indians?"

"Right. Choctaws. Dublin it was. You have a good memory."

"A good memory, but not many good memories. Your story about those Indians is maybe the best memory I have, and it's not even mine."

"Well, Mister Macombie, I guess it is yours, now, since you remember it so well." Paddy is touched and pleased that his story -- a mere footnote to an article he'd written in defense of Irishmen in America – has stayed with a man through his awful ordeals. "Inspiration is contagious," he adds, and is pleased with his phrase.

Something about this face, like one out of the Old Testament, holds Paddy. He says, "Listen, Mister Macombie. I'm hoping to talk to some of you men about what you've been through. And about going home. Might I start with you? I'll bet my Irish friends who keep the saloon on this boat would be honored to buy you a drink."

"That'd fit with my circumstance, Mister Quinn, my circumstance bein' I can't afford to buy myself one. But I wouldn't want t' impose. I'm not an officer, y'see...You're an important man, and, and I only meant to thank ye for that story..."

"Officers aren't particularly my cup o' tea, soldier. Let's head down."

*

The first round is, as usual, on the house for Paddy Quinn, and also for his guest, "even though ye be a Scotsman," as Jamie O'Hara joshes the gaunt old soldier. It has been difficult to get to the bar, for there are now about two thousand souls on board the *Sultana*, and hundreds of them are thirsty soldiers who somehow have come through their ordeals with a bit of drinking money in their pockets. The din of voices makes Paddy wonder whether he'll even be able to hear the poor fellow's soft voice. But everywhere else on the boat it is as crowded and noisy as it is here. As diners leave their tables, more arrive, and in the meantime the officers are making their nests on the cots that have been set up for them along the walls of the Grand Salon.

At the other end of the long salon, a troupe of blackface minstrels, who call themselves the Chicago Opera Company and came aboard at Vicksburg on their way to an engagement in Memphis, are building up their own lively clamor with banjos, tambourines and jews harps, singing and playing what they deem to be comical darky songs. Their faces are lampblacked parodies of goggle-eyed Negroes.

Paddy has only his notebook to write notes in, having decided it would take too long to squeeze through the crowd and go to the cabin for his wooden portfolio. The portfolio is too big and bulky to use easily in such crowded space anyway.

"This is good indeed for my profession," Jamie O'Hara says, indicating the crowd with a sweep of his fat hand. "I can only pray we don't run out of our commodity on some long stretch of the river where there's no distillers or warehouses to replenish the supply. We did roll aboard a few kegs here at Vicksburg, when we perceived how our clientele would be for growin'. And it is growin', ain't it, Paddy?"

"Too much. I think Captain Mason's gone greed-crazy, frankly."

"Ay, well! He did *finally* come to his senses. Tried to close the gangplank a while ago, protested he won't carry another soul because he can't. Too late now, though. The Army said he's to take every last man because it's damn near midnight and the rosters can't be changed."

"Here it is about that," Robbie Macombie says. "Won't do any good to try to put any of these boys off onto those other steamboats anyway. They wouldn't go." Both Paddy and Jamie tilt their heads and look at the pallid wretch, who still has half his whiskey because he's sipping it so cautiously.

"Well, they could be *ordered* off, I suppose, by the guards that escorted 'em aboard," Paddy opines.

"No, sir," Robbie insists. "They've got this mite closer to home, can't be made to take a step back. You'd understand that, if y'd been on the journey they have."

Jamie straightens up his great bulk and stares along his nose at Robbie. "*Mister* Macombie! You don't know what journeys we been on, in our time. We, the *San Patricios?* We trod all the hell over Mexico, to and fro. That's flinty ground! And that Reb prison o' yours could'na been worse than where the Army put us -- those of us they didn't hang! The Rebs didn't keep you chained to a dungeon wall, now, did they? When I came out o' there I was skinnier than you, believe *that* or no. And a damn sight lousier, too, I bet.. Now, if ye'll drain the rest o' that glass before I turn to me one thousand other impatient customers, I'll pour ye another... but be quick about it!" Robbie obeys, sets the glass down. O'Hara refills it, growling, "That one's on me, but if ye tell anybody I give away whiskey to a Scotsman, I'll say you lie." After a moment, the man Macombie leans close to Paddy's ear and says, "Sir, did I hear Mister O'Hara say 'San Patricios'?"

"That he did. Some Irish troops y' maybe never heard of..."

"*Heard* of? By God, sir, they damn near *killed* me!"

"You? What? When..."

"Buena Vista, then at Churubusco, in forty-seven..."

"You were in *Mexico*?"

"I was. Indiana Infantry. This isn't my first war, Mister Quinn."

Paddy raises his left arm. "Mine either. Buena Vista's where I left that hand. One o' those very same Saint Patrick bombshells, in fact."

Robbie Macombie draws back and squints at Paddy. "'Scuse me, sir, but you look too young to..."

"I wasn't a soldier. Just a boy then. So, eh? We've both been under John Riley's cannons!" He shakes his head, remembering one of the worst days of his life. Robbie has a faraway look in his eyes, too. He says, after a while, in a voice even softer than normal:

"I saw 'em hanged, sir. All those Irishmen."

Paddy has a chill up his neck and jaws. "I was at those hangings, too. Good God, Mister Macombie! You and I have been on a long parallel path, and didn't even know it. I'd say we have a good bit o' storytelling to share."

*

In order to hear the words of this specter he is interviewing, Paddy has to lead him out of the din of the saloon. As they pass along, a soldier greets Macombie: "Hey there, Hangman."

Macombie frowns, nods at him, and comes on. They squeeze through the crowd in lamplight and shadows. Paddy watches for a sight of Felice as they move back through the Grand Salon and the corridor to the staterooms. Paddy explains to Macombie that they are honeymooners, then asks him about his family.

"Still married, far as I know. Two sons about grown. Don't expect I'll see 'em, though."

"What? But you're heading home! Aren't you?"

"I don't fool myself, Mister Quinn. I won't make it to Pennsylvania."

"This close and you won't give it a try?"

"It wasn't tryin' that got me this far, Mister Quinn."

"I don't get your drift," Paddy says, putting the key in the stateroom door lock. He raps, but Felice doesn't answer. Where might she be? he wonders. Ladies' lounge? He leads Macombie into the cramped space, which smells faintly of her soaps and sachets. "Have a seat on that trunk. I'll pour us a nip. I'd like to hear you about this not getting on home business. And what's this 'Hangman' thing?"

The old soldier sits bent, a forearm pressed across his waist, wheezing and running his tongue over his teeth. "I had a dollar bet on, with the last man of my company still alive then, that we wouldn't come out that prison gate alive. Well, he won. We came out, him hanging on my shoulder, claimed his dollar, then slid down on the road right there and died on me. See, he must've set freedom from that place as his line to reach, and I reckon he didn't bother to see past it."

"Oh. So now you've set yourself a line, and it falls short of home, is that it?"

"My bet, remember, was we wouldn't even make it out the gate."

"Well, I for one am glad you lost that bet, Mister Macombie. And your wife and sons will be glad, too. Surely they know by now you got out alive."

"No. I reckon they think I'm long dead. Knowin' Tildie, she's likely got remarried by now. We never wrote each other. I never believed the Rebs sent our mail out."

"You haven't written her since you got out?"

"Guess I could've, but why? Not sure I want my ghost to show up in somebody's life. Might not be welcome."

Paddy shakes his head. Maybe he's afraid of what he'd find if he did go home, he thinks.

Or maybe he feels he really is down to his last days. "I heard some one call you "Hangman' back there. What's that about?"

"Due respect, Mister Quinn, I'll tell you, but only if you promise you won't write it. It's something I'd rather leave behind." His expression is so earnest, Paddy promises, but with reluctance. In his experience, what people don't want published is often the best part of their story.

"Well, here it is about that," Macombie says, leaning close as if there were someone else in this tiny stateroom to overhear. "I doubt you ever heard we had our own little war *inside* the prison? About the trial we had? About hanging six of our own Yankees for their crimes?"

A shiver spills down from Paddy's scalp. "No."

"Well, you'll hear about it from these fellows, if not from me. Want you to know, I was against hanging anybody, even those alley rats. I was just the only carpenter in there who wasn't too sick to build the gallows. I *hate* hangings."

"Me too, Mister Macombie. Seeing those brave good Irishmen hung in a row in Mexico, for no worse a crime than following their own Catholic conscience, that was enough for me, for a lifetime."

"Well, Mister Quinn, here's what else I didn't mean to tell you. I helped build *that* Godawful big gallows, too."

"No!"

"I seem t' get that detail whatever war I go to. It's what I get for being a good carpenter, I reckon. Jesus was a good carpenter, they say. What d'you bet those Romans made him build his own cross?"

By God, Paddy thinks. *There's* a subject for a lecture if I ever heard one!

The dorknob rattles, turns, and Felice sidles in,. bringing a surge of loud voices in with her, then shuts it out. Robbie Macombie rises to his feet quicker than a dying man could be expected to, and bows his white head without taking his eyes off her face. Paddy hugs her to his side, noticing that she smells more like coal smoke now than like a scented bride.

"Felice, dearest, this is Robbie Macombie, a wise man who's telling me intriguing stories. Robbie, here's my bride."

"Good evening, Mister Macombie. I was wondering," she says to Paddy, "where you'd gone to."

"We came in here to talk, so we could hear each other. I was beginning to worry about you, too."

She unties her bonnet, takes it off, slaps soot off of it. "I've been on the foredeck. We're setting up a sort of ward there, for the really sick and lame ones. Fresher air, and the deck's warmed by the engine room below."

"Good. And 'we' are your Merciful Sisters?"

"Ah, those angels," Robbie Macombie exclaims. 'God bless 'em all. And yourself, Mrs. Quinn."

"My Felice was a hospital ship nurse," Paddy tells him. "Every bit the angel she looks to be."

"God bless you for that, Ma'am," Robbie says with a reverential look on his ashen face. "Lord knows we need help." He says it so fervently that Paddy is moved, and he swallows hard, both with pity for the sufferers who crowd the *Sultana,* and with pride in her. After so many years in this trade, he seldom allows himself such feelings, and the ache is almost good. He's truly proud of her, but if she's to be nursing the sick, that will take away honeymooning time.

But what honeymooning time will they have anyway, if Paddy's to interview these veterans? The fact is, he knows, he's still a war correspondent.

He can see that Felice is preoccupied. "Some of them," she murmurs, looking down, "won't get off this boat alive."

"Amen," says Robbie Macombie, and she looks up at him, taking a quick breath.

"Robbie here doesn't seem to think *he* will," Paddy says.

"Why not?" she asks the veteran.

"Oh, that prison, Ma'am. I'm poisoned. But don't concern yourself with me. I guess I'll live as long as your good husband needs me to."

"Goodness!" she exclaims, seeming to see him for the first time. "I pray I can say the same!"

And Paddy, surprised in some unnameable good way, wonders: What does he mean by *that?*

The *Sultana* 's steam whistle screeches, startling them, then sounds two more times.

The vessel begins trembling, rumbling, clattering. A roaring cheer from hundreds of throats fills the night.

"We seem to be getting under way," Paddy says. "We'll continue our interview, but shouldn't we step out on deck and say farewell to Vicksburg?"

"You two go do that," Felice says. "I'll rest a bit here." Paddy suspects she needs a moment of privacy to use the chamberpot.

Stepping out proves more easily said than done. What had been a long, open promenade deck outside their cabin, allowing them to stroll the length of the boat almost alone like the honeymooners they are, is now packed with ragged, yelling, coughing men, reeking of sweaty, sooty, pissy clothing and tobacco, standing shoulder to shoulder along the rail, sitting or leaning against the bulkheads, many lying on the deck in their blankets so close together there isn't room to step between them, hundreds talking and yelling at once, their haggard faces and bony frames here and there crosslit by lamplight from the cabin doors and windows. Most are looking toward the lamplights of the Vicksburg riverfront which now seems to be slipping sideways as the *Sultana* leaves her moorings and turns her prow out into the strong night-dark flood-current of the Mississippi. The huge port sidewheel in its arched housing a few feet away churns water with a loud, fluttering, rushing noise, and windows of Vicksburg buildings up the slope reflect the flame-tinged, spark-spangled coalsmoke that belches up from the boat's twin smokestacks into the night.

There's no use trying to press through the noisome mass to get a place at the rail, so Paddy soon turns to squeeze through the mob and go back to the cabin. He's surprised that Robbie Macombie isn't beside him. There's something uncannily important about this man, and Paddy doesn't want to lose him. But soon he sees him squeezed up near a bulkhead close by the cabin door. Macombie has struck a light for his tobacco pipe, and his pale face and silvery hair glow in the matchlit eddy of pipesmoke, giving him the aura of a wraith among the dingy Shades of Hades. The man's clean, wan look sets him apart. Though he's as shabby and frail as most of these hundreds, his threadbare clothes appear to have been washed so often they are almost white. Robbie salutes Paddy with the pipestem. "Mister Quinn, sir, I shouldn't occupy you and your Missus the whole night long. I'll bid ye goodnight now and go find me a place to lie down."

"No, please! I mean to share a flask with you and go on with our interview. We've only just got started. And also I've a favor to ask."

"Such favor as what, sir?"

"We'll talk inside." Paddy glances around to indicate the curious ears all about.

Robbie puffs on his pipestem and nods. "Well. But let me finish this pipe here. And then I've a call of nature I need to heed. With any luck, I mean." He tilts his head toward the stern. Of course he couldn't use the chamberpot in the Quinns' stateroom. How long has the poor fellow been holding in? Paddy wonders. God knows his guts might be volcanic, judging by his obvious distress.

"Our door will be open, Robbie Macombie. As will my flask."

But Paddy wonders whether the poor fellow will come back for more questioning. He had seemed a bit uneasy talking of himself, all that about the gallows. And how eager might any survivor be to recollect that ghastly incarceration in the death camp? He might not come back. But likely he will, knowing another free dram awaits him.

If he doesn't, there are hundreds more such stories as his. They've all come from there.

But this particular man Macombie is growing in Paddy's mind as just the one to play a peculiar role that Paddy has been inventing to make his *Harper's* story even more poignant than it is already. The notion is growing, seeming more important by the minute. Paddy stands thinking and watches as the pale figure edges and squirms his way aft through the crowd.

This Robbie, maybe twice the age of most of the enlisted men, seems resigned to any fate. Married, he claims, but loath to go home to the connubial bed.

What Paddy hopes he's found, among these two thousand or so desperately homing wretches on board this steamboat, is a veteran soldier who can be shown to honor the martyred

Abraham Lincoln so highly in his heart that he will take a detour from the homeward beeline, a detour of several days and two or three hundred miles, to go up to Springfield, Illinois and pay his last respects to the Commander-in-Chief for whose cause he has suffered so much. How Paddy's mother Moira Colleen Quinn would applaud such an act of devotion by a sick old soldier!

And of course Paddy Quinn, famed correspondent of the War Between the States, writing his *exclusive* story about these incredible survivors, these dead men returning to life, Padraic Quinn on his final assignment of this war will have discovered and interviewed this devoted veteran, will have sketched a portrait of his remarkable face -- it truly is that! -- and the orgy of national remorse will be manifest in one pale, saintly visage, a soldier among soldiers, son and grandson of American patriots, delaying his homecoming in order to pay homage... Paddy's hand is all but itching to take up pencil and start drawing that face.

Come back, he thinks, feeling the vibrations of the *Sultana*'s machinery through the soles of his boots, watching the lamplights of old battered Vickburg diminish off the stern quarter beyond the *Sultana*'s churned wake. The flask awaits you, and we two have a story to tell!

Rapping at the door so he won't catch Felice over the chamberpot, he gets no reply from within. He enters, and sees that Felice isn't here. Maybe she's already gone up to help her Sisters of Charity tend to the soldiers. That would make his interview with Macombie easier in the tiny room, and their drinking less inhibited, but he's a bit irked that she didn't tell him before she left. This *is* their honeymoon, after all. And now he notices that she's left the inner door ajar. That's carelessness. Everything they own is in this room, and that door opens into the public corridor.

As he steps over to shut it, he gets a glimpse of the fabric of her dress just outside.

Paddy finds Felice standing in the corridor, facing a tall, dark-complexioned, rail-thin young man in the tunic of an officer. Her right hand is up on his shoulder inside his shirt collar and her face is almost on his chest. He is speaking softly down to her.

Paddy gasps; he staggers in the doorway. Then an Irish fury like a bombshell flashes red inside his head.

It has been nearly a year since Paddy Quinn struck any man, and that time he was drunk. Though he has only this one hand, he has used it to put out the lights of several arrogant asses, including some of those swollen-headed correspondents and photographers of the so-called Bohemian Brigade, in bivouac between battles everywhere east of the Mississippi. Even with just one fist, he was the acknowledged pugilistic champion of that motley band by war's end, nicknamed "the Mighty Fist of Saint Padraic." More significantly, certain *real* fighting men, officers and enlisted alike, who triggered his sense of outrage one way or another -- including one pompous colonel of cavalry who impugned his mother's reputation -- had awakened to find themselves with altered facial symmetry or lacking a few teeth. Paddy Quinn has never been one to seek or provoke a fistfight or a duel; the pen is his weapon of choice. But when someone or something detonates that latent bombshell of Irish ire, there is the blinding flash...

Thus it is that Captain Walter Elliott of Hanover, Indiana, erstwhile lawyer and onetime commander of Company F, 44th Infantry Regiment, while having a chronic skin condition on his neck and shoulder anointed with Choctaw Indian beargrease salve by the prettiest of the Sisters of Charity in a crowded corridor of the *Sultana,* perceives in the left margin of his vision something or somebody swiftly approaching. Before he can even flinch, there is a yellow flash in his head, followed by a woman's yelp, darkness, and a sensation of falling through space.

*

Robbie Macombie sits with his skinny bare butt on one of the board seats of the newly-built "Big Sultana Shittery" in darkness with the lights of Vicksburg almost out of sight astern. Although his stomach hurts and boils relentlessly, he's passing nothing this time. Most of the other soldiers are noisily and reekingly filling the barrels and slopjars almost as fast as one unfortunate Negro crewman can empty them into the boat's wake, but Robbie's call of nature seems to have been a false alarm.

A dark shape sitting at Robbie's right says, in some hill-country sort of accent, "Reckon this's what them sailor boys mean when they talk about the poop deck?." Robbie grins. Productive or not, it is luxury just to sit here in a clean latrine, just breathing a river breeze, airing his ass and puffing his pipe, instead of squatting ankle-deep in soupy excrement listening to the moans and sobs of dying men in that reeking shit-swamp at Andersonville. One thing about that place, he thinks, it makes any other circumstance seem better by comparison. He could sit here a while just rejoicing in the humble pleasure of trying to defecate in a place that isn't already all shit.

But there are men waiting, many, many of them, for a chance to sit here, and most of them do still have diarrhoea; after Andersonville, they might have it as long as they live. Can't sit here and strain while men are clenching to keep from messing their trousers, but this is a genuine pleasure and he hates to give it up. If that whisky boiling in there suddenly does move something, this is the place to be when it happens.

"Aaahhh!" says a voice nearby. "The most overpraised thing on earth is a fuck, and the most underpraised thing is a good shit!"

A voice from farther down on the boards responds:

"Man, either you don't know how to fuck or I don't know how to shit!"

Laughter comes from those waiting in the darkness. Some voice says, "Hell, who even *remembers* how to fuck?" More chuckling.

Another voice: "My compliments to the proprietors, for providing wet cobs. I just cain't stand them dry ones anymore like at Fisk Camp."

"You pore delicate thang."

Robbie remembers a thought he'd had a while back, and decides to venture his own joke into the darkness, he who seldom is a jokester:

"Boys, if this was a sternwheeler, we wouldn't even *need* cobs! We'd just sit up on the taffrail here and get our hineys *rinsed* clean!"

He's pleased by the hoots and laughs evoked by his remark. He vacates his place, buttons his trouser waist, squeezes out between the lifeboat davit and the press of sooty-smelling men.

He moves away from the Poop Deck, pauses to fill and light his pipe again. He considers whether to wend his way back to the cabin of that Quinn couple. It's way past midnight. He thinks they surely don't really want him back there. Just being polite, probably.

Wouldn't mind another snort out of his flask, though. And he did say he has some kind of a request of me. Won't meet many such genteel people. He doesn't act a bit like he's famous.

The only other famous persons Robbie has ever met before were Generals Lew Wallace and George McClellan, and they'd paid him only the attention that generals give to a messenger to encourage him to get through. Robbie's own uncle Alexander Macombie had been somewhat famous in Indiana, a member of the state legislature. All that meant was that half the people in town treated you well as a boy and the other half griped about your uncle's political leanings. But to you he was just another uncle you'd have to help on the farm in season.

So Robbie starts forward. Spring breeze from the west is cool with riverdamp but gentle, and keeps the stink of the Poop Deck and the dirty men and the swine below` blown off.

It's hard to avoid stepping on people. Robbie creeps along the railing, getting closer and closer to the great sloshing noise of the paddlewheel. Keeps thinking of those Quinns: remembers that heart-melting story about those poor Indians sending money away to the Irish folk. What a fine man to write such a kindly a story! He envisions the couple: that handsome, strong-jawed Padraic, in his prime, maybe thirty years of age with his keen eye and that poor stump of a forearm he uses so deftly it hardly seems a handicap at all, and that Mrs. Quinn, Lordy was there ever a prettier lady! And she must be a perfect angel for kindness, too, was a war nurse, and comforts the boys as one of those Sisters of Mercy. She doesn't have to go to all that bother about other people's misery. Doesn't have to deal with us sick and lame, us infected and infested. He thinks what a contrast she is to his own wife Tildie, who wouldn't get within fifty feet of a sick and dirty man to help him, if she had her druthers, for fear of having to see scabs or pus or getting a louse in her blouse.

Robbie has made his way forward past the paddlewheel now and can see out into the darkness again. To the unseen horizon there is not a speck or glimmer of light except that cast out on the river from the *Sultana*. He shivers.

My God, he thinks, this boat's a whole world all in itself out here on the dark water taking us all home from hell, look at those sparks from the smokestacks blow off in the breeze and wink out over the river yonder... Guess going by God's time, a spark is about as long as one our lives lasts. Makes you wonder why we think we're so much, or our troubles amount to any more than a patched boiler in some damned steamboat going along under those stars up there. What are stars, anyway, some other kind of sparks? An old Indian once had told Robbie that every star in the sky is the spirit of a person who died. Wonder if Mister Quinn ever heard of that notion.

This Mister Quinn said he's going up to the President's funeral, up in Illinois, so he can write a story about it and draw a picture. Robbie thinks, well, if his story about Indians sending money to Ireland can make you feel so lifted up, I guess he can do some good for our hearts by telling of a funeral that goes all across the country.

Illinois gets to bury Mister Lincoln. But he got to be what he was by growing up in Indiana. We Hoosiers have a better claim on him than Illinois, Robbie thinks. Wish they could bury him in Indiana, there by the Ohio River.

Wish I could've made him a casket. I'd hollow it out of one big walnut trunk, like a dugout canoe. With some curly maple inlays on the lid. And real silver fittings. Robbie envisions the beautiful but simple casket as he squirms forward through the lamplit masses on the promenade deck, and as he sees it in his mind, he feels his hands using the adze to hollow the wood, and can even remember that dense walnut wood smell.

Wish I could've made his casket. But that's a pipe dream if ever there was one.

Veterans along the port rail are singing a tune that comes familiar to Robbie's ear, a song that they had started composing at Camp Fisk as rumors of war's end came in, a song that was revised day by day.

We'll be livin' again
In the tall sweet clover,
For th' shootin' and stabbin'
And killin' is over!
Ah, the dyin' is done,
My fine feathered friend.
The war's at last come
To a glorious end!
Dear wife! Sister! Mother!
We've laid down our arms
And we come marchin' home
To your heart-warmin' charms!

Shouts and fretful voices issue from the passageway to the stateroom corridor just ahead; some disturbance happening, up there near the Quinns' berth. Robbie Macombie wriggles through a knot of intense, fast-talking men and beholds a confusing scene in the lamplight:

On the carpeted deck of the corridor there lies a long skinny man in the frock coat of an Union Army officer, his head resting on the baseboard. The beautiful Mrs. Quinn kneels over him, holding against his face what appears to be a wet towel. Standing above her and the fallen figure are two imposing men, one of them Padraic Quinn, and the other Robbie recognizes as the steamboat's captain, Cass Mason. They face each other, tense and livid. Robbie is astonished to hear that the famous journalist is being scolded by the captain:

"...will not abide brawling on my vessel, sir! I already had one brawler thrown off at Vicksburg..."

But Captain Mason's voice is overridden by Mr. Quinn's louder and angrier one, saying, "By God, Cap'n, you'll retract that remark and apologize!"

"What? Apologize to a brawler on my own boat? I'll do no..."

"Your own boat, is it? Damn you, man, it shouldn't be! You're not worthy of the title of Captain, a man who'll overload 'is vessel fivefold!"

The captain rears back, blinking, mouth agape.

The Army officer on the floor is stirring to consciousness. When Mrs. Quinn removes the towel from his face, Robbie recognizes the supine man as one of the officers who had been a prisoner: an Indiana captain. The officer is struggling to raise himself up on his elbows. Stepping over him, the journalist Mister Quinn advances on the boat's master and continues berating him:

"I know personally every general from Grant on down, and unless you apologize for calling me a brawler, I'll see to it your dereliction is reported all the way up! D' you hear me?"

Alarm shows in Captain Mason's eyes now, and he blurts: "You can't blame me for that! I...I tried to stop it! I told them to put the rest on the other boats! I argued, but they..."

"Whoa! Whoa!" the man on the floor exclaims. "Cap'n Mason, please just do apologize to Mister Quinn, why don't you?"

"What?"

"He didn't mean to hit me."

Robbie glances at Quinn and then Mrs. Quinn and sees that they're as bewildered by that statement as Captain Mason is. The man clambers to his feet, saying, "Mister Quinn was just demonstrating how we whipped the Johnny Rebs, and I happened to walk into range at the wrong instant. I'm sorry you were summoned for this trifle."

"If you say that's the case..." Captain Mason looks as if he doesn't believe a bit of what he's hearing. Padraic Quinn looks bewildered himself, but presses on Mason:

"Well, y' hear that, then? Now do you apologize for calling me a brawler?"

"Then I guess I must..." He nods and sidles away up the corridor as bystanders open a way for him.

"Apology accepted, Cap'n Mason," Quinn calls after him. "And I don't have to apologize for calling you a tinselled fool, because I *didn't* call you one, did I now?" Some bystanders laugh nervously at that.

"What the hell?" says a man nearby. "I saw with my own eyes, sir, he tried to knock your noggin off!"

"Don't be silly," says the thin officer, laying his left palm gingerly upon his cheek. "Mister Quinn wouldn't deliberately smite one of his most earnest admirers!"

Paddy, now half-smiling but with a look of perplexity in his eyes, glances around, notices Robbie, gives him a welcoming nod. Finally, he says, "Why don't we just go in our little cubby here and clear the hallway? Let's make up over a refreshment, eh?"

Shutting the door behind them, Paddy shakes his head and rolls his eyes, turns to see them, Felice, Robbie and the bruised Army captain, standing squeezed together staring at him with bemused or inscrutable expressions, and says, "Sir, what apologizing needs done here is mine to you. My wife let me know good and well I misperceived something. We've just now met, rather roughly, too, but not formally." He extends his hand. "To whom am I addressing my rueful embarrassment?"

"Mister Quinn, I'm Walt...I'm *David* Elliott, 44th...I mean, *76th* Indiana." Paddy looks at him with a frown, as the officer hurries on, his speech a bit indistinct due to the swelling of his face. "No apology necessary, but accepted in good humor. I'm astonished that a hand that writes and draws so finely also carries such brute power."

"Sir, after such praise, I'll have wear a bigger hat. You're all right? Nothing broken?"

"No, Mister Quinn. I go down quite easy." He raises his hand to touch his cheek again, showing that the end of his ring finger is missing.

Paddy wags his head and reaches into his luggage for his flask and a spare bottle, not yet letting himself look at Felice's face. He says, "Captain Elliott, allow me to introduce a fellow Indianan, Robert Macombie. Born in your state but enlisted in Pennsylvania. Not an officer, but a gentleman. If you won't drink with an enlisted man, then I'll not be so sorry I hit you." He begins pouring whiskey, hands a glass to each man and fills the flask cap for himself. Robbie says:

"I could leave you gentlemen, and find me a place on deck."

"Indeed you won't," says Captain Elliott. "In real life I'm a lawyer, not an aristocrat. I'm honored to drink with one of you. You enlisted fellows bore so much more than we did. The Rebs kept us officers separate, you see," he says to Paddy, "for fear that we'd organize the soldiers and overturn their Goddamned pigsty with an uprising, pardon my language, Ma'am."

"Oh, but in actual fact, sir," says Robbie with a little hard edge in his voice, "we peasants organized ourselves somewhat, no officers present at all, made us a sort o' government when we needed it. Once we formed a court, tried some criminals that the damn Reb warden wouldn't control. Hanged 'em, we did. No officers involved. We did it just fine. I built th'..." Now suddenly he blinks and bites his lips shut, as if he hadn't meant to say so much.

"That's a story I'll be askin' ye more about," Paddy says, turning to the officer, still holding up his little flask cap, "but there's another one that must really be interesting: It's why you don't seem to know your own name or unit, Cap'n Elliott."

"What, sir?"the captain looks almost frightened.

"You say you're David Elliott of the 76th Indiana. But first you said Walter, of the 44th. Now, I happen to know the 76th is with

Sherman. And, I remember one David Elliott, who could pass for you, but not quite. And the 44th are Negro troops. Just between us, sir, no charade, who are you?"

The man shakes his head, looking down. "No wonder you're the journalist you are! What *don't* you know? Well, here it is. Please, may we keep it to ourselves. I *am* Walter. I did command a company of coloreds. I was captured, thought the Rebs'd kill me then and there; to them I was worse than a Negro. Somehow by God's grace, though, they let me live. I was exchanged, paroled. Went back to my headquarters, was ordered back to duty - then damned if I wasn't captured again, by Hood's boys near Nashville. So I had to assume cousin David's name, or I'd've been shot for violating parole. May I beg you not to reveal who I really am?"

"You think you need to keep up the disguise still? The war's pretty much over."

"Mister Quinn, you know there *are* Southerns on this boat. I did march armed Negroes against their cause. That's unforgiveable, to them. So, please understand my anxiety? I want nobody to know who I am until my feet are firm on Indiana soil, in my home town of Hanover. Home safe!"

"Hanover!" Robbie Macombie exclaims. "Why, sir that's not five miles from where my Grandpa's buried, at Saluda!"

The captain raises his eyebrows and peers thoughtfully at Robbie. "Really! Your grandfather's name was...?"

"Joseph Macombie."

"The Revolutionary solder?"

"Yes, sir. He was."

"His son, Alexander Macombie, was in the Legislature! I knew him! Is he your father?"

"No, my uncle."

"Well, damn!" Paddy exclaims, "let's not stand here holding whiskey in our hands and talking about acquaintances and coincidences. God knows how much good whiskey evaporates while people do such small talk! I say let's drink to your brave grandfather, and to all the other departed spirits thronging that road to Heaven like herds o' sheep! As for your alias, Cap'n, it's our secret, uhm, *Dave* Elliott!"

Paddy's flask-cap cup is held aloft toward the other soldiers' glasses, and his throat is eager to be christened with the fuming nectar, when Felice slips quiet as a ghost behind him, and her delicate hand lifts the cup from between his thumb and forefinger.

"Peace," says she who has never to his knowledge taken anything stronger than a sherry.

And before he can turn, she has placed the silver vessel back in his hand, empty, and he hears her emit a shuddery exhalation.

"Dear," she says, I'd like a word with you at your convenience."

*

PADRAIC QUINN'S DIARY

Aboard Sultana

April 25 wee hour

Holy Mary Mother of God, at last some uplifting news!

I, Padraic Quinn, to be a father! Felice thinks we've conceived.

M'Love well might not have told me yet if she'd not taken my whiskey to toast our guests. Amazing change in her demeanor:

When they left, I feared I'd be doing big penance for pole-axing poor Elliott in my jealous fit. But she seemed to forgive me as graciously as he'd done. When we were alone she seized me with bold ardor and beguiled me to mount her in that mode by which, as she so quaintly says it, she "can't see me coming." Then in the afterglow of our frenzy, she murmured to me her belief that she is early with child, and in less than another minute was asleep with utter bliss lining her face.

I pray I can be worthy of this creature and the gift she is giving me. I vow to try.

*

Such an enigma this Macombie. Does he believe he's moribund? Yet he's not truckling for sympathy or attention. Had to extract his promise for further interview tomorrow. Declined remedies Felice suggested for his gut. Can he make it to the funeral if I do ask him?

Got to ask. He seems perfect for the role. (If he lives.)

*

Sultana throbs onward, patched boiler and all. Must try to sleep a bit as I'll be all day interviewing these amazing wretches. After the Hell they've endured, I still hear some of them singing & laughing out there under the cold stars! Songs of going home.

The joy of going home. Must be wonderful, say I who never had any home but Army camps and bivouacs and hospitals and steamboats and hotels. Shall have to make a proper home by & by if I'm to be a worthy father.

A home where? New Orleans, near Ma? St. Louis, near Felice's family?

More likely New York, where the weeklies are. And the best lecture halls.

The poet Whitman told me New York is the destined home for a man of my ilk.

God damn, the sight of these fellows would wring his heart out!

*

Could it be she's wrong? I asked her how she was so sure and she said by the count of days. Mysterious creature!

Must try to get a keg from O'Hara & McGinty. Would help get the gents a-talking. The way to a man's heart is down his throat.

McGinty saw to it I got a St. Patrick's Medallion; he'll see I get a keg.

Viva Riley! Viva McGinty! Viva O'Hara! Viva Macombie! Viva Quinn! Viva Felice! Viva the son of Quinn! Or daughter?

I'll drink to that, even!

CHAPTER SIX

Aboard Sultana

April 26, 1865

Paddy's notion of obtaining a keg of whiskey, for priming the poor soldiers' memories, has become an obsession, causing him to rise and dress in the pre-dawn darkness of the cabin, even more stealthily than usual, so as not to disturb his sleeping bride and their embryonic son - or daughter - still more reason for the desperate wakefulness of his mind.

He knows that the barkeeps McGinty and O'Hara sleep in the quarters up on the texas deck, and he feels he must get to them and borrow or buy a keg before they open their saloon for the day and run out of whiskey altogether. He knows it will take time to get up there to their quarters, picking each footstep among the hundreds of exhausted and enfeebled soldiers who lie hip to hip and head to heel on every square foot of all the decks and even the stairwells and closets and the cargo hold. Some two thousand souls on a vessel meant to carry three or four hundred at most! His contempt for Captain Mason burns in him whenever he thinks of that.

He's no better than any of the damned war contractors who've fattened themselves on the gore of this war. Five dollars a head and he'll risk any number.

Paddy has thought often of war contractors. He had used to discuss them with Grant.

One night during the Vicksburg siege, sharing a bottle and both seething about the quality of some equipment, Paddy had said:

"Riddle: What d'ye get when you cross a pig with a buzzard?"

"What?"

"A war profiteer."

"Well said!" General Grant had exclaimed with a bitter laugh.

But then Paddy had drunk a few more shots before coming to an unpleasant realization:

I profit on this war myself! Paid to write of it!

But even that thought doesn't soften his contempt for Captain Mason. At least, a war correspondent doesn't put two thousand souls like these at risk for the greed of it.

Paddy has tiptoed like this among sleeping soldiers much of his life, in the last Seminole War and then the Mexican and finally this war between the states: countless men become shapeless bundles of blanket wool in the darkness on the ground, acres of snoring, coughing, groaning, muttering soldiers exhausted by marching, as if the earth itself were susurrant, a match flare or two always flickering here and there as those who couldn't sleep lit their tobacco. Just before and just after battles there would be those untented fields of bodies underfoot. After the battles they likely would lie crying or screaming with pain of wounds, or silent in death, but the earth beneath them was always a still bed, its limit a dim hill or line of trees, a rail fence, a roadside, a surgery, a stack of dead comrades.

But here they lie not on still soil but on a throbbing bed of deck planking, this monotonous tremor of motion, with the swish of water all about, stars high overhead winking through coalsmoke, on this reverberating leviathan swimming against the current in its own nimbus of lanternlight, a bed of dreams and nightmares and northward yearning. Sometimes looking down for a place to put his foot Paddy sees a glint of light in an open eye, and he thinks: Another one like me, one who lies awake. Here and there a higher hummock of blanketwool: a man sitting up, exhaling pipe or cigar smoke, or a pair of men leaning together murmuring in conversation.

Paddy wonders where that man Robbie Macombie found a place

to lie down. A man grown so important to him. Must not lose him. Paddy has jotted important specifics about Robbie in his notebook and certain elements of his story: A veteran of the Mexican War before this one. After two wars, still just a private, tho' was corporal and sgt. "several times." Never hit in battles except by pieces of other soldiers. (I told him it was a flying piece of skull that took my arm off in Mexico, and he just nodded.) Saw his brother killed at Fredericksburg. Obsessed with cleanliness after the filth in the prison. Wry wit. Fatalism. Once or twice dared guards to shoot him in the "dead zone" along the palisade, hoping it would end his misery, but they didn't shoot or the gun snapped. He seems to bear the Rebs no grudge; he says, "Well, sure they starved us. But, hell, they couldn't feed their own soldiers." He's just 41. Says his hair went white at Andersonville. In replies terse but evocative, he's begun describing a place of unmatched misery and squalor. Men rotting alive. Turds in the creek they got water from.

Trading buttons to guards for a turnip. No shelter summer or winter, just holes in the ground.

And his is just one story among these hundreds! A full day and night of interviewing could likely yield a *Harper's* story like no one's ever read before. Paddy thinks: Must have plenty of whiskey to make their stories flow. Must get this all on paper, words and sketches. And then on to Father Abraham's funeral. Well, well. Peace might not be too tame for an old war correspondent after all.

After struggling up a dark companionway where a soldier sleeps on every stairstep, he arrives at the door of the texas deck living quarters at last. Darkness is just beginning to fade in the east, far to starboard, but no horizon or shore is yet visible. Under the edge of the door is a dim line of lamplight. Beside the door stands a sentry, one from the contingent that escorted the prison survivors aboard at Vicksburg. The sentry seems to be asleep on his feet, propped up by the jamb behind him and his musket in front, head down so far his cap bill is almost touching the muzzle. Paddy moves his hand in front of the soldier's eyes.

"Yes, sir?" says the sentry.

"Ah, you're awake! Good for you. Do you know whether Mister O'Hara or Mister McGinty are up and about yet? The barkeeps, I mean."

"I'm supposin', sir. I heard the fat one's voice in there just now." He says this in a whisper, as if a speaking voice would disturb soldiers who are sleeping through the throb of engines, thrashing of paddlewheels, the loud drone of snores and mutterings, the uncushioned hardness of boat decking under their swollen joints, and the chill of river dew all over, the moans and yelps of the real sufferers down on the foredeck.

"Would you be for violatin' the duty of your post, if you were to peek in and tell him there's someone here to see him?"

"Seeing as it's you, Mister Quinn, sir, I reckon you could just walk on in."

Aha, the dividend of fame again, Paddy thinks, and, patting the soldier's elbow, then reaches for the door latch and steps into the hot, dimly-lit room where cigar smoke and rancid sweat compete with the smell of overbrewed coffee. At a long table in front of the woodstove sits O'Hara himself, penciling in a ledger, round as a toad, in a collarless linen shirt that appears not to have been laundered since perhaps the War in Mexico. Glancing up at the influx of night air, he frowns, then breaks into a smile. "Paddy, m' laddie! At this hour! What, sir?"

"Top o' the mornin', Jim O'Hara. Glad to see you up already. Most barmen I've known sleep late."

"I would if I could, Paddy, but the officer traffic through here is lively enough to wake a deaf man from a two-pint stupor."

"A two- pint what? *Stupor*? I always heard two pints make one *cavort.*"

That pun precipitates an eruption of wheezes and spasms from the barkeep. When O'Hara does recover his breath, he goes solemn, raises one eyebrow, then the other, and crooks a forefinger. Paddy leans closer over the table.

"What's keeping the officers agog," he murmurs, "is an untiring rumor that some incorrigible Reb has brought a bombshell on board this tub and means to blow two thousand Yankees to perdition." O'Hara squints ominously, watching for Paddy's reaction.

Aside from a shudder at the mention of a bomb explosion, Paddy demonstrates the *sangfroid* one would expect of an old San Patricio, even just an honorary one, and replies in a flippant tone, "Is that so? Why don't they just throw the Reb overboard before he lights the fuse?"

"Why, because he's incognito. If he even exists. He could be any adult civilian we took on from New Orleans to Vicksburg. The crew's watching 'em all. Any cavalier dandy lights a match, one of our crew tromps in to report that the gent was lighting a cigar in a most sinister manner." Grinning, O'Hara interlaces his fingers on his great belly and says, "Aside from our imminent doom by a cigar bomb, which is beyond my control, what can I help ye with, m'boy?"

"All I need, Mister O'Hara, and I do need it bad, is a keg of plain but decent whiskey – or rum or brandy, but preferably whiskey. And a bung to dispense it with, if you've a spare."

O'Hara retracts his chin into his other chins, eyes darkening. "A keg, is it? What size of a keg?"

"I estimate two or three gallons would give me a good start, five get me finished."

"By God if it *wouldn't* get ye finished! I've underestimated you, m' lad! Forgot you're Irish." He chuckles at his own wit.

"It's for the boys out o' the prison, not all for me."

"In that case, y'll need a hundred gallons. But may I remind you: I'm the official whiskey-vendor aboard this tub, lad. I sell it to 'em."

"*We* do," says the voice of Thomas McGinty, the other barkeep, through the half-open door on the left. He appears in the doorway in nightshirt, gray hair wildly mussed. "What are you up to, Mister Quinn?"

"I'll buy it from you, wholesale if I can, retail if I can't, and I'll be givin' it to 'em, not selling it. Most of 'em don't have any drinking money."

"How generous," says McGinty. "But just bring 'em to the bar, and treat 'em there to a round, why don't ye? That's where the true drinkin's supposed to be done on this boat."

"With all due respect, gents," Paddy replies, "your saloon's too rowdy a place for genteel discussions of the finer things in life such as getting through it alive. I need to talk to many of those poor fellows, quietlike, one or two at a time. And it's mostly in the hours when your saloon's not open for business anyway. I need to hear what they say, when I can make them feel like talking. You're veterans, You know how it is."

Both the Irish whiskeysellers are now looking at him with full comprehension. He *is* the very man, the only journalist in America, who ever bothered to find the truth about their beloved leader John Riley in that war in Mexico, the only time it was ever told in a fair and sympathetic way, showing that great man as something other than just a murderous traitor. That's why these two gave him the San Patricio medal. Now they seem to realize that Paddy is on another right-hearted search for truth, with another mighty story to tell rightly.

"I suppose," McGinty says to O'Hara, "we could let him have that cask of rye at cost. We can replace it when we get to Memphis."

Paddy clutches the gold medal in his pocket and has to blink rapidly at the sudden moistening of his eyelids. "Gentlemen, let's work out a transaction here, then. What I can't afford out o' my own pocket, I guess I can finagle out o' *HARPER'S WEEKLY*, and pay when we get to St. Louis."

"O what fools we are," O'Hara says to McGinty with a wink. "Sellin' whiskey to an Irishman on credit!"

*

It's daybreak when Paddy is back to his cabin door, exhausted by the effort of squirming and tiptoeing through several hundred blanketed wretches while carrying under his good arm an unwieldy and increasingly heavy oaken keg of rye whiskey, with nowhere to set it down and rest, fearful that it might fall from his grip to crush the skull of some poor sleeper on the deck. He regrets that he'd not thought of using his coat as a sling to carry it in for easier handling.

Now he must set the load down to find his door key in his pocket, and easing it down with his cramped right arm and the stump of his left forearm, barely avoids dropping it on his own foot. He rolls the keg into the tiny cabin, panting for breath, and in the half-light sees Felice up on one elbow in the lower bunk. She's been awakened by his clumsy, bumping entry, and he wishes she had slept through it, because her first two sleepy questions are, "Where have you been?" and "What is that?"

He upends the keg inside, shuts the door, and sits on the keg with his back against the jamb, regaining his wind and trying to flex the cramps out of his biceps muscle and his thumb.

"Top o' the mornin', my darlin'!" he gasps. "How did you sleep, you and our little embryon? Or embryonette, if that's her destiny?" Felice says nothing for a moment, perhaps just remembering that she's pregnant. She sits up, having to tilt her head under the upper bunk.

"What is that?" she repeats. " Is that a barrel?" The tone of her voice is not as dulcet as he'd like to hear it.

"It is a keg of some uncommonly heavy chemical element. On a par with molten lead, or maybe even mercury. Its specific gravity is in fact so great that I suspect it might be rye whiskey. As y'know, the gravity of whiskey is sooo great, it sometimes is known to bring a man down."

Aware of her growing concerns about his drinking penchant, sensing that she well might not be amused, he nevertheless recklessly jokes onward: "Seeing how you took to my liquor last night, I was afraid we might need this," he pats the keg under his haunch, "to last us up to Memphis tonight." He's recovered his breath, but still has to twist his right arm because of its insistence on cramping. Under the floor, the great steam machinery throbs and clanks like the overtaxed heart of an aged Vulcan. Felice has a very distasteful look on her face. Finally, Paddy hoists himself over to the bunk, sits on its edge and pulls her to him with his aching arm.. "The whiskey's for the poor soldiers, Darlin', not for me. I need 'em to let down and say what's right in the core o' their hearts, and this is what'll best bring it out of 'em."

She shudders within his arm.

"You know as well as I what they've been through," he murmurs, thinking of the countless wounded who died on her hospital ship despite her nursing.

She answers nothing; he can feel the depths of her musings as she leans into his arm.

"Men's dying words," he goes on, "are pretty much just like what they say when they're drunk."

*

Three blasts of the ship's whistle and a change in the timbre of the engines jar Paddy out of his stupor. He must have been only minutes in dozing, as he's still half-sitting, his arm still around Felice. Her eyes are open, and he thinks she might have been talking to him, as her voice is in his head, but he has no idea what she might have been saying.

"Where could this be?" he mutters, aware that the three whistles mean a docking. The boat isn't due at Memphis until this evening.. "Get dressed, Sweetheart, and I'll go get us some coffee. If this place has a telegraph, we might find out where Mister Lincoln's funeral train's got to by now." He clambers achingly out of the bunk, looks down at a rosebud nipple revealed in the slack of her lacy neckline, yearns to sink back down upon her and lick and nibble toward ecstasy. His organ is hardening, yearning like a compass needle. But the voices of hundreds of soldiers outside the cabin, beginning to hail the shore, remind him that he has their story to tell, and he stands up to adjust his clothes. Felice is now face to face with the protrusion in his trousers; she blinks, puts her hand against it, shakes her head, and pushes him away, her touch nearly triggering an ejaculation. Heart swooping, he blows out a sigh through pursed lips. "Coffee!" he reminds himself. "Telegraph!" He picks up his notebook and slips it into his coat pocket. And as he squeezes out between the whiskey keg and the door jamb, he tells her, "If this town has a telegraph, I'll step ashore."

"Just go on," she says. "I can get my own coffee from the Ladies' Parlor."

"Lock the door if you leave," he says, signaling his meaning with a glance down at the keg. "And hide those lovely titties."

"All your treasures will be properly secure, Mister Quinn."

*

The rough little town is on the larboard side, telling him that this is the Arkansas side of the river. Huge faded letters on a warehouse declare the place to be Helena. Scores of townfolk are already on the plank sidewalks to watch the boat's arrival. Women have gathered their skirts up to keep them out of mud puddles. Flood water is up to the boardwalks and there are dingy brown old highwater stains farther up the walls of two whitewashed dockside buildings. Little boys with muddy bare feet gape at the great, churning paddlewheel and up at the horde of gaunt soldiers. These lads would have seen steamboats most days of their lives, but surely never one so crammed with the ruins of humanity.

Paddy sees the boat crew foreman standing by down forward at the gangplank, thinks a moment until he remembers his name, then calls down in his battlefield voice, "Mister Rowberry!" Hearing over the drone of voices and the clamor of machinery, the foreman looks up, sees him waving, and cups a hand behind his ear. "This town have telegraph?" The foreman shakes his head and turns back to the docking, yelling at deckhands who are hauling at the pulley ropes.

So much for that, then, Paddy thinks. No other reason to get off here. Time better spent talking to these soldiers.

Even better, he thinks with that heart-swooping desire again, go back in and catch Felice before she gets clothes on.

No! Get coffee!

As he turns away from the dockside hubbub, he looks up and sees that the entire roofline over the Promenade Deck is festooned with shanks and ankles and feet both shod and bare, some swinging rhythmically, some crossed at the ankles: the soldiers on the deck above are sitting along the edge, best seats for watching the mooring and the crowd of townfolk, for shouting merry greetings or jovial taunts about their recent foes, the Arkansas Rebs. Paddy's spirit is borne up by an onrush of admiration for such men who have emerged from Hell with the ability to laugh and tease.

Suddenly a huge eruption of laughter comes from nearby. Paddy turns to see a dense pack of soldiers enjoying a spectacle:

The boat's captain, that stiff-neck pomposity Cass Mason in full uniform, apparently unable to make his way through the solid mass of soldiers filling the companionway by the paddlewheel housing, has climbed up on the rail to crawl past them on hands and knees! His face is livid with the effort, or in reaction to their hilarity at this undignified spectacle. It is a precarious maneuver; one slip and he could fall down into the water by the still-turning paddlewheel. Paddy is delighted to see his discomfiture and his slow, painstaking progress. As the captain creeps closer, Paddy pulls his notebook from his pocket, balances it expertly on the stump of his left forearm, takes out a lead pencil, and with the practiced adroitness of a battlefield sketch artist, makes a sketch of him. Some of the soldiers lean in to watch, exclaiming over his deft pencil work, their breath and body smells a stinking miasma. By the time Captain Mason has attained the top of the stairwell railing and started to dismount, Paddy is right in front of him, and says loudly:

"What, sir? This boat a bit too crowded for you, is it? I wonder why!" And he holds the notebook in front of the captain's florid face to show him the sketch. Paddy couldn't have dreamed up a more fortuitous way to heckle the boatmaster. Captain Mason glowers at the drawing but says nothing, turns and heads forward along the deck, squeezing among soldiers.

"Y'all, lookee yonder!" a loud, twangy voice calls from somewhere

above, "there's one o' them pitcher-snipers a-settin' hisself up to shoot us!" Another uproar of hooting and laughing rolls out. Paddy knows the term "picture-sniper." It was one of the names the soldiers had for those photographers who followed the armies everywhere with their wagons of equipment, their tripods, their black hoods and curtains, always carefully aiming their cameras with a sniper's care. Paddy scans along the boardwalk and riverbank, and finally sees, off the stern, the familiar sight of a photographer wrestling his big boxy camera atop a wooden tripod. The man is back so far that his obvious intent is to catch an image of the whole length of the *Sultana* and its enormous load of humanity. It makes Paddy a little anxious; this boatload of Andersonville survivors is *his* story; his great *Harper's* story; he thought of it first. Not that a black and gray photograph would be anything like the words and drawings he's going to use to tell of their awful sufferings and now their homeward yearnings, their redemption in peace at last. But it is *his* story.

As the distant photographer fiddles and adjusts, now ducking in and out of his black shroud, soldiers come crowding the already packed larboard rails, every man of the two thousand seeming intent on getting in the photograph, as if this were some formal regimental portrait . Even Paddy himself instinctively smooths his lapels and his temples with his palm, vain motions so ridiculous that he makes himself blush and mutter, "Damn!" Due to his fame as the war's picturesque one-armed correspondent and his constant proximity to photographers of the "Bohemian Brigade" during the war, Paddy has been photographed as often as some generals, more often than most, and his reflex is to pose. That is probably just what is happening all over this overloaded vessel, even though any individual face in a picture of this scope would obviously be too tiny to be recognizable. Each man's self is his own soul's focus, so why not a camera's as well? Paddy realizes this in one moment, and in the next moment he feels a vertiginous imbalance and sees the dockside and the town of Helena rising before his eyes. The voices of hundreds suddenly change to a vast moan.

Good God, we're turning turtle! He thinks, trying to tilt for his balance, feeling the weight of other bodies shifting against his back. Some men are involuntarily teetering and staggering toward the rail. Straight below now, the swift, cold, brown water eddies. Pigs squeal, horses whinny. Heavy objects can be heard scooting and bumping, down within the huge vessel.

He understands at once: the weight of hundreds of men suddenly on the port side is turning the enormous steamboat over, rolling her portside down; she's listing ten degrees, fifteen, twenty...

Voices are rising to a quavering howl of dismay. Paddy finds his own voice, his deep-lung battleground voice, and bellows desperately:

"Go back! Get back to the other side! Back!"

And another powerful voice, from directly above, up on the texas deck, also begins giving the same order, and gives it again and again.

The shuffling and straining of weakened men shoving back against the weight of hundreds of other men begins; just perceptibly the tilting slows and then stops; men gasp and climb back up the slope of the deck. Paddy hears a thunder of footsteps overhead, a terrible creak and groan of timbers and beams. Only now does Paddy notice the *Sultana*'s great long shadow cast by morning sunlight over the whole waterfront of the town of Helena, the shadow silhouettes of countless moving men projected on the wall of a warehouse, the shadows of the smokestacks angling far up the street.

For a moment there is a palpable equilibrium, though the slow surge of bodies around and above continues. Paddy thinks of Felice and the fright and confusion she must be feeling in their cramped cabin, where the heavy trunk and the whiskey keg might have toppled and rolled against her. He hears water cascading somewhere - probably inside the larboard paddlewheel housing, he presumes by its hollow resonance - and then he feels that slow, subtle shifting of gravity, sees the upper edge of the boat's shadow begin to rise on the warehouse wall...

The tone of the great collective murmur is changing all around him, fear settling to relief. Paddy looks back to the photographer onshore. The man is transfixed behind his camera, his black shroud still held above his head by both raised hands, gaping, blanched face discernible even at this distance. Paddy thinks, as if the intensity of feeling might send the thought to the man:

You might have recorded a catastrophe of your own making, were you not such a slow bumbler with your apparatus!

*

Squeezing through the mass of excited, jabbering soldiers to return to his cabin, Paddy suddenly finds himself face to face with the swollen, purpled, lopsided visage of Capt. Elliott, the gentleman he smote so powerfully last night. The captain has just clambered down the ladderwell from the texas deck in a high, flushed state of happiness, and he cries, "Mister Quinn! Sir!" and fervently grasps the hand that knocked him unconscious those few hours ago; his grip hurts the stove-up hand, but Paddy grins over his grimace.

"Mornin', Cap'n. A bit scary there for a moment, wasn't it?"

"Was it ever! And correct me if I'm wrong, but I thought it was *your* voice down here first warned them to shift the weight back?"

"Well, I did yell...I..."

"It wasn't till I heard you that I understood what to do. I'd nearly slid off the edge myself. Well, at once I took up your call, started yelling orders , and they started for the other side. You've saved the day, sir!"

"Oh, I'm sure everybody would've realized..."

"Not soon enough, they wouldn't have. The credit's yours, sir. I'm going to say so to everybody, the skipper foremost! And if there's any way I can ever, *ever* be of service..."

Damn me, Paddy thinks, if everybody I knocked unconscious woke to love me this much, I'd sure go cloutin' just about everybody! But he says, "Cap'n, there is in fact a way you can be of service..."

"Good! How, Mister Quinn?"

"Just by sending soldiers to talk to me. I want to hear their stories, about that Reb prison. About surviving it. I have whiskey for those needin' to be primed. Can you help me?"

"Anything, Mister Quinn. I personally am ready to unload my soul, to begin with."

"You don't object to a nip in the morning?"

"In your company, sir, and that of your lovely bride – and healing angel – I'd gladly breakfast on whiskey."

"It's rye, Cap'n. Best I could do."

"Rye and coffee are good together, Mister Quinn."

"Well then! If the coffee urns didn't all topple and spill in our recent bobble, Cap'n Elliott, rye and coffee it shall be. And the rugged truth."

"You're my kind o' man, Mister Quinn!"

Here, Paddy thinks, is a fellow who'll relish being seen in print.

"Let's go, then. I'm worried how my bride came through the listing."

*

Felice has survived the scare with aplomb, having guessed its cause at once and bracing herself. When Paddy and Captain Elliott arrive at the cabin, she has already rearranged the tumbled contents and is dressed to go join the Sisters of Mercy in their humane ministrations.

The stateroom is almost too cramped to serve as an interviewing room, containing the couple's baggage, Paddy's portable desk, and the whiskey keg. But anyplace else on the overloaded vessel is much more crowded than this, and noisier. Felice will be out much of the day, and with most of the baggage stowed on and under the bunks, there is room for Paddy to sit facing his subject, desk on lap, and scribble notes in his *sui generis* shorthand, or to sketch portraits, without the subjects being able to see which he's doing. Paddy knows that someone aware of being sketched might feel self-conscious, and not speak from the heart.

So now Paddy is listening to Captain Elliott, and pretending to take notes but actually making a quick sketch. The captain surely wouldn't want a portrait showing the destructive effects of "the mighty fist of Saint Padraic," but Paddy is unable to resist drawing it: the swollen, purpled jaw, the mouth askew. Circumstances had never permitted him to sketch anyone he'd ever punched before. Of course he'll not show this to Elliott; he will also make a handsomer sketch, leaving out the damage.

So far, Elliott's account is a bit of a disappointment, not a vivid description of Andersonville's squalid conditions, as officers weren't kept there, but in a more habitable compound some miles away. But he has lawyerly opinions on the culpability of the Rebel officers in charge of the prison. "Their Major Wirz," he says, shaking his head slowly and setting his lip in what might be a sneer – though the swelling makes any facial expression hard to read – "that wretch deserves to hang. Not that he had the resources to make the place a *decent* lodgement, even if he'd wanted to. But he was one of those little men who try to enlarge themselves by a cruel exercise of their powers. I don't know, Mister Quinn, he just seemed to hate everything – probably, above all, his posting in charge of that vile slough – and maybe that's why he never erred on the side of mercy. If I sound like a jurist here, well, law was my profession, you know, and will be again, now that peace has come...Anyway, if there's justice in the world, he'll hang..."

Wirz to hang, El't predix, Paddy jots on the edge of the sketchbook sheet, then slips the drawing under the hinged lid of his escritoire, and then starts a notebook page with Elliott's name. "May I quote you on that prediction, Captain?"

"Eh? Well, you *are* putting my ramblings down for posterity, aren't you? I keep forgetting that. Must be the rye! Ha, ha." It is indeed apparent that the captain has little capacity for libation.

"I wouldn't quite call *Harper's* 'posterity,' but it's likely to be read just about everywhere."

"Maybe you'd better not quote me on that, then. A lawyer shouldn't pronounce judgement before a trial even begins. I did say 'deserves to hang,' didn't I?"

"'If there's justice,' you said."

"Right! Well, hell, then, Mister Quinn, quote me! I'm certainly qualified to have that opinion! Ah...keep in mind, now, that I'm *David* Elliott, not *Walter,* until we stand on Union soil, Mister Quinn. Heh, heh! Rather complicates the journalism, doesn't it?"

"No, it'll all come out," Paddy says, trying to hide impatience. "Now, er, *Dave,* something I'm so interested in is, what was it like when news came that General Sherman was coming through Georgia? And how did you learn of it?"

"Ah! That was a day! Let me put it this way. If we'd had a keg of this amber liquid there, we'd probably have raised the roof off with the pure force of our joy! The way the news came was like everything else: panicky rumors that we'd hear every time the guard changed. Oh, you can't imagine what ignorant louts those guards were, Mister Quinn! Even their dogs must scorn them, they were so low on the scale of humanity! The only thing they could pass their meanness down onto was us: Yanks. Yank officers. Myself in particular. I was never sure my alias had fooled them. I always thought they *knew* about my Negro troops..." He pauses, sips whiskey, goes on. "I think as much as real hatred of us, though, frankly, was just the repute they might gain among their stupid peers if they killed a Yankee. Understand, those were such wretches they weren't fit to serve in their real army. Too old, too runty, too simple-minded, or plain crazy...but as armed guards they might get a chance to put a notch in the gunstock. Try to imagine being watched by such as them! I could feel their sights on me, as itchy as chinch-bugs."

Paddy jots down these ramblings. Though they've wandered far off his question about Sherman, they're such details as readers will remember long after battle strategies and dates are forgotten. Fear. Bedbugs.

At the same time, Paddy is becoming aware that the captain is presuming to describe a place he didn't really know. Officers weren't in the pen with the enlisted men. Elliott didn't even have soldiers of his own command in the place, as he'd commanded colored troops. The man is so bent on being quoted, he's describing what he could have only imaged or heard.

This man is a bit false and desperate, Paddy is thinking. I need to be talking to the enlisted men. But this man's been listening to them so much, he might halfway believe he survived with them.

Paddy has seen things like this happen to men's minds in the hodgepodge of war. It can be rather like trying to remember what you've done when you were drunk, believing you were in something you only heard of.. It's why he himself likes to get only so toped up and no more. A good journalist has to know what he's actually seen.

"I hope to talk to somebody who tried to escape," Paddy says. "Do you know of anybody on board who tried?"

"Some never tried, some never quit trying. Some did get out, but most of them were soon enough caught and thrown back in. Georgians grow up varmint-hunters. Hard to elude people like that!"

"How *did* people get out? Tunneling?"

"That was one way. A few succeeded, tunneled under the stockade. But then the Rebs foiled 'em by building a second stockade farther out. Some diggers suffocated underground, some died by cave-ins. No, Mister Quinn, the commonest way to escape was to play dead and go out in the Corpse Wagon. Playing the role of a dead man was pretty easy. We all looked the part." The captain pauses and laughs. "Many still do, as you can plainly see."

Paddy nods. "But I never saw such cheerful and energetic cadavers as these."

Captain Elliott sips, absent-mindedly touches his bruised jaw. The shuddering racket of the steamboat engines throbs on; hundreds of voices drone outside the cabin: talk, songs, a loud laugh. "Homegoing," he murmurs, "is a life-force in itself."

Well said, Paddy, thinks, and writes it down.

But I need to get him out of here and soldiers like Macombie in.

*

CHAPTER SEVEN

Aboard Sultana

April 26, 1865

A short, swarthy, rank-smelling youth without a tooth visible in his mouth, mottled like someone once tarred and feathered, gives his name as Private Wilson Crowley, 40th Indiana. He relates that he was among those captured in the Nashville campaign by General Hood's Rebs. Scurvy, he says, turned his gums to sponge and his joints to knobs.

"Don't need teeth, though," says he, eyes glittering, "to drink this here rye, thankee, sir."

He raises the little cup in a toasting gesture to Paddy. "I got so weak in that hog sty that I couldn't hardly have lifted this to my lips. Wasn't 'til ladies brought onions and turnips to Camp Fisk that I thought I might could live after all. I misdoubt my own mama'll know me when she sees me. She makes the best soup. Pa makes the best cider. Reckon I'll not starve, teeth or no. Just put a funnel in my mouth an' pour in what-all I need, soup or cider. Well now, Mister, just what is it you wanted to know about that damn place?"

"Whatever you remember that was most important to you. Lean back and shut your eyes if it helps you remember."

"If I shet my eyes now, you'd just hear me snore. Well, sir, it was like when you got there you was an onion, an' kept gettin' peeled off. You had a dollar, a blanket, a penknife, tobacco maybe, a watch, a razor, hat, shoes, socks, sewing kit, anything...it got stole, first off, by th' Rebs that captured us. Then we was picked over by that gang o' New York thugs in there, them that we finally hung...

You traded off anything for a chunk of jowl, some corn meal, or a clump o' radishes. Them Reb guards were dimwits, but they's smart enough to know what a starvin' man'll swap for two taters or a clutch o' spindly carrots. One layer at a time peeled off you, 'til you'd got nothin' left. And them guards was so poor themself, hardly ever got paid, even in that worthless Reb scrip, why, they'd covet even your coat buttons. Last vittles I got in there, it was a pocketful of them slimy pod things the Southrons call gumbo okra, that I paid for with two eagle buttons. Them backward sons o' bitches hardly ever had a factory-made button in their life, even before the war, I reckon. They tied their clothes shut with strang, they did, 'til they got buttons off 'n us. So it was like that, sir, everything you owned stripped off. Clothes rotted away...

"And then it was your *person* that got peeled off. Flesh wastin' away. Teeth fallen out. Vanity gone. Then strength. Then self-respect. Then even any concern for your fellers. Got down t' every man f'r his self. Then one day you knew you'd lost any hope at all. Once in a while there'd come a decent pair o' shoes or a shirt from some well-to-do corpse that you'd get, and live off its value 'til it was gone."

Well-to-do corpse, Paddy scribbles.

"Another thing'd keep us goin' a while. Now and then there'd come a rumor -- Sherman's reached Atlanta! – or some new rumor of a prisoner exchange...you'd dare to hope a little, but that'd soon wear off too, when nothin' happened. Sometimes there'd be an escape plot, and we'd have a little while of hopin' that would succeed..."

Paddy Quinn writes swiftly as Crowley rambles on.

> *Strain thru latrine overflow for undigested morsels...strip corpses...wells dug seep excrmt...new arrivals "fresh fish"...*
>
> *Page 2 w crowley 40th Ind n.b.: peel onion analogy...center rot'n & holo...gumbo okra...admits cheat others get for self...*
>
> *More rye...cry'g now*

It's while he's in his weepy stage that the boy Crowley brings up the subject of the rooting hogs.

"Our graves, I mean th' graves they hauled our dead off to, they were upslope, maybe half mile northwest o' the stockade...Fifteen, maybe twenty thousand graves, all of 'em dug too shallow. Hogs bein' hogs, they uprooted God knows how many o' them poor graves to get at... you know...flesh, what there was of it. If we could of eat them pigs, they'd of been less of us *they* could eat...It was awful when the wind came down from that way. I mean, if we could smell anything smellier'n *ourselves,* just think how putrid it had to be!" He shuts his eyes and shakes his head. Paddy writes:

> *This, & shit-strain'g for morsels – too vile for readers? Consider omit.*

*

This boy Crowley, like most of them, has black pores and a dark gray cast to his skin, on face, hands and arms - everywhere skin is visible. And over him there hangs a tar smell. Paddy recognizes it: pine soot. These prisoners had for months been permeated in pinewood smoke, darkened and scented like smokehouse meat, with no way to wash it off. In various campaigns, Paddy himself had taken on the smells of campfire smoke. But he was accustomed more to oak smoke and hickory smoke, because hardwoods had been available where most campaigns were fought. Those woods burned clean, almost smokeless when dry, but nevertheless would leave their odor in clothing. And he had usually been able to bathe and get his clothes laundered within a few days.

But Cowley's odor evokes in Paddy some older recollections: the Seminole War, when he was an errand boy in the Army camps in Florida . Pine smoke, pine soot. He remembers a kind of pitch pine that could be lit with one match and not any kindling needed.

But at least there was plenty of clean water there in those Everglades, and a person could wash off.

Paddy also recalls, from other times, the pungent smokes of mesquite and arbusto, the shrubs burned in the Mexican War campfires all over that brutal and beautiful land. In that war he had also become familiar with the pleasant grassy smell of dried cow chips burning under the coffee and cookpots. And he can remember now the smell of rattlesnake meat cooking over a mesquite fire. As a boy he had killed the dreaded serpents in the camps, getting a bounty for each one, then had eaten their tasty flesh, and sometimes an officer would buy a rattlesnake skin from him to send home as a souvenir of Mexico. Mesquite gave a fragrant smoke and he can still remember it.

Strange, though, the cleanest and best-smelling fuel in those camps was dung. There was, in those often-hungry years, the delicious aroma of coffee, or bread baking, or of sizzling meat, but distinct from the food was the smell of a cowchip cookfire, which smelled like grass because that was what it was. Digested grass.

Other smoke smells made him remember: Rank, gritty coalsmoke from trains and steamships he'd ridden to and from the arenas of slaughter. Tobacco in its various forms, cigar or pipe or cheroot. Paddy doesn't smoke, and when people offer him tobacco, he likes to say, "Thanks, but I gave it up when I was twelve." Startling but true. He had smoked anything he could get until he lost his left hand . After that, filling a pipe was too much bother, and he couldn't shield a match in a breeze anyway without that hand.

And of course that other, unvarying smoke smell that he had known at every age of his life, perhaps the very smell of Hell itself: the sulphurous stink of gunpowder. There was always that smoke to remember. And while campfire smokes evoked comfort or respite, gunsmoke evoked, always, glorious terror.

Paddy lays down his pencil, picks up his whiskey glass, and looks at the filthy, smelly, toothless little soldier who sits across from him, head cradled in palms, face down, half-drunk, quietly weeping. Paddy swigs down his rye whiskey, thinking:

The glory of war.

*

Hours later, the next soldier arriving at the door is a welcome sight. It's the gaunt, pale, almost numinous figure of Robbie Macombie, seeming to gleam like nacre. He takes Paddy's hand, squeezes it lightly, looking down at their handclasp thoughtfully before letting go and looking up. "Good day, Mister Quinn."

"Glad you came back! I hope you've rested well enough. Are you comfortable at all?"

"Tolerable. And I've got you to thank for a particular comfort."

"Me? For what?"

"Well, Mister O'Hara the barkeep treated me to a dram today just because he knows we've been talkin', sir."

"Did he now!"

"He esteems you way high, Mister Quinn. That raised me up to his notice, it seems."

Paddy puts his hand in his pocket and feels the San Patricio medallion. He'll show it to this soldier someday, try to explain why it's sacred to him. "When you talk to those two, by the way, I'd suggest you don't mention that about building the gallows for the deserters. They, uhm, barely escaped that themselves."

"Oh, yes sir. I'd figured that out already on my own. And I thought a lot about that, and about all those places we were at the same times. Like fate, sort of, and here we are again."

"Sure it is. And you're here to tell me more stories about that prison. I've interviewed several today, Indiana, Illinois soldiers. But you in particular, I'm glad you're back....I told you I have a proposal..."

"I *have* been a-wonderin'."

"See, it's about President Lincoln's funeral..." *No, don't ask him yet,* Paddy warns himself.

A brighter gleam has appeared in Robbie Macombie's sunken eyes. He raises his hand and looks at the palm. "Just think. You've shaken Mister Lincoln's hand. And I've shaken yours!"

"I guess I could get rich selling handshakes," Paddy says with a chuckle. "Not that I would, though. Gave me a wink, too." Paddy is always cheered a bit by remembering that longago handgrip.

That and the wink had been like getting a medal. His has been a turbulent, hard and violent life, but he owns that. That and his new San Patricio medallion. Some honors. He'd started life with few prospects of ever getting honors. Now he has these.

The man Robbie has tilted his head and looks at Paddy's eyes, almost smiling. "Gave you a wink, y' say?"

"Just like this," Paddy says, imitating it, right eye shut, a sly smile.

The soldier looks incredulous. "Winked! Well I never ever pictured *that*, as many times as I thought of that man. Even *dreamed* of him, I did sometimes."

He's dreamed of him, Paddy thinks. It might be easier than I thought to persuade him to go to the funeral with me!

Paddy sees that the man has drawn a tiny oilcloth packet out of his clothes and is untying a string that binds it. "What I have here," Robbie says, "it's been wet and dried so many times a body can hardly read it. It was written by a fellow who said he traveled with Mister Lincoln, and what he wrote here, well, I wonder how he ever came by this." He carefully unfolds a fragile, creased old clipping and hands it to Paddy. In the margin is pencilled:

> *Written by Sut Lovingood*

Paddy chuckles, recognizing it.

"Lovingood's a pen name," Paddy explains. "Real name's Harris. He's a humorist. I've seen this before." He reads, smiling.

> *"Of all the durned scary-looking old cusses for a President I ever seed, he am the durndest. He looks like a yaller ladder with half the rungs knocked out."*

Paddy chuckles and returns the clipping to the frowning soldier, who folds it carefully and puts it back in the little packet, and reties the string. "I always wondered if he was insulting Mister Lincoln in a mean way," Robbie says, "or, you know, a teasing way?"

"I've heard it put this way," says Paddy. "'When Abe was born his mama threw him away and kept the stork.' He liked that one himself. For all we know he made it up about himself."

Macombie appears ready to laugh, but then sets his lips, as if laughter about the martyred President would be sacrilege. Paddy goes on, "Maybe he was 'scary-looking,' if the sight of an undertaker makes you feel your mortality. But not once you saw him smile and wink."

Robbie Macombie unties the string on his little packet. He crumples the faded clipping and drops it in the spittoon. "Thanks for tellin' me. Had a hard time picturing him as a yellow ladder."

"Picture instead a rawboned old Indian chief, with big ears. Teeth white and straight as piano keys. Put a frock coat and stovepipe hat on that old Indian, and you've got your President."

Paddy wishes he had his "Abraham Winkin'" sketch to show Robbie, but he's left it with his mother in New Orleans. Of course he could draw another one from memory to show him. But instead, he thinks:

Now's the time to ask.

"Mister Macombie, your feelings being as they are, how would you like to go with me to Springfield and see Mister Lincoln for yourself? Pay him your last respects?"

The soldier's face is blank for a moment, then suddenly transformed. Wrinkles disappear; he looks almost like a hopeful youth . "Go with you?"

"It'd take a few days. And I understand you might not want to be detoured from going home..."

"Mister Quinn, sir, never mind 'detoured.' Home'll be there whenever I get to it -- *if* I do -- so a few days one way or t'other won't matter. But Father Abraham, he can't wait. If I'm ever to see the man I went to war for, it has to be before they throw th' dirt in over him. Or over *me*. If you can help me see him with my own two eyes, even if it's just the carcass of 'im, why, I'll be forever in your debt."

"Robb Macombie, it's a deal. So help us God."

And the misty-eyed soldier clasps Paddy Quinn's hallowed hand. Paddy can't say anything for fear he'll choke up.

*

Aboard SULTANA near Memphis

Wednesday, April 26

My Dear Mother,

I pause in my labors to pen this, which I'll post in Memphis this evening for the next boat down to you. I can't contain this news.

You'll remember inscribing in the new Diary you gave me as a wedding gift: "Make me grandchildren."

Yes, Ma'am! No sooner said than done!

Aye! My Felice believes she is with child already, presumes it by counting days, as she says. Of course I, despite my reputation as a writer, can't compose a sentence adequate to express my wonderment and joy. Would I were poet instead! I don't know whether she would want me to tell anyone this yet, as there might be disappointment. But in my very bones I believe it'll be. If you'll believe it with me, how could it not be so?

Too busy to make this a long letter. An astonishing circumstance:

The management of this vessel so succumbed to greed, they took aboard some 2,000 veterans, at $5 per man. With about 100 civilians & 80 crew, our ark rivals Noah's for a living load. The 400 soldiers originally authorized would have doubled the legal capacity; we carry maybe five times that. I took it upon myself to reprimand the captain for his recklessness.

Those in authority will hear of this, as the numbers will be told in the article I'm writing now: I'm interviewing scores of these brave scarecrows about the atrocious prisoner camp in Georgia. It'll be for Harper's, with sketchwork.

Their accounts are so appalling, I'd be too morose to keep on with it – were I not inspired by their own homegoing joy. After their years of peril and defeat and suffering, at last they have hope.

As do I: that of a father to be!

With devotion as ever, your son,

Paddy

P.S.: Two of J. Riley's old veterans, the barkeeps, declared me a San Patricio, honoris gratis, presenting me with one of the real Mexican gold medallions. My head's so swollen with pride, I can't wear my hat!

*

The mass of soldiery seems to understand how they nearly caused the *Sultana* to capsize at Helena, and so they no longer surge to one side or another to look at anything – neither towns nor southbound vessels – but the steamboat still tends to be perceptibly unstable when she turns in the riverbends or runs into turbulent currents.

"Feel it?" Felice murmurs. It is the slight shifting of balance. She and Paddy, alone in their cabin for a few minutes' rest, sit facing each other, two cups of black coffee sitting on the head of the whiskey keg between them. The coffee tilts in their cups visibly with the boat's movement, like spirits in a level.

"I feel it," Paddy replies. "Wintreger told me we're top-heavy, with all these people up here and no real cargo below for ballast." Wintreger, the chief engineer, and has twice now on the voyage approached Paddy to express his unease about Captain Mason's management. He seems to want his grievance on record in case anything goes bad. It is not comforting.

Felice has been spending most of her waking hours with the Sisters of Charity on the bow end of the cabin deck, caring for the sickest and most crippled of the soldiers. Paddy gazes at her for a moment, marveling at her selflessness. "You still feel pregnant, I hope?"

"Dear, it's not that I *feel* pregnant. I just believe I am." Faint lines of perplexity appear between her eyebrows, and she shakes her head. "I can scarcely believe I told you. You're making so much of it before we really know...."

"Well, whether *you* feel you are or not, *I* feel you are. And I couldn't be happier."

"I'm glad. But now, we'd both better get back to work, hadn't we?"

"It's about three hours before supper. Not expected to get to Memphis before dark. Come, Dearest, I'll escort you to the foredeck. I should talk to some of the really sick ones... Wait. Before we go, look at this sketch of our new friend Macombie." He opens his portfolio and brings out the sketch.

"Oh, yes," she breathes. "That *is* the man. You've captured the...the *Biblical* cast. He's so clean, compared with the rest..."

"I have something to tell you about him," Paddy says as they leave the cabin. They close and lock the door and begin squeezing through the odorous, packed crowd, moving forward along the port deck, murmuring, "Excuse me...excuse us...pardon me, soldier..." And those dirty, bristly faces brighten when they see her. A gust of fresh, cool wind comes from the west, where distant thunderclouds are piling above the horizon, outlined by sunlight.

"Here it is about Robbie Macombie," Paddy tells her. "He'll be traveling with us."

"What!"She stops and looks up at Paddy.

"On to Springfield. To the President's funeral. He wants to see Mister Lincoln's body before it's interred. It's his most ardent wish."

"Instead of going *home*?"

"*Before* going home."

"What did he...how...Is he asking you to buy his passage, or...?"

Paddy grasps her hand, and shoulders a path through the masses along the deck, leading her along. "It was my idea.. I invited him. I want him to see his commander. It's a part of the story, you see...A soldier whose reverence for Mister Lincoln supersedes even homesickness!"

She stops. "Isn't that rather...*using* the poor fellow?"

"No more than he'll use *me* to get *him* there. We both want it. And it won't be out of pocket. *Harper's* will reimburse his fare. Think of it, Darling! This is a touch of true pathos!" The look she gives him is not a look of pure adoration. She doesn't really understand the practical devices of being a star journalist. "Listen, Dearest," he says, "those things the badly hurt soldiers tell you, any really remarkable things they say, about how it was, about the way they *felt,* why, keep them in mind, will you? For me? With their names and what regiments they were in? Which battles they were captured in? I can only talk to so many before the boat gets to Illinois. You can help me learn what they've been through. I'm sure they tell you things from the heart.."

"What they tell me from the heart is private."

"No, please, you know what I need...You know what *readers* would want to know...This will be, rather, you know, my *last* story of this war? It's, well, with the President's funeral, the finale of the greatest American story. It has to be the best I'll ever do. It has to be something they'll always *remember* me for!" He wants her to understand how quickly one's fame could be forgotten, how easily the great tragedies and consequences can banish his name to oblivion in the national memory. For Paddy is already thinking beyond the *Harper's* article, to a future time when such pathetic reminiscences as these will perhaps fill a memoir, or, better, make lecture hall audiences moan, weep and applaud . *Immense* audiences! Paddy feels the substance of his adventurous past, heavy as a bag of gold, as elaborate as a tapestry. This is one of those times when he believes his life is a rich and unique commodity, and that he himself will be its sole and rightful distributor.

And that poor, wan soldier on a pilgrimage to see Father Abraham will be, as a conveyor of tragic dramatic power, as vivid and memorable as General Grant or General McClellan, or General Taylor or General Santa Anna, or even John Riley of the San Patricios, among the true *personae* in Paddy's eloquent reminiscences. My biography hasn't come easy, Paddy is thinking. I won't sell it cheap.

"I do understand, Paddy," Felice says in a quiet, cool tone. "But you're the journalist. They tell you facts. I'm their...their...What they tell me are like *confessions.* We're not in the same business, Dear." He decides not to press the point now. He thinks: Then I'll just get it from her later. Pillow talk. Whatever she tells me will just broaden and deepen the story.

*

Paddy rises from the foredeck where he has sat interviewing a very sick Indiana soldier, one too sick even to sit up, one who doesn't know the names of half his own diseases. Six months in that damnable Georgia prison has killed that soldier; he just hasn't stopped breathing yet because he has to get home first. Getting up is painful and awkward, as he's been sitting here so long, and because he has only his one hand to brace himself on. The wooden portfolio strapped on his left arm is useful for his writing or drawing, but can be an encumbrance when he maneuvers from one position to another.

Now standing, a bit dizzy from the effort of getting up, he has to take a couple of deep breaths and blink away what look like stars under his eyelids. He knows from long experience what this means. He is very tired, *too* tired.

"Mister Quinn," says a voice beside him. The chief engineer stands there.

"Eh? Ah, Mister Wintreger! All's well, I'd guess? We're still chuffing along..."

"So far," the engineer replies, but he appears even more sullen than usual. "I wonder," he says, "if y'd like a look at the boilers, being as y're this close by. I'd like if you could see the little iron patch they stuck on at Vicksburg. Just so y'll know what it looks like, in case anybody ever asks.." Paddy knows what he means: If anyone, such as a board of inquiry, might ask the journalist what he knows of the chief engineer's concerns on this dangerous voyage. Maybe after they take a look, he and the engineer can stop at the bar.

"Lead the way, sir." Paddy looks across the deck, sees Felice on the far side kneeling over a recumbent soldier, pauses until she looks over, and waves to her. Then he follows Wintreger down a staircase that seems like the entrance to Hades. Sulphurous-smelling heat rises up the companionway like a desert wind. Yet, even in this blowing funnel, there are soldiers, sitting crowded on the steps. They scoot and press aside to make room for Paddy and the engineer to descend into the sweltering darkness.

Paddy has been in the boiler rooms of steamboats and steamships before, and to him they are indeed the manifestation of the mythical Inferno. Muscular, sweating stokers scoop coal from the coal bins and pitch it far into low iron maws where roaring fire gleams almost white. Other stokers spread the fuel with long, iron-handled rakers, iron doors clank shut. There is a steady, powerful rushing, roaring like a great waterfall, and the intimidating odor of superhot iron. The ceiling is so low that a tall man like Paddy must stoop. Underfoot, all is coal and coaldust. Paddy sees that an emptied coal bunker is full of cots with men on them, and some soldiers even lie on blankets on the filthy black floor itself. Evidently these veterans can tolerate any kind of living conditions for the few days until they get home.

Nathan Wintreger lifts a lamp from its wall sconce and leads Paddy into a dim aisle between two of the massive boilers. Each boiler is perhaps eighteen feet long. From farther astern comes now the rhythmic metallic pulsations of the great, long, horizontal pistons that drive the paddlewheels. The engineer stops and holds the light up near the radiant iron side of one boiler. Over all the roaring and clacking, Paddy can just hear him shout into his ear:

"Here it is! Our little patch!"

The repair that has been a troubling image in Paddy's mind for half the length of this voyage is now right before his eyes, and it is little different from what he's imagined. It is a sheet of three-quarter-inch thick steel plate, about twelve by twenty-five inches, riveted onto the surface of the boiler. Paddy knows that the steel of the boiler itself has to be considerably thicker than that of this patch, which means the repair itself is a weakness riveted over a flaw.

Despite the heat, he shivers. To him the actual sight of this boiler is too much like having a bombshell suddenly appear close in front of his face, with no way of knowing about its fuse. That circumstance has happened to him more than once in this war just past. Fortunately, they were duds. He never even saw the one that took his left hand off in the Mexican War. That one had exploded in the air and blown part a soldier's head off nearby, and part of that soldier's skullbone tore off Paddy's hand. He hates and fears things that explode - a severe handicap for a war correspondent.

Gradually he remembers that he's looking at a steel patch on a steamboat boiler, not an actual bombshell.

"It was put on over a bulge," the engineer shouts in his ear, moving the lamp so the shadow of the irregularity shows. "I wanted the captain to lay over at Vicksburg until the whole boiler could be replaced! Damn this contraption anyway! Had trouble with 'em every trip!" Wintreger goes on. "Too much sediment in Mississippi water! Shouldn't use tube boilers on Mississippi boats, is what I say!"

"Then maybe you should work for a company that doesn't," Paddy suggests.

"Speak up! What'd y'say?"

"Think it'll hold?" he says instead.

Wintreger shrugs, scowling. "Maybe will if we sail steady. When we list, water drains. Get air in them hot pipes, and..." He shapes his lips as if he'll say "BOOM'" but instead just shakes his head.

`Absit nomen absit omen, Paddy thinks.

When they've moved back out of the suffocating din and into light, Wintreger fills his pipe bowl. Paddy watches the tension and the anger and the tics in the engineer's face, and when the engineer puffs out tobacco smoke, he also exhales the words:

"At Memphis we'll load off twenty tons of sugar, a hundred cases of wine, and the hogs and livestock. There goes what little ballast we have. If you think we're top-heavy *now!* Well, Mister Quinn, I just thought you should know how it is on this boat. If you and y'r lovely lady was to debark at Memphis, I wouldn't blame you."

"Thank you for all that, Mister Wintreger. But I need to hurry on to Illinois."

"Sure you do. But if you *did* decide to get off at Memphis, why, I hope you'd remember my concerns that I've told you of. Thanks for your attention, sir."

Paddy has changed his mind about having a drink at the bar with the dour engineer, so he doesn't invite him. He leans back against a bulkhead after Wintreger moves away, taking deep breaths to clear the hellish boiler-room residue out of his lungs and the dread out of his soul, and watches the towering clouds build up over the flooded bottomland to the west.

Everything is so big outdoors here: the river, the endless wooded riverbank, the high sky...And this is but one horizon, nothing compared with the thousands of miles of rivers and roads he's traveled over from battleground to battleground, from horizon to horizon on this vast continent...

Enormous, enormous, enormous!

By contrast, one little sheet of riveted steel down in that steaming, hissing, clanking hellhole:

One foot by two. No bigger than one wing of that buzzard soaring up along above the Arkansas shore over there. What a bother, having to worry about a little steel patch just because speed and profit are deemed more important than living souls!

Well, he thinks. When the cargo ballast is unloaded, the hold will probably fill up with soldiers going down to look for indoor sleeping space anyway. That might even alleviate the top-heaviness instead of making it worse. That Wintreger really *isn't* a positive thinking fellow.

Now I need to get back to work, he thinks, looking around.

"Soldier," he says to a short, freckle-faced lad beside him leaning on the bulkhead, "if you're thirsty, that's something you and I have in common."

"Yessir. That and bein' short of a limb." He turns his torso and Paddy only now notices his empty right sleeve. He seems to have no right arm, nor even a shoulder.

Holy Mother of God! Paddy thinks. He says:

"Well! A comrade-in-*arm!"* It's a pun he'd coined during the war while drinking with an amputee in General Grant's staff. This soldier shows no sign of being either amused or offended by the joke, so Paddy assumes he just didn't get it. The soldier is looking with curiosity at the portfolio strapped to Paddy's left forearm. "Tell you what," Paddy says, "I do carry my wallet where I can reach it with my good hand. I might buy you a swig." He tilts his head toward the saloon.

"Sir, I'll buy *you* one, if you'll draw me my picture like you've been doin' those other fellows. I never ever had my likeness put down on paper."

"Why, son, I believe I could. I could draw you pretty well. I practiced up by drawing President Lincoln himself one time, and you're not *near* that homely...What's your name?"

*

Standing at the bar, being served whiskey by a cheerful McGinty, Paddy learns that the soldier was a Michigan cavalryman, shot in the shoulder and captured at Raccoon Ford on the Tennessee River last fall. His name is Hamblin, and he is a wry one. "My shoulder was busted pretty bad, and hurt me fierce," he says. "I think it would've healed in its own good time, but that Reb doctor I guess needed amputation practice, and I wasn't able to prevent 'im from it. So here I am, Mister Quinn, like you: only able to drink one-handed."

"Just think how we could drink with *two* hands each!"

"Well, I reckon it'll just take us longer one-handed. Well, now, Mister Quinn, where'd you lose your own hand, sir, if I may ask?"

Paddy explains, and the cavalryman is astonished that it wasn't in this war, but seventeen years ago, in Mexico. As Paddy tells the story, he's sketching Hamblin's bony face, trying to make it look as he imagines it might have if the soldier hadn't lost half his body weight by the combination of amputation, starvation and sickness. Other soldiers at the bar lean in to watch. They look at Hamblin, then at the sketch, back at Hamblin, and nod approval. With the whiskey, Hamblin has begun to talk about the prison ordeal.

"What I feared most, all that time," he says, "was, that prison was so foul, one little mosquito or louse bite could start a festering skin ulcer, and you could die of it. People's limbs would just rot off, once they started. A man might lie so long sick that the maggots'd be under him before he even died. Cut up and stitched together as I was, I was so afraid I'd get festered from my shoulder and rot to death, well, it damn near crazed me. Never was any clean water to wash in, 'cept when you could stand in the rain. Oh, don't ever take clean water for granted, Mister Quinn! There's been times I'd've chosen it over whiskey."

"I guess I can understand that, though I've never *quite* reached that stage myself..."

"Big as this Mississippi River is," Hamblin goes on, "I bet if you could turn it to run it through Andersonville, it'd take it a year at least to rinse all the corruption out of that pen. Thirty thousand men can sure make a mess. Especially if they're all sick. Listen to me, sir! Only liquid in that place was a creek running mud, pus, puke and diarrhoea, diluted with piss. Tell you what I can't wait to see, Mister Quinn, is those lakes up home. Water as clear as air! You can lean over the side of your canoe and count the scales on a bass ten feet down!"

"Mister Hamblin," Paddy says, "you make water sound near as good a blessing as whiskey." He turns to McGinty, and calls, *"Hola! Cantinero!"* and holds up two fingers. *"Dos mas!"* McGinty laughs, and shouts:

"Better stick to English, Mister Quinn! Two more coming up!"

*

Paddy can't keep spending pocket money to treat his informants at the bar, so he considers moving his interviewing operation back to his stateroom, where the keg is. But now he feels a light hand on his back, and turns to see a familiar face. Always better at remembering names when he's reached this ideal level of inebriation, he makes the recognition, lays his pencil in his open notebook on the bar and shakes the man's hand. "Good afternoon, Captain Brown!" It's the scrawny but elegant Ohio infantry officer who introduced himself at the table last evening and carried a tray of pastries up to his soldiers. "Alexander Brown, isn't it? "

"What a memory, Mister Quinn! Thank you for remembering. Well, am I interrupting something? Looks as if you're working."

"I am. Just enjoyed a fascinating talk with this gentleman here. Capt. Brown, 2nd Ohio Infantry, meet Corporal Hamblin, Michigan Cavalry." The captain extends his hand, for an awkward little fumble on realizing that here is another amputee.

"I've been looking for you, Mister Quinn. Captain Elliott said you're trying to round up informants. I have three fellows from my regiment who have a few things to tell about where they've been and what they've done. One of them helped in the hanging of the gang, if you know about that. I'm happy to buy a round or two for you all while you talk. I do believe we all deserve a celebration, eh?" Paddy smiles to an imagined Saint Patrick up in the chandelier. The timely arrival of fresh drinking money is uncanny -as it often has been in his lifetime.

There is already much more celebration going on in this boat's saloon than one would expect from hundreds of men fresh out of Hell. Men with merry and harmonious voices at the other end of the bar have been composing a song of tribute, and after several false starts it now pours out:

O mine eyes have seen O'Hara.
He's as noble as a lord!
He's a generous dispenser
Of his amber liquid hoard!
He is lavish at the bung, and
He's the sweetest man aboard!
His soul goes marching on...

Paddy looks down the bar, sees the rotund barkeep flushed, sweating, and trying not to show his delight. "Either he's been treating some of those fellows, or they're trying to get him to," Paddy laughs. The old Irishman is certainly worthy of the tribute. Paddy fingers the gold San Patricio medallion in his pocket, and his eyes tear up when O'Hara finally throws his white-thatched head back and laughs aloud. The inebriated choristers sing on:

Glory, glory Jim O'Hara!
Glory, glory, Jim O'Hara...

Captain Brown is shaking his head, with a rueful half-smile. He takes a deep breath, exhales, and says, "Almost sacrilege, isn't it, though, that song? From John Brown the martyr to O'Hara, a barkeep?"

That reminds Paddy of something, a powerful memory. A face, a mighty voice, and his heart feels squeezed in his chest.

"Eh, well," he says. "I've had the honor of knowing 'em both, and either one's brave as the other..." He had interviewed the abolitionist before the war, just days before he was hanged, and can still see every angle and weathered line of that face, like the God of the Old Testament. That man whose uprising against slaving some said brought on the war. "John Brown told me that this nation's sin would have be washed out with blood," Paddy muses. "And wasn't that the truth.." Suddenly he yells, "HEY! HEY!", and waves his whiskey glass over his head. "Come on, boys, let's sing it again for Mister O'Hara! Let's hear *The Bottle Hymn of the Republic!"*

Far down the bar, O'Hara has turned to look at Paddy. He rolls his eyes, then roars with laughter until he's wheezing and coughing. Other voices are repeating it: "Bottle Hymn of the Republic!" "Bottle Hymn! Ha haaa!" And when O'Hara recovers his breath, he raises a bottle over his head and yells into the uproar of hilarity:

"This round is on the house!" Then he turns a fake scowl on Paddy. "Goddam you, Quinn, for makin' me feel generous! Ye're a bad influence!"

*

In frightful detail, Captain Brown's soldiers have been describing to Paddy the murderous gang of thugs and bullies, mostly from New York, that terrorized, plundered, and humiliated their fellow prisoners in the prison compound for months. Paddy and Captain Brown have moved the men from the noisy saloon to Paddy's cabin. Here it is even more crowded, but the noise is lessened, and the source of the whiskey is now the keg of rye that Paddy bought from O'Hara and McGinty at a generous discount. Captain Brown seems relieved that he's no longer buying the drinks. Like Paddy, he had gone deep into his pockets to keep lubricating their narrative. Paddy is writing rapidly in shorthand, trying to record this appalling tale of ruthlessness, and the three soldiers keep interrupting each other in their eagerness to omit no part of the tale. Each time one takes up the narrative, another fills his pipe with tobacco and puts a match to it, to begin puffing away and thinking what he'll say when he has a chance to speak again. The air is hazy and rank with smoke and body odors, and at least one of the soldiers is a silent farter, thickening the atmosphere every five minutes or so. Paddy realizes that these men aren't sensitive to bad smells after their months in the unworldly stench of Andersonville.

"Them sons o' bitches in that gang were more our enemy than the Rebs sentries were," one says. "The guards, they'd just *let* us die of neglect. The gang, though, s'posed to be in our own Army, why, they outright robbed and killed us..."

"Fresh fish - I mean by that, new prisoners right off the train -" another interjects, "they were grabbed right as they came in the gate, stripped of whatever they had: bedrolls, boots, cash, grub. Took by force. If you tried hard t' hang onto it, you'd get beat plumb to death!"

"That gang had every sort of weapon. Knives, derringers, cudgels, brass knuckles... Nobody else had more'n a spoon to fight back with, if that. Hell, if y' did have a spoon, or a tin cup even, y'd have to sleep on it or it'd get stoled."

"What-all they looted from us they traded to the guards for food, for booze, for favors..."

Paddy says, "Then what you're saying is, the prison authorities knew about all that lawlessness but didn't try to stop it?"

"Why, hell, Mister Quinn, They agged 'em on! Sure they could see down from those watch towers, every little thing that went on, and them varmints *enjoyed* seein' us Yanks fight 'mongst ourselves for scraps or whatever. It was their entertainment! Onliest thing more fun to 'em than that was maybe catchin' a Yank at the dead line so they could shoot 'im. Sometimes them guards would stand up there and *cheer* the gang when it was stompin' on some poor helpless bastard..."

Paddy shakes his head, still scribbling. None of this really surprises him. All his life he's seen soldiers at their worst. In the Everglades and Mexico he saw them rape and kill Seminole girls and senoritas. As a camp boy he'd had to defend himself against drunken buggerers as often as against plain bullies. And he remembers how the crudest individuals in any encampment would eventually find and congregate with their own kind. In an army of millions, there are thousands who are criminal by nature, and army life brings out the worst in them.

"It shows why *discipline* is so necessary!" Captain Brown pipes in. He has been quietly sipping quite a lot of whiskey and not saying much; his gaze is erratic, his lower lip slack. Now he's seen an opportunity to make a point that he deems important. "If they'd put us officers in there among our men to maintain discipline..."

"Well, I beg to differ, Cap'n," one of the soldiers says. "Them *thugs* done had the discipline! They had a damn *king,* is what their damn ringleader was! When we hung that son of a bitch, it was the closest thing I ever seen to true justice. And *we* done that, *we* caught and tried and hung him and his henchmen, it was all done by us enlisted men, no help from officers whatever. With all due respect, Cap'n, an officer don't have no authority in a, in a damn *zoo* like that place was!" Captain Brown scowls and opens his mouth to argue, but the soldier goes on: "Think of it thisaway, sir, if y' will. If one o' them scruffy Reb guards up there in his tower saw you get too close to that dead line, he don't need to call down, 'Requesting your permission, Mister Yankee Cap'n, to shoot you now!' "

Paddy grins, lowering his head further over the notebook so the officer won't notice his amusement. Soldier, he thinks, you are so right!

Just now the cabin door is pushed ajar from outside, bumping Paddy's shoulder. He looks up. Half of Felice's face is visible, one beautiful eye peering in through the opening. Tobacco smoke catches the air current and visibly flows out past the door jamb. "Ah!" Paddy exclaims, trying at once to hold onto his pencil, keep his notebook from falling, and rise to move the keg he's sitting on to make room so he can open the door and let her in. But having passed his ideal level of inebriation by at least a pint's worth, and finding his right leg gone numb, he loses balance and topples against the door, slamming it in her face, and slides to the floor between door and keg, blurting out, "Well, *shit!*" The soldiers packed in the little room, every one of them more drunk than he, watch him tumble, finding it more comical than alarming, and begin hooting with laughter, and one of them breaks wind as loudly as that can be done. The captain, trying to hop up from his seat on the lower bunk, hits his head hard on the bed rail above and spills a full glass of whiskey on his knees, which elicits from him a loud epithet, citing the Lord's name.

Paddy isn't too drunk to realize how Felice will take this disorderly greeting at her own door. He struggles to extricate himself from the jumble of baggage, keg and portfolio, rising to free the doorway for her. The soldiers don't know she's out there, still aren't aware of anything except Paddy's pratfall, which to them seems funnier with each flailing move he makes. One soldier decides to add to the hilarity by uttering farts of many syllables.

On his feet at last, Paddy scoots the keg out of the way and opens the door. Felice stands there waiting, shielding her nose with a kerchief against the stinks pouring out of the room, and she looks like anything but an adoring bride at this moment. Captain Brown just now sees her and, struck by her distressed expression, sees that an escape would be advisable. He at once takes command of the situation while Paddy is still standing there with a sheepish grin. "Good afternoon, Mrs. Quinn," he says with a slight bow. "Your husband has just concluded a thoroughly satisfactory interview with me and my men...and I believe he was just ready to run us out and fetch you for suppertime! Good day, Ma'am! Come on, boys, out!" She has to stand backed up against Paddy to give the four men space to stagger out of the stateroom, each of them in turn breathing a rancid word of respect or apology into her face as they squeeze by.

The couple are left to stand in the stench of whiskey, unwashed bodies and flatulence.

Paddy braces for her anger and disdain, certain that he deserves it. Who is he, to take a refined and kindhearted wife like Felice, but now to act so indifferent to her honor and comfort as to pollute her living space with foul tobacco smoke, spilled whiskey, and probably, too, fleas and lice from the soldiers' clothing? Who is he indeed?

A besotted son of an Army camp laundress, don't even know my own father's name - and a cripple, too, that's who I am..

Paddy had evaluated himself in those very words just a few weeks ago, had even written them inside the cover of his old diary, while weighing his chances of winning her hand. It was an honest self-appraisal, but he had never articulated such doubts to her. His aspiration, his vow, had been to make himself worthy of her, to be a better and more respectable man, a successful gentleman of letters and oratory - even, he'd hoped, a more sober man. Indeed, all this scheme of interviewing these wretched soldiers has been a means to work toward those good purposes.

But he has performed miserably. He has kept boozing, and she is becoming aware of how bad his problem is. He has been ignoring her concerns while charging ahead like a blindered warhorse to do this job for *Harper*'s, just as he had done on every assignment throughout the whole damned war. "Quinn," General Grant had told him once, "you're just like me. Won't ever quit." And Paddy had replied with a laugh, "I'll drink to that!" Paddy's mind is grasping now for the right thing to say in his own defense - maybe something humorous, maybe some excuse about the soldiers' intemperate thirst for liquor, their desperate need to express their tumultuous feelings or tell their awful stories... Or, maybe, just his own sincere and abject apology is what she really needs to hear...

Felice turns slowly around to face him, one hand pulling the ribbon of her bonnet to untie it. The anger he expected to see in her eyes is not there, but her eyes swim in tears. Her face and demeanor are, in fact, so forlorn and stricken that all those defensive thoughts are swept from his mind, and he says instead, "What... in the world? What's wrong?"

She looks in his eyes, slowly shakes her head, pulls off her bonnet and backs away to sit down on the edge of the bottom bunk. There she sniffles and drops her face into both palms. For a few seconds she says nothing. Suddenly sobered by alarm and pity, he puts aside his notebook and moves over to sit beside her and put his arm around her. "What is it, sweet?"

Her voice is small, almost strangling. "Why did we have to get on *this* boat? It's just...it's just...oh, it's all just so *awful!*"

"This boat? What's so awful? Tell me..."

She emits a long, quaking sigh. She lets her hands flop into her lap and gazes unseeing at the wall.

"I never wanted to do this anymore... They're so sick, those boys... Another one died - one leg gone, just a boy! - died while I was reading *Psalms* to him...And I felt, Well, what good is this?" She puts her face down in her hands again, and her shoulders heave. Paddy remembers first meeting her on the hospital ship *Red Rover,* where hundreds of soldiers had died under her care, all those tender ministrations gone futile every time a man died. Sometimes he forgets what she's been through. And now here she is again, with ruined men and boys dying around her. After a while she raises her head.

"Not one priest aboard for last rites...Well, the boy wasn't Catholic, but still...And...and just then, it happened that we went past an ironclad on the river...I looked up from that dead boy and there was that war boat, hideous as a snapping turtle...rusty armor, cannon ports... a boat made just for killing and destruction!...And I just couldn't *stand* it anymore... *Damn* you all! You...you... your strutting generals...your bugles, your victories...your *glory...*" Her face is contorted. He has never imagined that Felice could look ugly.

"You know how glorious war is, Paddy? It's just as glorious as *cancer!*. Oh, *such* a glorious thing it is! Isn't it? You men just *wallow* in death and violence! You'd drink to your manly glory with the seepage of rotting wounds! God, you are all *demented!*"

He's stunned by the truth of it. This is all too true, he knows. He knows. He has seen men ground up like sausage by cannon shells and cannister shot. He's been in the midst of it all his life. He's had these very thoughts, and they have kept him sleepless, and he has tried to drink them away. *Holy wholly holey*...But, coming from her mouth...

They sit on the edge of the bunk, she finally allowing herself to slump back against his shoulder, while the boat's machinery throbs below, river water over the paddlewheels and the voices of thousands of men talking and singing make a susurrus outside their room...

"I know," Paddy murmurs. "But the war is over. It'll be all right now." He's stroking her shoulder. His heart is a deep, wide ache.

"You think so, do you? But no, it'll never be over. It's what men do. It's what they've always done..." She breathes softly, leaning against him. He can't see whether her eyes are open or closed. After a while she says, "Just think." Her voice sounds calmer now, less strained. Her calm is a relief to his bewildered and fretful soul.

"What?"

"Your beloved Mister Lincoln? Up there in his casket on the train? Your War President?"

"Mhm?"

"Think how rotten his body must be by now. Reeking. Seeping. Think how he must smell! Not just by his own rot, but by the rot of half a million dead in his war."

The thought shakes him. He would never have wanted to have

that thought.

And now, even more to his astonishment, she starts singing. He realizes that he has never heard her sing anything before, not even hum a tune! But now she has begun to sing, barely above a whisper: *"Old Abe's body lies a-moldering in the grave..."*

Oh, God, he thinks. *The Bottle Hymn of the Republic...* Without voice now, just breath, he is laughing, though weeping inside.

But gradually, by some miracle, the miracle of exhaustion, it's over, gone, and they manage to doze off again, sitting up, leaning together.

*

He can barely see the innumerable faces out there beyond the footlights but he can feel the great pull of their anticipation. They are the whole multitude and they are hungry to hear his words. They have been arriving for hours, from everywhere. Behind him on the stage in a row of chairs sit people who loved or befriended him before they died. Though they are at his back and he faces those who still live, the select few behind him are the ones who will know how true his words are. The most palpable presence in that row of chairs is a brawny Irishman wearing the light blue coat of an American infantry private at one moment, or in another moment, the elegant dark blue uniform of a colonel of the Mexican Artillery, a man handsome except for the slick pale scar of the capital letter "D" branded under each cheekbone. Paddy yearns to turn around from the lectern to ask John Riley why he's here among the dead ones because he's supposed to be alive, but instead he must keep facing the great, buzzing audience out beyond the footlights. Paddy is not to begin his lecture until the chairs at both ends of the row are occupied, and he waits. As the audience quiets down to hear the opening words of his speech, Felice enters from stage left and sits in the last chair of the row. Paddy is astonished and terrified that she has joined those select few. Then from stage right the President enters and, winking at Paddy, seats himself in the last chair at that end.

This place seems to be the lecture hall of the Cooper Union, but more vast by a thousandfold in order to hold the masses who have come to hear him. It is the culmination of his ambition to orate to all mankind here in this revered hall.

"Ladies, gentlemen, distinguished friends," he begins. "I AM A MAN." There follows a soft murmur of millions of voices, which subsides to stillness again, and he continues:

"I am a man. That is not a boast. It is a confession."

There is silence in the enormous audience in front of him, but those few in the row of chairs laugh. He turns to show them he was being serious, that he was not trying to be amusing.

They have all rotted to carrion.

"What, dear?" Felice's voice cries over the throb of the engines. "Are you alright?"

He is sodden and prickly with sweat. His neck and shoulder are cramped and hurting from sleeping slouched against the bulkhead. Felice is standing naked and soapy beside the ewer and basin, her alarmed face turned toward him, holding a washcloth under her chin.

"Thank God those are just dreams!" he groans, sitting up, licking the stale whiskey taste off his teeth, twisting to loosen the ache in his neck.. "Yes, I'm alright. But..." He pauses, staring at her. "... Have I come from a bad dream to a wet dream? Godalmighty, what a vision you are..." Despite his aches and weariness, the sight of her is arousing a tingling cockstand.. Only seconds ago she was a decomposed corpse in a nightmare chair, but now she is life itself, the horror gone with a shudder.

"Please don't get notions just now," she says. She turns away to rinse the washcloth over the basin and wrings it out, and now begins wiping her ivory skin with it. "I thought I could get bathed without waking you. I couldn't go to supper as dirty as I felt... Please, Paddy, don't come at me just now..."

He stops, halfway up from the bunk, astonished by those words. She has never put off his approaches. But maybe she isn't really opposed to an impromptu romp. Surely she can be teased into it, as she always has allowed herself to be. He doesn't sit back down. "I wonder," he begins, "whether our son-to-be, in there..." he gestures toward her abdomen, "... would like, ahm, if it wouldn't be too much of an intrusion, would like to 'meet his maker,' as we could call this thing I have here, as it really *is* just that..." Already the tumescence is easing his headache as his blood rushes from his brain to the expected place of engagement. He begins unbuttoning his sweaty clothes. But she takes up a towel to cover her nakedness, frowning at him, shaking her head.

"Please, no. Sometimes, one just isn't in that state of mind. I'm awfully upset. I tried to tell you...the boy dying...all that...And one other thing, dear. We do have fleas in here now, as I expected we should. They woke me up. That's why I needed this little bath. We should get some vinegar when we go to eat."

"Oh, no! Not a case of the bodyguards!"

"I'm afraid so. At *least.* You'd best clean yourself up, too. Now."

*

Groggy and weary though he is, Paddy is moved deeply by a sight on the starboard riverbank a few miles below Memphis.

On a high bluff, a troop of Union cavalry lined up in the gold light of sunset salutes the *Sultana*'s human cargo with cheers, their weapons raised overhead. The nature of the *Sultana*'s cargo must have been wired ahead to Memphis. The mass of homebound soldiers roar a grateful and merry response back up at the horse soldiers.

Paddy and Felice watch this exchange of honors from the dining salon entryway as the steamboat thrums along the base of the bluffs, and he doesn't look at her, remembering her abject outburst about military glory. Shadow softens the ugly, angular shapes of old barges, rotting flatboats, broken ironclads, sternwheel gunboats, and derelict packets that line the levee, some half-sunk. The immensity of war waste is staggering, even to one who, like Paddy, has seen whole armies strew their wreckage over battlefields the size of counties. This city of Memphis had been the Confederacy's major shipyard, where its gunboats and ironclads were built, until the Federal fleet defeated the Reb flotilla in this stretch of the Mississippi and seized the city in June of 1862, the second year of the war. That battle had been a grand and terrible morning spectacle for the citizens of Memphis, who thronged the high bluffs and watched the Federal ironclads demolish or capture seven of the eight rebel vessels. Paddy had missed that battle, being in Virginia with General Hooker's Division at the time. But he had heard it described in detail by eyewitnesses he met elsewhere as the war dragged on year after year, and he had envied those who saw it. It was terrible and thrilling in his imagination: the thunderous, smoky broadsides as the warboats maneuvered on the broad river, the clang of cannonballs ricocheting off armor plate, close-quarter cannon-duels, and awesome collisions of ramming boats against the Confederate ships. "A marvelous show!" a young gunnery officer had exclaimed with sparkling eyes. "Imagine, a full-out naval battle smack in the middle of America, hundreds of miles from any sea!" How Felice would have hated those exultations!

Memphis had fallen to the Union immediately after that battle, and the Federals thereafter had controlled the length of the Mississippi, except for Vicksburg in Mississippi and Port Hudson in Louisiana. That autumn, Paddy Quinn had departed from Virginia to come out here and join his old acquaintances Grant and Sherman, in order to cover their campaign against Vicksburg.

Felice is more familiar with the city of Memphis than Paddy is. She had been here often with her parents before the war; then the *Red Rover* had plied this stretch of the Mississippi, taking on sick and wounded soldiers by way of Memphis, whereas Paddy had been here only once before, en route down to join Grant at Vicksburg. Early on this honeymoon voyage, she had talked of leading him on a walking tour when they stopped here.

But there'll be no time for a such a stroll now. It is nine o'clock by the time the *Sultana* is moored at the levee. Gaslights show the way of the streets up the bluff to the city, and the major buildings of the downtown are dark rectangles silhouetted against a sky of lamplit haze.

An order has been passed that no soldiers will be permitted get off because the stop here will be hardly more than an hour. Paddy and Felice will hurry ashore only to fulfill two errands. He will go to the telegraph office and send a telegram to his editor at *Harper's*, explaining the growing scope of his exclusive story about the two thousand ex-prisoners. There also he might learn the latest on the progress of the President's funeral train, and of General Sherman's drive against the Rebs still resisting in the Carolinas. While Paddy is at the telegraph office, Felice and several others of the Sisters of Charity will hurry up to the Soldiers' Home, an establishment of the Federal Sanitary Commission, to obtain baskets of sweets, sundries and remedies and carry them back down to the boat. Their supplies have dwindled almost to nothing.

The breeze is cool, reeking of fishy mud. Negroes are rolling sugar barrels out of the cargo hold, across the crowded deck and down the gangplank to a stage on the levee, and from the stage they roll and wrestle them onto wagons that are already lined up in the lamplight. One hundred and twenty tons of sugar are being put off here. A couple of barrels are broken and empty, having been raided by sugar-starved veterans on the trip up from Vicksburg.

"There goes our ballast, dear," Paddy says.

Other stevedores are lined up like a bucket brigade, passing cases of bottled wine from boat to shore. Soldiers crowd the gangplank, putting on a bathetic dumb-show, some wringing their hands and miming great despair over the loss of the wine cargo.

Now the soldiers find another object for their high spirits as the whole herd of squealing, grunting hogs is driven down the gangway and along the levee into darkness. And one last uproar rises as the minstrels of the Chicago Opera Company get off the boat with all their trunks and instrument cases. They are booked for several nights of performances here in this major city, and the soldiers sing them ashore with some of their own darky songs and bawdy ditties.

But warmer and deeper songs are being sung, too. Paddy hears coming from somewhere amidships one of his favorites, perhaps a score of male voices crooning:

There's never a bond, old friend, like this!

We have drunk from the same canteen.

It was sometimes water, sometimes milk,

Sometimes applejack, fine as silk.

We shared it together, in bane or bliss,

And I warm to you, friend, when I think of this:

We have drunk from the same canteeeeen...

Despite the order to stay aboard, some soldiers are slipping through the mob and sauntering down the gangplank. Paddy can guess where they're going. Their biscuits and salt pork rations on the *Sultana* have been eaten cold, for the most part, as there's just one cookstove available for two thousand men, and the Soldier's Home will have hot food for them. Then there are the many waterfront saloons. Though McGinty's and O'Hara's bar on the boat is stocked with anything they might want to drink, it will be closing in an hour or so. Besides, it lacks barmaids and whores. A life among soldiers has taught Paddy that some of them will disobey any order and take any risk to follow their lust. Memphis has been a celebrated whores' nest for much of the war because of the vast numbers of soldiers staging through the city.

At this moment, a loud voice somewhere in the lower town begins yelling something, something unintelligible at first, but so insistent and excited that the drone of voices ebbs and attention turns to the bugle-like voice. And Paddy hears the words:

"They shot Booth! They got the assassin! Caught 'im in Virginia! They shot the God-damned son of a bitch that kilt Abe Lincoln! They..."

Before the words can be repeated, an incoherent roar of cheers goes up from hundreds of men on the boat and the dock, now followed by an absolute Babel of emotional voices, yodels, whistles and laughter.

Heart suddenly swollen, blinking at tears, Paddy turns to look at Felice. She is looking up at him, fingers of her left hand pressed on her lips, first nodding, now shaking her head, now nodding again. And now he sees tears trickling down beside her nose. She seizes his arm and says something to him, but he can't hear her over the uproar . Her mouth pronounces again, but still not loud enough, and he leans down so she can shout into his ear:

"I guess your mama will be glad!"

"By God, won't she though!" He remembers how frantic his mother was that morning, just a week ago, in her hotel in New Orleans when this boat brought down the news of the assassination. He had never seen her so unhinged before in a lifetime of griefs and disasters.

By the mighty fist o' Saint Patrick, she'll be happy at this! As am I!

"Come on, sweet!" he yells into Felice's ear, and presses a way for them through the shouting mass of soldiers toward the gangplank. "I need to get to that telegrapher! God knows what else is going on in this poor damned country!"

*

By the time they press through and get close to the gangplank, the shouting has died down, but the name of Booth the assassin is circulating. Paddy and Felice hold hands to keep from being separated in the smelly crowd of soldiers crowding the rail. Many of the men are gawking at something down on the landing.

A few well-dressed civilians, men and women, are milling about on the dock, waiting to board the *Sultana*. Among them undulates a tall, richly-attired woman of callipygian form and siren's visage, a stylish, glossy hat pinned atop her upswept auburn curls. She looks disturbingly familiar, but Paddy, his head a-whirl over the news of Booth, can't quite place her in his memory. She stops, caresses down her skirts, and seats herself on a large, costly, brass-trimmed trunk. Even in the emotional storm over the news of the assassin, the sight of her has struck much of the soldiery into a state of wordless awe . As Paddy looks at her and searches his memory, he begins to feel Felice glaring at his profile, and he quickly looks everywhere else, feeling vaguely embarrassed, even guilty for staring at another woman. Instinct tells him to trivialize the moment. In as insouciant a tone as he can muster, he says, "Do you see the odd hat on that lady's head? Reminds me of a pony saddle I saw in Mexico City once! That woman sitting down there."

Felice replies in a flat voice, "You're staring at her *hat*?"

Glad that his flushed face is in shadow, he quips, "Oh? What else?"

"There's much else, dear. I think you noticed."

"Well, now that you mention it, that's an impressive piece of baggage she's sitting on."

"Yes. Everybody *does* seem impressed by what she's sitting on."

At that he can only laugh, and it is such a big, genuine laugh that it seems to dissipate Felice's little fit of jealousy. She's smiling now, shaking her head in that familiar gesture of fond amusement. "I would rather see your smile," he says, "than anyone else's impressive baggage."

"Thank you, dear. And congratulations on blarneying your way out of that one."

Sensing that it would be good to say no more on it, he takes her elbow. "Let's see if we can get through the crowd. We don't have time to spare. There are your Charity Sisters waiting for you."

There stand four of them, carrying empty baskets and net bags, and behind them stands a homely, but well-dressed, young man carrying a knobby blackthorn cane. At the gangplank, Felice introduces him to Paddy. "This is George Safford. His father is on the Sanitary Commission, sponsor and supervisor for the Sisters."

"Pleased to meet you, Mister Quinn! My father suggested I escort the ladies up through town."

"Good, Mister Safford. I hope you'll not need to use that shillelagh o' yours. I'll help you guard the ladies through this iniquitous waterfront, but only as far as the telegraph office. Doesn't that knock your hat off, about them shooting Booth!" Mister Safford responds with a wan and uneasy expression. Of course, Paddy thinks. These official saints don't approve of anybody being shot. Not even John Wilkes Booth!

As they make their way down the gangway, as if struggling across a crowded bridge, Paddy becomes aware of that big, elegant, familiar woman again. Maybe, if they pass her close by in the gaslight, Paddy will see her well enough to make a recognition. But that thought in itself makes him uneasy. Whatever the association is, it doesn't feel like a good one. *Bottle fog* is his term for this condition of his memory. So many images from moments in his tumultuous life roll forever through his head, but with so little recollection of where and when he saw them. Sometimes it's troublesome. Other times it's merciful. He has seen too many things he'd rather not remember at all. It's odd that the sight of a voluptuous woman would feel like one of those.

Felice is talking now with the other Sisters as they near the end of the gangplank, but Paddy doesn't think for a moment that she isn't aware of the lady on the dock. He himself steals glances at her, trying to remember, but he's careful not to let Felice to see where his attention is going.

Because of his fame as a correspondent, his physical appearance itself, and his empty sleeve cuff, Paddy is accustomed to being perused. Especially by women. And since his marriage to the exquisite Felice, he now walks with an even greater attention-getter. He is aware now that several of the people on the dock are looking their way. The beautiful woman is one of them. She's not only looking right at Paddy's face, she is rising from her seat on the trunk, and the fingertips of her gloved left hand are on her cheek. It's as if she recognizes him, too, or is, like him, trying to correlate a face, a place, a time...

He's five paces from her when she glances down at his empty coat sleeve, and her face comes alive with recognition. The lost hand has verified for her that she knows him, and as if both their memories have connected in the space between them, it comes back to him too, just as he gets a whiff of fishy riverbank mud:

It's as if his forearm stump itself has a memory. He feels it ensheathed to the elbow in moist, warm vaginal flesh. In memory's eye he sees pale nakedness undulating above him in the light of a hotel chandelier. A drunken memory so shameful that it returns in his nightmares.

He almost stumbles and his face flushes hot.

Oh, no! The bacchante at Hooker's orgy! And she's spotted me!

And a long-forgotten name surfaces in his mind: *Fanny Foremost.* That amusing *nom de theatre* under which she had exhibited her whole flawless self writhing before a painted sylvan backdrop, on a dais in a room at the Willard Hotel. As her encore she had *backed* nude off the stage, down into the audience, and there engaged those privileged stags in whatever sport her Venusian posterior inspired them to, that is, those not too impaired by drunkenness to rise to the occasion. Paddy himself had been one of those thus impaired, until she found that use for his erect forearm. And *repleted* herself upon it, to use her own word.. Paddy is now almost aflame with that shameful memory. A few prominent men, officers and tycoons, still live in this country, he knows, who were in that room that night and watched him and laughed at him in that unholy moment, though their own involvement would probably restrain them from ever mentioning it, even if they *can* remember it. But here is Fanny Foremost herself, whatever her real name... How would this maenad from that longago debauch recognize him, one man out of however many there must have been?

Yet why wouldn't she? He was famous then and is now. Many people recognize him.

But he wishes she hadn't, because his alert bride has noticed this moment of recognitions. She brusquely jerks her hand out of the crook of his elbow. He turns to see anger in her eyes. Or is it *fear?* Fear of what she doesn't know of his raffish past? Fear that she has recklessly married a brawler, a drunk, whose weaknesses become evident to her bit by bit along this voyage... and now whatever she might be inferring about him and this obvious *demimondaine* who approaches gazing into his face as if about to speak...

Surely this Fanny Foremost person won't say anything. Surely she notices Felice beside him and won't be that indiscreet.

Paddy tries desperately to think. But he's still half-besotted and stunned by the sudden recall. His mind had been on the assassin Booth, unprepared for such an encounter as this.

They walk past her and she says nothing. Paddy finds himself holding his breath, as he used to do when cannonballs came whistling in.

He knows better than to turn and look back at her. But Felice has pivoted, maintaining that suspicious, even challenging, appraisal. Paddy prays that the woman isn't still looking after him. Felice whips her head around to face forward, not looking at him, and her eyelids and mouth look hard and thin. After only four more paces she says in a hissing near-whisper, meant for his ears only, not for her Sisters of Charity walking alongside her, "That fancy woman was certainly ogling you boldly enough."

"Fancy woman?...Oh, you mean that lady with the odd hat?"

"She knows you."

"Dear, I *am* known! You've remarked on that yourself."

He feels her wanting to say more, but she can't quibble with that, and he hopes she won't. He wants her to forget the woman. He himself wants to forget her. He prays Felice won't ask the next question: *Who is that?*

Paddy wants a drink, as he usually does after a scare.

And this woman is going to be on the same boat!

*

They find the telegraph office two blocks up the street, a storefront, still open, lighted by many lamps, crowded with soldiers and travelers. Next door and across the street Paddy notices two saloons, with soldiers from the boat thronging their open doors. The name of Booth is loud and frequent in the uproar. And this dingy little telegraph station, this one anonymous man with his finger on a black key, is the tiny mouth of the funnel through which the most significant news of a vast, desperate country must be squeezed. So often Paddy has had that notion; near blood-muddied battlegrounds, revolutions, fleets sailing, political rallies, he has thought:...

God's voice itself on Judgement Day will come in dots and dashes! It's one of those lines in his notebook, destined to be a part of a lecture someday in a crowded odeum, or perhaps the theme of a chapter in a book he will write...

"Sure enough I'll have to wait," he says. "You ladies go on up to the Soldiers' Home and get what you can. But hurry. We have to be back aboard within the hour." He puts his hand to Felice's cheek and turns her to look in his eyes. There's still a little of that edge on her expression, but he senses that his hand so tender on her cheek is softening her. He leans to kiss her ear, and murmurs, "We mustn't either one of us miss that boat, dearest, unless we both do. You and I are together for good. I'll never have a kiss for anyone but you." Her eyes soften and she puts her hand over his.

"We may be back before you get to the telegraph," she says, tilting her head at the queue.

"If so, I'll help you carry down your loot. 'Til, then, dearest, I'll miss you."

"Please behave yourself," she says.

Paddy gets into line, turns, watches Felice and her companions in their pale calico dresses go on up the street, Mister Safford ahead of them, passing from the glow of one gaslamp to the next. Up Main Street, above a confectionary, Paddy remembers, from the time when General Sherman was governing the captured city so adroitly, the City Medical Inspector had used to give out medical certificates to undiseased prostitutes, $2.50 each, the proceeds going to support a new hospital wing for "ladies," up on Exchange Street. Only by such means did Sherman bring under control the hordes of Soiled Doves who followed the Union troops into the occupied city. By that policy, Sherman had diminished the epidemic of clap and syphilis that debilitated so much of his army. That damned Sherman can do anything well, Paddy thinks.

But the people of Memphis had hated every day of the Yankee occupation, even when it was improving their civic life and prosperity. The good Southern ladies here had blamed Sherman for bringing a mass immigration of prostitutes to their city, because it was his army that the prostitutes followed. Not that there hadn't been plenty of them before, when the city was the

Rebs' boatbuilding center. Paddy smiles and shakes his head. Those Southern women! The Passionate Pissing Patriots, they were sometimes called, from their practice of saving the urine from their chamberpots to send in railroad tank cars to the Reb munitions factories, where ammonium nitrate was extracted from it for making gunpowder. Paddy even remembers a song about it, something like:

When Lady Reb lifts up her skirt

She kills another Yankee!

It was rumored that one reason the Memphis belles had so hated Sherman was that he prevented the shipments of their pee to the munitions makers.

Remembering all that, Paddy now turns to look back down toward the docks. He is half expecting that Fanny Foremost, as she was known in Washington, might have followed him up here. He's relieved, but, oddly, a little disappointed, that there is no sign of her. The *Sultana* lies down there at wharfside, looking as big as a town at the river's edge with all her lamps and lanterns burning, people and wagons milling on the dock, the excited hubbub of the recent news of what may be deemed justice...

I doubt the people of Memphis are quite so happy about the shooting of Booth, he thinks.

Now he'll be their martyr.

The last trace of sundown has gone from the western dusk, but a few faint lights twinkle on the far shore, at the coal yard on the Arkansas side of the Mississippi. The vessel will have to cross over there and take on coal before continuing up the river. A few tons of coal in the hoppers will at least restore a little ballast, he thinks.

That boat. *Tub of Doom.* It swarms like an anthill with its two thousand desperately hopeful homebound survivors of war and suffering. That vessel which was to have given him and Felice their carefree honeymoon voyage. He tries to see if the woman and her fancy trunk are still on the dock, but at this distance can't make out such detail. He can hear the drone of hundreds of men talking, can hear bits of song.

"Sweet Hour of Prayer, Sweet..."

From the saloon nearby, a barmaid's bawdy laugh, the loud voices of men animated by drinking...

And *"Booth...Booth...Booth..."*

Paddy sees that he won't have time to work his way to the head of the line and spell out his telegram to the key operator before the *Sultana*' s bell summons everybody back aboard. And he wants a taste of whiskey as much as he wants to send his message to *Harper's.* He pulls his notebook from a pocket, then a pencil. Bracing the notebook on the bannister of the stoop, he writes:

> *Telegrapher – Enclosed: Urgent message to A . P. Guernsey, Editor of HARPER'S Weekly, New York City, also a generous gratuity to you for its swift transmission. God knows you're busy:*

And under that, his message to go through the tiny channel of telegraphy, back to the East:

> *STEAMBOAT SULTANA CRIMINALLY OVERLOADED SICK PRISON SURVIVORS.*
>
> *2000 SOULS OVER CAPACITY. AM DOING EXCLUSIVE INTERVIEWS.*
>
> *LOYAL YANK HERO RATHER GO ABE FUNERAL WITH ME THAN HOME.*
>
> *MY BEST STORY EVER. MORE FROM ST. LOUIS OR SPRINGFIELD. P. QUINN*

Such a feeble attempt to convey the pathos of the story, he feels, but you can do only so much by Morse's code. He tears the page from the notebook, folds into it enough paper money to cover his estimate of the transmission cost, adds ten dollars gratuity -- or bribe – for the telegrapher. It is a hard task to tear and fold paper with one hand and a numb stump, but with his tongue in the corner of his mouth he completes it, then pushes and apologizes his way to the front of the line, saying, "War correspondent. This is urgent. No, I'm just going to hand this to him. Thank you. Excuse me. Thank you, sir. I won't delay you at all. Excuse me. Thanks." A tall soldier near the head of the line starts to challenge him, but somebody else in the line, a civilian in a brown suit, says:

"Hey, now! I know who he is. Let him in. It's sure to be important!"

"Thank you, sir," says Paddy.

"Hey, hear the latest just come in?"

"About Booth? Sure."

"But this, too: Gen'l Johnston surrendered to Sherman today, in North Carolina!"

"Really? Really! My God, what a day! Peace at last! Real peace, maybe..."

The telegrapher, seeming annoyed at the interruption, takes the paper, looks in, looks up at Paddy and nods once.

"It is crucial," Paddy says.

"All right. What isn't?"

"One more thing: where's Mister Lincoln's funeral train got to by now?"

"Left Buffalo today." Paddy feels relieved, quickly calculates days and distance in his head. We'll still get to Springfield before Father Abraham does, Paddy thinks, and gives a sigh of relief. Then he steps back out through the door, takes a deep breath, looks up the street toward the Soldiers' Home, sighs, dodges around a passing carriage, and walks across the street to the bar.

Just one, he promises, a promise more to Felice than to himself.

*

Robbie Macombie is among the many soldiers watching the voluptuous woman come up the gangplank onto the boat.

"Lord a mercy God!" someone exclaims .

"Big 'un!" another says. "Reckon she's an operetta or somethin'?"

"I claim 'er," another voice groans. "I swear she's mine 'cause I created her in a lifetime o' wet dreams!"

Robbie is impressed, too, but his peculiar interest in the lady is piqued by what he saw when she and the Quinns passed close by each other on the dock. It was plain that his important new friend Paddy and this woman either know each other, or sure would want to. And that angel Mrs. Quinn is alarmed by it, whatever it is. Robbie saw her turn around on the dock and catch the woman looking after Paddy. He saw that the big lady almost turned to follow them up the street.

No business of mine, Robbie thinks. But she better keep her distance from them.

Robbie has a deep concern for both Paddy and Mrs. Quinn. As he sees it, he and Paddy are now partners in the telling of an important and terrible story, and the great journalist intends to honor Robbie by taking him up to Mister Lincoln's last funeral day. Nothing must divert those important plans. They're on a path together now that is the first thing in a year Robbie really wants to live for, and besides, there's enough strain already on those newlyweds, what with the different kinds of work they're doing with all these miserable, desperate veterans. And Paddy's boozing.

He didn't do himself any good with her by knocking out that Captain Elliott, either.

Robbie wants this boat trip to be over without any complications, and he wants to stand at the funeral with this Irishman who personally shook the President's hand, and he wants Paddy to write a story that will touch and lift hearts, like that story about the poor Choctaws sending their money across the ocean to the starving Irishers over there. And then when that's all done, then those Quinns need to get back to their honeymoon and learn to grow together into a good marriage.

Because by God Robbie loves these two good young people, and, apart from Abraham Lincoln, it's been so long a time since he could feel love for anybody or anything that they've just *got* to have a happy marriage. And they're a part of his love for Mr. Lincoln, too. Robbie Macombie and Paddy and Felice Quinn wouldn't even be on this boat together if it weren't for Father Abraham!

The big beauty, followed by two Negro porters carrying her fancy trunk, is now so close to Robbie at the rail that he could speak to her. He could warn her to let the Quinns be. But of course he doesn't. Robbie has learned over a long lifetime that there are times when it's best to be invisible and silent. He's very good at invisibility. It's one reason why he's still a private after years in the armies. He's not fool enough to create a scene, by speaking a warning to a woman who's being devoured by the ravenous longings of hundreds of poor ragged soldiers.

Robbie will guard the Quinns, and his vested interest in them, by staying invisible and keeping an eye on her. He'll be like all those steamboat crew members who scrutinize every Southern gent coming aboard as if he might be carrying a bomb.

This big lady won't know Robbie exists unless she tries to get too close to his friend Paddy Quinn.

He begins making his way along behind her through the crowd. Just at this moment, the big bell begins clanging on the hurricane deck, summoning the passengers in town to get back aboard for departure. Startled, Robbie squints up the gaslit streets of downtown Memphis for a sight of the Quinns and the Mercy Ladies coming back down. Dread rising, he thinks: What'll I do if they take too long up there and miss the boat?

The answer comes quick and simple:

Just have to jump ship here, I guess.

CHAPTER EIGHT

Memphis Waterfront

April 26, 1865

If Felice can smell the two fresh shots of tavern whiskey on Paddy's breath - yes, two despite his vow to have only one -- she says nothing about it, probably because of Mister Safford and the Sisters walking down the steep street alongside her with their baskets and bags of favors and notions. In fact, she hasn't even sneaked Paddy the reproving look he knows he deserves.

It might be that he just isn't reeking any more now than he was *before* they walked up into Memphis. After all, he hasn't been truly sober since...

Well, since he can't remember when. He has lost track of nights and days. It all runs together: scribbling shorthand notes, drawing, pouring and sipping whiskey from the keg, asking questions, in their tobacco-stinking stateroom or boat saloon, in the engine room, on the decks, dozing off, waking up sometimes with Felice in the room, sometimes not; in his mind's eye a dismal parade of pain-wrinkled, sooty, scabby soldier faces with their mouths open, recounting their odyssey in Hell, telling of spewed shit and pus and maggots and cadavers, but also of brave men dying with dignity, comrades they know they'll never forget or cease to love; telling of dreams of home and of their mothers and their wives, or of those they hope will be their wives, and of the rich earth they yearn to turn again with ploughshares forged from swords, as one soldier had said it with tears glinting in pious eyes ...

This blurred flow of powerful impressions and fatiguing recollections isn't new to Paddy Quinn, though. All his life it has been like this, hardly ever orderly and lucid. Involved in wars since childhood, a drinker since boyhood, he has always lived half-scared, half-thrilled, half bone-weary, usually uncomfortable, heatstricken or shivering, high or hung over.

This steamboat voyage, which began as an enraptured honeymoon, has evolved into something like another war campaign: endless lines of soldiers slogging through a long, desperate story. And Quinn the war correspondent, gathering details into a panorama, one pencil line at a time, listening for the phrases that tell the most, watching for the crumpled chin or the eagle scowl that can best convey a soldier's soul onto paper...

The big difference in this campaign, though, is that the commander isn't General Grant or General Meade, General Sherman or General McClellan or General Lee, the commander-in-chief is neither Abe Lincoln nor Jefferson Davis. Paddy Quinn is in total charge of *this* campaign. This story, his last campaign of the war, will be what his genius can make of it. He means to make it unforgettable. That would be hard for a dry sober man to do. Grant taught him that lesson.

These are the flows and eddies of his thoughts as the little party hurries down the street to the Memphis waterfront after ten o'clock, summoned by the bell of the huge, glowing, smoking, teeming sidewheeler *Sultana,* the floating theatre of operations for this pathetic, triumphant campaign which will be his last and greatest story as a war correspondent. By willpower he has subdued the shock of seeing Fanny Foremost on the dock half an hour ago. He will work on through the fatigue and the roiled confusion of this campaign until at last, after Abraham Winkin's funeral, after the funeral of that great man whose assassination has been avenged this very day, his story will go to *Harpers Weekly* and become a closing chapter of the history of this enormous and ghastly national fratricide euphemized as The War Between The States. Paddy sighs as they come to the teeming gangway. "What?" Felice says, looking up at him, having heard his sigh.

"I'll tell you sometime," he replies, and he thinks:

Sighs are so eloquent. But they're inarticulate.

Must remember to write that down.

*

Robbie at last sees the Quinns and their party coming down toward the dock, passing from one pool of lamplight to the next, and he breathes deep with relief. They won't miss the boat. So now he begins squirming through the crowd to follow the beautiful lady.

The admiring soldiers make a path for her, but not a wide path. They hope to be close enough to ogle her closely, perhaps get a scent of her, maybe even be brushed by her billowing skirt as she comes by, followed by the Negroes carrying her trunk.

Robbie sees that where she's going is the clerk's station, the little cubicle at the forward end of the salon, with its brass-grilled window, and he slithers through the mass of people to station himself by that window so he can see and hear her. On a brass plaque on the wide sill of the window is engraved WILLIAM GAMBREL, CLERK. Mr. Gambrel looks up from a fistful of papers, sees the vision standing outside his window, makes himself tall, pulls in his prolapsed abdomen, smiles, and says, "May I help you, Ma'am?"

"Please. I need to secure some valuables in the safe."

"Certainly. And you'll be with us how far?"

"St. Louis."

"All the way, then. Good! And may I see your boarding ticket?" She slides the card to him under the grate. "Mrs. Willard. All right. Now, as they told you, no staterooms are available until after Cairo, but you should be comfortable in the Ladies' Parlor until then."

"It'll do. I must say, I've never seen a boat so crowded."

"And let's pray you never shall again. Twenty-four hundred passengers. No vessel on any river has ever carried so many, I believe." He sounds proud of it. "Now, what is it you wish to deposit with us, Mrs. Willard?"

Mrs. Willard, Robbie thinks. Willard, if I heard right. Remember..

She slides a long, velvet bag across. "Some cash," she says, "a deed, and some jewels."

"And how much currency would that be?" Mr. Gambrel asks, leaning to put his ear confidentially close. Robbie's own hearing has been diminished by warfare and sickness, and he strains to hear without seeming to eavesdrop. At this moment the boat's bell rings again, the machinery begins rumbling as the casting-off begins, and the voices of hundreds rise in a babble of exclamations, but Robbie is sure he hears her say, "Five thousand dollars Yankee."

As the clerk writes on a cardboard receipt ticket, the woman in her turn leans closer to him and asks a question that Robbie hears clearly: "Mister Gambrel, does there happen to be a passenger on board by the name of Quinn?"

"Why, yes, in fact. The journalist fellow...May I ask why you inquire?"

"I *thought* I recognized him. How far is he going?"

"To St. Louis. Would you wish to leave him a message, Ma'am?"

Robbie, now intensely interested, watches a half smile dimple her mouth, then she bites inside her upper lip and replies, "No...You're busy. I'll see him if I see him...Thank you, Mr. Gambrel."

"You're most welcome. Bring me this receipt when we reach St. Louis. You'll need it to redeem your valuables. And in the meantime, if there is anything, *anything,* I can do personally to enhance your pleasure on the voyage, Mrs. Willard, don't hesitate to come find me..."

As the woman turns away from the window, she's looking right at Robbie's face, from no more than an arm's length, but he can see in her eyes that she doesn't see him. He hasn't lost the knack of invisibility.

So they do know each other, Robbie thinks.

He doesn't follow the woman now. It seems more important to go and find his friend Paddy Quinn. He doesn't know quite why he wants to tell Mr. Quinn what he's seen and heard. It just seems he should.

*

Several officers are already waiting by the door when Paddy returns to his cabin, all talking excitedly about Booth and about Johnston's surrender to Sherman. He greets them with a smile, but cringes inside. Now that officers know he's interviewing, many of them will be hoping to get their names into his article. But he doesn't want officers. He sees the true stories of Andersonville in the enlisted men. He has to be polite to the officers, of course. But what he wants is to go into the stateroom, take a swallow from the whiskey keg, maybe lie down and rest a moment, then get back to interviewing the soldiers who survived the horrors of the prison. He certainly doesn't want to dispense whiskey to officers, who for the most part can afford to buy drinks in the saloon.

Felice has gone directly to the foredeck with her fellow Sisters and by now will be giving out treats and sundries and homilies to the feeblest of the survivors. Her absence would have let him have his whiskey bracer without guilt and in privacy, except for these officers seeking a bit of fame.

"Good evening, Mister Quinn," says a snub-nosed Army lieutenant with a seeping red rash on his chin. "My name is George McCord, and I have some very interesting tales to relate, if you've a moment..."

But now Paddy sees a more welcome face just over the lieutenant's shoulder. It's Robbie Macombie. Paddy says, "Lieutenant, I'll be happy to talk with you, maybe tomorrow sometime, but at this moment I need to finish an interview I've already begun..." He reaches over to take Robbie's hand and pull him forward. "Glad to see you back, Robbie."

The lieutenant's face reddens as he sees a private soldier get priority over him, but he decides not to pull rank, and nods. "About nine in the morning, perhaps?"

"Make it ten. I hope to get some decent rest, then have a leisurely breakfast with my wife. Believe it or not, sir, this is supposed to be our honeymoon!" He turns to the other officers who are hovering near, and adds, "You gentlemen too, maybe toward noon? Just straggle in as you will. I'm too tired to schedule reservations. Good evening, gentlemen."

Inside the cabin with the door closed, Robbie shakes his head and says, "I just can hardly get used to bein' put ahead of officers. Some o' those gents looked to have hurt feelings, Mister Quinn."

"If so, maybe they won't come back and try to waste my time in the morning. Well, Robbie my friend, thank you for showing up in time to run off some fame-hungry popinjays. My God," he sighs, "am I tired and thirsty! Here. A little shot of the old tanglefoot." He runs a trickle of whiskey into one glass for Robbie, then another for himself. "I did get a wire off to my editor about what I'm doing with you fellows. That is, I trust it'll get to him. You can't be sure unless you tap it out with your own finger."

"Lord a mighty, sir! You can run a *telegraph*?"

"Oh, sure. Learned as a boy in Mexico. Before there was a telegraph in that whole country, in fact! It's just another way of writing. Well, here's to Samuel Morse, a man who changed the world -- though a brass-plated anti-papal bigot he was. I hear he's atoning as a big do-gooder in his old age. Here's to 'im, anyway." Paddy and Robbie touch glasses and drain them. Paddy waves Robbie to the chair, then sits on the lower bunk and slumps back to lean his tired shoulder on the wallpapered bulkhead.

"I think," he says, "you'll be my last informant tonight. I'm just too whipped to work through another night. After we coal up and get going upstream, I think I'll just go drag my Felice away from her *agape,* and make her get some sleep, too. Just about have to *force* that woman to stop doing for others."

"She is a true angel, sir. If you don't mind me sayin'..."

"I don't. But I do mind you saying 'sir' to me..." Now Paddy pauses, brought up speechless for a moment by the misty-eyed adoration he sees shining in Robbie's face, making him look even more like a saintly Biblical elder.

"I hear the boys and they all say, 'That's an angel!'" Robbie goes on. "She'd go comfort *lepers* if we had any on board! Couple o' those syphilitics on the front deck there might's well be lepers. Y' seen 'em? I can hardly stand t' look at 'em, but she comforts 'em as if they were poor orphans...Oh, yeah, that's an angel you've got, Mister Quinn." And at that, Paddy himself suddenly feels his weary, cynical spirits lifted up. He recognizes the reverence that this poor Robbie is trying to express. He's reminded of the gift that came to him in the graceful form of that elegant little woman who is his own wife. And remembers that vow he's taken to himself, to be worthy of her. A vow he hasn't upheld very well, God knows. Almost feeling foolish, he has to swallow a groan, and sniffs.

But now too he remembers what he's tried to shove into the back of his mind: that flash of jealousy he saw in Felice when they walked by the harlot on the dock. He shudders at the old booze-blurred memory, both thrilling and repugnant, of that voluptuous vulva devouring his pathetic stump of an amputation...

"Repleting."

That was the word that woman had used and he has never forgotten it. *Did* she actually come to satisfaction in that obscene moment? That old doubt has made her his succubus. He's dreamed of it, almost the way he's dreamed of explosions and of seeping piles of rotten corpses on battlefields. He would like to banish her from his memory, but now she's apparently on the same boat with him and his bride.

And at this moment, as if reading his mind, Robbie says:

"Mister Quinn, 'scuse me, but I ought to tell y' something that's somehow got me all beside m'self. Though it's none of my business. I hope you'll forgive me if I mention that, ah, that Mrs. Willard."

Paddy blinks, confused, yet sensing what this soldier's apologetic preamble refers to. In their momentary silence, the tempo of the steamboat's machinery is slowing, resurging, again subsiding. The vessel must have crossed to the Arkansas bank and will be coming ashore now to fuel up at the coaling station. Soldiers' voices outside the cabin drone, as usual commenting on the process of any maneuver. Paddy himself feels a sudden urge to refuel, and he trickles more whiskey into the two glasses. He sips, aware of a rapid heartbeat of dread, and finally says:

"Who, pray tell, is Mrs. Willard? " As if I didn't know, he thinks. And calling herself Mrs. Willard? The Willard Hotel! He almost laughs at the odd aptness of it. That's almost as funny as Fanny Foremost!

"You don't know that lady, Mister Quinn? She knows you."

"I really don't know anyone by that name."

"Well, damn me, I'm embarrassed! Well sir, there was a right fancy lady got aboard at Memphis just now, and I got the feelin' you know each other. She asked the boat clerk about you."

"Did she now." Paddy pauses, wondering what she asked and what the clerk told her.

"Well, Robbie, here it is about that. She's somebody I've seen somewhere, but I don't know her name. People do recognize me from my work, many I don't know..." Paddy is trying to be as dismissive as he can, but Robbie looks a bit skeptical.

"Well, it's none of my business, sir, and I'm sorry I brought it up."

"And as I said, Robbie, don't call me 'sir,' but you can say anything else you like. Now, let's just get on with what you were going to tell me about people trying to tunnel their way out of the prison. Did anybody ever succeed in that, to your knowledge?"

Robbie pauses, apparently surprised by the change of subject, then shrugs and replies:

"Rumors had it that a few did, once in a while. But we were never told. Would've given us hopeful ideas, y'see. But we did get told about those that failed. Some got buried in tunnel cave-ins. Lord only knows how many were scratchin' away under there. It was like a yard full o' moles. Lots of Union soldiers'd been coal miners, it was natural to them. Fellows still strong enough would find something to scrape earth with, start digging a well, they'd say. Then turn off aside from it, a-headin' for the stockade. Dirt had to be brought up at night and scattered, so sentries wouldn't see it being piled up. 'Course, it was all dirt in there. Dirt and shit. No grass, nor even a weed, could grow in there. You've seen a pigsty, all churned and trodden? Like that."

Like yard full of moles, Paddy scribbles. "And you, were you ever down there digging like a mole yourself?"

The soldier smiles slightly, looking down into his whiskey glass. "I was no miner, Mister Quinn. I been a carpenter and a millwright. I could've shored up a tunnel real well, if there'd been any wood to be had. But any stick that got in there ended up firewood. That's one reason there were cave-ins. Sometimes the give-away was when y'd see stockade posts sink down or fall over, and ye'd know some poor soul'd tunneled that far..." He shakes his head and sighs.

"So, anyway, Major Wirz by an' by got tired of all such diggin', and he rounded up darkies from the farms thereabout, and he made 'em build another stockade a long way out around the outside of the main one. That was discouraging, almost near stopped all the tunneling..."

Paddy takes notes in his peculiar shorthand. Now and then he turns to his sketch of Robbie, and adds a line or a shading to improve his depiction of the soldier's expressions. During one such pause, he remarks, sounding as insouciant as he can:

"Did I hear you say that fancy lady asked about me? What did she want to know?"

"Well, whether there's a passenger named Quinn aboard.. Mister Gambrel said yes, a journalist by that name is. He asked her why she wanted to know, and she just said she thought she recognized you. Oh, and he asked her if she wanted to leave you a message..."

Paddy's scalp prickles. That's the last thing he and Felice need: a message from the woman who is under her suspicion merely because she looked at Paddy. But Robbie goes on:

"She told him don't bother, that she'd see you if she saw you."

"I guess that'd be so, wouldn't it?" Paddy squints, pretending to concentrate on what he's penciling.

"She asked him to put her valuables in the safe. About five thousand dollars, she said. Yankee dollars. And said she's going to St. Louis."

"By God, Robbie," he laughs. "The Army'd have used you better as a spy than a courier!" But he's trying to hide his astonishment. How does a whore come to be at large in the South in these times with five thousand Yankee dollars?

He thinks of women who spy across the lines, for the Rebs and the Federals both.

Also he remembers hearing about all the boat-bombing fears. Might she have got that much money for bringing a bomb aboard in that brand-new big trunk? God, I've got to be numb-brain tired to worry myself about such things!

"Well, my sharp-eyed friend," Paddy says after a pause, "there might've been a time once when I'd've been delighted to hear a mysterious beauty with big moneybags was looking for me. But I'm a married man now, and I wouldn't forsake my dear virtuous bride for *fifty* thousand Yankee dollars."

Now Robbie's wan face blooms with the biggest smile Paddy's yet seen on him, and he says, "Mister Quinn, I'm *so* damn glad to hear you say that, I could about dance a jig!"

"Well, I'll drink to that!'

And so they drink to that.

"Listen," Paddy says. "Who's singing out there?" They get up to look out the door.

Under the coalyard lamps, they see that some of the skinny soldiers have joined the muscular roustabouts to help them shoulder and carry burlap bags full of coal up the gangplank. Like ants they labor up the long ramp to the deck, singing cadence. They're helping to get this boat fueled in a hurry so it can proceed up the river toward home. They work in a warm drizzle of rain, but here and there a star blinks through the overcast. Again Paddy marvels at the spirit of these wornout men who have been through all kinds of hell, for months, for years, and yet are helpful and cheerful.

This is a part of the story that readers will hardly expect after all the hateful drama of the long war. But if he can convey this marvelous spirit through the power of written language, it will be a tribute to these men, and readers will never forget it. This, he knows, is something like his longago story that his friend Robbie likes so much, that of those Indians pausing in their desperate journey to collect coins for starving Irishmen far away. He turns to Robbie, who is just putting a match to his pipe bowl, his pale, kindly face glowing in the matchlight, and says, "You know, old fellow, there's man at his best."

"What is, sir?"

"Your comrades working down there. That Burlap Brigade."

"I hope you write that in your story, sir. Make us look good."

"Just what I mean to do. But didn't I ask you not to call me 'sir?'"

*

Forward on the upper deck, near the steamboat's flagstaff, sitting with a basket beside her, Felice peels waxed paper off a nugget of red rock candy and holds the treat in front of the soldier's eyes, which are looking up at her with an adoration so intense she can hardly stand it.

"William," she says, "I'll put this sweet in your cheek so you can taste it, but promise me you won't breathe it down and choke. Do you understand, dear?"

"Ng hn." He's lying flat on his back on a blanket, a long linkage of fleshless bones, his head a scurfy skullbone almost hairless, his facial skin looking like yellow oilcloth tight over the ridged cheekbones and nose. He doesn't have to open his mouth for the candy because his mouth is permanently open, a crusty, stinking aperture almost filled with a swollen tongue. It takes all her resolve to reach in and place the piece in his cheek, which feels scummy. He just keeps gazing at her and holding her other hand with his bundle of fingerbones. She knows how this is. If she withdraws her hand from his grasp he'll probably just let go and die.

God knows what he's dying of, but he's not going to make it home to Ohio.

"Sometimes," she tells him, "the clouds blow away and you see a star. See them? Last night you told me you love looking at the stars."

"Unh uh oog uh oo."

I love looking at you. That was probably what he said . Those had been the last words of other soldiers, too, back on the hospital ship, some coherent, some like this.

She struggles not to cry because it would trouble him if she cried.

Gracious Lord please don't let another single one die holding my hand. I thought I was done with all this.

She thinks back on Paddy's request, that she tell him what these extreme sufferers say to her, for his magazine article. What could she pass on to him? They just try to express their love and gratitude. They don't speak of other things much.

Well, they say some things about the prison, maybe explaining how they got this sick or lonesome, but it wouldn't be proper to write such things in a story. Like being so hungry they'd pick through what has come out of someone else not quite digested.

Or like that soldier who admitted that he held a dying soldier in his arms and wept because he had loved him more than he had ever loved his wife.

These aren't stories, they are deathbed confessions.

As if she, just because they love her desperately for holding their hands and caressing their brows, could absolve them.

Felice thinks of the soldier Robbie, his eyes always full of adoration, who intends to go with her and Paddy to President Lincoln's final funeral, up in Springfield.

Does that man really love Mister Lincoln more than he loves his wife and children?

I wonder what all he and Paddy said in coming to that agreement.

Or maybe Mister Macombie thinks he can live long enough to get to Springfield but not to home.

That could be it.

Felice tries to imagine what it will be like to stand looking at the President's corpse, with Paddy and Robbie. And maybe her parents too. She won't want to look. She learned as a child how not to see things she didn't want to see, just by putting her eyes out of focus.

That's going to be an awfully seasoned corpse. *Old Abe Lincoln lies a molderin'...*

Felice knows she upset Paddy by speaking so about the Presidential carcass.

She remembers now the joyous uproar of cheers when the soldiers heard Booth was caught and killed.

It disturbs her that she can understand a Southerner having a vengeful passion to kill the President at such a time. What she can't understand is how he could actually pull a trigger and kill him from behind as he sat with his wife.

God could have kept men from wanting to do the things they do to each other. Couldn't God the Creator have made men less cruel?

She sits on the deck, hip aching, holding the bony hand of the man named William, and a voice croaks nearby in the shadows, "Missus Quinn? Could you come here a minute?"

"What do you need?"

"Need t' tell ye somep'n, Ma'am."

"About what?"

"Bout you and me."

"I'll be there in a bit. Try to sleep."

What would I tell Paddy about what these poor men confide in me? Would he understand enough not to feel jealous?

Maybe feeling a little jealous would be good for him. As long as he doesn't hit anybody.

Jealousy is so silly! Compared with all the rest of this!

Despite the silliness of jealousy, Felice keeps worrying that Paddy and that statuesque woman on the dock actually know each other. She's almost certain that they do, and is afraid that they might even now be looking for each other on this boat.

If he's used to women like that, she thinks, why would he even *look* at me?

But I'm the one carrying his baby.

She's sure that baby is forming, down there where her hips hurt from sitting lopsided so long on this vibrating boat deck holding the hand of a soldier name William Something.

It's while she's trying to remember William Something's last name that she realizes that he isn't alive any more. *Hail Mary Mother of God. Another one!*

Anyway, it isn't as if he choked on the candy ball she put in his mouth.. In lanternlight she still sees the lump of it under the thin skin of his cheek, like a tobacco quid.. She knows he's dead because he isn't gazing at her anymore. His eyes are open as if he'd been looking toward the stars. There are no stars to be seen now, though; misting rain falls on his unseeing eyes.

Maybe the last thing he saw was the sparks rising from the smokestacks.

I'm sorry, William. I didn't mean to let you go away all by yourself. While I was thinking of something else.

Now she can let loose of his fingerbones and cry a bit and it won't trouble him.

*

The lights of Memphis are dim and far astern in the mist now as the *Sultana,* refueled with a thousand bushels of coal, throbs and churns up the Mississippi through a sifting rain. Paddy and Robbie, tired and not very sober, slump in the cabin, each with a fresh dram in hand. Paddy looks at his watch, thinking of going forward to fetch Felice, and sees that it is near one-thirty in the morning. He winds the watch and slips it back into his pocket, where it clicks metallically against something. The San Patricio medallion, of course, he remembers with a twinge of gratitude toward the old bartenders who gave it to him. McGinty and O'Hara will have closed their bar by now and gone up to their quarters to count cash. God bless the old rascals for selling me this keg, he thinks.

"There's a set of islands right along here called Hens and Chickens," Paddy says. "They ordinarily require sharp piloting to get through them. But high as the river is, we'll probably pass right over 'em. We might floating be over some sunken island right now. I've seen hunting camps and cookfires on those islands, when the river's normal. No campfires now, though, under two fathoms of water.... Don't know about you, but that notion spooks me a bit." He shudders, clenching his jaw.

"I do know that feelin'. Any time I'm on a boat I try not t' think what's passin' under."

Robbie shakes his head, a strange, fearful look in his eyes. "Odd, huh? A body'd think, why, after what all we've all been through, we shouldn't get scared of, of just ...*figments*...Is that the right word, Mister Quinn? Figments?"

"Figments it is." He sips whiskey, thinking, somehow almost panicky: Probably never so many men in such a small space who've shared as much hell as these two thousand. I bet the only thing they fear, most of them, is not getting home after all that hell. "Tell you what,my friend. I am worn out. I think I'll go up forward where my good Missus is, and see if she's ready to quit for the night." The urge to have her close by is sudden and powerful, so strong that even as exhausted as he is, he wants to go where she is, despite the difficulty of wending a way through this tight press of wretched veterans of Hell. "Why don't you just drain that glass, Mister Macombie, and we'll go up there and see her."

"Why, sir, I...."

"What did I say about you calling me 'sir?'"

"Sorry. I was just fixin' to excuse myself anyway, Mister Quinn. It's nice of you t'ask me, but you don't need me along. I've taken up so much of your time already...both of you..."

"Oh, but I *do* need you along. I need you to carry the whiskey."

"Uh...Carry the whiskey, sir?"

"Those poor mutilated bastards up there, they need more than the damned gingersnaps and clean hankies all those Sisters of

Mercy in the world could ever bestow on 'em. They need some of what's in that keg. And I can't carry it and my desk both, not with just this one hand. You should've seen the trouble I had hauling it down here!"

Maybe Robbie won't think himself so perishing weak if he's got a toting task to do.

Robbie grins, blinking. "Well, all right, sir! They *would* be thankful, for sure!"

"Come on, then. Up off your ass, soldier. If you get to call me 'sir,' then I get to order you around!" He staggers to his feet, one shoulder bumping the bunk, the other the doorjamb, and over the rumbling of engines he hears something he realizes he's never heard before: Robbie laughing aloud.

Paddy opens his writing portfolio, lays the sketchpad and notebook in on top of his diary, then shuts and latches it, and straps it to his stump so that he can carry it hanging flat by his hip through the crowd without dropping it or spilling anything from it. Robbie stoops over the half-empty whiskey keg and lifts it to his waist, still chuckling. Paddy feels a deep, bittersweet affection rising within himself and then brimming out to enfold this gaunt, Biblical figure holding a booze keg, then expanding out over this whole unwieldy, chuffing, clanking Ark of survivors shuddering through the night over dark, cold, deep waters, over old, extinguished campfires, then to his wife who is known as The Angel - one of those upwelling, maudlin tides of compassion that have lifted him up, from time to terrible time in a lifetime of wartime boozing, the *agape* that is always in Felice's soul, though she doesn't need drink to raise it because it's her whole nature.

Extinguished campfires in wet blackness two fathoms below, yes, but between Paddy and the riverbottom a fire still does burn, a roaring inferno of coal in a flawed steel boiler...

Don't think of that. *Absit nomen absit omen.*

But he *has* thought of it. Now he needs to be with Felice if anything happens.

*

Felice is trying to arise off the deck to find Mister Safford and tell him another soldier has succumbed, but both her legs are asleep, tingling and useless, and she can't stand up yet. She is on hands and knees far forward on the foredeck surrounded by sleeping, sick soldiers, trying to regain sensation in her legs, about to reach for a stanchion to pull herself up by, when she is thrown down upon William Something's bony carcass by a mighty jolt, and for a moment thinks she has gone deaf and blind and breathless. When she can turn onto her side and look up, she finds herself in some sort of hot, red cloud, pelted with stinging drops and sharp particles.

Then things start falling all around: boards, glass, furniture, and the legs and arms of people. Men with clothing afire fall out of the sky, onto the deck or into the river beyond the deck rails. When she can at last draw a breath, everything smells scalded. She begins to hear, first, a loud seething noise. Then screechings. Then voices wailing in pain and terror.

Paddy is somewh...

A chair falls on her and knocks her back into darkness.

*

Paddy has survived enough shellbursts to know an explosion the moment it happens.

The floor surges up under his feet. His breath is compressed out of him at the same instant that he is deafened by a clanking percussion and blinded by steam and light. He feels as if he is being flayed off by hot claws and his nostrils burn with the blacksmith smell of quenched red-hot iron.

He soars, legs feeling stove up into his hips, soars turning as in a backward somersault, through a scalding space full of hard and sharp fragments. The bright yellow behind his closed eyelids darkens as he careers through hot space.

He knows it was the boiler even before he knows whether he's alive or dead.

Now he is aware that he's falling instead of soaring. The name *Felice* is in his mouth, but he has no air in his lungs to cry it out.

When on the Buena Vista battlefield in the long ago war with Mexico his left hand was blown off, he had immediately gone unconscious. Now he is not going to have the mercy of fainting. He will have to bear this. He falls and falls, ears still ringing, body still hot.

The shock of plunging into cold water causes an involuntary gasp. His lungs, forced empty by the explosion, suck in Mississippi water. Going to drown! O, shit!

No, I mean *hailmarymotherofgodblessedartthou...*

Something is pulling him by his left arm, pulling him upward, it seems, toward the surface, though deep in this cold darkness he can't really tell which way is up. His lungs want to expel water, to cough. The Hail Marys do nothing to quell his panic. The face of the Mother of God forms in his mind and it is Felice's face. All he can think is:

Have to find Felice...

Now his head breaks through the surface and he heaves a weak spasm of exhalation.

Water spews out of his mouth and nose and he gasps air in. It makes him cough still more violently.

Another breath. Maybe he won't drown after all. But something big and heavy - a body, it seems to be - falls on him and drives him deep under a second time, the impact hurting his neck and driving the breath out of him again. It is a man, and the man's hands get hold of Paddy's torso and try to climb up him to the surface, which drives Paddy further under in the deep current. Paddy with all the strength of his right hand tears the other's hands off of him and now he is free of the desperate grappler, and again something is pulling him up toward the surface, as if the Mother of God heard his Hail Marys and is rescuing him.

As he surfaces this second time he is turning in the strong current and though he can't see yet, there is a vast bright yellow blur in front of him, but it darkens as the eddy turns him.

He blinks water out of his eyes, and when the current turns him again he sees that the brightness is a blaze on the *Sultana,* on her port side forward of the paddlewheel, twenty feet away and towering over him. There where his cabin was. Even soaked in cold river water he can feel on his face the heat from the burning decks and bulkheads. Everything above the boiler room is gone. Flames, sparks, smoke and steam billow up, and pieces of wood and debris are raining out of the night sky, hissing as they fall in the river around him. A severed human leg tumbles into his vision, splashes into the water, and bobs inches from his face, boot sole up.

Every part of the gigantic boat is swarming with yelling men, hundreds of them, trying to move away from the flames. Scores of soldiers are leaping or dropping off into the river, many with clothing aflame. As Paddy's vision and sense return, he sees bobbing heads everywhere around him. He is bumped from behind by something, and turns his head to see a dead mule drift by, two sobbing men hanging onto it for dear life. Paddy, legs kicking and right hand paddling, floats easily because his watertight desk is still strapped to his left arm. He understands now that it was the buoyancy of the desk that had kept pulling him by his left arm toward the surface.

The firelit water all around him is being churned by people leaping in, people flailing to swim, people grabbing for each other and fighting each other off. A lanky soldier with his coat aflame plunges in not two feet away from Paddy but doesn't surface. Paddy feels something bump against his leg, feels a hand grasp his trouser leg and start pulling him down. He kicks at the invisible hand with his other foot and then is free. The burning man must have sucked in water at the shock of the cold water, as Paddy himself had just done, and is down there somewhere, drowning.

Also tumbling down from above are chairs, doors, boxes, boards, rails, even sections of stairways, all being thrown in by men who must be hoping to jump in and seize them for flotation. But these objects are hitting men in the water. And as soon as a wardrobe chest or a plank splashes into the water, several swimmers grab onto it and begin fighting each other for it. In their panic, these old comrades are drowning each other.

That noise he had been hearing for days, the steady rumble and clatter of the engines, has been silenced. The noises now are random and hellish: burned men screaming, people shouting and sobbing, the flames roaring like a bonfire, the creak and crash of collapsing ceilings and decks and bulkheads, the splash and gurgle of the river, Paddy's own desperate wheezing cough as he tries to get the rest of the water out of his nose and gullet. The huge, blazing boat is no longer churning upstream against the current but drifting upon it. The great paddlewheels have stopped turning.

Even by the bright light of the towering flames there is no river shore to be seen. The water seems so limitless that this catastrophe might as well have struck in mid-ocean. And all this water is numbingly cold. Though this is April, the Mississippi itself is still frigid with the melted snow and ice of its headwaters far to the north. Whiskied though he is, Paddy keeps gasping with cold, and his heart races. He feels that if he doesn't drown, he'll shudder to death, or just wink out like a spark.

But even in this whirl of awe and despair, Paddy is gathering himself to think and to do something. Felice is somewhere, either on the boat or in the river. Either alive or dead. He has to know. He has to do something about her.

And where is that good soldier Macombie? Did the explosion kill him? He should have landed in the water somewhere here near Paddy, they were so close together in the moment of the blast. But he was so frail, he's likely dead, or near so by now, Paddy thinks. Or down there below me somewhere.

Hail Mary Mother of God...

He turns in the water, scanning the enormous boat and the chaos on and about it. The *Sultana* is still prow upstream, it seems. A steady wind from upriver is feeding the blaze like a smithy's bellows, the roaring flames whipping sternward. Felice was far up on the foredeck with the crippled and sick soldiers, so she might yet be safe, upwind from the conflagration.

Unless she was coming back to the stateroom when the boiler blew.

Don't think of that. See what happens when you think something!

Now hearing a deeper roar and a metallic screech, Paddy looks and sees the two towering, flame-spewing smokestacks slowly buckle inward toward each other and crumple onto the superstructure with an enormous burst of flame, sparks and debris.

McGinty and O'Hara, he thinks. That came down right on top of their quarters. God rest their souls. My San Patricios!

San Patricios, hell! We're all going to die!

A powerful wave of despair and indignation almost squeezes the breath out of him. What kind of a vicious God would do this now to these poor bastards who have already been dragged through years of blood and pain and shit!

What kind of a Goddamned God are you?

No, I mean Holy Mary Mother of God, Blessed art Thou and...

Through the uproar and splashing Paddy hears a voice moaning just behind him. Turning in the water hoping to see Robbie, he sees instead something that looks like a wad of raw meat, floating an arm's length away from him. It is sidelit by the bright inferno, red and gray and gristly. And an eye. A hole opens on the front of it, showing white teeth, and a voice rasps, "Mister Quinn! Oh, God, man, I can't stand this!"

It is a man with the skin scalded off his head. No hair, no eyelids. Paddy grows weak at the sight, but is just too cold to faint. "Robbie? Is that you?"

"Oh! God! *GOD!*"

With that quaking cry of agony, the man sinks out of sight; his hand rises above the water. Paddy grabs for it with his right hand and gets a hold on it. But the skin slips off like a loose glove into Paddy's grip and then the man is gone. With a shudder of revulsion, Paddy tries to shake the clammy tissue off his hand. He is quaking almost too hard to breathe.

Have to breathe! Have to!

If that was Robbie, God rest his poor soul.

But if he got scalded, why didn't I, right beside him? Maybe that wasn't Robbie.

May never know who the poor bastard was. Better off drowned.

The blazing superstructure of the steamboat seems as bright as daylight, and every human figure or piece of furniture or wreckage that comes hurtling off is a dark silhouette against the flames. Several times Paddy is almost hit by something or someone.

Everyone in the water seems to be trying desperately get away from the inferno, but Paddy can't just swim away from it. Felice is surely still aboard, up forward, or in the river somewhere up that way. As long as he thinks she might be alive up there, he can't swim away from the boat.

Hundreds of frantic, yelling, coughing soldiers are in the river all around him by now, almost as densely crowded in the river now as they had been on the boat Many are sobbing or cursing and fighting each other for planks and doors to hang onto, and trying to paddle to safety on such flotsam. More seem to be drowning than not. He hears one after another crying "I can't swim!" He sees many slip under, sees others drown themselves by struggling to get out of their coats and boots in the water.

Paddy keeps gauging distance by looking at the high, semicircular housing of the paddlewheel with its huge, painted letters:

SULTANA

He starts swimming toward the bow of the vessel, where Felice was. But the current is bearing him downstream faster than the ponderous drift of the flaming vessel, and he will have to swim hard just to stay abreast of it. So he snugs his portfolio up close to his left shoulder, leans upon its buoyancy, and begins reaching and paddling upstream with his right hand, also propelling himself with kicking legs. He had been a strong swimmer when he was a lad with two hands. But he is weighted down now with wet clothes and his shoes. The cold is sapping his strength, and he had already been in deep fatigue before the explosion. And now his course through the water is impeded every few seconds by something or someone floating down: now a broad section of deck or bulkhead with dozens of human figures lying or sitting on it sobbing and wailing, while dozens more in the water try to cling to its jagged edges or climb on. Now a charred corpse in a nightshirt. Now a horse swimming along strenuously with a man hanging to its mane, two more men hanging on its tail.

Maneuvering past such things, Paddy almost collides with some agitated object, splashing and churning and grunting, brightly backlit by the sweeping tower of flame beyond. It's a moment before he realizes what it is: a man trying to stay atop a barely-floating keg, a keg which keeps revolving under him. In these dire straits, a pathetically comical sight. But then:

I know that man! I know that keg!

"Macombie! Robbie Macombie!" Paddy gasps, and grabs for him, getting some cloth. The pale man, sputtering and spitting, stops trying to mount the keg and lays one arm over it. Gets his eyes focused on Paddy.

"God be praised! Mister Quinn!"

Paddy almost yelps in desperate gratitude. He shudders mightily in the cold water and holds the skinny soldier's shirt sleeve, not wanting him to drift away. The man's wet white hair is slicked to his skull and his face is gaunt with exhaustion, but he keeps nodding at Paddy and looking right into his eyes. Then he glances at the blazing steamboat, and shakes his head.

"Now we all die? After all that, we just drown like rats?" Then he tries to haul himself onto the little keg again, and again rolls off.

"Not you and me," Paddy says. "We're going to see Mister Lincoln, remember?"

Robbie stops struggling with the keg, hangs onto it by fingertips, chin in the water, and stares at Paddy. In the light from the roaring boat fire, something changes in those pale blue eyes.

"We... we are?" He is barely audible over the roar of flames and the cacophony of desperate voices.

"Didn't I promise you?"

"I reckoned you meant God willing. Don't look t' me like God's willing!"

"We don't know that, not yet! Can you stay by me?" Paddy tilts his head toward the boat. "Got to find Felice." His voice is quaking with cold.

"Can't get back on that ship, sir!"

"Don't know. But I have to find 'er!" He begins stroking against the current and kicking with numbing legs. Robbie yells something, but his words are overridden by the pandemonium. Paddy yells back, "Just stay close!"

Paddling upstream with his right hand, he has to swim facing away from the flaming boat. The dark water is full of debris and flailing swimmers. Paddy feels so spent that he doubts he is making any progress. He stops after every few strokes to turn in the water and look at the floating conflagration. Yes, he is gaining, but so little it seems futile.

The vessel's prow is still holding upstream and straight into the wind. Everything but the forestructure is curtained now with bright, roaring flame, fed and fanned aft by the wind from upriver. The huge semicircle of the sidewheel housing is now smoking, faintly silhouetted against the nearly white-hot blaze, the name *SULTANA* fading in shadow and smoke.

God let Felice be upwind of the fire. God keep her safe until I...

Holy Mary Mother of God, blessed art thou and blessed...

Chest heaving, gasping and spitting, he strokes and kicks onward. Robbie is still coming along, keg under one arm, face white and gaunt. A few more strokes and Paddy pauses again to look at the boat.

Here near the prow, fewer people are yet in the water. But the foredecks, the last refuge from the holocaust, are thronging with hundreds of desperate men yelling, crushing, trampling each other, some with clothes ablaze, some climbing the handrails and leaping off into the river. Cripples are being lifted over the railing and dropped into the water. Those falling from the promenade deck plunge some eighteen feet before hitting the water headfirst, feetfirst, flat or contorted. Those on the lower deck have no more than seven feet or so to fall, and don't plunge in so deep. None but suicides would leap from these forward decks if the paddlewheels were still running, but on this immobilized hulk now the dangers are only burning or drowning. Or eventually, chill.

Paddy, now in a state of almost breathless chill himself, looking everywhere for a sight of Felice, sees a swarm of activity around the jutting gangplank. Men are hauling on pulley ropes, clumsily shoving and manhandling the long, heavy gangplank, trying to get it positioned to lower it into the river, where it might serve as a big raft. It could support dozens of people. Paddy gains a bit of hope from the sight. If Felice is still up here on the lower deck forward of the flames, she has a chance to be one of those boarding the gangplank and floating away from the boat before it's entirely burned up. Surely, if she's still alive, those men will aid her and make a place for her, those men who have been praising her as an angel of mercy.

Above the roar of their yelling, Paddy hears a shout beside him:

"There she is!" It's Robbie's voice. Paddy turns and sees him pointing.

Pointing up.

Oh God no!

There he sees her, in that elegant pale dress, forward on the promenade deck, far above the water. She is on the wrong deck to get to the gangplank even if it *can* be launched. Paddy takes a gasp of air and bellows, *"FELICE!"*

But even his battlefield voice is faint in this uproar of shouts and screams and the flue-like roar of the fire.

Suddenly now a tremendous grating, creaking sound overrides the general noise, and a column of flame and sparks climbs skyward. Paddy looks back toward the middle of the vessel and sees the near paddlewheel slump away into the river, its curved housing ablaze, tons of flaming wood and red-hot iron falling amid the men and horses swimming there, hissing and spewing steam as it collapses.

Now the conflagration on the huge wooden boat is almost complete; everything burnt up aft of those last remaining bulkheads, doors and windows that separate the superstructure from the foredecks. As the inferno is whipped aft by the breeze from the north, the whole vast wooden superstructure is burning nearly down to the waterline. No one back there could be alive who hadn't already gone into the river. The scene seems bright as daylight. Bobbing heads and anguished faces and flailing limbs in the water are visible for hundreds of feet in the fire glare, only those far off looking like dim dots in the dark distance. Sodden as he is, Paddy can feel the flameheat on his face.

He looks again to the foredeck. There Felice is still, near the rail, moving amid the stampede of desperate men, and he yells her name again, and then again, waits as if he believes she will hear him and turn to see him.

"FELICE!" he bellows. *"I'M HERE! COME HERE! JUMP!"* She's a swimmer. She should jump.

If she hears him, there's no sign of it. She's still up there, head and shoulders barely visible to him. Paddy feels something bump against him in the water. It's Robbie clutching the keg, Robbie whom he'd almost forgotten.

"She can't hear you!"

"She's got to hear me! I want her to come here! *FELICE! FELICE! HERE..."*

"Lookee, sir. It's turnin'!"

Paddy sees what's happening. The collapse of the one sidewheel has altered that equilibrium of wind and current, and the huge, flaming mass is beginning to yaw. Her prow is coming around. Having sat nose into the wind since the explosion, the *Sultana* is slowly swinging around crosscurrent to face the west.

And as she comes broadside to the breeze and the river current, her plume of fire whips off this near side, and the blazing hulk begins drifting faster down the river.

Soon Paddy and Robbie have to backpaddle from the looming prow. The gangplank, which is still being manhandled by desperate men, could fall on them at any moment. Paddy's strength is flagging in the chill water. But he keeps stroking with his pain-throbbing right arm, trying to stay in a position where he can see his bride up there. Men all around her are still shoving, waving their arms, shouting, wrestling with each other for whatever in their crazed minds seems advantageous. Some are still hoisting the cripples over the rail and dropping them overboard.

Paddy remembers a time, in some Army camp somewhere, soldiers had pulled up an old oaken fence post to burn in their campfire. Its lower end was full of ants, and as the rail burned, the ants swarmed madly from the oncoming flames, until the entire post was burning and they were all dead, even those that had fallen off the post into the embers below. There are now men up there on the foredecks as numerous and frantic as the countless ants in that campfire, and they are behaving just as those ants did, and their fate seems the same.

Until now, the foredecks have been shielded from the inferno by the fore bulkheads as the conflagration was whipped astern by the wind. But Paddy realizes now, to his horror, that as the vessel pivots, the flames will soon be consuming that bulkhead near where Felice stands. Inhaling all the breath he can take in, he bellows up at her, there where she stands scarcely ten yards above him:

"JUMP, FELICE! JUMP! NOW! I'M HERE! JUMP!" With one strong leap off the rail she could hit the water within ten feet of him, and he and Robbie could grab her and keep her afloat with them. And then somehow they could all three together deal with the matter of staying alive in the river. Actually, all four! It comes

back to him suddenly just now that she's nurturing the embryo of his offspring!

Holy Mary please let her see I'm alive and I'm here. Then she'd come to me!

*

Felice had thought that there couldn't be steadier, braver men anywhere than these veterans, but now they are all stampeding in panic. They have knocked her off her feet several times, and the ones who can stand and run are trampling upon those who can't get up. They come yelling and stumbling onto the foredeck in droves, fleeing from the inferno behind them. Many are horribly scalded and some are on fire even as they come charging onto the foredeck. Some fight their way to the rails and climb over to jump off into the river. Others struggle with each other trying to wrest life vests or any other buoyant objects from each other, screaming that they can't swim.

Through the bulkhead windows she can see the conflagration raging back there. Everything back there is ablaze. Back there where their cramped little stateroom was. There where Paddy went to continue his interviews. Their little room must have been shattered and flung skyward when the boiler first exploded.

For that's what happened, all the survivors know by now. The boiler, maybe all the boilers, blew up like a bombshell and then fire rose and spread astern like wildfire in the strong breeze from upriver. Indeed, the fire had sucked at the wind and funneled it aft, roaring and crackling ever louder, and surely, she thinks, surely nobody back there beyond this bulkhead can be alive.

Surely Paddy can't be alive, she thinks with plummeting heart. No use hoping for that.

She feels she is telling that dismal truth to the embryo of his child within her. She stands with the misty wind blowing its river smell cool on her face, the heat of the fire intensifying at her back, and what she sees on the deck before her is Dantesque, a frantic melee in Hell. These are the damned now and they are, almost all of them, out of their minds. These old comrades are fighting each other to grasp some last advantage.

But somewhere up forward, she can hear the sounds of *something* being done, something still rational: men's voices calling queries and commands and answers to each other, heavy things being moved, the sound of a windlass creaking. Someone is still trying to do something, save somebody perhaps. She hears the word *gangplank* yelled out once, then again, looks forward and sees block and tackle moving.

Yes, oh, why, yes! If the gangplank can be let off into the river, what a great raft it could be! She knows of wrecks in which that has been done, and has saved lives. If they can get the gangplank off soon, there's hope for at least some of these. Unless they all kill each other first...

Must calm them down! she thinks. There's no hope if they don't calm down and help each other!

And so she begins trying. She grabs struggling men by their sleeves and shoulders, makes their deranged eyes turn to her, shouts into their wild faces:

"Stop it! Shame on you! Don't hurt him, *help* him! PLEASE! CALM YOURSELVES!...*YOU! HELP ME WITH THIS MAN!"*

One at a time, two at a time, then in a widening circle around her, they begin paying heed to this woman whom most of them recognize. "Go down and help them with the gangplank! Can you get down there?"

"No, ma'am! Stairs is all afire!"

To Felice now, that is really the end of hope. Except for those willing to go over the rail and drop twenty feet into the cold, dark, turbulent river, this upper foredeck is the place of doom. As the blazing wreck yaws across the wind, the bulkhead behind her is rattling and roaring with the wind-driven conflagration. The foredeck is now so packed with people that they can't even cringe away from the seething, smoking bulkhead any more, they can only press toward the dreaded railings. Someone's hand gets a hold on her elbow and she is pushed firmly toward the port rail.

I'll go over when I need to. But not before.

Oh, Paddy! I'm so sorry we're not together!

*

"She's comin' t' the rail, Mister Quinn!"

"Yes! Yes. *Felice! FELICE! Here we are! Jump! COME ON!"*

As if she's heard his voice, Felice now turns to the railing and puts her hands on it and she is looking down and she sees him. Or she seems to be seeing him. He waves his arm and shouts up at her: *"HERE! COME ON!"*

He sees her wave a hand at him. At last! She calls something down to him, words he can't hear, just the sound of her voice in the thunder and screaming, and nods at him. But instead of climbing on the rail to jump over, she turns forward again and begins yelling at the soldiers, grabbing their shirts and crying, "Be calm! Help each other! Be..."

The smoking bulkhead behind her bursts. She is swallowed and obliterated in billowing flame and twirling fragments. The foredeck is swept with a yellow blaze. Soldiers fall with their clothes afire. Men in flames keep struggling against each other now to get over the rail and leap.

Paddy is breathless with disbelief. One moment ago she was there looking at him and now she has been wiped away by a dragon's tongue of flame. His vision blurs and fades, his heart quakes.

Holy Mary Mother of God...

I'll come too...

CHAPTER NINE

Robbie Macombie would just let go of the keg and let himself drown, if he didn't feel he has to keep this Mister Quinn alive.

Robbie's heart went cold when he saw that angel Mrs. Quinn vanish in flame.

What in hell's the use?

That was what he'd thought. Maybe he'd said it aloud. He didn't really know.

But who'd even want to live any longer in a world where that could happen?

Half of the able-bodied men in America dead and mangled and sick from a plague of war. Saints like Mister Lincoln murdered by haters. People delivered from a latrine of a prison camp only to be scalded and blown to bits and drowned in a cold river. An angel of mercy just burnt up like a moth in a candle flame. Right before her husband's eyes. This good man's eyes.

GOD DAMN IT ALL!

Robbie had already nearly used himself up, just keeping himself from slipping under and choking on river water. Now he has to use one hand to keep Mister Quinn's face up where he can breathe. He's got a grip on his ear. Mister Quinn isn't conscious. Apparently he fainted when he saw what happened to her.

Can't do this much longer.

Wake up, Mister Quinn. Help me. Just wake up and float.

Wake up and tell me what you want.

If you want to die, I'll let you.

I'll even do it with you.

Just wake up!

The big boat is still burning, though the blaze is dwindling because there's so little superstructure left to burn. The giant vessel had gone up quicker than an old hay barn.

The river is still full of people trying to keep from drowning or shivering to death. From all around come groans and curses and feeble outcries.

But it's growing darker as the fire burns down. As well as Robbie can see, the gangplank hasn't been freed yet to serve as a raft. The boat is crosswise to the current now, but farther away. This current is so strong and roiling that it keeps turning him and sweeping him every which way. Sometimes he's seen treetops nearby, treetops in young spring leaf, just showing above the water. Maybe these are the treetops of those Hens and Chickens Islands Mister Quinn said they were floating over. Such a treetop would be something to grab and hang onto until daylight, when other steamboats or fishing boats might come out and start saving people. How long it is until dawn he doesn't know.

But those few limber wisps of treetops Robbie has seen are already claimed by wet, desperate men, hanging on by scalded hands or crooked elbows, perching like crows, yelling, crying, cursing, fighting to keep others from crowding them off.

And beyond these treetops that he passes so swiftly, there is nothing but more water. Nowhere within this whole fading firelit range of vision is there a sign of land.

Sure the evilest of all the damn evil things I've ever seen is that angel Missus Quinn just erased by a gush of fire. O my heart!

I bet Mister Quinn'd rather be dead. After he seen that. O he loved that woman!

And no wonder! I'd've died for that woman my own self!

Robbie is crying now, and his mourning is so deep the cold and pain and fatigue don't amount to much. His old body is used to suffering.

He's just never had his heart hurt so much.

God damn ye, wake up, Mister Quinn! I can't handle this by myself!

You still mean us to go see Mister Lincoln?

*

"Let go o' me, you son of a bitch!"

Paddy shouts those words into Lieutenant Milton's snarling face and tries to stomp on his foot or kick him in the groin. The lieutenant has a steel grip on Paddy's ear and means to beat him for stealing his newspaper.

Paddy kicks as hard as he can, and suddenly he's choking and coughing up water and is cold and wet and is being buoyed up by some force on his left arm and a grip on his ear.

He blinks water out of his eyes. Instead of the snarling Lieutenant Milton in the Mexican sunshine, he sees faintly a wet, gaunt, white-bearded man with his head barely above water, holding onto a half-floating keg with one hand and tugging up on Paddy's ear and hair with the other. It is nighttime and there is firelight.

And now he knows where he is.

Now he remembers. He remembers that he isn't a boy in Mexico but a man in the Mississippi River and that he adored a beautiful wife who was going to give him a child but instead she just got burnt up. That realization returns so painfully that he can't even think of the name of this man here who has apparently been keeping him from drowning. It's all just too big and awful and his heart is as cold and dark as this river in the night.

The white-haired man says, "Mister Quinn, y' call me a son of a bitch! Why?"

Paddy shakes his head. Gasps. Spits out water. Shivers violently. "Not you. I was...there was...It was a dream..." The current turns them and Paddy sees the razed hull of the steamboat burning, far up the river. He looks at its guttering fires until the current turns him away. He groans.

Or did I dream that Felice died?

For a while the two men slosh and shiver and paddle in the dark water. Paddy wants to think Felice is alive, that somehow she was saved off that foredeck. That he just dreamed of that burst of flame. It comes back to him that this man with him in the water is Macombie, a soldier who lived through the war and then lived through Andersonville Prison. That this man somehow saved their whiskey keg. And now the whiskey keg is rewarding him by keeping him afloat while other men are drowning everywhere.

Paddy, with an awful jolt of pain in his left shoulder, tries to hoist himself high on his own buoy, the escritoire strapped on his arm. All the fitting and sealing he did with glue and rubber to keep his correspondence dry in the battlefields made it as watertight as that keg, and now it keeps him from drowning. He would have lost it in the explosion if he'd not strapped it on. That little keg and this little desk. Their life buoys.

It's easier to think of these little miracles than of what has just happened. It is hard enough to think of anything now, even to feel anything. His limbs are numb and his heart is numb. He has seen soldiers die in the field from less exposure than this. We can't last long, he thinks...

Robbie's voice, quavering and raspy, comes into his dim conscious over the slap and slosh of the water:

"What about Mister Lincoln?"

"What? What of him?"

"I reckon we won't see 'im?"

A shudder passes through Paddy, so powerful it seems almost to stop his heart. Then he has a giddy desire to say something laughable, some mockery in the face of all this grief. "Illinois's way up the river. We're floating the wrong way. We might... be back down in Memphis...by daylight...Be as cold stone dead as he is...likely..."

Dead will be alright. I've been almost there often enough already. If that's where I can find Felice, that's the place for me.

"Well," comes Macombie's voice. "I just wondered if you gave up on that promise."

"What the hell promise?" Words are such an annoyance, distracting him from the grief he deserves.

"You and me goin' to see the President."

Paddy squeezes his eyes shut tight and shakes his head. This is getting to seem ridiculous.

"Faith," he says, "and a thing or two's happened since then! Or haven't ye noticed?" His soul wants to plummet down where it can writhe in the exquisite agony of his loss.

Robbie says nothing else, for which Paddy is grateful, as he can now groan and weep for a while.

But soon the man's silence becomes a reproach, or so it seems. Paddy trembles violently, opens his eyes, sees Robbie still nearby, clutching the keg with one hand, and now Paddy realizes that the man is holding his sleeve with the other. If not for that, they'd have been swept apart by the swift waters. It's still darker now. The flames and cries on the hull of the *Sultana* are far away. There are still shouts and wails and splashings in the river all around, but fewer and fewer people still alive in the water, those few being dispersed over the unbounded flood of the river.

"Look, I try to keep promises. But, Godalmighty! You saw what happened! She was worth twenty Lincolns to me! God damn it!" he sobs.

He feels Robbie's clutch on his coat sleeve pull tighter. Robbie's voice says:

"To me too, sir." The statement grabs Paddy's heart like a warm fist.

After a while Robbie goes on, "If she'd lived and you didn't, I'd a-taken her home, and me an' my Tildie we'd've adopted 'er for a daughter. I swear to God! You're not the only one lost that angel! With due respect, sir."

After that Paddy can only press his cheek against his escritoire and cry. He weeps so hard it almost keeps him warm. But eventually he's all sobbed out and feels ice creeping into his exhausted core. He is a sodden bit of chaff swept along in darkness on a measureless flood . Into his mind comes some dim memory of something some educated officer taught him when he was a boy, so long ago. Yes. It was General Wallace, but when he was just a young lieutenant down in Mexico. Told Paddy about the mythical river called Lethe. The River of Forgetting.

If only this were the Lethe instead of the Mississippi...

It could be. All I'd need to do is drown.

*

Robbie has no idea what time of night it is, or how long they've been in the river. He knows from years of all kinds of misery that you can't judge time when you're suffering, hungry, or afraid.

Or drunk.

He remembers that it was after one in the morning, maybe even two, when the boat exploded, but since then four or five hours might have passed, or maybe just one. He's seen no sign of morning in the sky. There are no stars visible because of the overcast. At least two or three light rainshowers have spattered on the river, that he can remember.

Robbie has been colder than this, countless times. Lying hip-and-shoulder on frozen ground in the prison camp in midwinter all night long night after night without even a blanket. Nothing but the shivering soldiers against your front and your back to give any warmth. A coat of frost on you. In your armpit or under your scrotum you might be warm enough that lice and fleas could live there, and you'd feel them living their nibbly little lives down there. But even in those circumstances a body could get exhausted enough to slip off into sleep for a while. Here up to your chin in the Mississippi, though, you're too wet to be warm anyplace. Even your asshole's cold. And no matter how tired, you don't dare sleep. Got to keep a hold on the keg, keep your face above water, hang on to Mister Quinn so he won't drift off or slip away.

Can't even talk to him about the funeral of Mister Lincoln. He doesn't want to talk about anything.

Well, hell no. He's in shock.

After another long, shivering, shuddering spell that could have been ten minutes or another hour, Robbie is thinking:

Why haven't other boats come along? We were always passing them, every few hours, day or night.

You'd think somebody somewhere would've heard us blow up, or seen that fire. You'd think somebody'd come out here, even just in rowboats, to see what happened.

As the current turns him, he keeps looking for a light of any kind. A lantern on a boat. A lamp in a house window. Some glow from a town or city.

Hard as this current is, shouldn't we be back down to Memphis by now?

Oh, G-G-God damn!

Robbie's heart is just downright quivering, he's so cold.

He tries to warm it a little by thinking of Mister Lincoln. Or of Mrs. Quinn.

There is a little comfort in that. But the fact is, they're both dead. Robbie tenses his whole body to make it stop shivering. He shuts his eyes. He tries to remember Mrs. Quinn's face.

He begins to slide away. He was half dead before this happened, hardly a spark left in him even then. It's going out now...

*

"GOD DAMN ME FOR A MORON!" Paddy's voice croaks in the darkness.

Robbie is startled awake and sputters and spits out the water that had begun running into his mouth. "Huh? Pfffssh! Huh?"

"Why should our hearts freeze up when there's whiskey? Damn!"

These are words in total darkness. There isn't even a trace of fireglow from the *Sultana* anymore. Neither man can see the other. Nor can they see any of the people whose pitiful voices still come faintly over the cold waters.

"Tell me y've still got our keg?"

"Do, sir. It's my float."

"Then let's have at it. My cockles call for it! And by th' fist o' St. Patrick, Robbie Macombie, don't *ever* tell anybody it took me this long t' think of it!"

Already his voice is recovering its old plangency, at the prospect of it.

Robbie's voice says in the dark:

"Let's us be careful, though, sir. Without th' keg, I sink, remember."

"The good thing is, the less whiskey in it, the better a float."

"True. But, um, how d'we do this, sir?"

"First, stop calling me 'sir.' Get a hold on my desk here. It'll float you. Where's that keg?"

Paddy gets his right hand on the keg, gropes it, turns it in the water. He soon realizes that it poses a serious dilemma.

The keg's wooden bung in one end is the outlet for the whiskey. No device is more familiar to Paddy. Twist the spile in the bung to open it and whiskey flows down and out. The bung has to be down, and you put your glass under it. So simple.

But here in the river, the keg floats half submerged. If the bung's down, it's under water. Roll the keg so the bung will be above the water, and the whiskey won't come out because whiskey doesn't flow up.

"Wait," says Paddy. He needs to think. But his brain is waterlogged. "Now, wait...."

I need to get under the bung.

Easy to do on land. Even if you don't have a glass or cup, you can just lift the keg overhead and open your mouth under the bung. He's done that on occasion. He and General Grant himself once had to do that, during the Vicksburg siege, when they were without conveniences.

But Paddy has never before had to drink from a keg while afloat in water.

It's perplexing, but it's better than thinking about Felice. He says to Robbie, "This won't be easy. But where there's a will, there's a way."

Ever since he was an Army camp errand boy in Mexico, he always succeeded in getting whiskey -- or rum or tequila -- under the most trying circumstances. He was a bootlegger for the officers when he was twelve, and never failed them.

But then we weren't afloat in a damned river.

"Let me think."

After a while, Robbie asks, "What's the problem?"

"The keg's our buoy. We lift it up, we sink down."

"Oh...yeah. Damn."

"Might drown."

"Maybe would, yep."

"Might be worth it, for just one swig." Oh, how he wants that warmth to fill the cold vacuum in his bosom! He's been cold and sober for hours.

Went sober when Felice...

Shush! Got to think!

"Let's try rolling the keg up on my desk."

They struggle blindly, to the sounds of their own grunts and splashes and the hollow bumping of the desk and the keg, heads sometimes under water, then up and choking and coughing and spitting, but the keg's weight added to their own keeps sinking the desk, or the keg keeps rolling off, or Paddy gets a shoulder cramp that makes him helpless.. Exhausted at last by such futile wallowings, they give up that idea. They hang on to rest, panting and spitting.

There is no sign of dawn yet. There are still sad and desperate voices coming ghostly from far out over the limitless, cold river. Cursing voices. Singing and praying voices. Despairing wails.

"Say, there's that cork plug in the side," Robbie's voice says in the darkness after a while. "Maybe we could pry it out?"

Paddy evaluates that suggestion for a long time, then says:

"We'd still have to get down under to drink. And if we lost that cork we might sink the whole keg."

He fears neither of them is in a condition to engineer any sure way of getting whiskey out of the bung without just going under water and sucking from it like a calf under a cow. He can't even think clearly enough to know whether he can do that without getting water up his nose or down his gullet.

A body could drown himself.

He remembers that some of the soldiers who crossed the Rio Grande to desert in the Mexican war hid from sentries by lying under water near the riverbank and breathing through a hollow reed. So he knows one can suck on something under water.

But that was to inhale air. You don't want to inhale whiskey into your lungs. Rather drown in whiskey than water, but it'd still be drowning. Can I drink but not inhale?

Faith, you never know 'til you try!

"Friend, I'm going down for a drink. Don't let loose o' me."

"Got you, sir. Good luck."

As he submerges, his whole body and head in the cold current, Paddy has to hold back panic to try to think it out:

Got to get my mouth right on the spile and use my hand to open the spigot. Wish I had a free hand to hold my nose.

Ready. Now...

Suddenly he's in a strangling torment. He jerks his head up, coughing harshly, spewing water from his nose and whiskey from his throat. He hangs onto the keg for dear life and coughs and spits with desperate violence for a long time. Then he remembers to twist the spile and shut the bung before too much whiskey flows into the river or too much river gets into the whiskey.

As Paddy tries to figure out what he did wrong, Robbie's voice says, "Not too good, I take it?"

"Damn... near drowned..."

"Don't."

"*Did* get whiskey. *Can* be done. Think maybe I just shouldn't swallow it while my head's under." He takes a deep breath. " Hold on. I'm going down again."

"I'm prayin'."

Paddy had always been a good underwater swimmer, and instinctively blocks water from getting from his nostrils into his throat. The difficulty is simultaneously getting his pursed lips around the little spigot without water rushing into his mouth. He tries to keep oriented under the keg by kicking but his legs are too numb to know whether that helps.

Now he has it. Concentrating, he twists the spile and sucks until his mouth is full of whiskey, cheeks distended with it, resisting the frantic natural impulse to swallow or sniff. He sticks his face up out of the water, keeps his mouth shut while exhaling one breath and inhaling the next through his nose, and only then does he open his throat to let the whiskey go down. It is so incredibly harsh and wonderful!

"Straight to my cockles! Aaaahhh!"

"Y' did it?"Robbie's voice says.

"Did it! Felice, ye married a genius..."

Then he realizes what he said, and adds, "...Sorry..."

"It's good, I bet," Robbie's voice says after a while.

"Oh, yes, good! But it's b'God no natural way to drink whiskey! Scary as hell. Listen, I need to practice once or twice. Then I'll teach you."

"But leave me a little, eh?"

"Hah!" Paddy is astonished to hear a shuddery laugh come out of himself. "Robbie, you're funny! Sure and I'll leave some. There's more here than you can drink, it's that hard to do. Here I go, now. Here's mud in your eye..." And he ducks down in.

By remembering and concentrating, Paddy manages to go under two more times and come up with mouthfuls of delicious whiskey. But on the next try, he's careless with his epiglottis and snuffs a headful of water, and thus needs several minutes to recover from a coughing and gasping and retching spell in which he's lost a whole mouthful of the precious whiskey into the Mississippi.

By now, despite that mishap, he has enough down in him that the warmth of life is returning around his heart. He has even quit shuddering.

"Your turn, Rob. But be careful. Here's what you have to do..." He describes and explains, and in the dark he can hear Robbie practicing sniffles and gulps and glottal clicks.

"Guess I *understand* how,"Robbie says. "Just hope I can do it. Now, where's that whiskey nipple..." By feeling around in the dark, they get him situated. Paddy has a rush of pity when he grasps Robbie's skinny arm and feels the poor man's terrible shuddering.

"I've got you, friend. You should do all right. You've got a hand to open the bung *and* one to hold your nose." Robbie takes a deep breath and ducks under.

A moment of quiet explodes into flailing, wallowing, spewing and gagging. Paddy holds Robbie's arm until he's settled, but still hacking and moaning.

"Can't do it...Damnation! Just don't have any lungs left...or something...left 'em in Andersonville or somethin'...Can't do it..."

"Try again. It took me two tries."

"'Fraid to. Reckon that whiskey's ...yours, Mister Quinn. Really, go on.... I don't mind. You like it better'n I do anyhow..."

"No, damn it. You need whiskey, or you're a dead mackerel. Look, I told you, where there's a will there's a way. I'll just go underneath that keg like a whale and shoulder it up out o' the water and tip it so you can get a quick suck at it. Just take a second. And, oh, you'll feel like a new man."

He convinces himself and Robbie that it can be done, and they coordinate the motions of their plan. Paddy avers:

"I'll get whiskey into you if it takes floatin' down to Memphis and buying you one in a saloon. But 'til then, we do this. Now, be set to move quick."

But the whale maneuver doesn't work, either. Paddy can shoulder the keg up almost out of the water for a moment, but not long enough for Robbie to get to the bung. After a few tries, they're panting, Robbie still hasn't had a single drop of whiskey, and Paddy is really wanting more.

Then an idea comes. It's risky, but he really wants Robbie to have some whiskey in him before he just shivers himself to death. "Listen. In my desk here I have something that maybe we could fill from the bung, and then you could drink from it without goin' under water. It might work... Only trouble would be opening the desk to get it out..." The thought of opening it and having river water slosh in and ruin all his notes and pictures is terrible. Or, worse, taking a chance of swamping the very life-buoying thing that's kept him from drowning all this eternal night! But with luck, he could open the desk lid and grope for the thing quickly before any water would get in. He knows just where it is. He's kept it under a velvet false bottom in the lower right corner where Felice would never see it even when the desk was open.

"What is it you got in there, a cup?" Robbie asks in that quaking, weak voice. "How could we fill a cup... without liftin' the whole keg up? We already know... can't do that."

"It's not a cup... It's a, um, well, it's a french letter..."

Silence for a moment, then Robbie says, "A *condom* , you mean?"

"You know. Lamb gut. I, ah, I...before I married, I had...I..." And something comes rushing back up in his memory:

Had it on for that Hooker's Whore Fanny Foremost! But on my flaggin' cock, not on my arm! O Christ!

He'd not thought of her, the so-called "Mrs. Willard," once since the boat exploded.

Surely she'd be dead by now...

And though it's the very same expensive condom he'd kept all through the war, he could at least declare that it had never been inside "Mrs. Willard." He'd been too drunk to use that part of his anatomy that abominable night.

That condom had been a life saver, too, probably. Without its use, he'd probably have come down with clap or syphilis somewhere along his feckless path from Mexico and through the war. He should have discarded it when he married Felice; they'd never have used it. But those things are expensive, and, to tell the truth, that one had some sentimental value, memories that didn't rinse out of the device afterward. Still, he shouldn't have kept it.

Or, yet, maybe he was supposed to keep it for this unexpected purpose...

For a while now, Robbie has made no comment about the idea, and so Paddy explains, "It'd fit right snug over the bung...We could heave up the keg and in a second we'd slosh a dram in it at least..." It really does seem like a feasible plan. And they wouldn't have to risk drowning just to get a mouthful of whiskey.Though they might risk drowning by opening the desk to get the device. But he'd take that risk, to get some whiskey into his friend here.

In the darkness, Robbie's quavering voice says, "Is, uh, is it a *new* one?"

"New?"

"I mean, have you ever, you know, um, *used* it?"

"You want the truth, I guess. Yes. I've...used it..."

"With all due respect, Mister Quinn, and don't take it personal, but...I, I really don't just *have* to have whiskey."

"Sure. Nothing personal."

In a way, Paddy is hugely relieved. Opening the desk likely would be a disaster in itself. It's hard to think of it now, but in this desk are all the notes and sketches of the best and most terrible story in his life. His whole future might be dry and safe in there. Even without his beloved Felice to share it with, he might yet have a future.

*

Another immeasurable period of time has gone by in the darkness. During that time Paddy has gone down two more times successfully and come up with cheek-distending mouthfuls of whiskey, then let their caustic heat trickle down to warm his heart.

But poor Robbie! Sure and his candle's about to flicker out!

At once now Paddy has another idea. It comes to him in an image, a memory of something he once saw high on a mountain in Mexico. He thinks about it for a minute.

"Robbie, you're a real good man. I need you. What I'm going to do for you I'd never do for anyone else. I wouldn't do this even for my friend Sam Grant, if he was in such a fix as you are."

Robbie's voice comes weak and quaky. "Thank y', Mister Quinn. You do...know how ... t' make a man feel...important. What y' aimin' to do?"

Need to explain this right, Paddy thinks.

"Picture me as an eagle. You're an eaglet, in the nest, can't fly. But I can go down and get you what you need... bring it up in my mouth... transfer it into yours. Just a *transfusion,*" he says, liking the aptness of the word. He's managed to explain it all without using the word *kiss*. He hasn't wanted to think that word, and he doesn't want Robbie to think it, either. The old fellow might be as squeamish about that thought as of the condom.

"Mister Quinn...That's about as... as *kindly* a thing as I ever heard of. I 'd be *so* thankful."

"Right, then!" Paddy prepares to go under for the bung. Before taking a deep breath, he says, "This round's on me, soldier."

He means it as a joking remark. But immediately he feels a bitter, sad sense of what the word "soldier" really means.

A soldier deserves every drink he can get.

*

Robbie's heart and soul had been so shut down by cold and misery he'd thought he'd never be able to feel *anything* ever again. He had been preparing himself to let loose of Mister Quinn's sleeve and give him the whiskey keg and with no goodbye or argument just slip down away into the deep cold dark water of the Mississippi and be done with it all finally. That would have made it so much easier for Mister Quinn.

But now this famous Irishman with all his troubles and worries and his angel wife just now snatched out of his life... this really *important* man, damned if he isn't going to risk drowning himself... just to get me a drink of whiskey!

What he said he wouldn't've done even for General Grant!

By God, Robbie tells himself, and the swelling in his heart is starting to make him cry, you just better try to be worthy of a friend like this.

A moment later he hears Paddy blow through his nose. He feels Paddy's hand touch his shoulder, his neck, now his cheek. He smells a hint of whiskey. And now he feels Paddy Quinn's mouth touch his and press on it. He opens his mouth and sucks, and the transfusion takes place . His mouth fills with whiskey, whiskey so unexpectedly powerful that he almost spews it, but, no, he mustn't spew the precious stuff, especially after what Mister Quinn has done to get it for him! When Paddy withdraws from the contact, Robbie tilts his head back, lets a little of it trickle down his throat, then the rest. It fumes in his bosom, it begins to burn in that icy darkness within him. "Ohhh, good!" he whispers.

And now he hears something he'd have thought he'd never hear again: Paddy is laughing.

"By God, didn't I tell you I'd get a drink into you?"

Rob himself isn't laughing, but he's smiling such a real smile that even in his cold-benumbed face he can feel it. Down inside, he feels life beginning to burn again. Off in the distance, from several directions, there are still voices audible over the gurgle and rush of the river.

A pity, Robbie thinks. Those poor souls don't have anything to drink.

"You need a couple more," Paddy says. "I've had way more'n you. Goin' down again..."

It's even easier this time, and the next. When Robbie has swallowed his third shot, Paddy says, "This next one's for me. Don't want t' get ye *too* tipsy."

"Deed not! Mister Quinn. I'm so much obliged... One thing, though..."

"What?"

"I am glad it's still dark. If y'know what I mean..."

"I do know. So we'd best get our drinkin' done before daybreak."

They both are feeling alive enough by now to smile at their joke.

*

Paddy is as content in himself as a grief-stunned man might be in such dire circumstances. If he and Robbie can just keep their hearts warm with whiskey for a while longer, they might still be alive when daylight brings boats and rescuers.

It might take many more swigs to sustain them. There's no sign of daybreak yet.

We might be squiffed to the gills by sunup...

Gills! Lord, give us gills!

Hey, I'll drink to that!

In their cold and exhausted condition, he knows, they'll burn it up fast as an alcohol wick and will have to keep refreshing themselves much more often than anyone would normally.

Nice to have such a good excuse!

He has no idea how much of it they've drunk, or how much is left in the keg. But he knows that the keg grows more buoyant with every mouthful they take. And the emptier the keg, the higher it will float. Maybe it'll get to floating so high that they can suck the bung without having to submerge their heads, at least not so deep. Then Robbie could get his own whiskey without the mouth transfusions.

Paddy has a rush of melancholy suddenly, remembering something, something from mere hours ago, though it seems like another lifetime:

On that steep street in Memphis, in front of the telegraph office, bending to kiss Felice on the lips, saying, *I'll never have a kiss for anyone but you.*

It's especially appropriate, then, that they've been calling these "transfusions." Not kisses.

CHAPTER TEN

Before the whiskey, the utter physical misery had kept him from thinking too much about the fate of Felice. Now, though, enormous tides of grief overcome him, he sees her die in flame, and he feels so crushed he can hardly breathe. When those spells pass, he is so weakened he almost slips away.

With the challenge of getting the whiskey solved, the tedium of endless floating in endless cold water and endless night numbs his mind and saps his spirit. One could yield up everything and slip off into oblivion.

Stay awake, damn it!

"Robbie!"

"Uh? What?"

"Stay awake."

"I am... Just thinkin' real hard."

"What about?"

"About how many... Reckon any still alive?"

"Some. I hear voices out there, now and again."

"I 've heard nary a one, for a long time. But I don't hear so well. In that prison, my head got so clogged up by th' cold, I'd be deaf for days... Glad you still hear some...."

Robbie falls quiet for a while, and Paddy knows he's awake only by feeling that he's still holding his sleeve. Keeping himself up on the escritoire is cramping Paddy's shoulder almost unbearably, and he's about to pass out from the pain when Robbie's quavering voice says, "More'n two thousand of us. And I bet not a hundred left."

"I pray you're wrong." But thinking of all he's seen, Paddy can't be very hopeful.

Two thousand souls gone all at once? That many sparks of life extinguished in a river?

Just two of us still alive only because Fate gave *us* alcohol to burn?

"I need another sip," he says. "May I get you one?"

"Please."

Felice's face tries to form in his mind but he refuses to let it, or to think of her name, and submerges again, concentrating on how not to drown himself.

*

"Aw, *shit,*" Robbie mutters, an eternity later.

"Aw, what?"

"I shit my britches. Only meant to make bubbles... "

Paddy offers no comment. Robbie releases his hold on Paddy's sleeve and struggles in the water, likely trying to get his trousers off. "'Scuse me while I do laundry. Can't stand filth! I was a year up t' my knees in diarrhea in that prison. No more. Ever!"

"Careful you don't drown wrestling out of those clothes," Paddy warns. He's remembering something from the Mexican War, nineteen years ago: One Irish deserter who couldn't swim but was determined to escape across the Rio Grande. Tried the old sailor trick for making a float out of trousers: knot the ankles, swoop the wet trousers through the air to make bladders of them. A practical device, but the poor sod drowned himself trying to take them off.

Robbie gasps and sputters in the darkness. Paddy holds his collar to keep him from floating away, and feels he has to keep talking to him. "In Mexico, my Ma ... seamstress... laundress with the Army, d' I tell you that? Said she...she washed 'nough blood and shit out of soldier c-c-clothes to color Lake Te-Texcoco maroon...'s how she said it..." He remembers that fear he'd had that Felice would find out somehow about his mother's past. He nearly starts crying over that thought, tells himself again not to think of Felice. He stutters on. "Ma was li...like you...woul'n' stand f...filth. Kept me patched, smellin' o...of soap..."

Robbie seems to be done with his rinsing and hangs on the keg, panting. Maybe he didn't even hear what Paddy had been telling, and Paddy now almost hopes not. But now Robbie says, "Your Ma a laundress? Lord... I took y' for high-born!...'f ye don't mind me sayin'...."

"I...*was* high-born, being that woman's son..."

If I get through this night alive, first thing to do is write her and tell her so. She'll need to know that as soon as she hears about the boat.

Have to tell her about Felice, too...

Thinking that, he can't talk for a while. Something big and soft bumps against his shoulder, startling him, then floats past, leaving a smell like entrails. His heart races faster and faster with horror until he has to force himself to stop thinking about what it might have been.

This whole river's full of the dead. Calm down. It's only meat.

Only meat. But the souls are in the river too.

He shudders so hard he groans.

Robbie's voice sputters in the darkness. "S'pose that alligator got loose? I....don't like... be in a river with... alligators."

Paddy thinks, but doesn't say:

You keep worrying about that...might keep you awake.

After a while, the current becomes very turbulent, and starts swinging him around and trying to suck him under. He hangs on to Robbie's shirt and kicks with his benumbed legs to keep his face above water. He keeps reminding Robbie to hang onto the keg. Eventually the roiling current smooths out to run swift and straight. He is almost totally used up.

Somewhere in the distance now he thinks he hears a sort of rumbling, under the swash and gurgle of the river. It might be the engine of a boat. He peers out as the water turns him, but can't see lights anywhere. Even if there are boats out looking for survivors, he knows, this flood is so vast he'd be lucky even to see their lights or smoke for a long time.

Time to go down and draw up another dose of heart-warmer. One for me, one for Robbie.

*

Paddy opens his eyes sometime later and thinks maybe it isn't quite so dark. Still not a star, not a lamplight, not a glowing steamboat anywhere, but, turning in the fast, cold, roiling water, still clutching Robbie's collar, he seems to see that in one direction, the blackness is fading. Feeling the current, seeing the grayness, he orients himself.

There's East.

Think so anyway.

It doesn't help to know the direction. He can't see whether he's nearer one shore or the other.

From the speed of the current, it seems like midstream. The *Sultana* was midstream when she blew.

This now is probably right in the middle of the Mississippi and it wouldn't make sense to try to swim toward either side. There might be trees or a bluff nearby, and if he started swimming he might head away from them instead of toward them...

He thinks what a comfort it would be just get hold of a treetop. In a tree, one could just simply hold the keg and bend down under and drink from the bung, no scare of drowning.

With just a little dawnlight, one could find treetops if they were nearby, and try to get into one.

Daylight would show *something*.

But he's not sure he wants to see that something. What he'd see would be death and wreckage. The darkness is merciful, it is.

Maybe it is. But we can't be found or find our way out in darkness. Need day.

A lifelong insomniac who has seldom ever gone to bed really sober, he finally begins to feel, even here in this dire plight, the perverse yen at dawn for the sleep he never wants at night.

Don't dare!

We've had enough whiskey we might forget to remember not to doze...

"You awake?" he rasps.

"Yu-hu-hu-huh," Robbie chatters.

This is that margin between oblivion and the present moment. This is where one comes blinking out of dreams and makes a feeble effort to remember them. Almost always in vain. This reality and that other one don't yield easily to one another.

He begins musing on his Great Theory. The one he'll make shockingly humorous speeches on, someday, in the Great Auditoriums of America.

Odium in the odeum.

"Why y' l-l-laughin'?"

"Well, see, here we are... afloat in everybody's dreams...It's like this. Running water's where all the dreams are...*All* the dreams."

After a while, Robbie mutters, "Not sure I follow y', sir."

"Well, see... when you wake up... you remember you've dreamed, don't you? Oh, wondrous dreams!"

"Usually, uh huh."

"Then you get up and piss. And when you try to remember what you were dreaming, you can't remember. Right?"

After a while, Robbie says, "That's so. Uh huh."

"So where did those glorious dreams go? Down with your piss. Into the pot...down the creek... into the river. Down that river, into the bigger river, into the sea. Get the idea, my friend?"

"Keep talkin'. I ain't quite there yet." Robbie's voice is shuddering. He needs another dose of the Fuel of Life.

"Everybody between the Alleghenys and the Rockies, they all pee in this river. This is...this is, by God, Robbie, this is the Sewer of Dreams! The Mississi pee pee i! Ha! . And here we are, you and I, up to our ears in it! Think of it!... The best of everything in man's intellect and imagination pissed away in th' morning...and we're floatin' along in it like a pair o' blissful turds!"

"By God if I ain't a blissful turd! And I never knew it! Hey, I'll drink to that!"

And as Paddy goes down to fill his mouth from the bung, he gets a notion that almost makes him forget how he needs to breathe:

Whiskey! It's made from Dreamwater Streamwater...and then distilled! No wonder it's like it is!

*

After the latest whiskey transfusion they float trembling and gasping for a long time in which it doesn't get any lighter. Once Paddy shuts his eyes for a while but keeps reminding himself that he cannot go to sleep. He feels a tug on his hand that is holding Robbie's collar, and hears a hard, quick groan. Robbie says, "O, God, oh! Oh, my gut's goin' bad..." Then a quick, loud gurgle. Paddy opens his eyes, afraid Robbie might drown, though he's still got him by the collar. Then as the current turns him he begins to see a light in the edge of his vision. He comes around and sees a small, glowing line far away. Tiny. Wider than it is high.

It could be a steamboat. But if it is, it must be two miles off. It seems to fade, then brighten, then it glides out of the corner of his other eye as he turns.

"What...what's it about your gut?"

"Hurts...like a...knife in it...Gone all slumpy... just spewed m' britches again...Damn I hate that!"

Paddy guesses that was the odd gurgle he heard. Gassy spews. That's what they'd sound like underwater, he thinks.

In me glorious Sewer of Dreams, O!

It's alarming to think how sick Robbie is. How can he even still be alive?

But no surprise. They've been in a cold river all night with no food since he can't remember when; nothing in their stomachs but river water and whiskey. That could play hell with anyone's gut. Especially of some poor sod who lived a year in a swamp of wormy stool.

My own gut could go any time now.

He expects Robbie to start through his britches-cleaning routine again, but the fellow isn't doing much of anything, just floating and now and then yielding a groan. When Robbie does speak, he sounds surprisingly jovial:

"I'm sure not adding any turds t' your pissy Mississippi...Not a turd in that load! Heh ha! Just poop soup...Almost felt good! ... Warm, sort of... Might try it again, felt so warm..."

As they turn in the current, the tiny line of light again comes into Paddy's margin of sight. It's sure a steamboat over there.

Though it could be the lights of Memphis.

Robbie's groans change. Damned if he isn't singing:

"Oh, oh, that pissy Missi-ssippi!..."

Actually a decent singing voice, amazing to hear after all the croakings and sputterings of the long night. Paddy recognizes the tune. He says:

"Hey, Robbie! Hey, sing me a song!"

"I'll sing y' any song ye like, Mis...Mister Quinn...'Cause y're the best man I ever met since I got in th' goddamn Army!"

"Likewise! Sing me th' one called 'Way Down Up!'"

"'Way Down Up?' Odd name. Don't know that one..."

Paddy is astonished. This scrawny half-cadaver with knots in his guts is returning to life enough for a songfest! Paddy croaks out a chuckle and says:

"The hell you don't know it, you were just singin' the tune! Way Down Up...on the Swanee River..."

"Oh! I was , wasn't I? Ha, ha! Well, hear this:

"Way down upon th' Pissysippi, fart, fart away..."

Paddy laughs, an actual laugh, declares, "Robbie Macombie, b'God, y're my kind of a man!" and then takes it up:

"All my shits are O so drizzly, ever'ywhere aroma..."

They sing as the black of night slowly leaches to gray, and manage to keep making each other laugh. They take turns remembering favorite songs, maudlin songs, inspirational songs, punning on them as they go, now and then risking the water torture to effect another whiskey transfusion. By these means Paddy fends off, time after time, the image of Felice vanishing in a fountain of flame. Once, between songs, Paddy remembers a thought to share with this greatest of all comrades:

"Abraham Lincoln floated down this very Missipissy River, long ago... He's been *right here."*

Robbie's voice goes solemn. "He did?"

"Sure as hell! Flatboated from Rockport in Indiana, with a cargo to sell in New Orleans. At least once." Paddy is pleased that he can remember so much about the life of the dead man they're going up to see...

God willing.

He thinks, looking around for another glimpse of boat lights on the flood:

We might see him yet. One can hope. Though in dire circumstances such as these afloat in the Sewer of Dreams one might tend to be Pissimistic...

CHAPTER ELEVEN

A man's voice from a distance comes over the swash of water, over the desperate hilarity of their drunken singing of The Bottle Hymn of the Republic. "Listen," says Paddy, opening his eyes, heartened by the sound of another living human voice after all these hours in cold wet Purgatory. The voice calls:

"God damn you sacrilegious fools! Shut up!"

Morning is just graying enough that when Paddy looks around, he can make out the difference between the water and the air above it, and he can see dark irregularities on the water. Something floating. Many somethings floating, some large, some small, but all too indistinct in the gloom to identify. The man's voice comes again, deep but with a strange, gargling quality:

"People are dead! Dying!"

Paddy calls back, "Sure they are! You, you all right? You got a good float?"

"No business of yours! Keep away!" the voice cries. Paddy thinks:

Nobody willing to share his float. They'll let others drown first.

"Come this way," Paddy calls. "Have a drink!"

The answer is silence for a long while, but the voice comes again, closer now: "Did you say a *drink*?"

"I know that voice, don't you?" Paddy says to Robbie. "Cap'n Elliott?" he calls.

"Who you? Who knows me in Hell?"

"Quinn. Macombie's here, too." He remembers that Captain Elliott's voice has that odd glottal quality due to an old bullet wound in the neck.

"By God! Quinn? And still drunk, from the sound of ye. How in Hell..". The voice is closer now, and where it's coming from Paddy can see a low, long dark shape on the water. Whatever the captain is floating on, it's much bigger than a desk or a keg. Paddy prays that it might be a bulkhead or maybe a floor section big enough for three men to sit on and hoist a whiskey keg up and just take turns drinking right out of the bung without having to dive for it The officer's feet are splashing water as he propels his flotation closer.

"Is your..." the voice comes again, "...I pray your Angel of Mercy's safe here with you?"

The question hits Paddy right under his heart like a mule kick and he thinks he'll die. After a while he groans and says, "No." This is a problem he hadn't expected to come with meeting another survivor downriver here. His comrade Robbie has been here with him all this time knowing of his loss and they've absorbed it together with the whiskey's help. Now here comes some fresh fool into earshot bringing her death back to life and it hurts so much he has to grind his teeth.

Captain Elliott is close enough now and the overcast sky is light enough to show that what he's floating on isn't big and broad, but something irregular like a length of driftwood. He says in a hesitant and fearful gargle, "Not with you?"

"Thank you for your prayer for my Angel of Mercy but it's too late."

You're one of those lucky people, he thinks, who didn't have to see her go aflame. You're outside of this kind of grief....

"Keep faith, Mister Quinn. She might be on a..."

"She's gone, Cap'n. Please drop the subject?"

"I...I..."

Paddy, in the flurry of thoughts and images this newcomer has stirred up, remembers the sight of Felice anointing this very man's neck, and remembers knocking him to the deck in a wrongly righteous rage. And since then they've interviewed and been gentlemen together. He has an absurd thought: All this cold water should help the bruises I gave him.

"You're sure she's..."

"Sure as hell, God damn it. Now just heave to and have a drink with us."

"Hello, Cap'n, sir," Robbie interjects in his shuddering croak of a voice. There's just barely enough morning gray to reveal the driftwood trunk the officer is on, and Robbie reaches over and gets a handhold on a root. Now they're linked together, like two vessels meeting in midocean and passing a lifeline across.

"Hello, soldier. You're the fellow from Saluda, aren't you? How you faring?"

"Still alive, sir... thanks be to Mister Quinn... But sick and drunk."

"Sorry I cussed you gents," said the captain. "After what-all's happened, I thought you were just too merry. Didn't imagine you had whiskey."

"Couldn't be merry without it," says Paddy. "Probably dead. Care for a snort? This is the only saloon open at the moment hereabouts. I remember you like rye."

"Oh, would I! Took three whole doses of quinine but they didn't do much for my shakes. Your lovely wife gave me the qui..."

Paddy overrides him loudly.

"Can that driftwood o' yours support a keg? A keg near empty, not too heavy..."

"We can try 'er."

As they struggle feebly to lodge the keg someplace where it'll stay balanced up on the root bole of the driftwood tree, the officer says, "I think some saboteur Reb got aboard with a bomb. D'ye think maybe so?"

"No. Bad boiler's all... And a captain so stupid greedy he ran with it."

"Y' don't think sabotage at all?"

Paddy shoves and wrestles with the keg, being careful not to let his fragile desk get punched or split by a protruding root. "No villain blew up that boat but its own master. Don't argue nonsense.." For a moment he remembers his own suspicion that Fanny Foremost, or Mrs. Willard, or whatever her real name was, might have brought a bomb aboard in her trunk, but he's past thinking it was anything but the boiler. He tells Ellott, "Please, tilt the log a little your way, and I think th' keg'll stay up." The three are breathing hard, groaning and splashing.

"I hear engines. You?"

"Now and then," says Paddy. "Way off. Saw one's lights a while ago."

"Some men got in treetops. Pray they can hold on 'til boats come. I had a word with a neighbor, a Tolbert. One you'd talked with." Paddy vaguely remembers that soldier, who had been through the whole war with a comrade-in-arms from the same Indiana town. Chin gnarled by a wound. But remembering is hard now. All the facts and details endure now only as written notes in his writing portfolio, this buoy strapped on his arm, this life saver.

Life saver like the whiskey keg.

They've got the keg lodged between two root protrusions now, and they begin trying to roll the log a few degrees to lift the keg out of water. It promises to be a delicate struggle. They still can hardly see what they're doing and are almost too weak and shaky to exert any force.

"Tolbert," Robbie gasps. "Cavalry...from Saluda... My family town... Maddox not with 'im in that tree?"

"Lost him in the explosion, he said..."

"Damnation." Robbie's voice sounds weaker and more depressed, and Paddy worries whether he'll still be alive when the boats come with daylight.

"By God, Robbie," he exclaims, "I do believe we got that bung up where we want it! You're the first thirst. Suck away, but leave us some!"

"Come to me, ol' oaken titty!" Robbie groans, and struggles in the roiling current to put himself in position, groping in the darkness to find the bung. After a long minute of bumping and gurgling noises, he emits a long sigh. "Oh, *thank* you!"

"Did you turn off the spigot?"

"Oops! Sorry! ... There."

"Have you court-martialed if you waste any," Paddy jokes. "Cap'n? Your turn."

It proves not so simple for the officer, who is on the opposite side of the log from the bung, and is straining to keep it from tilting back to its natural balance. When he releases his handhold to work his way around the log's end, it rolls slightly, and the keg slides off into the river, Robbie's fingers still on the spigot. It starts veering away in the swift water, taking him with it. Paddy hears him moaning with fear, lets loose of the log and tries to swim after him, to recover his hold on his collar or sleeve. There is just enough light now to see that the water is really turbulent here, swirling and swelling. A long, dark shape swings through Paddy's vision, probably a line of treetops, though still too vague in the gloom for him to be sure. Another swing around and he sees the distant lights of either a boat or of Memphis.

But he can't see Robbie. Paddy is alone again in the vast, cold river, numb except for the throbbing pain in his left shoulder where he has been lifted and pulled, forever it seems, by the buoyant writing desk. Somewhere in the distance he hears Captain Elliott calling from his ponderous driftlog:

"Where are you? Where'd you go?"

"Robbie!" Paddy calls with all the volume he can force from his quaking lungs. "Robbie! Let me hear you! Where are you? Let me hear you! Say something! Don't you even *think* of going away!" Robbie has been so ready to give up and slip down into the deep river, Paddy is afraid this separation will make him lose heart again and just end his misery. He knows Robbie has been at the very verge of his spirit for so long, he could just die at any time now.

"Robbie Macombie! Let me hear you!"

Surely he's not floated clear out of earshot this quick.

Maybe he's deliberately not answering because he doesn't want to try anymore and I make him keep trying.

"Answer me, damn you!"

There is no answer. Somewhere now Paddy can hear the engines of steamboats, more than one, it seems, as the sounds are coming from two different directions.

"Robbie! Hey! Answer me!"

I know what...

Paddy yells, "You promised you'd go with me to see Mister Lincoln, damn it!"

That ought to get an answer from him.

Paddy waits and listens, twirled round and round by the eddies. The darkness is fading enough that he can now see distant shapes that must be treetops. He can see indistinct shapes floating everywhere in the dismal grayness.

Come on, Robbie. Come back here with my whiskey.

Then he thinks:

That's mean.

"Robbie! You going with me to see Mister Lincoln?"

He hears only faraway steamboat engines. Sees lights maybe a mile away, toward what he takes to be the Tennessee shore, though the swirling currents confuse his sense of upstream or down. Next time the lights swing into his vision, he thinks he sees a dark plume of smoke above them.

"ROBBIE! MACOMBIE!"

Now Paddy feels like lead, heart sinking, face quivering, snot running. If he's lost Robb, the loss of Felice will come slamming back on him. The living presence of that good gray soldier, the drinking and the singing with him, has been like a buffer against the monstrous shock of that other loss. The notion of being alone with that despair is too frightful to bear. Better just to give up if you've lost your last living friend. His numb right hand is still cramped from its hours of holding Robbie's collar, but he aches to feel that sodden clutch of cloth again. The hand is too weightless without Robbie and that keg pulling on it. Now the only tug Paddy feels is his own weight attached to the buoyancy of his desk. What a relief it would be just to unbuckle the damned wet leather straps and let that damned thing go!

He dreams for a while of effortless, sinking oblivion.

In the River Lethe.

But he can't sink with this damned thing buoying him.

A box made to keep papers and pencils in...a box he made himself... the only thing left of his whole life and everything he's done...a box that won't sink or let him sink unless he opens it...

Paddy doubts he has enough strength left to unbuckle or pull his arm out of the wet leather straps. But opening the hasp would be easy. He could just pry it up with his thumb and lift the lid. Lethe would fill the box and down he'd sink, papers lifting away and drifting away in the dark water, ink dissolving, all that writing gone...diary, letters, notes for future lectures...all those words the soldiers told him about surviving the war and the prison, all their stories dissolving into Lethe along with his own memories of a life of wars...

Then there'd never be another thing I'd ever have to do anymore...

But he remembers that there's one other thing in this box: The pencil sketch of Felice bathing. And, not being ink, it wouldn't dissolve off the paper. It might float in the river until someone found it and gazed at it and saw his name and hers on it.

That mustn't happen.

He doesn't really know *why* that mustn't happen, just that it mustn't.

So he flexes his shoulder with a groan and twists his neck to move the pain around a bit, rests his left cheek against the lid, shudders so hard it wrings a sob out of him, and keeps trying to stay alive..

Hail Mary full of grace the Lord is with Thee; blessed art thou among women and Blessed is the fruit of thy womb, Jesus...

Say it out loud, you damn backsliding ninny!

"Holy Mary... M-Mother of God, pray...for us sin-sinners now and at...at the hour of..."

"Hey! Hey!"

"...at the hour of our..."

"Hey there, Mister Quinn!" The voice is faint, but nearby.

"What? That you, Robbie?" Hardly any voice left now that he really needs it. He sucks air in and croaks: "Say something... so I can hear... where you are!"

"I"m in this damn river, know that!"

Paddy's heart is starting to frolic in his cold chest. Mirth rising. He says:

"River, eh? Which river'd...that be, eh? The Lethesippi?"

He shakes, half-laughing, half-crying. His legs are so numb he can only presume they're responding as he tries to propel himself in the direction where he thought he'd heard that voice.

Lethesippi...

He doesn't know if Robb would even get the allusion. It doesn't matter. He just needs to get to him.

"Robbie, I need a drink, I'm bone-chilled...Bring me my keg... soldier, and I'll make ye famous..."

But he almost panics now, knowing how much stronger the turbid currents are than even a strong swimmer, afraid that in their feebleness he and poor Robbie probably can't get back together unless the Mississippi chooses to rejoin them...

The Mississippi or maybe God in the Mississippi...

And now he sees a shape in the grayness not ten feet away, and the shape says, "I see ye, Paddy Quinn! I see ye there...Come reach me a hand..."

In a burst of joyous eagerness, Paddy strokes with his arm and kicks with his legs , struggling toward him. It's good to have enough light finally to see what he's swimming for. It's a rounded dark shape on the water, the keg, with a smaller, lighter shape just next to it: Robbie's gray head, the head of that old sick exhausted soldier who well should be dead by now, but somehow isn't. How has he clung by mere fingertips to that keg all these hours!

But despite their exertions Robbie seems now to be moving farther away instead of getting closer. Maybe because he's lighter than Paddy, and the keg's so empty by now that it's more buoyant than the little writing desk, the current seems to carry him faster.. Paddy croaks, "Swim, damn you, Robbie! Come this way!"

"Doin'... my best..."

I pray you, damn river! Stop playing with us and bring my friend here!

And he wonders if he's gone fully crazy, praying to a river.

But as if complying, the currents now swirl him to his right, turning him full circle to come jarring against a hard object which he sees at once to be the whiskey keg. As the keg moves by, there is good old Robbie Macombie hanging onto it, looking the other way. Paddy flails out with his right arm and grabs for him. The edge of His hand touches Robbie for an instant, but gets hold of nothing. He hears Robbie utter a startled "Eh!" And then Paddy feels a tug on his own coat sleeve. Robbie has reached out and caught him.

For a moment they float together without a word, just gasping. Paddy prays, to God or the river:

Thank you.

Then he seizes the shoulder of Robb's threadbare, baggy shirt and twists his clenched fist into it as if to make a permanent hold.

"Wish this could be a hug, old boy," he rasps.

"Uh *huh!*"

The eddies are so strong now that the two men feel as if they're being whirled apart. The force is so powerful that Paddy fears Robbie's shirt will just tear off in his fist. As the two swing about like a pair of dancers, they bump against things just under the water or at the surface, and it is now light enough to see that they are in a floating graveyard of corpses: here one in dark clothing, there one in a loose, billowing shroud of pale cloth that must be a dress or a gown, here a wan, thin, naked body with dark hair, there something human-shaped but its skin all in tatters...

Another burnt one, Paddy thinks, and suddenly it all returns to him, the fiery catastrophe that hurled them into this cold, wet purgatory and burned up his wife, so long ago it seems like a historic age.

That last thing could be Fe...

He begins shaking and shuddering as if in a mortal fit, eyes squeezed shut, feeling so compressed he can't draw breath, until Robbie speaks:

"I'd... plumb given up us goin' to... Mister Lincoln's funeral. Sure glad t' see you!"

Paddy at last can inhale. "Let's drink to that," he gasps. I'll drink to that I'll drink to that I'll...

CHAPTER TWELVE

The pain in Paddy's left shoulder sharpens until it forces him awake.

To his astonishment, he isn't cold and wet, but warm and dry. He lies supine on a soft mattress, feels bedding over him, feels the vibrations of an engine, though he hears nothing. His mouth and nostrils feel raspy and and raw, his nose is running, and his head aches and feels as big as a pumpkin, his legs and feet feel aflame. He realizes that he is naked. And that his writing desk isn't on his arm.

What in Hell?

He opens his eyes, and though his vision is blurred he can see that he's in a small room with white window curtains and red wallpaper, that he's lying on one narrow bunk, under another. This can mean only one thing: he's in a passenger cabin on a steamboat. A vague figure in white stands beside his bunk.

In a moment it comes to him: That he's in his stateroom on the *Sultana.* That the horrible explosion and the night in the water were only a nightmare! He gasps with the sense of relief. Heart racing, he tries to blink away the foggy vision and look at Felice, the figure in white beside his bunk.

But the figure standing beside him is not Felice. It's a slim man with a black face and white hair.

The man is holding an armful of folded white cloth and gazing out the window. On the floor across the room there is Paddy's desk, its wet leather straps hanging down. The desk sits on top of a small oaken keg. Now it comes to him that although he can feel the familiar tremor of steam engines under him, he isn't hearing them.

"You," he says to the man. Saying the word hurts his throat, but he doesn't hear himself speak.

But the black man jerks, turns to face him, bends closer and looks into his face. The black man's mouth opens and his red lips move, but Paddy can't hear what he's saying.

The man sets the armload of cloth on the bunk by Paddy's knees, takes a white kerchief off of it and holds it toward Paddy's face, again saying something he can't hear.

What? Wipe my nose? His mother had done just that when he was a snot-nose boy.

Paddy takes the kerchief, and the mere grasping of it hurts his hand. All his knuckles ache. He wads the cloth under his nose and blows. He hears a squeak in one ear and a pop in the other. He blows again, hearing squeaks. Now his head feels like a smaller pumpkin.

And now he can hear the engines, can hear excited voices and shouts outside the cabin, and can hear the Negro's voice saying:

"...Lord watched over *you*, sah! Eh, I go fetch the Mate. He ast me tell 'im when you come awake."

"Wait. Wait... What's going on out there?"

The man rolls his eyes. "They fishin' up drown people, sah. Hunneds o'm. We got carcasses caught in our paddlewheels, tha's when we first learn 'bout you boat. Mercy!"

So it wasn't a dream after all. Oh, God!

"Wait. There was a man with me... Older. White whiskers. Did he..."

The Negro smiles and glances up at the upper bunk.

"He sleepin' one off, um? You two was in a treetop singin' and cryin'. Now I go get th' Mate, sah." He pats the cloth bundle he'd put on the bunk. "Dry clothes 'ere if y' 'cide t' git up."

"Wait. What boat is this? Where's it headed?"

"*Belle of Memphis*, sah. Goin' to Saint Louie. But first got to turn back down t' Memphis. Hospital."

"Hospital? Some still alive, then?"

The Negro shakes his head and looks at the upper bunk. "You'n him, sah."

Oh, God.

*

How sweet it had been for that moment to believe it had been nothing but a nightmare and that he had awakened from it.

So he shuts his eyes to try again. He remembers being cold in the water and cold in his heart because he saw Felice die. He can't stand seeing and feeling all that, so he opens his eyes again. For certain now, it wasn't dreamed. He is, no doubt about it now, alive. On another boat. Rescued.

And Robbie rescued too. He wants to get up and look in the bunk overhead and see that Robbie really is there. But one effort to move a leg makes him doubt he can get up. Feels as if every bone and joint has been heated in a forge and beaten with a hammer.

Good God! Should be dead by now!

His lungs feel squashed. Drawing a breath is hard. Everything hurts. Feet hot, and his hand feels inflamed. He wonders whether he might have been burned in the explosion, and tries to raise his hand to look at it in daylight and see if it's burned.

It's not. But just raising it has hurt his whole side, his shoulder, his neck.

"Robbie! You awake?"

No answer. Voices still coming from outside the cabin, but too muddled by the roaring in his head to make sense. He wads the handkerchief and blows his nose again, ears popping and squeaking.

"Robbie, y' damn bung-sucker, wake up if you're alive, and tell me so!"

No reply.

Paddy doesn't want to lie here alone and think of what happened to Felice. During the long night in the river, just keeping Robbie alive and having him to talk to had made it bearable, had kept it from crushing him utterly.

Kept each other alive is what we did.

He wonders how Robbie could even have stayed alive through that night, weak as he'd been from Andersonville.

He's so quiet up there he might be dead.

"Wake up, damn you!"

All he hears is a shout from out on the deck somewhere:

"Shit! His skin's comin' off!"

*

Nothing left but...but what?

Nothing left but what I've got to do.

And that would be?

What I was doing.

He seems to remember that the black servant who'd been in here had gone off to get somebody – the mate, he said. – but nobody's come.

Too busy fishing up corpses. Sure and that's it.

Going back to sleep would be the best thing to do, but he can't. What he feels in himself now, aside from the worst pain and exhaustion ever, is that trotting-heart insomnia he's lived with all his life, through war after war.

Only thing good for it is liquor.

Like when he was with General Grant.

We had that demon in common, didn't we? And we both knew it.

Sometimes when Paddy Quinn couldn't bear to do anything, one thing he could do was get liquor.

Keg's right over there. Maybe we left some in it. Wish that darky'd come back. I'd have him pour me one. Then I bet I could move. But he's not back. Have to get it yourself.

He takes a deep breath, though that hurts and makes him cough, and the coughing hurts more. He struggles to sit up and let his feet to the floor. That hurts still more, and knocks the clean clothes off the bunk. Bending to pick them up would hurt even more, so he leaves them there, reaches up to grasp the rail of the upper bunk with his right hand, and with an effort so painful it makes him gasp, pulls himself to a standing position. His weight on his feet creates such a pain in them that it makes him forget the pain in his shoulder. For a moment everything in the cabin blanks out as is he were in a blizzard, but after a few breaths he can see again.

He turns to see Robbie in the upper bunk, and there he is, looking like an old man's corpse in a coffin, head on a pillow, mouth agape. The corpse snorts and shuts its mouth, so Paddy knows Robbie's alive.

The cabin is so narrow, Paddy can touch the other wall with the stump of his left arm and thus steady himself in order not to fall when he lets go of the bedrail. He stands there naked and woozy and racked with pain for a minute or so, then reaches down for the wet leather straps of his arm-desk. It feels so heavy he's afraid its contents must have gotten wet. He swings it over onto his bunk and turns back to the task at hand, which is getting to the rye whiskey. He knows he'll have to get the keg up onto his bunk so he can put a glass under the spigot. For a moment it all seems to be too daunting. The oaken keg, even if it's almost empty, will be heavier than his desk. And he doesn't even know if there's a glass or a cup in this cabin. He stands looking around for one. He can still hear footsteps, shouts, and bumping and scraping noises outside on the deck. His legs feel so weak he thinks they'll fold under him.

On a shelf above the wash stand there is a white china cup.

That find gives him the fortitude he needs to deal with the keg. It's going to be a major job. It will be not just heavy, but awkward. With only one hand, he'll have no way of hoisting it onto his bunk except by grasping the bung and swinging the keg up and sideways. With his shoulder in this condition, that's going to hurt. He considers instead just waiting until somebody comes to lift it for him. But he really doesn't want to wait. It could be a long time before anybody comes. From the sound of it, everybody on this steamboat is plenty busy getting who knows how many corpses out of the river.

He tells himself:

You got whiskey to Sam Grant when there was a man specially assigned to keep it away from him.

You got whiskey from this keg floating in the river. This can't be any harder than that. Come on.

"Nnnng!"

A blinding flash of extreme pain, clenched teeth, and then a loud wooden clunking and banging sound. "Oh, shitdammit!"

He finds himself tottering off balance with just the bung in his hand. The keg tumbles on the wood floor, whiskey sloshing out. The lifting has jerked the spigot right out of the bung hole. Before he can move, the keg rolls against his bare ankle and knocks his footing out from under him.

Paddy hits the hard floor flat on his left side, rearranging every pain in his body. His first instinct is to keep the remaining whiskey from running out. He's aware that he's lying naked in a puddle of it, an experience even he has never had before. Quick as he can move, he grabs the rolling keg and halts it while the bunghole is up. He sits up, groaning. He sticks the wooden bung back into the bunghole, gives it a painful thump with the heel of his hand to wedge it in, then grabs it and tilts the keg up to stand on end beside the bunk.

The whiskey-spill crisis averted, he sits groaning, looking down at the ridiculous sight his bare body is: legs white as paper with reddish hair, the skin flaking, apparently from so long in the water. They look scrawny, with knots of sinew for calves. His legs had always been long and well-muscled; Felice once had told him during one passionate moment of the honeymoon that they were like young oaks, he remembers with a clenching heart. Can he have lost so much flesh from just one night in cold water?

Everyplace on his hips and torso he is now utterly fatless and slack-skinned like an old man, with an itchy scurf behind his knees and on his feet. His organ and scrotum in their sporran of red hair look normal but feel raw, probably from the hours of soaking and chafing in the watery ordeal.

If I'm down so far, what must be left of poor old Robbie, who looked like a cadaver even before?

Only two things he can think of will alleviate this dead-fish image of himself.

Cover up the outside with clothes and get some of that whiskey inside.

He decides on the whiskey first, then the pile of cotton clothes on the floor. It'll be easier to dress if he can just benumb these aches a wee bit.

And then he'll have to take a look at that desk that saved him and see whether he can save what's in it.

If water got in and ruined it, I don't want to be all sober when I see it.

Just the scent of the whiskey he's sitting in gives him strength for his next moves.

First he has to stand up. It hurts, but he does it. Then he grasps the bung again, tilts the keg over, and puts the stump of his left forearm under it, carefully lifts it and lays it on its side on the bunk. Now he has to stand holding the upper bedrail for a moment until a white blindness passes.

Now he limps a couple of steps to the shelf, and gets the cup, comes back and puts it on the floor directly under the spigot. He twists the petcock and is immensely pleased and excited to see the thin stream of whiskey obediently and neatly run right into the cup. It's a weak stream, meaning there's not much left in the keg, but he's glad they did leave some after last night.

Must've lost a quart when I dropped it. Damn!

While whiskey drains into the cup, Paddy looks at the two wooden objects he's put on his bunk: square desk, round keg. One containing words on paper, one rye whiskey.

Both life preservers.

O so true!

Ink and whiskey.

What you need when you're tired of all the blood.

When the cup is half full he turns off the spigot, and bends to pick up the cup. His hand is shaky, and so numb he can't tell whether his finger's through the handle. And now his knees are going wobbly and hurting too much. He's going to have to do this sitting down. So he rolls the keg aside, turns around to sit on the bunk between it and the desk, then bends down and picks up the cup from between his feet.

I can remember when taking a drink of whiskey was so easy you didn't even have to think.

At least I won't risk drowning myself for this one.

It's strange, suddenly remembering now how hard and frightful it was figuring out how to drink whiskey in the river. The recollection gives him a mighty chill. Now too he remembers having to go down and get mouthfuls to transfuse to Robbie. He feels as if he's about to cry.

Don't think; drink.

Good motto.

He picks up the cup with trembling hand. The sloshing whiskey is as turbulent in the cup as was the roiling river that had swirled them around all night willy nilly and had sucked so many down to drown. He remembers Robbie being twirled away and lost for a while, he and the keg. Now lifting the cup under his nose and smelling the magical pungency, he remembers calling for Robbie, and suddenly finding him. He raises his eyes to the underside of the upper bunk, and says:

"Want a drink, Rob? Answer now, or this one's mine."

No answer from the sleeper. Now, conscience clear, Paddy puts the cup to his lips and sips, swallows, sips again.

"God damn! Bphphphph!" In his parched and swollen gullet, the rye is hotter and more caustic than anything he's swallowed within memory. He gasps, tears in his eyes, and shudders. The spirits explode like a bombshell in his gut, bending him over.

But damned if he'll vomit it up. He takes two or three lung-racking breaths, clenches his teeth, then has a longer sip, nearly draining the cup.

Now by Saint Patrick I'll be human again. Give me a minute...

As it settles in and begins refilling him with the feeling of being alive, something crosses his mind, a fleeting something...

San Patricios

What's become of my medal?

For that matter, where's my wallet? My damn clothes?

He won't know until the servant comes back. Or the mate. Or whoever.

He sips what's left in the cup. His gut feels like a volcano now.

Better be a chamberpot in this room someplace!

There is. Under the edge of the bunk. Just in case he'll need it. So far, he doesn't. He maneuvers the keg and tries to refill the cup. It's a mere trickle now. Almost gone. An empty keg and he doesn't know where his wallet is. He takes another sip. Now he's ready to proceed to whatever seems to be next.He bends to look at the stack of clothes. Cotton shirt, full sleeves, no collar. Pair of cotton drawers with waist ties to make them fit. Not that he can tie a knot easily, with just one hand. But he can if he has to. Cream-colored linen summer trousers, and a pair of white cotton socks. All plain but clean. He gets all the clothes on, pausing between items for sips of the rye. He looks at Robbie from time to time and sees that he's still breathing.

Just as well let him sleep. No whiskey left for him.

Paddy rubs his dry palms over his face, all paper-dry, raspy. He sits with head forward, taking long, slow, painful breaths, each deep breath provoking a spasm of phlegm-moving coughs. He breathes a little easier after each fit, but the handkerchief is sodden. He blinks, squints dry eyelids tight shut and opens them. Blows into the handkerchief a few more times, and with each effort his hearing gets better. He can hear voices everywhere outside the room, can hear the modulations of engine speed as the boat is maneuvered about on the flood. Paddy isn't ready yet to go part the curtains and look out at what must be a stew of wreckage and corpses.

Even Felice's remains might be....

Can't think on that.

He shakes his head. No. He will not think of her except alive and in her full beauty. A grim thought begins to run in his head: Maybe half the people he ever knew in his life he's eventually seen as corpses, shot dead or blown up, or dead from diseases. He just will not see Felice that way. Not in reality nor in imagination. She is too beloved to see as a corpse.

He has yet to see another beloved face dead. Lincoln. Remembers Lincoln smiling at him and winking. He has the yet unfulfilled duty of seeing him as a corpse. That will be hard enough. Not Felice. She will never be a corpse in his memory.

Paddy pulls the desk onto his lap, and rubs the damp wood for a minute with his fingertips, marveling at the thought that this box kept him afloat all night long, that if he hadn't strapped it on before the explosion, he would himself surely be one of hundreds of corpses in the Mississippi by now. He remembers the dozens of Andersonville veterans whose pencil portraits and interview notes are in this box, and who in the last few hours have become the most recent of his countless friends and acquaintances who are no longer alive.

Only one of those poor bastards I know to be still alive is Robbie up there.

With a silent, quick prayer, he thumbs open the latch and tries to pry up the lid. It resists. Its rubber lining is wet and sticky, and the wood itself swollen. His fingertips are tender and it hurts to try to pry at the lid. He repositions his hand to hold a corner of the box with his fingers and push up on the lid with his thumb.

I need a damned oyster knife!

But it hisses and gives way, a hair's-breadth at a time.

Everything in here might be ruined, you know.

I know, damn it, I know!

Now the lid is fully open and he looks in.

Thank God!

There is no water in the box.

There lie jumbled the notebooks, the inked pages, the pencil sketches, his diary, just a little bit damp to the touch, all in disarray from the violence of the night before, but nothing wet or smeared.

All that he had nearly worked himself to death to record in those long, whiskey-fueled interviews day and night aboard the *Sultana*, it is all intact. He has everything he needs for his Andersonville story, all of it dramatic enough before, now tragically moreso...

He lifts out sheets and notebooks and lays them out flat on the bunk, smoothing them with his hand, seeing the sketches of those gaunt veterans, and one of the first is that of Robbie Macombie, looking like Da Vinci's self-portrait.

But all those others are probably dead now. All but Robbie.

And now up comes a picture that twists his heart in his bosom: that hastily-made sketch of Felice bathing. He remembers her consternation on seeing it.

Paddy looks at it, vision blurring with tears.

If only I'd posed her for a portrait!

He could have, should have, made a sketch of her face, not just her backside.

He had intended to draw her portrait eventually. But in the enchantment of their honeymoon, he had deemed it too early to try to capture her singular beauty. He had thought it better to wait and draw her after becoming familiar with all her moods, after seeing her in every kind of light, all the variations of her smile. Then he could have drawn the best portrait he'd ever done.

But she just didn't live that long.

Paddy sits on the bunk with the sketch of her graceful nudity on his lap, but not seeing it. Instead he is seeing in his memory the face he should have portrayed when he had his chance.

I can draw her face from memory.

Will maybe when I can stand to.

From the time he was an errand boy in the Army camps, he had been able to draw a person's likeness from memory, after seeing that person just a few times. In Mexico he had drawn Ulysses Grant as a 24-year-old lieutenant fresh from West Point, and had done it from memory. He had drawn Braxton Bragg and Lew Wallace, Zachary Taylor and Winfield Scott, after seeing them three or four times. He had sketched President Lincoln winking and smiling after seeing him only twice: once in Illinois before he had a beard, then that one time in Washington. Surely he could yet draw Felice, though it would be harder because he loves her and she is dead now. Felice had said she'd been photographed only once in her life, just once before their wedding portrait, and Paddy has never seen that picture. She had told him that he would see it when they went to St. Louis to meet her parents. She had said they kept it in a shiny frame on the mantel in their parlor.

I could draw her face without seeing that picture. But I want to see it.

He knows that's another terrible duty he has to do. Somehow he will have to go to the Beaulieus' home in St. Louis and tell them their daughter died, without last rites, on the *Sultana*. That is such a morose prospect that he almost regrets surviving.

That and the President's funeral. It's almost too much an onus to bear.

All the yet undone things begin crowding up in his mind now. If anything is found of Felice, he'll have to arrange a decent burial.

He'll also have to telegraph his mother in New Orleans that he's alive and Felice isn't.

He'll have to telegraph Alfred Guernsey at *Harper's* and forewarn him of this tragic new face of the story, and finagle some more expense advance out of him.

And somehow he must get poor Robbie Macombie to Abe Lincoln's funeral, and then home, even if he has to push him in a wheelchair or carry him pick-a-back.

And then immediately he will need to plunge into the huge task of writing and illustrating the most pathetic tragedy he's ever written in a whole lifetime of conflicts.

All this to be done within the next few brief days by a man who just spent a long night expecting he would never live to do another single thing!

What a time to be out of whiskey!

Paddy puts all the papers back in the desk, praying brief thanks for their miraculous deliverance, and shuts the lid. He stands, turns around with aches pulsing in every bone and muscle, and coaxes out another half cup by tipping the keg on the edge of the mattress and holding it there until not one more drop will dribble out.

He straightens himself and stands with the cup in his hand, looking at old Robbie who still sleeps gape-mouthed, gurgling and wheezing on the upper bunk. Looks at his profile a long time, at the gaunt head on the pillow, a skull with thin dry skin on it, like a whitened mummy.

"Well, Robbie, God's saved me life many a time, but you're the only *man* who ever did. I guess that makes you the best friend I ever had. Such a good friend, in fact, that I'd give you my very last dram of whiskey, if ye'd wake up and take it."

Robbie shuts his mouth and seems to be licking his teeth, eyes still shut. "I'm awake," he croaks.

"Damn! Wouldn't y' know it! All right, but y'll have to sit up and drink it like a man. I'm not going to give you a mouth transfusion ever again. You can sit up, can't you?"

"God only knows, Mister Quinn."

"Well, try, or I drink this m'self. And God only knows how, but you and I crossed the River Lethe alive, and we're safe on another boat. You ready to make another run for Mister Lincoln's wake?"

"I reckon that's what I'm still alive for...Nnng!" He is straining to get up onto his elbows.

Paddy sets the cup down on the lower bunk and puts his palm under Robbie's shoulders to help him up. The man is nothing but bones and Paddy wonders where he found strength to make it through last night.

Now he's sitting up. Paddy lifts the cup and places it in his skeletal hands.

"Try to keep it down. It's the last of it, from our... our Keg of Life."

Robbie puts the cup to his mouth, takes the most cautious sip, then swallows. He convulses twice, falls sidewise and spews frothy vomit over the side of the bunk. At that moment the cabin door opens and there stands a burly, square-faced man with muttonchop whiskers and the black coat and cap of a boat's officer. His nose crinkles, his brow lowers as he smells the reek of the little room and sees the two pale wretches hanging on the rail of the top bunk, sees the keg and desk on the bottom bunk, and now sees the pine floor slick with spilled whiskey and vomit. "Shee-ut," he growls. "*Yankees*!"

"Um, hate to tell ye, Skipper," says Robbie. "This Yankee just pissed your bedding, too. Sorry."

*

The waterfront at Memphis is now an outdoor morgue. Corpses lie in rows on the planking of the docks, some covered with sheets and tarpaulins, many still not. Every sort of boat, from Army packets and sidewheelers and sternwheelers down to rowboats and canoes, is unloading still more shabby, burned and sodden carcasses. And a few living survivors are being helped or carried ashore. Wagons and carriages come down and return up the steep street, bringing stacks of pale new wooden coffins down, hauling sick and hurt men up to the hospitals. Much of the town's population prowls the docks and streets, carrying blankets, pitchers, food baskets, clothing and stretchers. Many of these samaritans hold handkerchiefs over their faces as they work.

Paddy Quinn and Robbie Macombie watch all this morose activity from chairs on the main deck of the steamboat *Belle of Memphis*, as the vessel stands off waiting for a berth space to open along the docks. Paddy is still too weak and painful to stand at the rail long, and Robbie can't stand at all. Both are back in their own clothes, such as they are, wrinkled and damp. While the *Belle* was picking up corpses upriver, the clothes had been wrung out and hung in the boiler room to dry. The boat's clerk had conscientiously kept Paddy's wet wallet for him, and the gold San Patricios medallion also, much to Paddy's relief. He feels the medallion in his pocket with his fingertips. He thinks he would give up this treasure if it would bring back McGinty and O'Hara who presented it to him. But it won't, he knows. He saw the smokestacks come down smashing and scorching the superstructure where they slept. For a moment Paddy sings in his head the tune of The Bottle Hymn that the soldiers had made up in tribute to the barkeeps. It makes his dry eyelids sting.

Paddy wears his own shoes, which are still wet, but Robbie is barefooted. He had lost his shoes in the river while struggling to get out of his soiled trousers. But he won't be needing shoes for a while yet, as he's too feeble and sick to walk. Somehow Paddy will have to obtain a wheelchair for him when they get put ashore. The mate, despite his disgust at finding them whiskey-soaked, bepuked and pissy in their stateroom, was glad he had saved them, and was hospitable enough to have the Negro bring them from the galley a very good beef broth, which they'd managed to keep down, and then some chicory coffee with cream and sugar, just the kind Paddy had learned to love in New Orleans, the only non-alcoholic thing he likes to drink. But the mate had refused to bring them any whiskey. "We're too busy to keep mopping up after you Yankees," he had explained in a stern tone.

The *Belle of Memphis* has altered schedule and won't be going back up the river for another three days, but there is at least one steamer leaving upriver tomorrow, and when Paddy hears the name, his heart seems to jump up: The *St. Patrick!*

Paddy has dreaded starting again up the swollen Mississippi on another steamboat, after what happened to the *Sultana,* but the name *St. Patrick* is an almost magical reassurance. Paddy remembers how he had to overcome his intuition that morning in New Orleans on first seeing the *Sultana* and thinking *Tub of Doom.* If he had heeded that ominous feeling that morning, Felice would still be alive.

But now he's happy to be a bit superstitious. He scribbles a note, the first writing he has done since their rescue:

> *I am an honorary San Patricio. I have their gold medallion in my pocket, given to me by McGinty and O'Hara, rest their souls. I'm an Irishman. A boat named the St. Patrick is a Godsend and her decks are sure to be as safe as terra firma!*

Robbie, who is probably just as frightened as anybody about getting on another steamboat, might be relieved to hear about the name of *St. Patrick* when Paddy explains it to him. They have their promise to fulfill to each other, to go and see Father Abraham, and they have to be in Springfield, Illinois before the third day of May. Four short days of travel by steamboat and train, hundreds of miles yet to cover. There is just no time to lose by getting on an unlucky boat. The *St. Patrick* is bound to be lucky.

*

The deathly scene on the docks is rendered even more dismal by the peculiar quality of the daylight -- an overcast brightened by the midday sun above it – and Paddy's eyes are so dry his eyelids feel like blanket wool. He must squint and blink to see much.

Farther forward along the deck of *The Belle,* near the gangplank, there lie the dozens of corpses the vessel's crew pulled from the river this morning, some so scalded and mutilated that they're been covered with bedsheets. And there are, in deck chairs or lying on cots, about a dozen survivors, none of whom Paddy recognizes. They were pulled up still alive later in the morning, after Paddy and Robbie were rescued from their treetop perch, that lifesaving treetop that Paddy can't even remember.

As for the other wooden lifesavers that had kept them from perishing , Paddy's desk is at his left beside his chair, but the empty whiskey keg is gone, carried away by the Negro when he cleaned up their cabin. Paddy had thought at first that it might be a good souvenir for Robbie. But it's going to be hard enough to transport Robbie himself, without toting a heavy, now-useless oaken keg, regardless of its sentimental value. Now that they're rescued, a bottle at a time will suffice. Paddy's expensive flask, the one that he'd carried throughout the war, must now be somewhere in the vast brown flood, along with his luggage and Felice's trunk.

And Felice too.

He squeezes his eyelids shut and puts his chin down on his chest and he hears a high, whining little sound coming up through his own throat, coming up from his chest where his heart hurts just too much to bear.

I wanted to be worthy of her. What'll I have to live up to now?

Then he thinks:

Where she is she can see everything. Keep an eye on me. Now I can't sneak into a saloon or go behind a door and make an unworthy ass of myself.

He can't remember ever having that thought about anyone before: that someone might watch him from the other side. Although as many as half the friends he ever had are now dead, he has never thought any of them would be monitoring him from beyond.

But of course I wasn't married to them. I wasn't in love with them. I loved some of them but I wasn't in love with anyone but Felice.

He remembers a dream he had not many nights ago. The dream begins coming back in images:

He's before an audience of all the people of the world. In Cooper Union, but illimitably vast. All the people whom he knew before they died were sitting in rows of chairs behind him. He gets a feverish prickling sensation in his temples as he remembers that dream. It's odd that he remembers a dream he'd already forgotten. What does this do to his pet theory that all dreams trickle away in the first piss of day?

He tries to recall more of that dream. He senses that it was full of portent. Among the dead in his audience was President Lincoln; that image comes up in his memory. He shudders, remembering:

Felice came in and sat in the row of chairs with the dead, didn't she?

But it's all fading away again, disturbed by the hubbub of the docks, and by the building engine noise of a steamboat. He sees that a sternwheeler is churning water, pulling away from the dock. Now the *Belle of Memphis* can pull in and tie up and he can get off and get Robbie to the attention of a doctor and get himself to the telegraph office. The dream has gone away now, but it haunts him with an aching sadness so powerful he's not sure he'll be able to rise and do all the things he needs to do.

He dreads being led to any small charred corpse and having to say whether it's hers.

He's already vowed he'll never see her as a corpse.

*

Paddy and a Negro porter, one on each side, walk Robbie down the gangplank onto the dock.

Paddy leaves Robbie sitting on an empty coffin and, himself able to walk only with great pain and weariness, shambles down the dock, to see if he can book their passage on the *St. Patrick*. The boat's clerk looks him up and down, noting the writing desk under his handless arm, and says, "You one of them from the *Sultana*?"

"That I am."

The clerk gazes at him with what looks like a desire to ask many questions, but instead just says, "Congratulations. You made it."

"Barely. Sir, we need to get up to St. Louis as quick as we can. My friend down there needs to see a doctor and I need to send some telegrams, but soon as that's done, we have to start back up. I hope to God you've got a cabin, because he needs a bed. But if you have nothing but deck passage, we'll just have to settle for that."

"I have a cabin. You're in luck, sir."

"I expected luck, with a name like *Saint Patrick*."

When Paddy returns to Robbie, he sees a small, bald gentleman in a brown suit standing by him, talking to him. The man, his accent indicating he's a local, tells Paddy he is taking needful survivors up the Soldiers' Home, and points out to the street where there sits a two-horse buggy with seats for six passengers. Four wretches are already in the vehicle, waiting.

"I'll be for getting off at the telegraph office. But my friend Mister Macombie will go on up with you to the Soldiers' Home, if there's a doctor up there to look at him..."

"Of course."

"And maybe you can find him some shoes?"

"We'll certainly try. But so many have lost theirs. As well as most of their clothes, poor lads..."

"But we have to be back down here before the *Saint Patrick* sails."

The little man looks Robbie over, frowning. "Well, unless the doctor recommends..."

"No," Robbie interjects. "I have to leave with the boat, sir."

"Well..." The man is shaking his head and frowning.

"If you intend to keep him, we'll just decline your ride and find a doctor down here. With all due respect and thanks."

"I'll go up, Mister Quinn," Robbie says. "Sure do need something for my gut. But I'll be back down, don't you doubt it."

Paddy helps lift his skeletal friend onto the wagon, almost fainting himself from the effort, then hoists himself up. The buggy rattles up the steep street with its pitiful passengers. Paddy shakes his head.

Poor Robbie looks a hundred years old.

And I bet I could pass for sixty.

Along the sidewalks Paddy sees shabby men in wet blue coats, some even in nothing but long underwear, plodding, sitting on curbs catching their breath. He sees shopkeepers coming out of their stores, bringing them cups and glasses to drink from, cigars to smoke, trays of fresh-baked muffins.

Bet this is the kindest Yankees have been treated here in Memphis in three years.

"Any idea how many survivors?" Paddy asks the driver after a while.

"Too soon to guess. Still bringing them ashore. Alive and not. We have I'd guess two or three hundred in the Home and the hospitals so far..."

"More than I'd have thought could make it..Heard anything of Captain Mason?"

"Mason? The *Sultana*'s master? No."

"If he's rescued, he should stand trial," Paddy says. His contempt for the man is so great in this moment that he shudders. After a while he has a thought about the two Memphis newspapers, and starts wondering how much information about the disaster they might have amassed this morning. He could do well to go there and get whatever figures and names and essential facts they might have. But he doesn't want anything to do with the newspapers right now. He doesn't want them to be aware of him. He asks the driver, "Do the *Bulletin* and the *Argus* have telegraph, do you know?"

"I suppose. Don't really know."

Suddenly Paddy is anxious that those papers might transmit information that he considers his own. It's a throwback to his war correspondent attitude about exclusive interviews and reports. But now he shakes his head, disgusted with his own thought.

You don't own this tragedy, damn you. This belongs to everybody.

All he owns, he knows, are the words of all those interviews, and his sketches, and his own suffering in the disaster, and the life of this Robbie Macombie. These are exclusively his.

But he does hope to be the first to telegraph it to Blackie at the New Orleans *Picayune.* And to Alfred Guernsey at *Harper's.* He might already be too late. The Associated Press might already have it on telegraph up in the East and then it will be everywhere.

"I get off here," Paddy says as the buggy is slowed by a dense and noisy crowd in front of the telegraph office. Part of the mob is collected up the street a few yards, around a large, florid, white-maned gent wearing a linen suit, who stands on a mounting block and seems to be delivering an impassioned sermon, in resonant, drawling syllables, with upraised fists. The only word Paddy can make out over the general hubbub is "damnation."

Paddy painfully raises himself from the buggy seat and lets himself down onto the street, hurting his shoulder so much it makes him wince. He puts his hand on Robbie's wrist and says, "Remember, we're going to see Father Abraham."

"I won't miss the boat, sir."

"I'm not 'sir,' damn it."

"No, sir."

As Paddy remembers from what seems ages ago but was only yesterday, the telegraph office is across the street from two saloons. The crowd is now, as it was then, milling between the two sides of the street, though some attention is being drawn to the big man preaching nearby. Today the telegraph office is busier than the drinking establishments, and today most of the people queued up are in mild to extreme degrees of dishabille: many barefoot, some in wet, stained suits and uniforms, most gaunt, exhausted, unshaven, soot-smudged and stringy-haired.

Now this feels like a recurring dream to Paddy: the urgency to get ahead of the line at this place, to crowd others out. Instead, he decides to wait for the moment and see whether the line is too slow, and push in only if he really must. He can see that there are some *Sultana* survivors in the queue, and he has too much empathy for them to barge in ahead.

With his practiced one-handed dexterity, he opens the portfolio at his side and slips out his notebook and a pencil. As before, he will get a bit ahead by having his messages written by the time he's at the counter. Some men nearby watch curiously as he hunches over and braces the box and writes on it, but most are too absorbed in their own circumstances and pay no attention at all.

First, to Blackie at the New Orleans paper:

> *SULTANA BURNT, SUNK ABOVE MEMPHIS*
>
> *1,000-2,000 DEAD, MOST ANDERSONVILLE*
>
> *PRISON VETERANS. I SURVIVED, WIFE KILLED.*
>
> *PLEASE INFORM MY MOTHER MRS QUINN AT*
>
> *SHAMROCK HOTEL AT ONCE. I PROCEED ON*
>
> *TO MR LINCOLNS FUNERAL. MORE FROM THERE.*
>
> *P.QUINN*

As he finishes this message, a flurry of angry words and curses, and an exasperated growl, come down the waiting line. "You can't quit now!" someone near the front yells in a whiny voice.

"We can't wait, damn it to hell!"

"What's this?" says Paddy.

"God damn telegrapher wants a break. Poor little Southern boy's tuckered out!"

"Sit down and work, y'little bastard!"

Aha! Irish luck, is this? Paddy thinks, and pushes forward. "Excuse me! Maybe I can help. I'm a telegrapher." At the head of the line of angry men he leans on the counter, close to the operator, and says loudly, "Look, you remember me?" The distressed man turns to see him, nods, and says:

"You! Yeah, you're the *Harper's* man! You made it, eh? Congratulations. But I can't do anything for you now, sir. I'm sick. I'm worn out. I'll be sittin' in shit if I don't get out of here for a few..."

"You don't have a relief man?"

"He won't be here 'til two. And I can't last that long...Sorry..." Paddy can see that the man is not only sick and exhausted but probably worried that he'll lose his job if the office closes in the midst of this emergency.

"You're in luck, friend," Paddy says. "I've operated the key since I was a boy. I'll be happy to take over 'til your relief gets here. Unless you have some picky damn little rule forbidding it."

"There's rules, sure. But a rule's no more'n ass-wipe, in my condition. Come in here, sir, please do! Now, you're sure you're qualified..."

"I am. Just ask me." The men crowding the front of the office are beginning to understand what's happening here, and the ire in their faces is softening, and some of them are smiling at Paddy. He eases down in an armless swivel chair next to the key in the operator's cubbyhole, which reeks of sweat, spittoon, and perhaps even shit. The operator, shuffling with discomfort and apparently leaking farts, or worse, quickly shows Paddy where everything is, including the cash box, then vanishes, making a high-pitched groan as he goes. "By God," Paddy remarks to the men at the counter, "there's a trusting man indeed, eh? Now let's get going here..." He takes a form penciled by the first gentleman in line, lays it beside the telegraph key, and, pretending to read it, proceeds to tap out his own message to Blackie at the New Orleans *Picayune.* That done, he now sends the gentleman's message, and follows it with his own to Mister Guernsey at *Harper's.* The customers have not the least suspicion that he's interspersing his own business with theirs, and he's fast enough that they couldn't complain if they did know.

It feels good to be doing this again, he thinks. Another kind of writing. The world of information, funneled through a narrow wire...

Dah dah dit. Dit dit dah. Dit. Dit ditdit...

Right here under his hand is the clicking key. In the room are the voices and coughings and sneezes of the men waiting to send their messages. Outside in the street, more voices, including the roaring rants of the silver-haired orator. As Paddy works he forgets his pains and tiredness.

And he learns details. Old Mister Safford of the Sanitary Commission has been found alive. The *Sultana*'s first mate, Rowberry, the pilot, George Kayton, and chief engineer Wintreger are alive. A good number of the *Sultana*'s crew members escaped alive in the vessel's lifeboat, which knowledge arouses anger and suspicion among the veterans who have lost so many of their own weakened comrades. At the last known sighting of Captain Cass Mason, he was on the burning boat, throwing wooden shutters to desperate men in the river. It's something, but not enough to absolve him. Paddy hears that Walter Elliott, or Dave, as he preferred to be known, has been rescued from a float of driftwood and brought to Memphis alive and well by the steamboat *Jenny Lind.* His name brings up in Paddy a quick rush of memories: of knocking him unconscious, of interviewing him, and the more hazy recollection of meeting him and his floating log in the darkness before dawn this very morning, trying to share whiskey with him...

Here on the telegraph key with such memories in his head, he has a dreamy feeling of being both the storyteller and the story...

He hears plain statements and wild speculations as the men stand in line talking. Many are sure that the boat was blown up by some Southern saboteur or bitter malcontent, that Jefferson Davis was behind it. Paddy listens intently to an eyewitness who saw "that gorgeous lady who boarded at Memphis yesterday" leap into the river from the blazing stern of the *Sultana*, not to reappear. He hears that the boat perished with hundreds of thousands of dollars worth of silver in its safe. And he hears this:

"Why don't somebody in the town go plug up that crazy ranting coot out there on the corner? He got no right to say such mean damn foolishness!"

"What's he saying?" Paddy asks, looking up from the key. "I thought he was just preaching."

"Yeah, preachin', all right! Preachin' that the Lord killed a host of Yankees in the river for coming down South to turn his niggers loose!"

"That *is* nasty," Paddy says with a grimace. "Why don't *you* go out and shut him up?"

"Mister, I can't hardly stand up. That old bastard's got a crowd o' Rebs 'round him and makin' them madder by the minute. B'sides, I can't lose my place in this here line."

"All right. Well, you're next after this man."

Dah. Dit. Dit dah. Dit dit dit dah. Dit. Dit dah dit. Dit dit. Dit ditdit... leave for...

And intriguing telegraph messages come in, too. One from Springfield, obviously too late, says:

MME F WILLARD C/O STEAMER SULTANA

AT MEMPHIS

MADAME

TWO THOUSAND PRINTED ADVERTISEMENTS OF YOUR MAY THIRD CLUB ENGAGEMENT HERE

READY FOR DISTRIBUTION PER YOUR INSTRUCTION STOP

D V PEGG

Paddy pencils a note on the telegram and slips it into his coat pocket, thinking: Madame F. for Fanny, would that be? Surely she didn't plan to give a bawdy performance while Father Abraham lies in state!

But of course. There'll be thousands of men in town that day.

*

Robbie sits bracing against gut pains in a wheel chair on the lawn of a big brick house on a hill near a huge elm tree, vaguely aware that he's finally at the Soldiers' Home in Memphis. Something is really wrong. He's never had a stomach act like this, like a pot of soup boiling over hot flame.

It took a long time to get up here, the buggy having been delayed by a street crowd. Robbie had sat waiting with the other sick soldiers in the buggy, his stomach pain making him almost oblivious to what he was hearing, until at last he had become unable to ignore the invective of an orator on the street corner: a big-bellied, white-haired, senatorial-looking preacher whose red jowls quivered with the force of his fury. The man was exulting that the Lord God had burned and drowned a whole boatload of the Yankee devils who had sullied the honor of the South and molested its fair ladies and murdered its youth and destroyed its cities and countryside and wrenched its poor helpless niggers out of the caring hands of their masters; the ranter was rejoicing that justice had been wrought so directly and so soon; he was thanking God for the wondrous – yea, the *miraculous* -- thunderbolt of vengeance He had hurled at that vessel full of Yankee fiends...

That had almost made Robbie throw up again, but then he had only dropped his head forward and shut his eyes and wept in silence. He'd run his bayonet through young Rebs on battlefields, boys that he hadn't had any cause at all to hate, but there in the Memphis street was a mean windbag he'd have enjoyed killing, but he was too helpless even to get out of the wagon.

Just as well, I reckon, he thinks, sitting here in a wheelchair outside the Soldiers' Home. Could get in a heap of trouble killing a preacher in his own town.

There's a humid breeze here on this hill, and on the broad lawn, scores of shabby men sit and lie on the grass while women move like nurses among them. Kneeling beside Robbie now is a balding, mustachioed, pear-shaped doctor, who has been poking around his midsection and asking how his innards feel, and Robbie has answered as vividly as he can. He's just finished telling the doctor the history of his guts going clear back to Andersonville prison and forward through last night in the cold river with nothing inside him but rye whiskey, and about the sip of rye this morning that made him spew foamy vomit in the *Belle of Memphis* so violently that he pissed the bed. It has been a bit embarrassing to tell that because a nurse sits by his other side on a little camp stool, cleaning his face and hands with white cloths smelling of witch hazel. Robbie looks over at the nurse, who is perhaps as homely as Mrs. Felice Quinn was beautiful. He wonders whether this nurse knew Mrs.Quinn, thinks she surely must have, for she was up here just yesterday. Robbie is wondering whether he should tell this one that he saw Mrs. Quinn die in flames. He decides not to say it.

The doctor, who has been squatting beside the wheel chair, stands up with popping knees and a pained sigh, and says, "First, soldier, I'm going to give you some bismuth. Then we're going to fatten you up a bit. We'll find some victuals you can keep down..."

"Beggin' your pardon, doctor, but I have to be aboard the *St. Patrick* before she heads up for Cairo this afternoon..."

The doctor shakes his head and chuckles. "Oh, I hardly think so! Of course you're eager to get home. But you do want to arrive there *alive,* don't you? Well, a few days here will make that difference. We've cots, medicine, good food here enough for all you poor gents -- and on good, solid ground, for Heaven's sake!-- all courtesy of the Sanitary Commission. It's the least we can do after all your sacrifices and your..."

"Doctor, sir, with all due respect and thanks, but I've made a promise..."

"Of course you have. A promise to return home. And you shall keep it. A few days late, perhaps, but *alive.* Come along, Miss Betts. I'll fix a potion for you to bring him. Then we'll get this good soldier indoors before dark..." As they walk away behind him toward the big house, Robbie hears the doctor saying in a lower voice: "We'd probably better worm him, too..."

Well, Rob thinks, so much for the Soldier's Home.

The scent of tobacco hangs in the air. Men are smoking pipes and cigars all around and some are chewing and spitting. Sure would like my pipe while I figure how to get out of here.

The river had taken it, and his tobacco, as well as his shoes.

I bet Mister Quinn'll get me something to smoke before we get on the boat to Illinois. All I'd have to do is tell him I want it. Bless his soul.

After a few minutes of waiting for the nurse to come back with his medicine, he starts thinking that it might not be such a good idea to wait for her. She might not let him go.

Probably better just to walk away before she comes back. Nobody'll notice, I bet.

But when he tries to get up out of the chair, he realizes that he probably can't walk five steps, maybe not even two.

Well, damn!

He cranes his neck, looking this way and that to see if any of those buggies might be going down to town, like the one that brought him up here. There's none in sight.

Well, then, reckon I'll just use what wheels I got...

He puts his hands on the wheels of the chair and pushes. He is astonished at how weak he is. It's hard to make the wheels turn. As a carpenter and millwright, Robbie had had great strength in his hands, back in the days before he joined the Army. In the Army, where days and weeks and months were spent marching or riding around or waiting in idleness and card- playing, there had been no work that kept his hands strong. Then in the prison camp there was no work to do and there was hardly any food, so his whole body had weakened, month by month.

Then there had been last night in the cold water, fingers hooked on the rim of the whiskey keg.

The efforts to fight the currents, to swim after Mister Quinn or hang onto him, that cold eternity in the river with the center of his body burning whiskey like a gas jet to stay alive, all that had cramped his hands and finally used up most of the strength he'd had left. And, bracing against relentless pain is as exhausting as anything, and doing so now keeps wearing him farther down.

But he does get the wheels of the chair moving slowly. The lawn is level here, so he must push.

Thank Heaven it's most all downhill to the telegraph office and to the boat.

As Robbie expected, no one is paying him any attention. Not yet.

Pray I get beyond that gate and shrubbery before that nurse Miss Mercy comes out with my medicine.

The pathway, moist dirt and pea gravel, begins sloping as he approaches the gate, and he hardly has to push at all now. The wheels of the chair have oaken spokes and are neatly rimmed with iron hoops like small wagon wheels. It is a nicely-made conveyance, with a woven-rush seat and a footboard, and Rob the workman appraises it unthinkingly with his craftwise hands. It would be a costly thing if one had to buy it. So he has to tell himself that he's not *stealing* this expensive chair; he's just borrowing it from the Soldiers' Home, and they can bring it back up after he's finished riding down to where he needs to go. In the misery of his sickness he had paid little attention when the buggy brought him up, so he might take a wrong turn and miss the one the telegraph office is on, but that isn't much of a worry. He can ask somebody if he can't find it. Some kind soul might even get behind the chair and push him where he needs to go, if he gets lost. It seems that these Memphis people are polite and kind enough, even to the Yanks that have taken over their city.

How lost could I get anyway? The river's at the bottom of the hill and the boat's in the river.

Robbie smiles for the first time in a long while.

This is about as easy as you could ask for.

It has been a long, long time since anything was easy for him.

He's in the street now, away from the property of the Soldiers' Home, and rolling down a gentle slope. The ride is somewhat bumpy because the damp dirt of the street is soft and has been rutted by wagon and buggy wheels, but it's all downhill from here, he knows, so he won't need any strength to keep going.

But now coming to a stretch where the street is steeper, he begins to think that it might require some strength to stop. The wheels are now slick with mud and are rolling a little too fast for comfort.

His bony frame is all but rattling in the chair as it accelerates down the slope, threatening to slue, or even tilt over, every time it angles through a wheel rut. Robbie doesn't want to wreck this nice, expensive chair, nor does he want his own frail and painful body to go tumbling. Instinctively, he takes his feet off the footboard and sticks them forward and drops his heels to the road to brake. Sharp pains in his heels remind him that he didn't stay at the Soldiers' Home long enough for that gentleman to find him a pair of shoes, either. Also, when his heels drag the road in front of the chair, the back of the chair seems to rise a little as if to go into a somersault. So he lifts his feet, and begins moaning a little because of this precipitous acceleration, and is too busy trying to slow down to pay any attention to some pedestrians who have paused along the sidewalk to watch him speed by. Now he's watching for some streetside shrub or hedge to steer into for a softer stop, but sees no such thing.

So he understands now that if he's going to slow this thing down, he'll have to use his hands like the wooden brake on a freight wagon: by friction on the wheels themselves.

This is going to hurt...

Pressing his palms down hard on the iron tires, he feels the burning of friction and the abrasion of grit, and the agony in his swollen wrists. But it's working. He's slowing. Finally he locks his fingers on the spokes, and with one painful jerk he is stopped. He sits for a moment, panting, letting his fright subside. He gazes down the hill, over the roofs of houses farther down. Off in misty distance he sees a stretch of the mud-yellow, flooded Mississippi. He sees two small packet steamboats out there on the river, and some smaller craft, and he presumes they're still out there fetching corpses out the water.

I don't believe God did that to punish us. A boiler blew up, that's all. I believe in God but I don't believe He did that to us, like that old bombaster said. Fire and water and steam can blow up without God intending anything by it.

"Can I help you, Yank?" says a voice nearby, startling him. It's a homely young man standing beside the street in a flower garden, leaning on a spade, his knees dark with soil. His wornout, wrinkled butternut clothes suggest that he's a Confederate veteran. Robbie knows the remnants of his own uniform mark him just as plainly.

"If you could direct me to the telegraph office?"

"You're almost there. Second street down, it's brick paved, turn right. Takes you right down to it."

"Much obliged."

"You one o' them off the *Sultana*?" The man still rests on his spade, talking from the garden plot, not coming closer. This fellow looks just like any of those young Rebs he shot or bayoneted.

"I am."

"Glad y' made it. Goin' back North, are ye?"

"God willing," Robbie replies. Then he shakes his head and adds, "God hasn't seemed much willing, though, lately."

"Well, Godspeed. I do like t' see you fellers go back up. Nothin' personal."

"Thanks, soldier. Hope your peonies grow. I do like peonies myself."

Robbie grasps the wheels and starts his chair moving, but this time keeping his hands on to maintain control on the way down. It's pretty easy to keep it braking this way, weighing as little as he does. As he goes along he thinks about how good it was to talk to a Johnny Reb instead of running at him or getting shot at. As far as he knows, this was the first one he's talked to since the prisoner escort that took him into Andersonville last year.

They aren't The Enemy anymore. Just like that! Good God Almighty! That's just crazy! Got to talk to Mister Quinn about that!

At the brick street he looks down past a few old houses and there's the downtown , and farther down below, the docks, with several paddlewheelers tied up. About halfway down there are many people in the street, must be about where the telegraph office is, there where that crowd was that impeded the buggy going up. His stomach still hurts.

Waste o' time that was, going up to the Soldiers' Home. Didn't even get stomach medicine. Or shoes.

He imagines that nurse up there coming out with his dose of bismuth in her hand, looking around for him and the wheelchair. He wonders how quickly she'll go tell the doctor he's gone. Wonders if they'll come chasing down after him to get their chair back.

Probably way too busy. Must've been near a hundred of us up there. Many worse off than me.

That was one truth Robbie had arrived at long ago and again

and again, no matter how bad things got to be: There's just about always somebody even worse off.

Not that it helps much at the time, but it does some.

He lets himself roll slowly down the steep brick street, feeling through the vibrating chair the difference between its surface and that of the dirt street above. Now he's passing between ornate brick and stone storefronts, and there are several men and women walking along the downtown street.

A block down, he's becoming aware of the voices of many more people. And there is one familiar voice, overriding the murmur of all the others. Robbie thinks:

Why, it's that same big old windbag still a-carrying on!

A few yards down, he sees the loud man, standing up on a mounting block at curbside, shaking upraised fists, tossing his silver mane. He's facing downhill, away from Robbie, and maybe thirty men are standing there looking up at him and listening to him, occasionally yelling in response, "By God, yes, Colonel!" "Damn 'em all, they had it coming!" Pedestrians pause near him to listen, then walk on, some nodding, some shaking their heads.

And now Robbie is close enough that he can hear the oratory that echoes between the edifices:

"...yes, the great Mississippi is *full* of them, floatin' like dead catfish...Yankees who *dared* to descend on our see-ivilized and gen-teel Southland like Huns and Vandals...And look at them now! What are they now? *DEAD FISH* is what they are, stinking in the water right here at Memphis, where they brought their ironclad boats down and hurled cannonshot at our fleet...forced us to surrender to them...brought down their minions to rule over our fair city...brought *plagues of whores* to shock the tender virtue of our womenfolk.... Our Dear Lord, our God of exact justice and retribution, after the greatest patience...after the humiliating trickery to make our great General Lee surrender his sword... God has *punished* them just as they deserve!...Our God saw His moment! He has a finer sense of justice than do we His impatient children... Last night He saw a Yankee steamboat in the river packed with *thousands* of those heinous invaders, and He *smote* them all in one mighty stroke and turned them into carrion!..."

Up the street behind him Robbie is clenching his molars and starting to breathe deep and hard through distended nostrils, and now he hears the tantrum wind up almost to a scream:

"And, my friends, my fellow Tennesseeans, listen to me tell you why Our Lord waited until this moment: Do you know? Do you know?

"Because He means to bring retribution *all at once!* Yes! Think on this: You know that up North, at this moment!... across that cursed and dreary landscape!... in a casket on a railroad train!... the prime Nigger-lover of 'em all...that ugly backwoods ignoramus!... he who stole our precious servants from us all with a stroke of his pen... he rolls toward his *grave! Struck down for his abominable sin by the same just God..."*

During these last sentences, Robbie Macombie, heartbeat quickening, vision blurring with tears, has shoved forward the wheels of his chair with all his might, braced his shoeless feet on the footboard, and he is riding the accelerating conveyance down the steep street straight at the speaker.

"...That stinking, moldering carcass... of Abraham..." the old man is shouting, but then he sees a part of his audience looking past him up the steep street and beginning to scatter; in that pause of his tirade he hears the ringing rattle of iron tires on brick behind him, and turns his head to look.

Too late.

When the footboard of Robbie's careering wheelchair hits the mounting block, both Robbie and the chair pitch up and forward and bowl the portly man right off his pedestal. Robbie and the chair combined probably weigh barely half as much as the old slavemaster, but they are hard and angular, and he is soft, and they have momentum.

The fat man, the skeletal veteran and the chair, all in one wheezing, growling, clump of flailing limbs and twirling wheels, land with a rattling crash and tumble along on the bricks of the street, spectators dancing out of their way.

It is a softer landing than Robbie had been willing to suffer, the chubby orator being underneath, but the chair itself gives Robbie a painful whack or two before they all come clattering to a stop in the gutter. Robbie can't get up yet, but neither can the big man, who has come to rest with his head against a gaslamp stanchion, unconscious and bleeding from his nose and from a severe abrasion on the right side of his face. Robbie is on top of him, the wheelchair on top of Robbie.

The crowd is coalescing around this wreckage by the time Robbie is able to crawl out from between the chair and the big man's torso and sit up to look down on him. One of the spectators yells, "He's done hurt Reverend Blovill!"

"Git that li'l Yankee son of a bitch!"

But most in the crowd are laughing. Someone yells, "Good! He had that a-comin'." A pair of men in butcher aprons put their hands under Robbie's arms to help him stand up. They release him when he's erect but his legs go and he slumps to the street again. He sits staring at the big man, panting between clenched teeth, just beginning to see clearly again, and he says in a low, hard tone, "I wish you'd wake up, Reverend, or Colonel, or whatever you are. I want t' hear you apologize to President Lincoln."

"Amen," says someone in the crowd. "Such talk was *low* down, even for the Honorable Big Mouth!"

"And apologize to the drowned Yankees, too," Robbie hears Paddy Quinn's voice say, right beside him. The voice is music to his ears.

"Amen," say several other voices.

"Come on, Robbie," Paddy says, righting Robbie's wheelchair, then stooping to get his arm around him and raise him up and wheel him to the nearest saloon. "That Reverend Colonel is in no condition to apologize just yet."

*

"Not going to heave *that* up now, I hope?" Paddy asks, watching Robbie sip carefully over the edge of a beer schooner.

"So far, so good."

They're sitting across a table from each other in the saloon across the street from the telegraph office, where Paddy has brought him in from the crowd. Paddy looks across at old Robbie and gnaws inside his lip with perplexity. The old soldier looks worse than ever. Now he has abrasions on his hands, blood on his shirt, and lumps on his head. He still squints and leans forward with his gut pains. Paddy is irritated at him for not staying up at the Soldiers' Home long enough even to get stomach medicine.

And although Robbie hasn't admitted it, Paddy is sure he ran his wheelchair into the Big Mouth on purpose. It hadn't looked at all accidental. Paddy had come out of the telegraph office just in time to hear the orator maligning Mister Lincoln and then see Robbie's speeding conveyance hit the mounting block.

That collision had been a satisfying sight to Paddy, except for his momentary fear that his poor frail comrade might have killed himself doing it. It had split the frame and bent the axle of the wheelchair. Some people in the crowd had not wanted to let Robbie leave the scene until they knew how badly the fat man was hurt.

The victim, Colonel Blovill, Paddy has since learned, is an influential but not universally admired pillar of the Memphis community: a plantation owner who had been a Congressman before Tennessee seceded, a preacher in a big Memphis denomination since Secession. His appellation of Colonel he had bestowed upon himself, not by virtue of any military service but by having married the widow of a Mexican War hero. That title is one of the town's favorite jokes.

Though the Honorable Reverend Colonel Blovill is generally presumed to have been laid low by accident, Paddy half expects some officer of the law to show up looking for Robbie. Paddy also expects he might yet have to make some arrangement about paying for the damaged wheelchair, if someone thinks of that before the *St. Patrick* departs. But maybe no one will bother with such a small thing as a broken wheelchair, as the town is still fully absorbed in the horrific business of tending to injured survivors of the *Sultana* and finding and disposing of the hundreds of corpses the boats keep bringing ashore. It is evident that the people of Memphis are generally much more civilized and humane than their Reverend Colonel Congressman.

One favorable development is that Robbie has been able to eat half a bowl of buttered hominy from the kitchen behind the saloon, and keep it down. And it looks as if he can sip beer without vomiting. Paddy himself has chosen a nice, smooth Tennessee whiskey, for which his hours on the telegraph key created a severe thirst.

But something is much more troubling in Paddy's spirit now than queasy stomachs and broken wheelchairs, or even fallen Congressmen, as he gazes across the table at his half-dead friend.

Robbie now poses a moral dilemma for Paddy, because of something that happened in the telegraph office this afternoon. Paddy hates moral dilemmas; they always seem to arise just when one is trying desperately to steer a simple course or is in a state of spiritual exhaustion, as Paddy is now.

It's that damned Captain Walter - or David -- Elliott from Indiana. Damn him and bless his heart, Paddy is thinking. Never anything simple when he shows up.

Captain Elliott had walked into the telegraph office, tired and unsteady but intense, while Paddy was operating the key. Part of his pallid face still showed the bruising from Paddy's fist. Captain Elliott had a message he wanted sent to one of his law associates in Indiana, asking them to send a considerable sum of money to him at Memphis: enough money to book passage home for every Indiana soldier rescued from the *Sultana* disaster. Basically, Captain Elliott hopes to charter a whole steamboat at his own expense so the Indiana veterans can have comfortable rooms and dining accommodations all the way up the Mississippi to Cairo, and then transfer to trains or to Ohio River boats with comparable comforts. A really generous gesture, so kind - and costly - that Paddy could hardly believe the message he was transmitting. There might yet prove to be as many as two hundred Indiana survivors, maybe more. Captain Elliott intends to find and invite all of them except, of course, those too sick and injured to leave the Memphis hospitals yet. It's a grand gesture, but not surprising in a dramatic attention-seeker like Walter Elliott. It will ennoble him in the eyes of everyone who learns about it. It crosses Paddy's mind that Captain Elliott might have political ambitions on his return to Indiana. The captain had hinted that Paddy's story for *Harper's* might find this good deed interesting. But even despite the self-glorification, it's an admirable thing to do. Paddy gets out his notebook and scribbles a phrase he might use in a speech someday:

Altruism is the skimmed milk of human kindness.

The dilemma is that Captain Elliott, remembering Robbie Macombie, had asked Paddy specifically to make sure Robbie gets on that boat if he's not hospitalized, because Robbie's kinfolks are, after all, close neighbors to the Elliotts in Madison.

And if Robbie chooses to go on Elliott's boat, he won't be going up to Springfield for President Lincoln's funeral.

Paddy looks across the table now at the dear, sick wretch, and is feeling the moral obligation to tell him about Captain Elliott's humane offer. He knows quite well that Robbie just might not make it home alive if he *doesn't* go that easy way.

If I carry him to Mister Lincoln's funeral, I might then have to carry him on to his own, Paddy is thinking right now.

So I really must tell him about that direct and easy trip home.

But I want him to go with me!

And not just because he's so important to my *Harper's* story, though sure he really is about the best part left of it.

So now Paddy takes a deep sigh, and a similarly deep pull at his Tennessee whiskey, and says, "Listen, my friend. You remember Captain Elliott..."

Robbie looks up from the rapt contemplation of the bubbles in his beer, thinks for a moment. "Sure I do. The one you hit? Him we tried to give whiskey to in the river, but couldn't? I do 'member him, rest his soul."

"No elegy yet," Paddy says. "He's still amongst us living."

"You say he *is*?"

"Is. And he's doing a fine thing I need to tell you about, for your own sake..."

Robbie just sits peering, nodding, as Paddy tells him about the special boat for Indiana survivors. The beer seems to be sedating him. "Nice thing for him to do," he mumbles.

Paddy takes a deep breath and comes out with it:

"Mister Elliott wants you to be on his boat. It can take you right to Madison."

For a long time, Robbie sits silent, his eyelids more droopy, head starting to tilt toward the table. "Sounds mighty nice..." Then his head jerks up. "Can't, though."

"Can't? Why?"

"Cause I'm goin' to Springfield with you! You know that, Mister Quinn."

Paddy slumps with relief. It was all he could bear to lose Felice. He knows from those minutes when he and Robbie were lost from each other in the river last night that he needs this man's presence, desperately needs him along for the President's funeral, because in some unexplainable way their shared pilgrimage mitigates her loss. *Something* has to end where it was meant to end.

But he has to talk this out to leave his conscience clear. "Listen, Robbie. If you *don't* feel up to the trek to Springfield, just say so. I won't resent it. You're a whole lot sicker now than you were. Last night should've killed you."

Robbie is obviously wide awake now. He looks afraid, eyes widening. "Now, Mister Quinn, I can understand you not wantin' to drag me along, but..."

"No, no, that's not it. I just want you to make it home alive..."

"We have a deal, you know..."

"But I'm not going to hold you to it if it kills you, damn it!"

Robbie sits for a moment, looking down, looking as if he's about to cry. Now he raises his eyes to Paddy's and says, "Well, sir, we made each other a promise to go see Mister Lincoln. It's what kept me goin', in that river. But I reckon mine was as much a promise to Mister Lincoln as it was to you. So, if you don't want t' haul me along, I reckon I can get to Springfield *some* way on my own." He sits up straight, puts the heels of both hands on the edge of the table, sets his jaw and stares at Paddy. His eyes are as fierce as an eagle's but afloat in tears.

Paddy stares back at him. Shakes his head. Takes another slug of whiskey, which feels like a sunrise in his bosom. Now he chuckles. "Not stubborn or anything, are you?"

"We had a deal!"

Paddy leans forward over the narrow table and puts his hand on Robbie's. "Soldier," he says, "I could kiss you if you weren't such a pukey-mouthed old coot. Now let's see if that wheelchair's too busted up to take you down to the *Saint Patrick*."

CHAPTER THIRTEEN

On the Steamboat Saint Patrick

Friday 28 April, 1865

My Dear Mother,

This letter will not entertain you. I've no heart for cleverness, scarcely enough heart to keep living.

You will know by now that our beloved Felice was among near two thousand souls who perished early yesterday when the Sultana blew up & burned, near Memphis. There is no hope for her surviving; I myself witnessed the blaze that swallowed her.

I was blown intact into the river, & thus not wounded or burnt at all, but the ensuing hours in the cold flood tested me beyond anything ever before. I owe my life to an Indiana soldier, one of those prison survivors, who endured the ordeal with me & is barely still alive.

By this steamboat we shall go on to St. Louis; there we'll cross to Illinois and entrain to Springfield for the President's funeral. This soldier with me, named Macombie, is your peer in devotion to Father Abraham. He won't go home until he has paid his last respects to the President.

I interviewed & sketched scores of the soldiers before they died in the calamity. I salvaged my notes & sketches. You would try in vain to imagine their grisly fate as I witnessed it, or the dolorous tale I have to write. Its pathos is of course compounded by the sad progress of the martyred Emancipator toward his final resting place. He saved the Union, but that glory is tarnished by all that has ensued.

Mr. Guernsey at Harper's awaits this, the most poignant tale I shall ever write. I am daunted by the task & weakened by the loss of Felice and the child she carried. But never was a correspondent so fatefully placed as I was, so I must presume that our Maker arranged it so. And to be worthy of such a vicissitude, I must use all my skill & talent to tell the saddest story ever.

Pray for me that I can do this timely, & as well as it needs be done.

I must pause at St. Louis to notify Felice's parents. After the President's entombment, I expect I'll go by railroad from Springfield to New York, writing the tragic story en route, so that it and the sketches will be ready for Harper's when I get there.

I shall deliver my dear comrade Macombie to Pittsburgh on my way to New York, if he lives long enough to get there. I do believe he's really dying. I ask you to pray for him, too, please.

I am, Your devoted son,

Paddy

P.S. You would be proud to know, your daughter- in- law was a true Quinn woman, heroic to her last breath.

*

As if by an unspoken agreement, all the *Sultana* survivors aboard the *Saint Patrick* are on lookout for any trace of the vessel as the packet boat churns up the flooded river this evening, through the islands known as the Hens and Chickens. The vessel rumbles and the paddlewheels slosh endlessly with a sound like a cataract. It will soon be too dark. All that can be seen of some of the islands are treetops. The soldiers, some strong enough to stand at the rails, some on deck chairs, to a man they are out on the decks, watching the muddy river swirl by. Frightful as it was in the blind darkness, the actual sight of such a limitless roiling flood is even more dreadful. Paddy can only imagine their thoughts, though many must be similar to his. They lost their old comrades; he lost an angel. Every soldier on this boat endured the long, cold, desperate hours in the utter darkness after the glow of the *Sultana*'s fire was gone. Each man surely remembers his own suffering in some peculiar way, Paddy knows. For those who were scalded or burned, or wounded and bleeding, the pain and panic and despair would have been worse than his own. And as Paddy knows from those hours in the dark stream with Robbie, every soldier would have had his own way of fearing the invisible turbulence below his feet, which repeatedly tried to suck him down. Some are recalling that the fear of the alligator had terrorized them more than anything else all night.

No one knows just where to look for the hull of the *Sultana,* or whether any trace of her will even be visible. She drifted downstream burning for hours after the explosion. There is the chilling possibility yet that the *Saint Patrick's* paddlewheels will churn up still more bodies. The men can see garments and rags snagged in treetops, paper and charred wood occasionally floating by. They watch such debris, their eyes following each piece sternward, and each such shred of the disaster surely troubles every man in his own way. Such flotsam is thin and bloodless carnage compared with what they have all seen left heaped and strewn on battlefields. The flooding river can dispose of great quantities of corpses much more quickly and neatly than any number of grave diggers on a battleground could ever do.

"This Mississippi could have rinsed out all the blood and ruin of Antietam or Gettysburg in a day," Paddy remarks to Robbie. And then he writes the thought down. Maybe for a lecture someday.

After a while, Robbie replies from his deck chair in a gurgly murmur, "But even this river'd never flush out the filth of that damned Andersonville."

And Paddy thinks:

Somebody else said the same thing, just a day or two ago. It was... wasn't it that one-armed cavalryman. From Michigan...Hamblin? Got his sketch in here...Wonder if he lived...

Paddy is pleased that his memory for names and details is getting back up to normal after all the panic and confusion of the calamity, and the awful drain of physical and mental vigor during the long immersion in cold water.

He suspects that almost all of these *Sultana* survivors must be in awful states of fear at being back aboard another steamboat less than a day after that ordeal. One Indiana Infantry veteran, named MacFarland, was assigned a cabin, but wouldn't go into it. Instead, he has climbed into the steamboat's yawl, suspended on its davits over the stern, announcing that he will camp in it all the way to Cairo. Paddy has written down that curiosity in his notebook. It will fit right into the end of the story someplace, and make its point about the effect of fear upon reason.

Searching over this vast muddy flood for a trace of the *Sultana* seems futile to Paddy. There are no landmarks to remember by, because everything was dark when she blew up. Still, he has a feeling that it must have been right along here someplace.

And just now, as if reading his thoughts, Robbie says, "Too many people die in a place, it gets haunted. I think we're there." The statement gives Paddy a *frisson*. And then somebody forward shouts:

"Looky yonder! Jackstaff, I bet!"

At that moment the master of the *Saint Patrick* lets loose a single blast of the steam whistle, and a mate steps out of the wheelhouse, leans out over the rail and points off the starboard quarter. There, far beyond the upper end of a copse of willowtops marking a submerged islet, is a thin, straight something sticking up out of the water.

"Her jackstaff!" calls the mate. "Sure as hell!"

Might be and it might not, Paddy thinks, going to the rail and staring hard at it. But he feels all too sure that it is. It stands bare, its flag and halyard no doubt burned off. Some of the burned survivors who had been among the last ones off the *Sultana* had said everything had burned down and collapsed to the level of the hull by the time they'd got off, all but the brass jackstaff, which was at the windward end most of the time, and then the rest of the hull had flickered and smoldered in the dark like a charcoal works down to the waterline as they had looked back at her. Then there had been a long, loud hissing noise and the last glimmer was gone. To Paddy's mind, that means the scorched-out hull had just sunk flat, not rolling or pitching, and that would be why the jackstaff, if that's what it is over there, is perfectly perpendicular.

"By what's stickin' up, I'd judge she lays in maybe thirty feet of water," a voice says nearby.

In the late twilight, men at the rails are peering at it in silence. Paddy glances back to Robbie's chair and sees that he's gazing at it, too, with such a stricken look in his eyes that Paddy is sure he knows just what's in his comrade's mind. They had both seen it in that ghastliest moment, and both are seeing it again now in terrible memory:

Right there it was, just a few feet behind that pole, that great tongue of flame had burst out on the foredeck and swallowed Felice. It might have occurred miles up the river from here, but it was right by that jackstaff, that was where she perished. Right there was where the worst thing in Paddy's lifetime of terrible things had happened.

No last rites. No body to bury. No tombstone, just a jackstaff, and it'll probably be swept away by tomorrow. Gone down the Lethe...

"Mister Quinn, sir?" Robbie says, giving off a cloud of tobacco smoke from his new pipe.

Paddy sighs. "I'll talk with you when you learn my first name, Robbie."

"Um, Paddy, sir?"

"What did I say about 'sir?'"

"Paddy?"

"That's better. What?"

"Just wonderin'. You going to write about Mrs. Quinn when you write your story?"

By God, I think he reads my mind! She won't be all forgot if I write her in. But doubt I could stand to...

"Don't know yet, Robbie. I'll know when I get it going."

Which I better get to doing instead of just mooning over this river.

So many times, the only way he's been able to get control over grief or outrage has been by just putting the pen or pencil to paper and getting to work. So now it's time. He picks up his desk, sits down on the deck chair, and takes out a pencil, and a musty-smelling notebook, which he opens on his lap. By now the *Saint Patrick* has left the *Sultana*'s jackstaff far astern. He can't see it anymore.

"Robbie," he says, "I need your honest opinion. You don't think I can start writing about all this without a drink, do you?"

"Uhm... maybe you should try."

"Then how about your *not* honest opinion?"

*

By nine o'clock he has had two shots to prime himself but still faces a blank page. A crewman has come down the deck lighting lamps and beyond the lamplight runs that dark river.

Paddy has hardly ever had any trouble starting before. Even after days of cannonades and bugles and charges and mass slaughters, even after seeing certain victories turn into shameful defeats, even when sitting battle-weary under wet canvas with nostrils and lungs rank with odors of gunsmoke and gangrene and rotting horseflesh, he has always been able to put the pencil to paper and come forth with a good opening sentence and proceed almost without hesitation until the account of the battle has been finished.

The only time he can remember being unable to *start* writing was in '47 when he woke up in a hospital tent after the battle of Buena Vista in Mexico to find that his left hand had been blown off and it was several days before he could bring himself to tell about it in his diary. Twelve years old he'd been then, or was it thirteen? Army camp errand boy. Kept a diary and made a few cents writing letters home for illiterate soldiers. That's how he'd started writing, and writing had made him what he is now. The right words had always just *been there* when he needed to start writing.

That exception, all those years ago, was probably because of the shock of finding himself part gone. Maybe that's my problem now. Part of me gone. Best part.

Felice.

"Not gettin' much writ down, are ye?" Robbie observes.

"Sure not. Too much to sort out."

"Then maybe it's 'cause it's not finished yet."

"What's not finished yet?"

"That story you're trying to write. It won't be done 'til we go see Mister Lincoln, will it?"

Paddy finds himself delighted with that astute question, smiles at it, but also feels his eyes brimming with some huge, unexpected tide of melancholy. Finally he clears his throat and says, "Sure and I'm thankful we came up buoyant together, Robbie Macombie."

"Thank 'e. So am I..."

"Sometimes you get to things I can't figure all on my own. I may have to ask you questions now and then."

"That *do* make me feel important."

Paddy picks up his whiskey glass and glances out of the corner of his eye at Robbie's august profile in the lamplight, thinking.

Might be the only good way to start writing this is through him.

"I'll drink to that," he says. And he wishes Robb could have one with him and keep it down.

He's very worried about Robbie's gut. He's never concerned himself before with anyone's innards but his own.

Except those few days when Felice was...

When she...was with child...

*

Robbie sits in his deck chair and pretends that he isn't hearing

Paddy weep. He's not surprised that it's finally coming out. There's nothing for Robbie to say. He can tell that Paddy is trying not to be heard at it. He isn't caterwauling, or even sobbing aloud. All Robbie hears are sniffs and now and then a half-strangled moan. He could probably hear more if not for the throb of the steamboat engines and the rush of water in the paddlewheels.

Maybe *this* is what he needs before he can get to writing, Robbie thinks. He tries to imagine what it must be like to take all this that's happened and write it down on paper well enough that people can read it and know. *Small wonder he's having a hard time starting*!

Robbie sits here in the lamplight listening to the swash of the river, now and then looking at some tiny yellow light or another on the far riverbank, sometimes seeing sparks from the smokestacks whirl away to wink out in the dark. He remembers having just such thoughts of sparks a few nights ago, though it seems as long ago as childhood: the notion that stars might be sparks, and that lives are as brief as sparks in the long age of the world.

My spark should've winked out long ago and many a time. Mexico. Virginia. At Andersonville. Last night in this river. And many another time my spark could have gone out as easy as not.

Sure would've been out by now if it wasn't for Mister Quinn.

When he saw that angel Missus of his burn up, I reckon he'd just as soon died then and there. I do believe all he kept on for was to keep me alive.

Makes me feel real important that he wanted to keep his promise to me. A man like him.

God willing my guts won't kill me and this boat won't blow up, and we'll get there and see Mister Lincoln.

What must Father Abraham look like after two weeks dead?

Don't care, want to see him anyhow. God knows I've seen worse. Any of us in that Reb prison looked worse alive than Mister Lincoln could look dead.

I wish I could just fall asleep and wake up at the funeral in Springfield. Could sleep right in this hard chair if my innards would just let up.

Robbie hears glass clink beside him. That will be Paddy pouring another slug of the cure-all.

Only thing I'd want different about Mister Quinn is he'd not be such a jugsucker. Can't blame him, though, not just now....

Anyhow, he's stopped weepin', sounds like.

*

Paddy has had his cry out, such a one as he's never wrung out of his soul before, and now he lays out the notebook and tries again to start the writing.

He turns from a page of scratched-out beginnings, to a fresh page. Those false starts were all like war reporting: opening with factual statements conveying the enormity of the disaster, the pathetic condition of the homeward-bound Andersonville veterans, the estimate of the dead, the heedless might of the flooding river, the *Sultana*'s faulty boiler, the fecklessness of the authorities who so overloaded the vessel and of Captain Cass Mason, all that sort of relevant information.

But even with its declaration that this is being written by an eyewitness and survivor, the prose just does not convey what it needs to; it simply hasn't the pathos. This somehow cannot be told in the same manner of accounting as a battle.

Now Paddy remembers something he'd been thinking before the weeping came over him.

On the new page he begins:

> *We are at Springfield, Illinois.*
>
> *If testament is needed to how much any man can endure, and why he will endure so much, it is in the person of a gaunt soldier who stands beside me looking into the casket of the man he called Father Abraham. This is the story of how this soldier finally came to the funeral of his commander in chief.*

"Well, I have a start, Robbie. It looks good. And not just because of m' beautiful cursive."

"Good! Do I get to read it?"

"Not yet. Nobody sees my prose until I'm done and satisfied with it."

"That means I have to live that long?"

"That's what it means."

*

Paddy has been mulling on Robbie's wise statement that the story can't be written yet because it's not over, and it won't be over until, at the soonest, May 3rd, they will have gone to the President's funeral. In fact, this starting paragraph foresees that end of the story. Paddy has written ahead of the present – a trick technique he's never used before. As a long-practicing journalist, he's a bit uneasy with the style he's begun using here. It seems more like a panegyric than a magazine article. Writing it, he feels the way he felt writing in his diary as a boy, when he was learning to express feelings on paper. He wonders whether Mister Guernsey at *Harper's* will even print a story written in such an unusual form.

But it feels right to him now, and it *is* a beginning. And Robbie does personify the long odyssey of combat, imprisonment, sickness and terror that most every soldier on the *Sultana* had endured. Now Paddy can use this time aboard the St. Louis-bound *Saint Patrick* to compile and write, from all those interviews, the back stories of those many soldiers.

I didn't realize I was interviewing them for their obituaries, he thinks, with a shudder. And they hadn't known that, either.

Well, actually, everything *is* obituary, he thinks. Eventually. Then he thinks, smiling just a little:

Life does doom us to be humus.

He writes that in a margin of the notebook page. Maybe he'll use it in an oration someday.

*

The *Saint Patrick* is a plain, small, workaday steamboat by comparison with the *Sultana,* but clean, comfortable, not overcrowded, capably run and maintained by a polite crew and a captain lacking in pretension. Its saloon is operated by a corpulent, pink-faced old gent with a Germanic accent, not given to gestures of generosity like the dear departed McGinty and O'Hara, and so Paddy's patronage of the bar is infrequent and businesslike, with no special privileges expected or given. Paddy has three bottles of good whiskey that he bought before departing from Memphis, so there's little incentive to spend time in the saloon. Many of the soldiers aboard know who he is by now, and several already have approached him to talk about their survival or ask him to draw their portraits. Paddy really doesn't want very much to talk. He would rather like to be anonymous on this vessel, alone with his thoughts, so that he might get a couple of good days in writing and perhaps some healing sleep at night.

But with a weary sense of resignation, he gets himself ready for more interviews and sketches. He realizes that in order to tell this story fully, he needs to listen to these few who survived the explosion and the river, and not just listen, but interview them as avidly as he did the many before the catastrophe.

Who we are now is different from who we were then, he thinks. Keep that in mind.

So he braces himself for more intense work. He has all this to do, as well as the care of his sick friend. I'm like Sister of Mercy myself now, he thinks. And under all that runs the anxiety that some vicissitude - a mechanical problem, a collision with a snag, even a snarled troop transfer at Cairo - could foil the plan to reach Springfield in time for the funeral. There will be plenty to worry about. Plenty to wear him out. Plenty to stoke his infamous insomnia.

Even if he should have time for sleep, there probably would be the dreaded dreams. Those old dreams, of bombshells and bayonets, the newer dreams of drowning.

And, God forbid, that dream of orating to a living throng while his beloved dead sit in a row behind him, judging his truthfulness..

*

Between Memphis and Cairo lie no major stopovers, no places to disrupt his work. Most of the soldiers will be getting off at Cairo to catch Ohio River steamers, or to board trains going north and east toward their homes, so Paddy hopes to interview as many as he can before Cairo, and then bear down and get some of the writing done between Cairo and St. Louis.

He feels that it will be especially important to keep himself occupied with the writing as the steamboat travels that section of the Mississippi above the mouth of the Ohio. The absence of Felice might be just too poignant along that rugged and beautiful riverscape, because it was, as she called it, her very own "magic country." In her childhood she had been familiarized with nearly every mile of it by her parents, on steamboat excursions every summer before the war. They had traveled in style, with a Negro nursemaid to tend to Felice. On those excursions she had memorized the names of the bluffs, the islands, the settlements and their places in history. In New Orleans before their wedding she had regaled Paddy with rich lore about old Missouri settlements: Cape Girardeau and its old Shawnee Indian trading settlement, Ste. Genevieve and its lead mines, the old French Fort de Chartres. She had described the ancient mounds built by lost civilizations, and told of the explorers Lewis and Clark obtaining some of their supplies from her grandparents' emporium before they departed up the Missouri to go to the Pacific Ocean. Her father and mother had shown her an old leatherbound ledger in which her grandparents recorded every item they had helped the explorers obtain, and they had kept receipts and documents both explorers had signed after they returned from the West and lived in St. Louis as Governors. In another family story, Felice's grandparents had waited at the Ohio's mouth to see the first steamboat on Western waters, the *New Orleans,* come down the Ohio in 1811. And that very same night they had been nearly drowned by surging river waters and shore cave-ins when the Great Earthquake shook the Mississippi Valley. Part of the river's course had been changed by that immense upheaval, and Felice had promised to point out to

Paddy all the visible traces, as a part of their honeymoon voyage. The New Madrid Quake and her grandparents' adventure in it were a favorite part of her family history. But there was much more. Felice's father, as a young trader and interpreter, had ridden to treaty councils with General Clark when he was the U.S. Indian Agent for the whole West, and he had told her about those great gatherings of thousands of Indians from the Plains, describing the drums and cooking aromas and the smoking ceremonies and horse races. She could describe those great Indian councils as vividly as if she had been there herself. Being an only child, she had been raised like a son to be the eventual keeper of the whole history of the Beaulieu family. Paddy, who had spent his boyhood and youth with no relatives except his mother, had been amazed at the breadth and richness of family history she carried in her memory. He had joked one night that he could write a whole book without getting out of her family tree. "No. Rather," she had said, "*I* shall write it, if one's to be written." And she could have. She was in fact far better educated than Paddy himself. She could read in Latin, and sometimes had had to correct his pronunciation of the phrases he had picked up in his years of self-education. Felice could well have written still another book , too, a memoir of her nursing duties on the hospital ships in this war just past.

All that she might well have done, had she not died aboard the *Sultana.*

And it was *his* fault that she had.

*

This bright spring morning after an unusually deep and dreamless, almost comatose, sleep, Paddy leaves Robbie propped up in his bunk with a cup of tea, and he hobbles – his feet sting too much to call it walking – aft along the deck to the stern, with his writing desk under his arm. From the look of the distant riverbank, the Mississippi flood has receded a little. He sees stretches of bottomlands strewn with muddy driftwood, a woodcutter's cabin with water only up to its doorsill instead of its eaves, and great flights of buzzards drifting down to forage on the riverbanks for whatever has drowned.

Paddy stops beside the lifeboat yawl and reaches out to rap on its hull with his knuckles, as if he were at somebody's door. A dark, dishevelled head appears above the gunwale, looking at him with deep-sunk and fearful eyes. The man says, "Look, sir, it don't do no one harm if I stay here in this boat. Please leave me be."

"Easy, Mister McFarland. I'm not crew. Just want to talk a bit."

The man squints in the sunlight, then nods. "You're that writer and drawer, ain't you?"

"I am. Paddy Quinn. And you're Will McFarland, 42nd Indiana, they tell me."

"Yeh, and no matter what they say, I ain't crazy. I just mean t' be here in this boat already if anything happens. 'Cause I couldn't get in that other one, and I damn near drownded! Well, if ye want t' talk, climb in. I ain't gettin' out." And he adds, as Paddy climbs on the rail and swings a leg into the boat, "I am sure sorry about y'r wife, sir. I heard."

"Thank you. But I came to hear you tell how you got through that night safe."

So they sit in the swaying boat with the wake of the *Saint Patrick* gurgling and swashing far below them, and Paddy hears how the catastrophe looked to someone at the stern end of the *Sultana*.

Two general impressions unfold as the soldier talks, growing more agitated with every sentence he speaks. While those victims forward near the boilers had been instantly burned, scalded, crippled, trapped in an inferno of wreckage or blown into the river, the many farther astern had first become alarmed by a mighty percussion, an eruption of sparks and ruddy smoke rising into the night sky, and an immediate chorus of screams and shouts, and then their terror mounted as the windblown conflagration swept aft along the decks and through the salon and staterooms toward them. Theirs was a different kind of fright, a considered desperation that swelled to panic as every hope for deliverance fell away minute by minute. Paddy senses that, in a way, it must have been worse for them than instant death and shock for the others, and his hand trembles as he jots down Will McFarland's words and roughs out a sketch of him. And as the soldier describes the chaotic abandonment of the flaming vessel, his memory brings him to choking speech and tears of mortification.

"I didn't see hardly a one brave or decent thing done...it was jus' every man fer hisself..."

He now tells of men who had been comrades in war, men who had charged against Rebel gunfire beside one another, suddenly too crazed with fear of fire and water to help each other. Men who drowned other desperate men, and even women, to keep them from getting in the yawl, or to defend a piece of debris that might buoy only oneself. "Tell you what... Most o' the men th-that got away safe in that there life boat was *Sultana* crewmen! Oh, that was wrong! The strong 'uns pushing the weak out! If... If I'd had my gun, I'd might of shot a deckhand or two!"

Now McFarland goes on to tell of pathetic accidents he saw: a mother who tied a lifesaver on her baby and dropped it into the river, only to see that the flotation was too low and loose, and the child floated head down and drowned...Two civilian men who got onto a floating door, then were immediately swamped when a horse leaped overboard and hit the door...Two soldiers fighting each other for control of a floating door jamb until both went under and drowned...

"Oh, but the sorriest things I seen was wi... with the ladies!" McFarland stammers. "They, they come runnin'out of staterooms and out of the Wo...Women's Parlor back there...just a-shriekin', half- naked, some of 'em...One pertick'ler lady she jumped in th' river with a big bell skirt that floated 'er for a time, but when she begun t' sink, she stroke out t' get a hand hold on the rudder... But it already had cryin' men hangin' on all over it, men who couldn't swim, tryin' to stay down below the flames... and they pushed her away...then finally she tried t'get hold of one o' them by his collar... well, he swang 'round and hit her in the face with his elbow, an' then just plain pushed her under...I never seen her after that..."

McFarland's story pours out like a purge: people drowning all around him in the firelight, then eventually in cold darkness. He had stayed alive by floating rather than exhausting himself with efforts to swim. He had employed the old sailor's trick of making water wings of his wet trousers. "I'd be dead now if I hadn't knowed that trick...Look now, Mister, see these here patches? I'd sewed up some old rips and a bullet hole in 'em, down at Camp Fisk, jes' the day before we boarded that *Sultana*. Patched 'em so I'd look presentable, that's why. But if I hadn't, they'd not 'a' held air, and I'd o' drownded sure as hell. Was it the Good Lord that warned me t' patch them pants? I reckon I'll always b'lieve so...".

McFarland said he had heard men crying, praying, even singing in the river in those long, cold hours, now and then the voice of a woman. A few women passengers had been rescued alive when morning light came, but most of those then died from the effects of that long exposure.

At least, Paddy can be thankful that Felice perished quickly, probably with one scorching inhalation of breath, and had thus been spared such a gradual, numbing, terrifying fate as theirs.

In his broken and emotional narrative, McFarland keeps returning to retell the fate of the woman who was buoyed by her skirt, and each time he tells it, Paddy envisions the woman as the one who boarded the *Sultana* under the name "Mrs. Willard." It surprises and troubles him that he keeps imagining her. He's tried to keep that woman out of his mind since the disaster, as if Felice in her Heavenly omniscience might see that strumpet inhabiting his thoughts. But now he keeps envisioning the bawd struggling for life under the stern of the *Sultana*.

"I wonder who she was," he says to McFarland. "Could you see her well enough to, well, to describe her?"

"Oh, a vision to behold, she was! When she got on board at Memphis t'other night, she looked so big and elegant, I figgered she must be maybe an operetta...."

"An... operetta?"

"You know, the big main lady that sings in operas? But that was just my guess 'cause of the looks of 'er...I don't reckon she was an operetta, though, or she'd had a stateroom. But she was just back there 'mongst the ordinary women in th' Ladies' Lounge. I do s'pose if she was somebody famous, you'd of knowed 'er, wouldn't ye?"

Paddy shakes his head, having to hide a smile even though this is all too pitiful to be very amusing. He thinks:

Know her? In what sense, the Biblical? I can't even answer that!

He remembers Robbie telling him that "Mrs. Willard" had put five thousand Yankee dollars in the *Sultana*'s safe. He thinks of the wire he saw in the Memphis telegraph office, about advertisements. He had guessed that perhaps she was booking a club show to take advantage of the great crowds of men who will be in Springfield for the President's funeral.

If that's what it was, just as well she drowned. One more shameful memory down into Lethe...

"Anyhow," McFarland goes on, "th' way them men done her just t' save their own skins, it made me so mad an' so 'shamed, I get sick to think on it...That's why I'm in this boat, Mister Quinn. If anything happens t' *this* steamboat, and any poor woman needs in, why, I'm right here to save her a place, by God!"

*

Now in most of his interviews as the *Saint Patrick* churns on toward Cairo, Paddy detects that same deep hangdog malaise, of men disillusioned by their own behavior. Some look at their feet as they tell how they survived at someone else's expense. He understands these pitiful admissions; he remembers, himself, fighting off the clutches of men in the water. Others talk around it, but he can guess what they're hiding in their narratives. Some speak so directly of it that he feels like a priest in the Confessional. He suspects that most of these men, maybe including himself, will carry for the rest of their lives a guilt heavy enough to counterbalance the joy of surviving. He can imagine each man, in years to come, modifying the truth. Paddy has spent his life among soldiers, brave ones and cowards, some both, has seen some of them mature and grow old, and he has seen how their memories evolve over the years. He has, in fact, occasionally gone back through the musty, ragged boyhood diaries he kept in the Mexican War, to see how he described those events when they were fresh in his memory, and often has found that his recollections have changed so much in the last two decades that it seemed someone else must have written his diary.

Each of these veterans will have to deal with hellish memories in his peculiar way, Paddy muses. Some will rationalize, some will glorify themselves, some will simply try to erase.

Suddenly now, a thought gives him gooseflesh: a notion that he will, in the years ahead, have to cope with the memory of Felice's death. He'll always have it with him, as long as he lives.

At least, I'm not guilty of it.

Am I?

But she wouldn't have been on the *Sultana* except by his arrangement.

And he could have taken her off at Vicksburg when they knew the boiler was bad.

Or if he had been with her on the foredeck when the boiler blew, probably he could have saved her. Or at least they might have perished together.

Robbie was with me when we saw her die up there on the boat. What does he think of this, if he does think of it? Does old Robbie hold me guilty?

*

Now that Paddy has had that thought, he can't look at old Robbie without wondering whether he blames him for not being with Felice when the boat blew up. But he doesn't really want to bring it up. If Robbie hasn't already harbored such a notion, Paddy doesn't want to plant it in him.

They're in their cabin, now, just the two of them. It is midnight and Paddy isn't interviewing anyone at this hour. By lamplight he is trying to write. Robbie is in the lower bunk, now being too weak to climb to the upper. Except for an occasional groan and hard breathing, he's quiet, but probably not asleep. Unfortunately the *Saint Patrick* doesn't have a doctor aboard. Robbie hardly ever sleeps now because of his internal pains, and a fear that he'll mess the bed if he isn't awake to monitor his boiling bowels. That's a dire anxiety for him, made worse by his obsession with personal cleanliness after the filth of the prison. He seldom says anything, not wanting to interrupt Paddy's writing, which Robbie deems almost sacred. He responds when Paddy speaks to him. Theirs is a deep and compatible silence, neither man feeling he must entertain the other. Neither takes offense at the other's reticence. Once in a while Robbie will say, "Got t' try to use the pot," and when he says that, Paddy helps him sit up on the edge of the bunk, then steps out of the room to give him privacy, and, frankly, because the sound and smell are too unpleasant, especially in such a tiny room. Afterward Paddy takes the chamberpot out on deck and empties its stinking slush over the rail into the river. He fetches a cup of tea or glass of water whenever he hears Robbie start making a dry clicking noise on his palate. At mealtime he helps him into a wheelchair and pushes him to the dining salon, and gets for him the blandest stuff that can be had: grits, or mashed potatoes, or oatmeal gruel. If he keeps that down, Paddy rolls him into the saloon and gets him a glass of beer. Paddy carries in his pocket the cob pipe and tobacco pouch he'd bought in Memphis to replace the ones lost in the river, and Robbie might smoke it while sipping his beer, there in his wheelchair on the deck watching the changing terrain of the riverbanks. Maybe another beer in the evening. It's a new experience to Paddy, being rather like a nurse to an invalid, but he doesn't resent having to do it, even if Robbie needs something just when Paddy is trying to concentrate on the writing.

But just now, when the only sounds are Paddy's scribbling and the background rumble of the boat's machinery, Robbie clears his throat three times, and says:

"Sorry t' bother you, but I been thinkin'...'Bout a *what-if* kind of a thing..."

"What about?"

"Well, that if we hadn't been drinking whiskey in that cabin... talkin' all night with the soldiers... why, instead, we might've been up forward with your Missus when that ol' boat blew up, and..."

Paddy's scalp tingles. Damned if he isn't reading my thoughts again!

It is that very same matter he's been reluctant to mention to Robbie. He braces himself for what might have to be said. Robbie goes on: "S'pose if we'd been up there, we might've saved her?"

"God knows. We *weren't* up there, though."

"Course not...You with all that work t'do, but...Wonder what if maybe you could've been up *there* doin' your work..." There *seems* to be no accusation in his voice, though there could be...

"Believe me, Robbie, I've been ruminating on that same cud, and... well, I don't like the taste of it. Sure and I *could've* done my work up there where she was...Should have, maybe. But I figured the whiskey and privacy in the cabin would help them talk easier..." Sure... a true Irishman: blame whiskey for anything you're ashamed of...

"And when I sketch, it draws too many onlookers. That hampers an interview. Anyway, I felt she didn't *want* me hoverin' around up there. It was, well, like *priest* work she was doing for those poor souls." She'd told him that in just those terms. Paddy realizes he's got some tough rationalizing ahead for himself.

But he remembers that he *was* trying to go to her, just before it happened.

Robbie says, "Guess I never did tell you.... A time or two... when you were *real* busy...talkin' and drawin' in the cabin, I did go up there to see if she needed anything...or just to watch on 'er for you...Hope *I* wasn't intrudin' on her."

"No, you didn't tell me that."

"Well...Wasn't nothing to tell. Did do me good just t' see her comfort those poor boys... "

Paddy remembers the evening when she came back to the cabin distraught and frustrated because she couldn't keep a man from dying, or even give last rites.

"Well, anyway, thanks for keeping a better watch on her than I did." Saying this makes Paddy feel halfway between wanting to cry and to curse. He knows damned well that one reason he had done the interviews the way he did, with the keg in the stateroom, was because it was a good excuse to drink more than Felice would have liked. If he'd done the interviewing in the saloon, he could have got both his work and his drinking done, and that would have been much closer to where she was taking care of the veterans, and maybe he could have reached her...

But of course the saloon had been closed anyway by the time of the explosion.

And we were damn well meant to have that keg. Both be dead by now without it.

Paddy had vaguely hoped they'd have this conversation, hoped that it would come up and clarify his conscience one way or another, but now he wishes they hadn't started talking about it. It's making him feel as low about himself as some of these survivors feel about their own negligence. Now Robbie coughs in the bunk, really moving some phlegm, and after a while starts talking again, just audibly:

"Well, I reckon things turn out... the way the Good Lord means 'em to. If He meant her to live, why, we'd've been up there to rescue her when that boiler blew, maybe. But, well, you both, in your own different ways...you were both of you doin' us honor... and helpin' us... though you both could've just ignored us an' saved yourselves all that trouble. We all knew that, sure as hell." He pauses and expels a few more wet, wracking coughs, then goes on. "You ought t' been real proud of each other...And, well...her good work's done with, rest 'er soul. But you, well, you got a *long* row t' hoe yet."

The throb and rattle of the steamboat's machinery fill Paddy's ears after Robbie's voice falls still. Paddy sets his writings and sketches on the floor beside his chair, picks up his glass with an inch of whiskey in it, tips back and swallows, and puts the glass back down. He rises stiffly from the chair, goes to the outer door and opens it, looks into the vast darkness and smells the wet air and hears the constant swash of the river in the sidewheel paddles. Hardly anyone is on deck at this hour. Paddy shuts the door, goes back to his chair and scoots it closer to Robbie's bedside. He sits down, reaches out his right hand and puts his palm on the back of Robbie's cool, bony left hand, gives it a couple of pats and a light squeeze. Robbie opens his light blue eyes in their sunken sockets and looks up at Paddy, and nods. He says, "Y' know what you could do for me? If you'd hand me my pipe, help me sit up, well... I can't bear t' drink, but reckon if I smoke, and you drink, why, that'd take care of the vices, wouldn't it?"

"Yessir," Paddy says, blinking. "You and I together, ol' Robbie, we can do anything that needs done, can't we?"

By God I *was* going up there to protect her, just didn't get there in time. Got to remember that.

*

"Now you can see it," says a soldier at the rail, pointing out to starboard. "We'll cross in a minute. Come throw a penny in for good luck."

"About time for good luck," says another soldier. "I ain't had a bit since '62."

"Good luck for just a penny! That's a bargain!" someone else exclaims.

Paddy stands at the starboard rail in the morning sunlight, probing in his trouser pocket for coins. There with the small change is the gold medallion of the San Patricios, and he takes a loving look at it before dropping it all back in his pocket except a one-cent piece. If there has ever been a lucky piece in his pocket, that medallion is it. Maybe it's why he's still alive while the Irish barkeeps who gave it to him are dead. If they hadn't given it to him, maybe they would be alive now and he wouldn't. He leans on his elbow and watches the river water change. Eight feet below the rail, the Mississippi is suddenly flowing in two colors, along a distinct line: the familiar muddy brown, and alongside it a clear green current. Felice had expected that they would watch this phenomenon together on their honeymoon cruise up, this distinct line where the Ohio's clear flow shoulders into the Mississippi's muddy flood. It's this way, she had told him, because the Ohio comes down through a forested, green watershed in the east, where the soil is retained by the roots of trees and grasses and marshland plants, while the Mississippi bears mud and sediment swept into it by the long, uncontrollable Missouri, which constantly washes away the banks of the treeless western Plains. Above the Missouri's confluence, she had told him, the Mississippi is clean and green like the Ohio. She had been so eager to share with him her knowledge of these great rivers here in the middle of the continent, and this place of the two-toned convergence had been the most visible evidence of how God's rivers work in the land.

Though she had seldom talked about Catholicism itself, she had conveyed her devotion in two ways: her reverence for all vast Creation, and her tireless care for sufferers.

She's in Heaven, Paddy thinks, his throat tightening. Sure as hell she is.

She too had told him of the tradition that a penny should be dropped into this liquid margin. So, imagining her standing beside him, he flips the penny outward with his thumb.

"Mister Quinn," says a voice beside him.

At his left stands a swarthy, bony man in baggy Union enlisted uniform with no insignia of any kind, and a familiar face: chin and jaw a burl of scars from a badly healed battle wound. It's someone he interviewed one day on the *Sultana.*

"Well, good to see you," Paddy says, annoyed that he can't remember the man's name without looking into his sketchbook. "I didn't know you were aboard."

"Romulus Tolbert, 8th Indiana Mounted," the man reminds him. "Your pencil picture made me look good." He lifts his hand toward his mangled jaw and then drops it away, his gaze wavering for a moment. Paddy remembers having sketched him from the undamaged side.

"Well, congratulations on, well, being alive," Paddy says. It has become his usual greeting to men he hasn't expected to see since the night of the explosion.

"You likewise. And my condolence for your...loss...Reckon that lady's sure in Heaven if anybody would be...What I come to say, though, is... it's about that old feller with you, that Macombie. See, his family's place is just a few mile up th' road from mine, at Saluda, there near Madison?..."

"Sure. He always talks about it."

"Well, he ought t' get there as straight off as he can be got there, condition he's in...That's how I see it..."

"Sure and he ought to. He's so sick it scares me."

"But, sir, he told me you two's goin' way up to Springfield for the President's funeral."

"Right."

"Well, but if he went with us d'rec'ly, he'd be home among neighbors in just a couple days. We'd take care of 'im and see he got there. I doubt he's got more'n two days left in 'im without a good doctor and homefolks care."

"I fear that could be so. And it's a real Christian notion of yours to do that for him. Do I gather y've made him the offer?"

"Yessir."

"And?"

"Well, he's like all them people o' his. Stubborn-like once they're sot on an idee. The one that was in th' Legislature, he was famous for never changin' his mind..."

"I take it you haven't changed Mister Macombie's mind?"

"Well, that's why I come t' you, sir. I b'lieve he'd do anything you told 'im to. Thought maybe you could tell 'im he oughter come with us Jeff County boys and we'd perty sure get 'im home alive."

"Well, Mister Tolbert, two things: First, he won't really get *home* by stopping with his relatives there at Saluda.. He does love it there -- it being his birthplace -- but his wife and sons are in Pennsylvania. He enlisted in Pennsylvania, and that's where he'll get discharged. If he gets that far. Second thing is, he isn't looking that far ahead anyway. Only thing he cares about is seeing the President go to rest. He said he'll get there for that if he has to crawl to Springfield. I trust he'll keep himself alive that far. Hell, the whole Mississippi River couldn't kill him th' other night, because he'd still got that funeral to go to. And he still has. After that, God knows."

"Then you won't..."

"Not won't, *can't,* Mister Tolbert..."

They jump at the clang of the *Saint Patrick's* bell. Any loud noise since the night of the *Sultana*'s death is almost heart-stopping. The bell rings three times. "Look up there," Paddy says.

"That's got to be Cairo."

On a low bluff far ahead, its trees still bare in outline but tinged with the fresh green of budding foliage, are buildings with chimneys, and below sit so many steamboats they look like another city along the riverbank. Cairo has been an important supply and shipping town during the war because of its location just above the confluence, and Paddy knows it has telegraph. It was, he remembers, this town's *War Eagle* newspaper that first carried news on the President's murder down to New Orleans, that fateful morning that now seems years past. He remembers vividly the mate up on the deck of the *Sultana* shouting and waving that terrible newspaper, remembers standing there on the balcony at his mother's hotel, with Felice growing faint beside him at the news. Less than two weeks ago, but it feels now as if that day had been the beginning of his life.

As usual he considers debarking to go to the telegraph station and report in to his editors in New York and New Orleans, maybe a message to reassure his mother that he's this far and safe. But Cairo will be crawling with soldiers transferring to trains or to other boats, with shippers and brokers, contractors and agents and boat crews, so there's no point wasting time standing in the usual line waiting to send a message which reports nothing except that he's come this far. And he needs to keep an eye on Robbie. Paddy turns to the soldier, Tolbert, who is now watching the approach to the Cairo waterfront, and says:

"We'll be parting here. But you'll stay in my mind yet a while. Remember, you're in that story I'm writing for the magazine. And your kind intentions will be a part of it."

Private Tolbert nods, turns. Paddy glances at the puckered scar that had been his jaw, and sees that his chin is quivering. "My God Almighty," the soldier murmurs. "I cain't hardly b'lieve all the hell I been through since last time I seen this Ohio River!"

"Take a good long time at home to loaf and see if peace isn't too tedious. Godspeed."

"You tell that old Macombie I hope he lives long 'nough t' come visit us in Saluda. We got cooks in th' family that'll put some meat back on his bones."

"That'll sound good to him."

"And I'll be a-watchin' f'r that there Harper magazine. I know they sell it in Madison, seen it there many a time b'fore the war." He walks away shaking his head, and says, "The war."

*

It is dusk now as the *St. Patrick* raises steam and backs out from the crowded Cairo docks. The last rosy sunset hues have faded from the high clouds over Kentucky on the far side of the Ohio. All the homebound soldiers except Robbie are gone, marched away to board trains or other boats headed up the Ohio toward home. Several civilian passengers have come aboard, bound for St. Louis; a few mules and a team of oxen have been led on, two wagonloads of sorghum barrels rolled aboard, and a few score sacks of coal carried on by Negro and white stevedores. Paddy has pushed Robbie's wheelchair to the dining salon and ordered a bowl of bread pudding for him, with sweet cream to soften it, and a beefsteak for himself.

"That was one ugly town," Robbie says after he gets down the first two spoonfuls of his pudding. "A coalyard and an arsenal mixed together and left out in the rain, looks like."

"Fair appraisal," Paddy replies. "What can you expect of a war depot, though?" On the table by his plate is a new issue of the Cairo *War Eagle,* stacked with headlines about the *Sultana* explosion, about the President's funeral train visiting Indianapolis before heading up to Chicago for a stop before the last leg of its route to Springfield, and about the slaying by gunfire of his assassin, the actor Booth. There is also a story about the running Federal manhunt in the South for fleeing Confederate President Jefferson Davis, his entourage and rumored bags of gold bars. Davis and his staff are now alleged to have conspired with Booth and his gang in the assassination of President Lincoln and the failed assassinations of his Cabinet. Paddy shakes his head at that. He knew Davis as a young Army officer in Mexico and as president of the Confederacy, and his opinion of him is too high to imagine him part of an assassination plot. Of course many Northerners, and Northern publishers, want Jefferson Davis to be a consummate villain, so they are eager to believe the worst rumor and influence their readers to believe it too. Paddy gazes at the newspaper's masthead and muses, "I wonder what they'll call this paper now that it won't have the war to squawk about."

"The *Uglytown Peace Dove*?" Robbie ventures. Paddy laughs, feeling better than he has for quite some time about Robbie's chances of making it. *If he can state a joke like that...*

Paddy works his knife blade down through his leathery beefsteak, and says, "I might trade you this for your pudding. Think you could digest a boot sole?"

"Y'd have to chew it for me first. My grinders are coming loose."

"Well, look here now, old comrade. I was happy to feed you whiskey mouth to mouth. But meat? You're not my wolf pup, y' know... Hey, now, looks like company coming..."

The captain of the packet has been wending his way among the tables, speaking with other passengers but glancing often at Paddy, and now he's here, bowing slightly, one hand on the back of Paddy's chair. "Might I join you for a moment, Mister Quinn?"

"It's your boat, Cap'n. Surely you can sit anywhere you like..." That's not nice , he thinks. This *isn't* Cap'n Mason. "Honored to have you at our table. This is my best friend, Robert Macombie."

"I'm the one honored, gentlemen, to have you aboard. You've been through a lot, haven't you? Terrible!"

"Robbie much more than I. He went through the war, then through Andersonville, *then* the *Sultana*..."

"Yeh, well, but you saw more war'n I did," says Robbie. "Mostly I sat and guarded Gen'ral McClellan against his own imagination. You were at more fights than most any soldier I ever knew..."

"All of which I could have avoided, which indicates I'm not as smart as you."

"Indicates I'm not as brave as *you,*" Robbie retorts. "Given my druthers, I'd've avoided every one of 'em. You had your druthers, and went to the battlefields."

The captain chuckles. "It's plain enough you admire each other! Well, gentlemen, we're on the last leg of our run to St. Louis. God willing, there's still time for you to get to Springfield for the sad event."

"It's what we're living for."

"In Cairo I spoke with some of *Sultana*'s owners, on their way down to Memphis to look into what happened. I, ah, talked with a Robert Mason, a brother of her captain. He's going down there, too, to see if his brother might turn up somehow. Offering two hundred dollars to anyone finding Cap'n Mason, or his remains...I told him, from what-all I've heard, not to expect much..."

"No," Paddy replies. "The one good thing I can say for Cass Mason is, he went down with his boat."

"Could happen to any of us...It's always there in the back of my mind...But, well, now, Mister Quinn, here's something I've been wanting to ask you...well, your opinion, on something. Or, to be more direct, your help..."

"I'm pretty powerless to help anybody. What?"

"Well, sir, I wonder if you know of a certain Mister Eads. James Eads, an engineer in St. Louis?"

"Would that be the Mister Eads who made all those ironclads for the river fleet?"

"That he did."

"A considerable service for the Union."

"And a profitable one, I'd reckon." That remark, and the expression on the captain's face, make his antipathy clear. "I wonder if you know, Mister Quinn, that Mister Eads proposes to build an iron bridge across the Mississippi? Between St. Louis and Illinois?"

Paddy had known that such a bridge had been discussed as a possibility for years. Felice had sometimes expressed her awe at the thought of the first bridge to cross the great river. Paddy himself, before the War Between the States, had written of railroad bridges in the East, so he can anticipate this riverman's opinion on the topic. "I didn't know that was Mister Eads' ambition, no. It'll give him something to do now that peace is come."

"Swords into ploughshares," mutters Robbie, pudding-spoon in hand.

"Can you imagine," says the captain, leaning close over the table, "any more dangerous a hazard for riverboats than a *bridge*? My God! Piers in the river to run into? Spans to take your smokestacks, even your pilothouse off in high water time? It's madness!"

Paddy had heard such objections expressed by eastern boatmen. Some did genuinely fear such dangers, but their bigger fear was the economic one. Bridges put ferryboats out of business. And railroads, already taking overland freightage away from steamboats, would take an even greater share as they became able to span the rivers westward. In memory's ear, Paddy can hear Felice predicting that the riverboats that she loved were "doomed to diminish their sway." She had carried more understanding and foresight in that beautiful head of hers than most men, even the educated ones. This poignant marveling at his lost love has so distracted him that he just now realizes that the captain has asked him something and is peering eagerly at him. "I'm sorry," he says, "I didn't hear you over the commotion out there." Indeed, passengers on the deck outside are exclaiming over the confluence of the rivers, and tossing pennies in, as the *Saint Patrick* recrosses into the muddy Mississippi current in the last light of the day and turns upstream toward St. Louis.

"I was hoping," the captain says, "that you might write something sensible in your magazine about the hazard Mister Eads would create if he got to build that bridge of his. There are gentlemen up in St. Louis who know a great deal about the matter. Who speak better than me. And would be able to make it worth your while to write such an item."

"Worth my while. And what does that mean, sir?"

"Well...that they would...compensate you for your, your writing..."

It's a long pause before Paddy knows what to say to such a novel sort of offer. "That's an interesting notion," he says. "But *Harper's* editor pays me for what I write for *Harper's*. I've never been paid by anyone else for it. Why would they be wanting to pay me for work I'm already paid for?" He glances at Robbie, who is carefully dipping into one side of his pudding, as if he were so busy seeking some special spoonful of it that he couldn't possibly be hearing this discourse. But he knows that Robbie is listening carefully. "If I were to write about the matter of a bridge, Cap'n, I would want to inform the reader of its...its dangers, as you say, but also its very real advantages..."

"Advantages? Advantages to whom? The railroads?" The captain's face is reddening.

"Railroads, sure. Also, perhaps," Paddy goes on after a thoughtful pause, "to a sick man who needs to go from East St. Louis to visit a doctor in St. Louis, can't swim, and can't afford the ferryboat? But could walk across a bridge? Someone like that. Or, say, a farmer in Illinois who has a wagonload of turnips he could sell in the crowd at LaClede's Landing, but his horse is too skittish to cross a gangplank onto a ferryboat....Sure now I don't need to expound on the basic uses of a bridge, do I, even to a boat captain? There've been bridges built since ancient times, you know, for the most obvious reasons. Why, I'll wager old Charon himself would be out of a job if Mister Eads could build a bridge across the Styx to Hades..."

"You're taking the wrong side, Mister Quinn! We'd pay you to, ah, tell it *our* way..."

"Cap'n, bear with me while I explain how I am about what you call 'taking sides.' Now, I just spent the last three years writing about what was a much bigger disagreement than bridges versus steamboats. For me to get close to a battle, I had to make arrangements with generals. Of one side sometimes, and of the other sometimes. As it happened, I knew a good number of those generals personally, knew them from when they were lieutenants fresh out of West Point, down in Mexico. Knew them from both sides. Why, even Jeff Davis remembered me from when I polished his boots down there, and he authorized that I could go sometimes with the Reb generals, even though I was with a New York magazine! With Bragg, Stonewall, Joe Johnston... On this side, I spent many a month with Grant, Hooker, Meade, Wallace.

"Now, Cap'n, every general I ever rode with hoped I'd tell his side of the story. Make him look good, make his soldiers look brave, make his cause look right. And I did find all the good I could find. I'd write about a battle from either side, and next time, that same officer would be glad to see me again, because I'd written the truth about 'im.

"Only thing some of those Rebs didn't like was that I told the truth when I rode with the Union, too. And same with Union officers who thought I'd written things too good about some Reb a few months back." Paddy picks up his cup from the table and wets his dry mouth with tepid coffee. "That's a long sermon, Cap'n. But I hope you see the point. I can't write just half the truth when I know the other half too."

Now the captain, mouth shut firmly, eyes gone confused, puts his fists on the table and stands up. "You'll excuse me, Mister Quinn? I have a boat to run. But please think about the offer..."

"Thank you for giving us the honor and pleasure of your company, Cap'n. I would like to know one thing: just between us, sir, have you ever walked across a bridge?"

For a while after the captain's stiff-backed departure, Robbie sits taking dabs of pudding with his spoon. Then he smiles and says, "You're kind o' hard on steamboat captains, I notice."

"Yes. And him offering me money, at that. I tell ye, Robbie," he sighs, his slight brogue creeping in, "bein' an honest Irish quill-pusher's no way to get rich."

CHAPTER FOURTEEN

St. Louis, Missouri

May 2nd, 1865

Paddy Quinn pauses in the shade of the white-pillared porch a few minutes to recover his breath from the climb. He wipes his brow with a kerchief, bracing himself for this very difficult duty, and then twists the key of the cast iron doorbell at the Beaulieu Mansion. It is a two-storey, oak-shaded, brick Georgian house high on the bluff, with chimneys at both ends and four dormers, its wide, pine-floored front porch overlooking the St. Louis riverfront far below. The house and its setting are even more grand than had been evoked in his imagination by Felice's descriptions. It is no wonder she knew and loved the Mississippi River so well, growing up with this view of it. He can imagine her sitting in a gauzy white dress on one of these wicker porch chairs watching steamboats move to and from LaClede's Landing down there, but quickly he tries to banish that pretty image because he is going to need all the stoicism he can muster in order to introduce himself to her parents as their new son-in-law and then immediately inform them that their daughter perished in flames before his own eyes.

They will probably know who he is before he says a word, though, by one glance at his empty left sleeve cuff and the portfolio under that arm. She had told them in correspondence from New Orleans that her betrothed was the celebrated *Harper's* war correspondent Padraic Quinn, and like most well-read Americans they would have known him as the famous one-handed artist and reporter. He expects his reception will be cool enough even before he tells the tragic news, as Mister and Mrs. Beaulieu had not even been asked for their daughter's hand.

And, though he's of their Catholic faith, he *is* a lowly Irishman.

Paddy waits at the door with a breeze cooling his forehead and the shadows of new oak foliage trembling on the porch floor. He hears shod hooves and the grind of steel wagonwheel rims on the street cobbles nearby, the rumble of steamboat engines far down on the river, and, muffled by distance, the whistle of a train on the other side of the Mississippi, one of several leaving today to take mourners from East St. Louis up to Springfield for the imminent funeral. One train, said the newspaper, had carried an ornate hearse borrowed from a St. Louis funeral establishment, because in all of the Illinois capital city there was not one hearse deemed elegant enough for the occasion.

He twists the doorbell key again, hearing its metallic jangle on the far side of the door. As important as this call at the Beaulieau house is, he's impatient. There isn't much time to deliver this tragic message, hurry back downtown, fetch Robbie from the dockside alehouse where he sits in a cheap new wheelchair, and get on a ferry to the train station on the other side. Paddy turns and looks again at the river, and imagines Mister Eads's proposed iron bridge, tries to envision it spanning that wide, yellow flood, pictures black plumes of coalsmoke in midriver rising not just from steamboats but from railroad locomotives. If such a bridge existed already and he could board a train going straight from St. Louis to Springfield, he would be much less anxious about getting Robbie there in time for the funeral he's living to attend. He mops his forehead again and sighs.

"May I help you?" says a rich feminine voice behind him, and he turns from the vista to see what appears to be just an empty white dress and apron in the opened doorway. It is a negress, her face so ebon, indistinguishable from the gloom inside the vestibule, that she seems headless.

"Ah, good day, Miss. I need to see the Beaulieus."

He sees her white eyes look him over and when she sees the portfolio at his side, she says, "If you a drummah, sah, you s'posed go round to the side door."

"What? Oh. No, I'm not selling anything. I have an urgent message. Very."

"You have to leave it, nen. They not home."

"*Really* not home? Or just don't want to see a vendor? And you, you must be..." He tries to remember the name of their housemaid. Felice had spoken of her. "You're... Faith, is it?"

She leans toward him, into the daylight. Long neck, head shapely as an Egyptian queen's, a few white hairs in every tight curl, and peers at him warily. "How you know my name?"

"Faith, listen. I'm their son-in-law. I'm Padraic Quinn..."

"They don't have a...Oh! *Oh!* You one married Miss *Felice*?" Now she's looking intently at him, appraising. "Oh, gracious! Miss Felice here with you? My *honey*?" The woman's eyes are bugging with excitement all at once, and she's looking left and right down the carriage drive, toward the street. "You come in, tell me where my honey is!"

Paddy almost chokes on a huge lump of pity. And he fears that if the parents really aren't here, leaving his terrible message with this poor soul might be even harder than telling them face to face. If he can't see them right away, maybe he should leave them a written note about what happened to her, and let them tell this woman eventually, so he won't have to.

The servant leads him into a big parlor furnished with polished rococo furniture and velvet-covered chairs so plush they look swollen. The white-clad slightness of her form reminds him of his emaciated comrade Robbie: a skeleton in clean clothes. She stops him beside a divan near the fireplace and indicates with her hand that he might sit down, and waits standing as if to take an order. But he doesn't sit.

"Might I ask how soon Mister and Mrs. Beaulieu will return?"

"Sah, they up over to Springfield. F' Mister Lincoln's funeral, God rest his soul. Won't be home til 'at's over."

"That's where I'm going! Do you know where they're staying?" He thinks he might at least find them at some Springfield hotel and give them the terrible news.

"Some friends or other in Springfield will put 'em up, but they di'n' tell me who. Mister, whyn't Miss Felice with you, you just barely married an' all?"

"She's..." He can't think of anything to tell but the truth. But he can't bear to say it to her.

As for the parents, whom he had been ready to tell, he doubts there's much chance of meeting them in the crowds at Springfield. Suddenly feeling deflated, he steps back and drops his portfolio onto the divan, sits down with his elbows on his knees, bent far forward, his forehead in his palm, looking down at some ornate design in a rug of blue shades that keep flowing into each other and pulsating. He's so tired he's dizzy.

But he can still feel the presence of the servant and her unanswered question. Now he hears her walk a few steps. He looks up and she's gone to the mantel and is lifting something down, holding it in her hand and looking at it. She comes close to the divan and peers at him with deep vertical furrows of worry between her eyes.

"Did 'at Miss Felice leave you, so soon?"she says.

"Wh...No, she...Well, yes, in a, in a way..." Paddy grasps this as a way not to have to tell this woman, but without lying to her. He nods, looking back down at the rug. She *did* leave him, in a way.

"'At girl! Shame on her!"

"No, don't..."

"She jus' *never* had patience with no boy! One li'l fault an' she drap 'im like a hot stove lid! I said t' her, Honey, be that way, you *nev'* get married 'cause they's no such a thing as a perfect man, an'..."

Paddy lets the servant woman prattle on. It's probably her way of trying to make him feel better, he understands. Sooner or later she'll have to learn *how* Felice really left him. As she talks, she glances down now and then at the object in her hand as if addressing it. As she waves her hand around, he sees that it is an oval portrait photograph in an embossed copper stand-up frame. His heart seems to skip.

"Is that Felice? May I see it?" Faith stops talking, looks at the picture, and extends it to him. "I've never once seen a picture of her..."

That is, not one of her face. Just his nude sketch from behind, never a portrait, much to his shame.

In the image she looks much as she did the first time he saw her, on the hospital ship: wearing simple white cotton, as she had during her nursing duties. But in this picture the cotton dress and apron are crisp and clean, not smeared with soldier blood. Her thick, dark hair tied back. Stiffly held pose, like all the thousands of soldiers' photographs he's seen, having to be held from ten to thirty seconds for the exposure. The light on her face is from above, a sign that it was taken not actually on the hospital ship but posed in a studio with the usual skylight in the roof. The sharp detail in her eyes shows that she had neither blinked nor glanced about. But the first two fingers of her left hand are blurred slightly, and it reminds him of her habit of rubbing her fingertips with her thumb in tense moments. Some photographers would have considered that a flaw in the picture, but it pleases Paddy in a heart-clenching way because it is the evidence that she was alive then, not deathly still as the photographer would have liked. Only in one way is it deathlike: he never saw her face in monochrome. It was always suffused with the colors of life, flushed like a ripe peach, hues changing in the light, and often the glow seeming to come from within her.

The servant is watching him study the picture. Now she says, softly, "Don' look t' me like you mad at her for leavin' you."

"Mad's hardly the word for it, no..."

"When she come back, I will scold that li'l belle, you bet! You seem be a gen'man, sah. Might be you even good 'nough for *her!*"

Paddy had never thought he was good enough for her, but had meant to grow worthy. He has studied the photograph long enough now that he knows he could duplicate the image exactly in pencil, but it's beginning to blur now. He has a notion of asking to take it with him. He reasonably might, being her husband. But he won't take it from this woman, or from Felice's parents, as it is the only image they'll have of her from now on. Until the wedding picture comes, if it does. They need this. He can draw her face someday from all his memories, if he's ever ready to do it. He'll get pastels or oils and do it with all the colors of life.

With a sigh he gives the picture back to the servant, sits up straight and reaches for his portfolio. "What I'll do is write a note to her parents, and you can give it to them when they come home. I can't stay any longer."

"You like some tea or coffee while you write that?"

"Don't bother. This will be short." He opens the latch and lifts the lid, shielded from her view, not sure where his sketch of Felice bathing lies in the stack of papers.

"No bother at all, sah. Got tea water already hot." She returns the picture to the mantel, and passes from the parlor on silent stockinged feet, the only sounds in the room his rustling of papers and the *tock tock* of a tall clock. He wishes she had offered him whiskey instead of tea, to help him write this.

Tuesday May 2nd , 1865

My Dear Mr & Mrs Beaulieu,

I came today to bring in person news so sorrowful that I could not bear to telegraph it to you, though that would have informed you sooner. Now I find I have missed a chance to meet you here, to my profound regret.

My beloved wife, your daughter Felice, did not survive the destruction of the steamboat SULTANA on the morning of Apr. 27th. It grieves me to tell you not to entertain hope of survival, as she perished in my sight – mercifully, too much in an instant to have suffered. I was blown into the river & could not reach her, or I gladly should have given my life to save hers. She was bravely comforting & aiding others until her last breath.

We were coming to visit you here en route to Pres. Lincoln's funeral in Springfield, that other tragedy, which I am assigned to attend. I have little hope of finding you there, & must proceed

> *immediately from there to New York. I have no plans to return to this part of the country again, but someday when able, I shall come just to meet you, & share in your grief then, as I am, in my heart,*
>
> *your son-in-law,*
>
> *Padraic Quinn*

Paddy sips at the edge of the teacup as he reads his note over twice. He dips his pen again and adds:

> *P.S. Should you desire to write to me, do so in c/o Mr. Alfred Guernsey, editor, Harper's Weekly in New York City. Only he & God always know my whereabouts.*

He folds the letter in half, puts away his pen and ink bottle and closes the portfolio, glancing up and seeing that the servant is raptly watching how he manages everything with one hand. Now he stands and gives the letter to her.

"Give them this the moment they get home. How awful I missed them. They deserved at least a glimpse of the man who was married to their daughter, too brief though that was...." The woman is looking down, slowly shaking her head. "Just don' understand. I *tried* t' raise 'er right..."

At this, Paddy wants to tell her that Felice deserted him only by death. But it would take time to comfort her, and Father Abraham's funeral train will reach Springfield tomorrow morning. Time for getting old Robbie to the end of their pilgrimage is running out.

"You'll understand by and by. Thank you for your kindness. I see why Miss Felice always spoke so fondly of you. Goodbye now." His impulse is to bow as if to a grand white lady, and he does, then grabs up his portfolio and goes for the door without looking back at her face. The city of St. Louis below looks enormous, a harsh jumble of structures between him and the distant riverfront, the tall courthouse gray with coal soot. He has limped down past the great old oak and almost to the street, knees and ankles sparking pain with every step on the cobblestones, feeling exhausted and annoyed with himself for leaving the poor negress so misled about

Felice, when he hears his name being screamed from somewhere.

"Mist' Quinn! Mist' Quinn!"

He stops, turns, sees the servant woman running down the porch steps toward him, skirt flying around her skinny black shanks. In an instant she's caught up with him and stands with her face thrust close to his, and she is shaking, her lips trembling and her eyes looking as if they'll leap out of her head.

"What? What in the world..." he stammers in the face of this emotional storm before him.

"My honey *dead!* Why you say she jus' *left* you? Why you lie t' me..." She raises her hand and shakes his letter in his face. He is astonished and his face flushes hot.

"You...you *read* that?" It hadn't even occurred to him that a black housemaid could read. White people just didn't want their servants literate. "That was for her *parents,*" is all he can think to say, but it sounds too much like a reproof. He mutters, "I didn't want to distress you..."

"Sah," she says in a quaking voice, tears beginning to shine on her cheekbones, "I rether hear say she a *dead* girl 'n a *mean* one! *I reared that child!"* She bites her lips shut and stares at him, nostrils flaring at every breath. He reaches up and closes his hand over hers that holds the letter, just to try to stop its terrible trembling. She breathes hard a few moments, suppressing sobs, and then says, "I know I shou'n read their letter. But what that girl does, I *got* t' know, don' I? 'Sides 'at, it's her fault anyway. She *taught* me t' read, an' say, 'Faith, you jus' read *ever'thin'* you can get you hands on...'"

Paddy himself is about to cry, hearing that. The best gift he ever received in his wretched childhood was his mother's demand that he be literate. Here is another gift Felice gave some poor soul, a gift that was so unselfish and so good that he can hardly bear the way it twists his heart to learn of it. To keep himself from breaking down and crying on the street with this forlorn servant woman, he says, "Well, you...you *sure* didn't rear her up a mean girl! My God, woman, what you made there was an angel!"

"Nen you mean she wasn' bad t'you?"

"Never once. Nor to anybody else. She just gave and gave."

"You come back in an' tell me what happen? I can fix you some vittles. You hungry? My goo'ness, t' *think* you Miss Felice's *husban'*!"

"No, I've stayed too long already. I *am* glad I came up, even though I missed them. I got to meet *you*." He's surprised how deeply he is moved by uttering this simple statement. There have been generals and senators and dames of society who were not as significant to him as this bony little house servant. Swallowing hard, he says, "You give them that letter when they come home. It's up to you whether to tell them you already know what it says...And I *will* come back here someday – maybe just to see you."

She isn't crying anymore. Something is working inside that elegant ebony head. She turns away without another word and goes for the house at an effortless run, maybe too embarrassed to show any more feelings to a white man. Paddy has never heard any Negro express so much emotion, except once when a sergeant of Colored Troops tried to tell him how it felt to have a musket and a bayonet and how eager he was to point them toward the South.

Paddy's pocket watch went down with his luggage in the *Sultana,* but he can tell by the sun that he's running out of hours, and hurries down the street toward the river. He still hasn't recovered half the vigor he lost in that desperate night in the cold river, and his ankles, knees and hips hurt so much with every step that he has to clench his teeth. He wishes he'd rented a buggy driver to bring him up here and take him back down, but he had decided he couldn't afford that, with his steadily flattening wallet. He's already had to buy a wheelchair for Robbie, and even though a used one, it had been costly. He hopes that after the funeral in Springfield he might be able to get on the telegraph and wheedle Mr. Guernsey at *Harper's,* or even Blackie at the New Orleans *Picayune,* into wiring a bit more advance money. That reminds him of all the writing he has to do yet to earn it, and he feels even more weary.

*

Passsing along the downtown storefronts now, throat and nose irritated by the coal smoke drifting up from the steamboats, he becomes aware that someone is walking slightly back of his left shoulder. If it's a pickpocket, Paddy thinks, all he'll get is this Mighty Fist of St. Patrick, and for precious little. He turns his head just a little and picks up the light form of his follower in the corner of his eye.

"What in Holy..." He stops so suddenly, the follower almost collides with him. It is Faith. In her white dress. No apron now, but she has put slippers on her feet and tied a calico bandana on her head. She says, "Mist' Quinn, I am a-comin' along."

"Coming along...where?"

"To see Father Abraham, God rest his great soul. I got t' see that man."

He stands frowning, thinking. "I can't...I mean, won't you be in trouble, leaving the house?"

"I locked it all up."

"I meant, uhm, don't you need permission to leave?"

"Father Abraham says no slaves in this country, sah. Only a slave need permission t' walk away. 'Sides, I wasn' no slave anyhow. No slaves in Missouri, din you know?"

"Well, now... I think it'd be a fine thing for you to see the President. But I myself can't afford your fare to Springfield, if you're expecting that." This is a real concern, ferry boat and train fare.. And especially as she'd need a return ticket.

"I been hopin' you could. But I got me some money I save. I been paid help."

"How much?"

She squints and her tonguetip appears in the corner of her mouth. "I got fifty-eight."

"Really? You've saved fifty-eight dollars?" How long she must have scrimped to save that much, and then to spend it all on one trip to a funeral!

"No. Fifty-eight cents, sah."

"Look, Faith. I have to talk you out of this. Fifty-eight cents isn't enough. Why don't you just go back up and wait for the Beaulieus to come home?"

Her jaw muscles are beginning to clench, her only sign of distress. "I do need t' see Mist' Linkum."

"Maybe it'd be better you *don't* see him. He's been dead three weeks. And he was pretty scary-looking when he was alive. Believe me." Paddy hopes to play on the Negroes' alleged fearfulness of corpses to discourage her from coming. He already has one wholly dependent traveling companion, Robbie. True, she probably could help him nurse old Robbie along... But no. The company of a truant black housemaid would surely complicate an already desperate trip. Nor does he want to worry that she could lose her place in the Beaulieu household.

But Faith has cocked her head to the side and she stands with fists on hips, arms akimbo.

"Mist' Quinn, sah, I not scared o' dead men. I prob'ly seen more of 'em n' you ever did."

"Oh, I doubt *that*." His impatience is rising. Here he stands, a prominent war correspondent on his way to one of the most important assignments ever, arguing in the street with somebody else's house servant. He doesn't know what else to say that might discourage her, except by just being abrupt. "It would be nice having you along, Faith, but I do need to hurry, and I beg you not to follow me. Thank you for all you ever did for Felice. Goodbye." He turns away and starts on down toward the landing, suddenly more concerned about old Robbie's well-being than Faith's feelings.

Within two blocks he comes to the tavern where he'd left Robbie at a table just inside the door in his wheelchair, and pushes the door open and goes in. The dim space inside is noisy and smelly.

There sits the old veteran, like a skeleton in white clothes, white-headed, chin down, eyes shut, either dozing or dead, his pipe, match box, tobacco pouch and a glass half full of ale on the table in front of him. Everyone else in the dark place is up by the bar, talking or arguing loudly, drinking, filling the room with cigar and pipe smoke, Robbie alone looking as still and dead as the corpse in an Irish wake. Paddy lays his hand on his shoulder and shakes him, not sure whether he'll come awake or not. His head wobbles but he doesn't look up. He could have died sitting here and no one necessarily would have noticed. Paddy is bending down, looking into his face for a sign of waking, shaking his shoulder again, when he becomes aware of a sudden fading down of voices here in the front of the barroom. Then he hears a loud voice from the vicinity of the bar:

"Hey, get out of here!"

"No niggers allowed!" snarls another voice.

The door to the street is open. There in the doorway, a thin silhouette, is Faith, peering into the dim room. Christ, she's still following me, Paddy thinks, irritated. But his main concern is Robbie. He turns and bends back down over him and shakes his shoulder again. "Hey! wake up. We've got places to go. Got to go see Mister Lincoln, remember?"

"Hey, nigger bitch, git out!" Other indignant male voices are rising.

To Paddy's great relief, Robbie has opened his eyes and is looking up and about. The name Lincoln has worked its magic on the old veteran still again. Paddy turns back toward the door, but it is closed now, and Faith is inside, closer by, sidling toward Robbie's table, staring warily at some big men who are moving toward her.

"Don't know yer place, Nigra?" This is barked by a fat man in a wrinkled white shirt, garters above the elbows and a bar rag over his shoulder. He is Sam the barkeep, in whose care Paddy had left Robbie with instructions to give this celebrated war hero an ale any time he asked for one. To assure that Robbie would be well tended, Paddy had introduced himself to the barkeep and cited his own impressive credentials, making them perhaps even more impressive in the telling. The barkeep is bearing down upon Faith, his fat face gone crimson. Paddy had guessed that being followed to the funeral by this strong-willed little servant woman might create problems, and apparently this will be the first of them. The simplest thing to do now would be just to retreat from the saloon with Robbie and Faith, and send her back up the hill. There's no time or need for an altercation with bigots.

He understands that the barkeep surely has his rules to enforce, about Negroes on the premises and such. But despite his own present exasperation with the woman, he doesn't like hearing someone talk this way to a person who was loved and admired by Felice. He was called "Mick" so often in his youth that he doesn't care to hear a kind, dignified old woman called "Nigra" in a contemptuous tone of voice. Especially a literate one.

Dropping his wooden portfolio on the table with a loud clack, he steps quickly past her and stops, almost chest to chest, in the man's way. To the startled face he says, "I'd like ye to bring me a whiskey, Sam. One of those good Kentucky ones. Make that a double."

"Uh, sure I will, sir. First, though, 'scuse me while I put this Nigra out." He starts to move around Paddy toward her. But Paddy sidesteps like a boxer and is in his way again. "I'd like that whiskey now. We're in a bit of a hurry." He sees that several of the bar patrons are hovering near the table, some glaring at Faith, others watching him confront the barkeep.

It has been a while since Paddy has had to put himself into the path of possible fisticuffs.

Aside from that night on the boat when he felled Captain Elliott because of a misunderstanding, his one fist has been limited to writing and drawing, for perhaps a year at least. And he knows that since the ordeal in the river, he's less than half the man he used to be. Furthermore, he is more sober now than he's been within memory, and he hopes that the barkeep will see fit to bring him whiskey first and *then* the troubles, whatever they may develop to be. He has never been one for fighting sober. He looks straight into Sam's eyes, sees them start shifting. Paddy tilts his head toward the bar. "Whiskey, please?"

To his relief and surprise, the barkeep turns and goes.

Faith by now has edged her way around beside the wheelchair to get the table between herself and the menacing patrons. "Robbie," Paddy says, "meet Faith. She reared up my dear Felice. Faith, this is Robbie Macombie, my best friend. He's a hero of the war, and I promised him I'd take him up to see Mister Lincoln."

She stoops down and they look at each other, nodding. Then she lays a hand on Robbie's arm and tells him, "I goin' t' th' funeral too. Got t' see that man."

"Well, I reckon, Ma'am."

"Sam," announces a loud, deep voice nearby, "if you won't put this Mammy out, I will."

Paddy turns to face a very tall, long-jawed man with a mustache so droopy that it hides his mouth. He wears a threadbare, wrinkled suit with a vest, but no hat. His face is pockmarked and sunburnt, except the milky brow, which seems never to have been exposed to sunlight.

"Permit me to introduce meself, sir," Paddy says to him. "Name's Quinn. You'll notice I've got only one fist, but don't let that lull you into an overweening confidence. I should advise ye that in the Army's Bohemian Brigade, this is known as 'the Mighty Fist o' Saint Patrick,' and it held the championship for three years runnin'." He turns the fist to and fro, looking at it as if admiring a trophy. "I've come to believe this fist here has a spell on it, put there when President Lincoln himself shook this hand in 1862 at Washington. I don't know your political persuasion, sir, but a spell is a spell, and no respecter of parties." Paddy watches bewilderment and indignation flit across the face before him, and knows that his spiel is being enhanced by that tight Irish smile that always comes on his face when he's about to fight. The Smile was almost as renowned as The Fist.

The man is backing off slightly, which is what Paddy was hoping he'd do. That was why he'd given his Mighty Fist oration, to scare him off. A brawl here, and they might never get to Springfield. And now the barkeep comes back carrying a glass with Paddy's double whiskey and starts to set it on the table, but Paddy takes it before he can set it down, and drinks it in one swallow. He purses his lips and blows, shakes himself like a dog coming out of water. "Thank you, Sam." The bartender is already turning on Faith, scowling.

"Now, Nigra. Out!"

"Ooh ooh ooh, one moment there, Sam," says Paddy, blocking him again, smiling that tight smile. Just the taste of the whiskey is making him feel more like the old Champion. "I want you to apologize to this lady for your lack of manners and your language."

"*What*? Apologize?"

"That's right, Sam. Apologize."

"Goddamned if I will! Niggers aren't allowed in here!"

"Sam, Sam! This lady is the *nurse* of my friend here, the bravest hero to come out of Georgia alive! She has to take care of him. Y' wouldn't try to separate a war hero and the nurse who keeps him alive, now would ye? By th' Mighty Fist o' Saint Patrick, I'd hope not!" The expression on the bartender's face makes Paddy want to laugh. These are just theatrics now, as he's eager to get out of here anyway and hurry down to the ferry. The looks on Robbie's face and Faith's are also amusing to see. Paddy hasn't been in the mood to give out blarney and balderdash like this since the loss of Felice. If the crowd of drinkers gets mad and throws the three of them out into the street, it'll be just a part of the antics. But now Paddy sees that even Sam is losing steam in the face of this fancy, and decides to end it with a flourish. So he says:

"Sure now, Sam, ye wouldn't want me writin' in all America's newspapers and magazines that Sam's saloon in St. Louis is a dark and hostile place frequented by louts, an' his whiskey's cut with horse pee, now would ye? Plainly not, so I'll give you a piece of paper here, and all you need do is write an apology to this nurse for insulting her." As the bartender and his patrons stand scowling and gaping, Paddy opens his portfolio and lays out on the table a pencil and a slip of paper. "Her name is Faith. Just write, ' Dear Faith, I apologize.' That'll do it, and we'll pay our bill and be on our way. Well? You *are* going to write it, aren't you?"

Sam is looking down, grinding his molars, face aflame. Finally he says, "Mister, I can't write."

"Can't *write*? Aw, poor fellow! Well, you can speak. So just *tell* 'er you're sorry, then. Look 'er in the face and speak out, Sam. Politely."

To Paddy's delight and Faith's obvious astonishment, Sam looks at her from under his eyebrows and says, "Sorry...Ma'am."

"Nice, Sam, nice. Faith, would ye kindly write down that you accept his apology?"

Blinking and nodding, she picks up the pencil, bends over the table, and with her tongue in the corner of her mouth, writes as the illiterate white men stare dumbstruck at her black hand moving over the white paper. She hands the note to Paddy, who glances at it as he gives it to the barkeep. In a fair cursive, looking so much like Felice's, it says:

Mister Sam I axep your a pollagy.

Faith

*

Robbie is at risk of losing his wheelchair, it seems. The crowded ferryboat had barely had room for it, and now here at the train station in East St. Louis, the ticket clerk says the passenger cars will be too crowded with people going to Springfield to allow room for such a bulky thing as a wheelchair. It would have to go in the baggage car, if there's even room for it there.

"You'll have to guarantee he gets a seat, then," Paddy says. "He can't stand up five minutes. Sure as hell not all the way to Springfield."

"Mister," says the clerk, "I sold the last seat hours ago. This's going to be like a cattle train. People are goin' to Springfield, seat or no. They'll be squeezed in the aisles."

Paddy is near desperation. His double whiskey is wearing off. He barely has enough money left for the two tickets to Springfield, but now here it is three people and a wheelchair. He seems to be stuck with Faith; he couldn't send her home if he wanted to. He had managed to get her on the ferry without paying by touting her as the nurse of this wounded war hero, *Colonel* Macombie, a title Robbie didn't hear. Since Paddy defended her against the crowd in the saloon, she smiles at him every time he looks at her. And she has taken to heart her impromptu title of nurse. She hovers over old Robbie, wipes his face with a kerchief, adjusts the cushion in his wheelchair, and croons to him when he seems to be most pained. After his first surprise at having his own personal "nurse," Robbie seems very happy about the arrangement. Sending Faith back would be a setback to Robbie's morale, too. Anyway, Paddy can't afford ferry passage to send her back to St. Louis if he did want to. Until there's a bridge across the Mississippi, she can't just be sent walking home. So now he's got to get her on the train somehow without getting her a ticket. For that reason, he hasn't even mentioned to the ticket clerk that there's a third person. And the clerk is getting impatient. Paddy gets a desperate notion.

"Then do you suppose the Colonel could ride in the baggage car *with* his wheelchair?"

"That's not allowed. But..." The clerk rubs his thumb and forefinger together. "Under the circumstances..." Paddy understands. Critical circumstances create opportunities for bribery.

Such as 2,000 soldiers on a steamboat with a 375-person capacity.

*

"If the weather doesn't get too bad, this'll be bearable," Paddy says, as the train begins moving with a succession of clanking jerks. Coal smoke, full of tiny, eye-irritating cinders, blows in through the open sides of the overloaded baggage car. By bribing the clerk instead of paying two full fares, Paddy has actually managed to get them all three hidden aboard the baggage car, with the wheelchair, and has a few dollars left over. When they get to Springfield, they'll need that money as much as they'll need the wheelchair. It's a risky situation. He has no tickets, but the clerk did give him a baggage check which might keep them from being put off the train if some uncooperative trainman finds them riding here. Robbie's wheelchair is parked between two stacks of trunks, and Faith sits on a crate by his knee. Robbie still has no idea that Paddy has rhetorically promoted him to Colonel. Paddy stands back in a recess between other steamer trunks. The three need to keep out of sight as much as possible until the train is out of East St. Louis. And there will be many stops in the hundred railroad miles between here and Springfield. The train is to get into Springfield after dark. The President's funeral train is supposed to get there early in the morning, and his casket will be in the Statehouse all day for people to go by and look at him.

"Our pilgrimage is almost over," he says, and wonders whether Robbie even hears him over the chuffing of the locomotive and the steely gnash of wheels on rails.

"Pert near. Thankee. You've sure put up with a lot from me t' keep your promise."

"*Our* promise."

"True. *Ours.*"

"Thanks for going to the trouble of not dying on me," Paddy says. "A few times there, I thought you did."

Robbie nods. "Glad to oblige." He turns to Faith. "Ma'am, you ever smoke a pipe?"

She smiles, amused at the thought. "No sah. But my daddy, he let me fill his up for 'im."

"Good. 'Cause I was goin' to ask you if you'd pack mine for me so I can have a smoke."

Paddy laughs. "Why, you bossy rascal! Give you a nurse and you'll use her, won't you?"

And now he hears something he hasn't heard before: Faith is laughing. It's a brief, musical sound. She's begun pinching tobacco out of the pouch, crumbling it between thumb and finger, and packing it in the bowl, and as she does so, she's shaking her head and smiling. Paddy realizes that this is perhaps as much a pilgrimage for her as for them, and she must be happy to be going to see the man who freed her people. He wonders whether she was ever a slave, wonders how she got to Missouri and into the

Beaulieau household. Surely that would be another interesting story.

As if he didn't already have bigger stories to write than he might have the time and the stamina to do. And the finale of them all, the funeral, just ahead tomorrow.

God, have I got work ahead of me!

Faith puts the pipe stem in Rob's mouth and gives him his matchbox. "You c'n light a match all by you own self, can't you?" She looks out the door of the baggage car, then turns to Paddy with a sly sort of smile, and says, "Mist' Quinn, you know we just left the Devil's train station?"

"Devil's? No. Never heard it called that."

"See, just b'fore th' war start? Miss Felice an' her mama comin' home on th' train, got me 'long with 'em. They been talkin' bout the war comin', and I heah Missus Bo-yoo say, 'We are surely all headin' straight fo' Devil's Station!' An' I thought she meant that *railroad* station! I was scared t' get off the train, 'til Miss Felice 'splained t' me she said *devastation*!"

For the first time in a long while, Paddy hears old Robbie laugh aloud.

CHAPTER FIFTEEN

Springfield, Illinois

May 4, 1865

"Ever *see* so many people in one place?" Faith exclaims, gazing about, hand on heart.

"Only on battlefields," Paddy replies.

"Amen," Robbie says.

Night has settled; after a day of knelling church bells, midnight has come and gone, and in lamplight the queue of mourners stretches out of sight from the Statehouse down into the streets of Springfield. A guard officer told Paddy an hour ago that some sixty thousand viewers had already filed by the casket, and trains are still bringing them to the city, rolling into the Great Western Station. Every public building in town is draped with black crepe. Mister Lincoln's old law office above Miller's Store is festooned with ribbons and bows and a sign declaring HE LIVES IN THE HEARTS OF HIS PEOPLE. They had come past it on their way to the Statehouse. Now they have been standing in this endless, somber line most of the night, and are finally inside the capitol, this very building where Mister Lincoln had made his famous speech quoting St. Mark about the House Divided. Here he had averred that "this government cannot endure...half slave and half free." Paddy had been here then, reporting the 1858 Republican State Convention, one of his earliest *Harper's Weekly* assignments. He can't help remembering it now, the first time he had ever seen the Illinois politician. The words had been prophetic; many people recognized them as such even then, and Paddy had memorized them, had thought them over hundreds of times during the war as armies tore each other to pieces all over the land. It was as prophetic as John Brown's declaration about purging the shame of slavery with blood, which Paddy had also heard with his own ears. Interviewing that great fanatic had been another of Paddy's best early assignments. Paddy has personally witnessed so much terrible history in the making that his existence seems more like a drunken nightmare than a waking life. And now here he is witnessing more of it.

Robbie in his wheelchair says, "I never heard so many folks be so quiet. Guess this's what real honor sounds like."

Paddy writes that down in his shorthand. Somewhere in the notes he's been taking all night there will be some particular statements, and some particular sights, that will convey the essence of this day when he finally writes about it. He'll have thousands of words of notes, from which he'll write thousands of words of text, but a certain few words will go down as the very gist of it, as the phrase no reader should ever be able to forget. Paddy is a reporter, a respected journalist, and knows that a report must be complete and clear and thorough. But he is also an Irishman, which is to say a bard, and for an occasion like this, mere prose isn't adequate. He's keeping his ear open for the poetry which might come from anyone's mouth.

Just ahead, people of every description, whites and Negroes, in every kind of garb, farmers and rough workingmen twisting their soft caps in their hands, gents in frock coats coddling their stovepipe hats, women in black veils, move slowly up the ornate winding staircase leading up to the Hall of Representatives, while others come back down. Those coming down look stunned. Many are weeping. Soon Robbie will have to stand up out of his wheelchair and leave it parked on this floor in order to go up those stairs. He intends to do it. He has endured worse to get here, and Mister Lincoln is right upstairs there, waiting for him.

This really is the quietest crowd Paddy has been in, ever. Some of the people say nothing. Some murmur to each other. Women now and then sob into handkerchiefs; men blink back tears.

Some people read newspapers for a while, then fold them away and stand thinking. There is much to read; seven reporters from major newspapers have ridden the funeral train. Others in the line examine the souvenir badges, ribbons and funeral cards they've bought from the host of street vendors: pictures of the President, alone or with eagles and angels hovering over him, imprinted with newly composed odes, etchings of the funeral train, photographs of the elaborate hearses and the enormous funeral processions in the Eastern cities, quotations from his Inaugural addresses alongside excerpts from the Bible, fanciful engravings of Columbia holding the martyr across her lap like the Pieta cradling Christ - thousands of varieties of woeful mementoes printed on cardboard.

But even that plethora of print-shop entrepreneurship didn't astonish Paddy so much as a broadside advertisement that was slipped into his hand by a scruffy street shill outside the train depot:

> !!! GENTS ONLY !!!
>
> ** SEE THE GODDESS OF PEACE ARISE**
>
> APHRODITE, the Grecian Goddess of Peace & Beauty
>
> Will ascend in all her unadorned Glory from the Ruins of War
>
> In an Inspiring Tableau upon the Stage!
>
> Portrayal by Nationally Celebrated Actress
>
> FANNIE FOREMOST
>
> May 3, 1865 at 9 p.m. & 11 p.m., & Encores on Demand
>
> Pegg's Theatrical Club, on S. Grand

A shiver running down his jawline, Paddy had asked the shill, "Has this 'actress' actually *arrived* at your theatre?"

"Wull, I ain't seen 'er m'self, no."

"I hate to be the bearer of disappointing news," Paddy had told him, "but I suspect that Miss Fannie was diverted to a more important engagement. Maybe you should go and inform your Mister Pegg."

But what if she didn't drown? Good God!

Now as Paddy looks around in the waiting queue, he wonders whether many gents went down to the Theatre Club, whether she had by some miracle gotten there for her performances, or, more likely, how Mister Pegg handled the crestfallen crowd when she didn't show up, as she surely didn't. He's sure she's dead.

If she did make her show, he thinks, she might still be doing encores even now! What a sacrilege that would be!

For the first time, he allows himself to hope that she *did* drown.

In his notebook are some facts Paddy had heard on the street from a soldier wearing a silk mourning ribbon of the U.S. Military Rail Road: that in more than 1,600 miles the funeral train had been greeted by at least a million people, many of them waiting along the tracks by torchlight after midnight, in cities, towns, even in open farmland. And surely almost every one of them would have bought some sort of printed memento, some leaflet, some maudlin cardboard creation. Again Paddy muses on the many ways entrepreneurs find to profit on death.

Including journalists, he reminds himself. He has made his living and his fame writing about the carnage of battles. He will soon be writing about the violent deaths in the fate of the *Sultana.* And this funeral, too, is an outcome of a violent death. He is, like the souvenir traffickers, a maker of printed grief.

Sometimes reports and rumors come buzzing softly along the queue: that Jeff Davis is believed to have been behind the assassination, and President Johnson just yesterday announced a $100,000 reward for his capture. That most of Mister Lincoln's Cabinet is under guard from fear of more Confederate assassins. That in another casket the President's son Willie, dead three years, has been brought from Washington on the same train and will be placed in the same tomb as his father. That the hysterical Mary Lincoln had tried to prevent her husband's body from being brought back to Illinois, even that she personally had refused to vacate the White House. That General Fighting Joe Hooker will head the procession from the Statehouse to the tomb. The general's name reminds Paddy again of Fannie Foremost. She is always connected in his mind somehow with Joe Hooker -- because that orgy had been under his aegis – though the connection might be purely his own fancy. Might Hooker have had something to do with bringing her up from Memphis for a performance? Paddy knows this is not a charitable reflection on the general, but few of his thoughts are, since that drunken orgy at the Willard Hotel so long ago. He is annoyed at himself for having to force down the images of that night that keep arising in the midst of this reverent occasion. It was the Aphrodite advertisement that started those memories. And Paddy now and then envisions that woman's struggle to escape the burning steamboat, as if he remembers seeing it himself, although he knows full well that he had only heard it from soldiers who witnessed it. Like that odd fellow camped in the lifeboat on the *Saint Patrick*. He sees it more vividly than he sees that other death he really did see – Felice's – probably because he has tried so desperately to forget that one.

But such reveries are distractions, a troubling and unworthy train of thought in such a great and grave moment, and he turns his attention back to the black-draped Statehouse and the endless line of mourners. Faith has been pushing Robbie's wheelchair, a foot at a time, while Paddy stands with his notebook on his portfolio, writing notes, making quick sketches. Some people in line, hours ago, were curious about his work, and his strapped-on desk, and they peeked down aside at his scribbles, and he had at last explained to them simply that he is a reporter. This solemn occasion has made most everyone uncommonly polite, so they've quit watching him work. The reverence and sorrow that have been building up in their hearts as they creep toward the dead President are intense now, and they are too much enfolded in their own feelings to pay much attention to him and his old soldier companion and the Negress. But some glances do still come their way. During the progress of the queue, a mile or so by his guess, he has caught several women in the act of looking him over. Perhaps that means he is recovering enough from his ordeal in the river to seem a vital attractive man again. He was used to such flattering attention before. But he doesn't engage in any flirtation. His heart is still full of Felice. Now and then some gentleman coming toward him looks at him with a hint of recognition in his eyes, reminding him that he still has some fame in the country. Only two weeks ago he had been scheming to augment and rebuild that fame, as author, as lecturer, and these stories he is preparing for *Harper's* will of course contribute to fulfilling that aim. Maybe he will feel the pull of that ambition again when this last part of the pilgrimage is finished and he can begin writing about it. Just now, though, he feels too humble. He would prefer to be unrecognized.

All through the endless procession, Faith has kept watching for Mr. And Mrs. Beaulieu, but she hasn't seen them yet. Paddy wants, yet dreads, to meet them. Not only will he have to tell them of their daughter's death, for which he feels accountable, but he'll have to explain how he happens to have their truant servant in his company. If he finds them, they can take her back to St. Louis with them. The problem of sending her home otherwise had weighed on him much of the day, as he couldn't afford to buy her a train ticket. But he solved that problem a few hours ago:

While the queue was inching past the great hearse on Washington Street and Paddy stood sketching it with its eight clusters of black plumes on top, one of the hearse attendants struck up a conversation with him, boasting that it had been borrowed from St. Louis because Springfield had no hearse of sufficient elegance for such an occasion. In exchange for a sketch of the hearse, Paddy had obtained the attendant's promise that Faith can ride with the glorious conveyance when it goes back to St. Louis on the train and ferry. And he had written a note to excuse her absence:

May 3, 1865 Springfield

My dear Mr. & Mrs. Beaulieu,

This note is to explain that I took the liberty of bringing Faith here with me, so that if I met you in this crowd, she could identify you for me.

Also, I felt that she deserves to see the

Emancipator of her Race before he is entombed.

I pray you will forgive me for yet another brash act. I believe Felice would have abetted it.

With affection & respect, I am yours,

PADRAIC QUINN

"When I do see Mist' en Miz Bo-yoo," Faith said, "I be tellin' 'em Felice married a good man, yes, a *good* man." And the look in her eyes made him feel highly honored.

The one unresolved matter of business Paddy has yet to arrange is that of begging more advance money from the editor of *Harper's* – enough for his train fare to New York City, and Robbie's fare to Pittsburgh. Paddy didn't even try to get into a telegraph office here in Springfield. With all the other journalists in town, he'd have had to wait hours for his turn. His sworn duty today is not to wire for money, but to accompany Robbie to the President's casket.

He has nearly fulfilled that duty now. Just one curving flight of stairs to go. But that set of stairs will be a challenge to the feeble, sick old soldier.

A natty sergeant standing post at the foot of the staircase leans down over the wheelchair and asks Robbie in a low voice, "Should I get someone to carry you up, soldier?"

"I'll walk up to see him." So, with Faith on one arm and Paddy on the other, he stands, giving a groan. The sergeant rolls the wheelchair off to one side. "I'll watch it 'til you come back down."

"Yep. Just set it right there, and I'll slide down the bannister and land a- sittin' in it." This brings a chuckle and a nod from the guard, and Faith glances at Paddy with a puckered smile.

Robbie attains the first step mostly by being lifted by Paddy and Faith. He stands between them, wincing, and they wait for the line to move up and clear the second step.

"Let me try," he says. They keep their holds on him, but he does lift his left foot up onto the next step, leans forward over that leg and straightens it, then lifts the other foot up. "Heh. Whew."

It is a long flight of steps. He looks up, stands waiting for the next one to be clear. He says, "When I walked out of Andersonville gate...I was weaker than this...and holdin' up my friend Ned, t' boot. But...no stairs to climb, that day. Here we go...next one..."Again he does it, with Paddy and Faith steadying him but not having to lift. Robbie huffs. "Soon as Ned was outside that gate though, he... just gave up the ghost. Lived to be out o' there... that was enough, I reckon..."

Hearing this, Paddy suddenly is afraid. Coming to see Mister Lincoln was all that kept Robbie living, like his comrade living just long enough to walk out of the prison gate. Paddy imagines Robbie looking into the President's casket and then, like Ned, just giving up the ghost. He has the feeling that Robbie would know how to let go and just depart if he felt ready.

Don't you dare, Old Robbie. This might be as far as *you* want to go, but I want to see you home.

But Paddy doesn't say anything about it. He doesn't want to give Robbie the idea if he hasn't already decided that himself.

Step by step, stop by stop, Robbie climbs, flanked, but not carried, by his old friend and his new nurse. They are now coming up into a dense, cloying odor. It smells like an old battlefield in springtime, where blood and flesh are still in the ground, but equally strong here are the odors of flowers. The Hall of Representatives, like every place where the President has been exhibited to the public the last three weeks, is full of flowers. Even his funeral car had been kept full of wreaths, evergreen boughs, and bouquets. Calla Lilies. Roses. Peonies. Lilac. Every city where the train had stopped over for viewings, elegant pavilions and canopies had been built to display his casket in, and every city had tried to outdo all the others in the masses and varieties of showy, heavy-headed blossoms that had filled those structures. Mountains of flowers, their brightness contrasting with the miles of black crepe, their odors vying with that of the embalmed but long-dead corpse. It's been described in all the newspapers, that continuous floral extravaganza. Some women in the line now hold handkerchiefs to their faces, appropriate to their grief, but serving also as a discreet way to filter the odors. Robbie, as familiar as Paddy is with the smell of old death, looks over, catches his eye, shakes his head.

The Hall of Representatives now looks nothing like a public chamber; Paddy scribbles his impression as he enters the door – *glorious grotto of grief* – its architectural planes and angles obscured by cascades of crepe and ribbon and by a jungle of floral sprays and banks of bouquets, as formless and shadowy as a cave.

In its center stands what appears to be a hummock of ribbons and fringe, the catafalque upon which the polished, elegant casket sits, waist-high, lidless, partially covered with a blanket of tiny flowers, all illuminated by a chandelier above the foot of the casket. Army guards direct the mourners to approach from the President's left, go around his head, and then pass the right side of the casket in leaving.

There pillowed on satin is that craggy face: sunken dark eyesockets, big, coarse nose, whiskered chin. Moving closer, Paddy is more dismayed by the sight with every step. The President's face is neither weathered and ruddy as it was when he shook his hand, nor is it death-gray, but rather a ghastly waxen white. The mourners have all been warned not to get close enough to try to kiss the corpse or touch it, or even to touch the casket, or place any cherished token into it. Paddy's right hand, though now holding a pencil and notebook, tingles with its memory of that warm iron handgrip from years ago and he would love to feel that once more. But what the undertakers have produced is nothing one would want to touch. The face, darkening by decay, has had to be powdered over again every time the casket was opened. It looks no more human than the face of a Dresden figurine.

Paddy doesn't want to look at this bizarre effigy any longer. Instead, he passes around ahead of Robbie and Faith, turns to stand at the head of the casket, folds his notebook to a fresh page, and sketches the scene that he has imagined so many times, this scene that he himself caused to occur:

Robbie Macombie, the fragile but indestructible little old veteran of a thousand perils and miseries, gazing down at the body of his Commander-in-Chief. This sketch must be done in mere moments, like that furtive sketch of Felice bathing. But it must be done just right, because this will depict the final moment of this story of a pilgrimage.

Paddy's concentration is so intense that he doesn't even try to imagine what is in Robbie's heart at this moment. But he knows he is recording something of dignity and reverence so deep that his most bardic prose is inadequate to convey it.

Now he has the sketch. He has foreseen it so often in imagination that he could well have drawn it just this way days ago - probably, even, at the moment he invited Robbie to come with him. Except for one detail, one that he couldn't have foreseen in the beginning, and he has only seconds to add it before the stream of Time carries them past this moment:

It is that skinny black nurse holding Robbie's arm and looking down at Father Abraham too.

CHAPTER SIXTEEN

Terre Haute & Richmond Railroad

May 5th, 1865

Paddy has long believed that one's most profound and poetic prose can be written while riding on a railroad train. He believes that moving forward through space toward a destination inspires a like result in the writing of a narrative. It's good to believe that, as he has had to do it so often, traveling from one theatre of war to another. In support of this belief, he can argue that Abraham Lincoln penned his Gettysburg speech while traveling on a train to that place. And Bishop Simpson had written his heart-rending funeral elegy for the President while on a train. Ships and riverboats are conducive to the composition of excellent prose also, riding smoothly on water instead of shaking and clacking over rail joints, but they provide too many pleasures and distractions. On the train, there is nothing else to do but sit on the wooden seat, facing forward, with daylight from the window on his left lighting his little portfolio, and concentrate on writing this narration of three weeks at the end of a war.

What was to have been only the objective account of one man's funeral, however, has become such a complex weave of ordeals and tragedies, with himself woven into the fabric of it, that he's finding it hard to write in a narrative line proceeding forward. His story should be moving ahead as if on rail tracks toward its destination. Instead, he feels as if he's immersed and drifting in it, up to his chin, at the mercy of its flow, as he was on that dreadful night of fire and death in the Mississippi River. He now has three big stories to tell -- the forlorn saga of the homeward-bound war prisoners with Private Macombie their prominent representative, the *Sultana* catastrophe, and the pilgrimage to Mister Lincoln's funeral - and those three stories cannot be separated from each other, nor can he observe any one of those stories from outside because he has been within them from the beginning.

On the seat opposite him sits old Robbie, reading a newspaper sometimes, gazing out at the sideslipping countryside sometimes, sleeping sometimes. Sicker still, but still alive and now homeward bound after paying his respects to his Commander-in-Chief.

After pondering on the structure of his story from every angle, Paddy has come back to his old notion that Robbie is the key to keeping all the narratives on the same track. Only through him can all the aspects of the story be carried along, with all its meanings intact. A homecoming story, beginning with Robbie's release from the prison and Father Abraham's release from his mortal flesh.

The story thus written will not just narrate the soldier's homegoing, but also honor him for keeping Paddy alive and moving when grief would have stopped him dead. He pencils in a margin:

If you owe a man your life you owe him a tribute.

Here is the sketch of Robbie looking into the casket. This is a visual picture so eloquent that it must be used. This veteran and his pilgrimage *have* to be the central theme.

The story will have to tell of him getting up from his wheelchair and climbing the long staircase in the State House.

That wheelchair is not here in this crowded passenger car. There's no room for it in the narrow aisle. It is once again back in a baggage car. It won't be needed until he gets off the train, in Pittsburgh, if he lives long enough to get that far. He didn't give up the ghost after seeing Mister Lincoln, but he remains weak and scrawny and his gut is still full of pain. Robbie's gut has long been a source of anxiety, but has not been as difficult as it might have been. The visit to the president's bier would have been complicated and embarrassing, if not impossible, if he'd had the spews in Springfield. "God in his mercy plugged me up because he meant me to see Father Abraham," was the way Robbie explained it, as if it had been a Biblical miracle. But he now remains plugged and has been for a worrisome long time..

Paddy looks out the train window at the light green spring foliage of the western Indiana farmland. The Wabash River, boundary between Illinois and Indiana, has been left behind and the train is rolling eastward from Terre Haute toward Indianapolis. Here and there are the white blossoms of dogwood trees, with black coalsmoke from the Terre Haute & Richmond Railroad locomotive drifting away among them. The country is flat. Between copses, woodlots and drainage ditches lie fields of freshly-plowed earth, rich and dark as devil's-food cake, but most of the fields are fallow, coming up in pastel shades of prairie flowers, green in grass and weeds. There will be more plowing done now that the soldiers can come home. No battles had been fought here in Indiana, except a Rebel cavalry raid by John Hunt Morgan into counties down along the Ohio River, but almost every family had sent and lost soldiers. At the onset of the war Governor Oliver Morton had vowed that Indiana would send more soldiers *per capita* than any other Northern State to preserve the Union, and it had done so. The state also claimed Abraham Lincoln as its own, bragging that Indiana had made the boy into the man, whereas Illinois had only made the man into a politician. Paddy remembers Robbie himself expressing such a sentiment not long ago.

Paddy leafs through his sketches from the Oak Ridge Cemetery, and his shorthand notes on Bishop Simpson's tombside eulogy. He had scribbled the notes while Faith again searched the crowd for Felice's parents, to no avail. The Bishop had started off well enough, in a plangent voice, saying, "A mournful silence is abroad upon the land...Far more eyes have gazed upon the face of this departed than ever looked upon the face of any other departed man." While Paddy sketched the tomb and the crowd, the bishop had told of the million Americans who came out to watch the funeral train along its 1,600-mile journey "by sunlight, dawn, twilight and by torchlight." The most moving part of his elegy had been his reading of Mister Lincoln's own words: his almost poetic second Inaugural speech, calling for "malice toward none" and a resolve to carry forward the work so nobly begun.

But then the Bishop had sullied that very magnanimity, veering into the language of vengeance and demanding that "every Senator who aided in beginning the Rebellion, and every officer who turned his sword against his country, be doomed to a felon's death!" At that point, Robbie had tugged Paddy's sleeve, and said, not very softly:

"I reckon Father Abraham just rolled over in his coffin, eh?"

Some people nearby had growled and shushed him, but a few had uttered, "Amen!"

After the president's casket, and his son Willie's, were locked inside the tomb and the crowd strayed away, Paddy and Robbie had delivered Faith to the men in charge of the hearse, making them restate their promise to deliver her back to St. Louis. Paddy told her not to forget to give his letters to the Beaulieus, and she took them out of her dress pocket to show she still had them. Then she had said her farewell in a manner proper to a Negro servant, not reaching to embrace them in front of these strangers, only holding their hands tightly for a moment, blinking against tears. "Lord bless y' both," she said. Then she turned from them and went to stand by the hearse, a tiny, plain, slight figure beside the ornate juggernaut. And, Paddy pushing Robbie in the wheelchair, they had moved away in the dispersing crowd, heading for the telegraph office downtown, nearly two miles away.

He'd had to wait several hours in a crowd there to send his message and request for more travel money. During the wait he learned that the "Aphrodite" performance had been cancelled for lack of its star, who had never arrived. Finally Paddy had fallen asleep sitting on the floor, back against a wall, waiting for the response from New York:

> *QUINN*
>
> *TRAVEL ADVANCE TRANSMITTED*
>
> *NEED YOU HERE WITH SCRIPT AND PICTURES BY AM OF MAY 8 AT LATEST OR ELSE*
>
> *ALREADY MADE PICTURE OF BURNING BOAT*
>
> *FOR NEXT ISSUE*
>
> *GUERNSEY*

The editor's telegram means that Paddy has less than three days left to arrive in New York with the manuscript finished and his sketches ready for the engraver. If he fails to meet that, the story will be too old by the next week's edition, no matter how good it is. The editor already has enough facts by now from the Associated Press and other sources to report the *Sultana* disaster and the President's burial as news items. The picture of the burning boat will have been made by a *Harper's* artist drawing flames on a steamboat of the *Sultana*'s design, and it will be good enough to illustrate the magazine's account of the disaster as a news story. Alfred Guernsey is a good enough editor to understand the appeal of Paddy's whole eyewitness account with all its interviews, portraits and scene sketches, and to pay his famous correspondent adequately for them, but only if they are timely. It was almost a week ago that the steamboat blew up, and that has been reported in dailies all over the country. Since then, there is no shortage of news to fill the weekly's pages: more Reb holdouts have surrendered; the manhunt continues for Jefferson Davis and his staff who may be fleeing with five million dollars in gold bullion; a trial of the assassin's suspected conspirators is being prepared; and a nation is trying to reorganize itself for peace. An editor has too much to choose from to wait for a story that's going stale day by day. Mr. Guernsey's stated deadlines are never mere suggestions, as Paddy well knows from having missed a few. Exhausted as he is, he expects to write almost around the clock on this hard train seat, while also tending to the most important friend he's ever had, trying to keep Robbie alive as far as Pittsburgh, where the Army will take over his care, perhaps doctor him, discharge him, and transport him upstate to his wife and sons. From Pittsburgh on to New York City, Paddy will occupy both facing seats and will be able to use Robbie's vacated one as a work table, spreading out his manuscript pages as he likes to do to peruse his manuscript for its final draft. Those last 400 miles, from Pittsburgh to New York City, should provide him enough hours - ten or twelve - to do the kind of polishing he likes to do before he turns his manuscripts in. Even if he has no sleep in that last long surge, he can keep working well with a properly managed combination of whiskey and coffee.

He glances over at Robbie, who is awake now watching the

Indiana farmland slip by, but with a forlorn look in his eyes that indicates he isn't really seeing the delicate springtime out there. He's looking inside himself, not outward. Paddy knows him well enough by now to know that he's like the Mississippi: calm on the surface, but deep and full of unseen currents. This blind gaze could mean that just about anything is going on down deep there. He could even be deciding that it's time to give up the ghost.

Robbie has been like this, almost wholly silent, since they came away from Springfield. If getting to see Mister Lincoln was a great satisfaction to him, he hasn't said so in words. He praised the workmanship of the casket, but hasn't said a word about the condition of the corpse, that powder-caked death mask with its black chinwhiskers and thick eyebrows. Robbie hasn't even mentioned his nurse-for-a-day, though it had seemed at the time that they had a fine appreciation of each other, even a bond.

Paddy would like to know what's at work deep down in his friend. But he feels that asking him would be like asking the Mississippi, "How deep are you today?"

He turns his notebook pages until he comes to the sketch and notes on Romulus Tolbert, the 8th Indiana Cavalry veteran with the disfigured chin. The one who had approached him at the rail of the *Saint Patrick* just before it docked at Cairo, he who asked him to let Robbie go straight up to Saluda with him instead of taking him to the funeral. Here are the notes about Tolbert, taken on the *Sultana* with the help of that keg of rye whiskey, the background history of how Tolbert was wounded and captured in Georgia. He's one of the few Indianans who survived the explosion and the night in the river. Paddy looks at his sketch, sighs, and begins a paragraph:

> *Romulus Tolbert knew Robbie Macombie's family long before the war. They had been neighbors living on the beautiful Ohio River bluffs near Saluda, Indiana...*

*

By the time Paddy is finished with his Romulus Tolbert segment, the train is approaching Indiana's capital, Indianapolis, creeping through warehouse districts, neighborhoods of sooty houses, and now past a vast stockyard. He looks up at Robbie and is startled to see him apparently in a state of distress from something or other, though he hasn't said a word. His eyes are wrinkled all about and his lips are parted in a grimace, his teeth on edge.

"Robbie, what's wrong?"

"I hate t' say it."

"Say what?"

"Well, it's this. I can't go t' Pennsylvania.."

"Can't go *home*? After all you've been through, you don't want to go *home*?"

"I do want t' go home. It's just, well, Pennsylvania's not home."

"But that's where Matilda and your boys are."

"I know. But...Y' see, home, for me, is Saluda. That's all there is to it."

Paddy uses the blunt end of his pencil to scratch his temple. "You mean, up there on the bluff, the old place you told me about? Where your grandpa's buried?"

"Lookin' down on the Ohio. Yep. That's home. It's the first place I thought of when I knew Andersonville hadn't killed me. Thinkin' of it made me decide to live a while. Then you came along, an' gave me Father Abraham t' live for. Now I can go home and die. But there, not in damn old Pennsylvania."

Paddy starts putting papers back in his portfolio, trying not show how perplexing this is. "Look, Robbie, damn it, we have your ticket to Pittsburgh. It's paid for. We'll be there Friday. It's all set..."

"I have to go to Saluda. I can change trains here, be down in Saluda by tonight. I looked at the train schedules."

"Well, sure, you *could* do that. But what you *should* do is go home to Matilda. Get well. Then you can *move* to Saluda, with your family, if you're so determined to get there."

"I'm not goin' to get well."

"Don't talk that way, damn it!"

"Just tellin' you the truth. Maybe you noticed I can't even *shit* anymore? Well, it's shit or die. That's God's law. I'm real sorry t' tell you this, after all y' done for me. But like I said, *my* part o' your story's all done. Y' don't need me any further..."

"Well, damn it, you may not know it, but I *changed* the story. It doesn't end 'til you're home safe..." Paddy feels like he'll cry if he doesn't argue Robbie out of dying short of home.

Wincing, Robbie shifts and leans forward, reaching out. "Give me your hand." Paddy reaches, and Robbie's hand is like a paper sack full of cold chicken bones. But its grip tightens as Robbie talks. He's looking down at their handclasp as he says, "Yep, I can feel Father Abraham in that hand o' yours. Couldn't shake his hand at the funeral, but I can do it thisaway. Now, listen, and pay attention. I know you're a better man than me, Mister Quinn, and a whole lot more important, but I am your elder, so hear me out:

"This needn't trouble you a bit. I get off in Indianapolis – I bet they still got their Lincoln decorations up, from when he they showed 'im here, what y' bet? – and I just swap a long ticket for a shorter one, ride another train down to Madison. My uncle down there, he can come get me in a wagon, and haul me up t' Saluda Cemetery. My Grandpa Joseph lies there. I want t' visit him, take a look over the Ohio from up there. That's all I need."

"And then what? Just die, in an old cemetery? That's what you want?"

"Uncle Alex keeps a pick and shovel in his wagon. That'd be real convenient, eh? Other hand, it might be that cemetery'd heal me. Prob'ly not, but God's in charge o' the whens and whethers."

Paddy wouldn't admit it, but damned if Robbie might not have here the only right ending for his own story. Paddy just isn't ready for it. Robbie continues:

"So I go where I want, and you just stay on this train straight on to New York, get there on time with your story all done. Awful important story. Like that one 'bout the Choctaws an' th' Irish.

You *got* t' get that written. I've done what I needed to." He lets go of Paddy's hand.

The railroad car darkens as the train pulls slowly in under the vast train shed, where several other trains sit on parallel tracks.

"Well," says Robbie. "This's where I get off. Can you kindly get my wheelchair off the baggage car for me? Just think. Mister Lincoln was in this train station. Both on his way t' Washington and on th' way back, wasn't he? Hey, ol' comrade. We got a deal?"

Paddy nods, and stands up. "Don't run off. I'll go get your chair."

*

Robbie sits waiting, thinking:

That was easier than I expected. That Paddy Quinn's no fool. He can understand a thing pretty quick whether he likes it or not.

There's a friend I'm going to miss real bad.

A pain like a bayonet through the bowels blacks out his vision and wrings a groan out of him. When he can see again, the aisle is empty. The passengers getting off here are already off, and Robbie is glad, because he doesn't like the ways people react to his fits of pain, either the solicitous ones or the ones who pretend they don't notice. The few still in their seats are distant enough that they really didn't notice.

He feels jolts as another locomotive is connected and the train is made up for the East. The train his most important friend ever will ride away on while he finishes writing his big story.

Robbie almost strangles on a swelling of profound gratitude for whatever force put him and Paddy Quinn together. Paddy Quinn and that angel wife.

To distract himself from the gut pain, Robbie turns to anticipating the Saluda Cemetery. That bright, beautiful, high place, the enormous oak and maple and chestnut trees. No people up there to get embarrassed at the sight of an old dying soldier's pain. Ever since he started thinking about that place, when he was walking out of the Andersonville gate last March, he has found peace in the image. Respite from pain. He remembers just what corner of the graveyard his Grandfather Joseph Macombie's headstone stands in, and that's where he'll go first. The only Revolutionary War veteran in that whole cemetery, his own grandfather. He has always had pride in that. He remembers the smell of the plane shavings when he helped make his coffin.

The pain comes again, the blindness.

When he can see again, he looks out the window for Paddy, and notices there is indeed still crepe up on the depot building, crepe from the President's stop here, and what look like silvery stars on the crepe. Stars probably representing the states of the Union he held together. Now Robbie's memory turns to the President's corpse and its powdered white face and the mixed smells of death and blossoms so overpowering they might have toppled him over if that Negress, Faith, hadn't steadied him. He thinks of that sketch Paddy did so quickly, of him standing over the casket beside the only Negro woman Robbie ever knew to speak to, the only one who ever touched him. Amazing how fast that man can draw.

Robbie thinks of him now as "Paddy," though he still tends to call him "Mister Quinn."

Remember to call him Paddy when he comes back. He wants me to. Important people must get tired of being talked up to. He doesn't think he's so important. Doesn't even think he was good enough for Mrs. Quinn. I don't know anybody but him that was, though! Just hard to call a great man like that by first name. But it'll be the last time I call him anything.

I know what. I'll call him Son. I'm old enough to be his father, that's sure.

Other people, all civilians, men and women, are climbing into the railroad car now and finding seats. As the car fills, a few passengers pause as if to take the seat facing him, but Paddy's writing desk and satchel are in it.

You're taking a long time to get that wheelchair, Son. Where are you?

Suddenly he has a thought that makes his scalp prickle:

By God, Mister Quinn, you wouldn't be just stalling around out there 'til it's too late for me to get off this train, would you? That would be a lowdown trick!

Robbie is at once suspicious, indignant and almost in a panic. He gathers strength to stand up. He'll get off this train himself if he has to. Damned if he'll get tricked into riding on to Pittsburgh!

He hears two toots of a train whistle. Hears someone yell outside, "Columbus, Pittsburgh, New York! All *aboard*!"

Robbie manages to stay up, weaving, sparks flashing in his head. He clutches at the seatback for support, and turns toward the aisle.

There stands Paddy, who says, "Glad to see you can stand up! Come on. Your chair's right out there."

As Paddy's strong hand closes on his arm, Robbie is ashamed of himself for having had that suspicion. With the help of a black man in a cap and uniform, Paddy carries him to the end of the car and down the steps and eases him down into the wheelchair. But then without even saying goodbye or giving him a handshake he turns away and mounts the steps into the passenger car again.

Robbie is stunned. He didn't even have a chance to call him "Son!" The wheelchair starts moving, pushed by the porter, away from the car. Robbie is about to cry. He must have made Paddy so mad with this Saluda surprise that he doesn't even deserve a decent farewell.

Under the high roof, deafening, a locomotive chuffs up power and cars rattle as the Eastbound train starts moving. Gradually, through his chagrin, Robbie grows aware that he isn't being wheeled toward the depot, but away from it, across tracks and toward another train. "Hey! I need t' go t' the ticket office! Where are we going?"

"This 'ere's your train t' Madison, Cun'l," says the porter.

"Colonel? I'm no colonel!"

The porter chuckles behind him. "Mist' Quinn said you a cun'l, an' the mos' modes' hero o' the whole Wah."

"Why, that's a damn lie! I'm just a private!" he snaps as they come to a stop at the boarding steps of a glossy green passenger car. It's the first time he's ever been mad at Mister Quinn and it feels awful. His heart hurts as much as his gut now.

But now he hears Paddy laughing behind him and saying, "Don't believe him. The son of a bitch just doesn't want to admit he's a damn officer!" Mouth agape, Robbie cranes to look back, and there sure enough is Paddy, with his satchel on his shoulder and his desk under his arm. "You...you.. Hey, what the hell? You're missin' your train!"

"No, I'm not. That one's going East. I've got us two tickets to Madison."

"But, you... You've got to..."

"What I've got to do is see a man who goes through Hell first, *then* to the graveyard."

CHAPTER SEVENTEEN

Madison, Indiana

May 6th, 1865

Paddy stands bone-weary on the loading dock at the railroad depot in Madison, leaning on the back of Robbie's wheelchair, watching the sun come up over the Ohio River, wondering if maybe this was the stupidest choice he's ever made in a lifetime of stupid choices. He can't even imagine how he'll tell Moira Colleen Quinn, his shrewd Irish mother, why he chose to get on this train and just forfeit the greatest story he'd ever had in his grasp.

On the other hand, it hadn't really been a choice. He couldn't just put his dying friend on a train alone and send him away down one railroad, and go himself on another railroad headed somewhere else. As he'd said, he couldn't end Robbie's part of the story until he got him home alive. Just a few miles down the river road is Saluda, the place old Robbie Macombie calls his home, where his uncle lives. Paddy has almost got him home.

Getting here took longer than they'd expected. Track repairs south of Indianapolis had kept the train sitting out in pasturelands most of the night. Paddy had tried to write part of that time by lamplight, but eventually lost heart for it when he finally admitted to himself that he'd just thrown away any chance of getting it to New York by the deadline.

Often during the night Robbie had apologized for making Paddy miss the *Harper's* deadline. Then he'd switch the blame to Paddy, telling him he was a fool to change his own plan. At last Paddy had just told him with a sigh, "A deadline isn't the end of the world."

"A deadline was sure the end of the world at Andersonville,"

Robbie had begun musing then, as if happy to change the subject from the lost story. "I think I told you 'bout that, didn't I? A line four feet inside the stockade, and anyone put so much as a toe over it, he was shot dead."

I just stepped clean over Mister Guernsey's deadline, Paddy had thought then. Best editor I ever had, or probably ever will have again. I should at least telegraph him when we get to Madison and say Sorry, no story.

"Some fellers," Robbie had continued, "they'd just go up and step over that deadline on purpose t'get put out o' their misery. Tried that myself once. But for some reason, the sentry didn't shoot me. It's like I said. God decides whether and when."

Such were the things they'd mused on and talked about as they sat in the stalled train all night hearing the other passengers snore or gripe, windows open for air, moths fluttering in around the lamp, mosquitoes whining. Finally Robbie had slipped away into such a still sleep that Paddy had to check now and then to see if he was still alive.

And now here they are in Madison, a bright spring morning. Below the town flows the broad, blue-green Ohio, known in French as *La Belle Riviere,* and in many Indian languages also "the beautiful river." And it is that. The craggy, forested bluffs of Kentucky soar on the far side. The town of Madison climbs up this north bank, from the river up the bluff, neat tiers of fine storefront establishments and mansions built by the wealth of steamboat commerce. Paddy sees the telegraph office up there, but just can't seem to make himself go up there and send Mr. Guernsey his dismal confession of failure.

Two sternwheel steamboats and a sidewheeler are moored at the quay, being loaded and unloaded, while another sidewheeler, one built on the same design as the *Sultana,* has just churned away headed upriver. Here at the train depot, tired passengers from the tardy train are plodding around or sitting on their luggage waiting for transportation or greeting people who have been waiting all night for their train. Now and then in their conversations Paddy hears the name *Sultana.* Some train passengers are going down to board the steamboats and some steamboat passengers are coming up to the train depot. Paddy has started thinking that he still might at least salvage something of his reputation, by doing the funeral story and a copy of the drawing and sending them by boat down to Blackie at the *New Orleans Picayune*, as he's supposed to do. He thinks he might be able to do them while Robbie is visiting his uncle and the graveyard.

The veteran himself is having a morning indulgence with his tobacco pipe, looking like a smoke-breathing skull. He's gazing around in quiet recognition of this familiar port, when a man's voice calls out from the depot:

"Mister Quinn! Mister Macombie! Hello!" It's a voice Paddy knows but can't quite identify, until he sees a tall, thin figure in officer's uniform hurrying toward him with folded newspapers under his arm, followed by two smaller figures in civilian work clothes.

"Well, I'll be damned! Robbie," he says, turning the wheelchair in their direction, "look who's here. It's that Cap'n Elliott. And your friend Tolbert."

Elliott hurries up, beaming, grabs Paddy's hand in both of his, then, eyes shining, tosses out decorum and wraps his arms around him, slapping him soundly on the back, laughing all the while. Then he stands back, craning backward to look him over, takes his hand again and says, "Ah, yes, that mighty fist o' St. Patrick! And don't *I* know how mighty it is!" He rubs the side of his face; there's no trace visible of the bruising from Paddy's blow. "You know Mister Tolbert here, I remember you interviewed him..." Tolbert nods to Paddy, then stoops to Robbie's chair and takes his hand.

"Welcome home, soldier. So, y' got up to see Mister Lincoln, did ye?"

"I did have that honor, thankee. Best day ever."

"This here's John Maddox. 'Member him? 8th Cavalry with me."

"Sure do. Glad t' see you, neighbor. But I'd heard the Mississippi got ye."

"They was just slow findin' my body. Then found out it was alive."

He and Tolbert exchange glances now, frowning apparently at Robbie's terribly wasted condition. Probably they're amazed that he made the trip all the way up to Springfield and back down here alive. Captain Elliott, in the meantime, seems impatient to be the center of attention again. "Well, as y' know, I chartered the *Belle of Memphis* to bring Indiana survivors up to Cairo. Then we came straight on, and here we are." Paddy senses that Elliott is reminding him of that generous deed in hopes of being mentioned in the *Harper's* article. Paddy doesn't deem it wise to disappoint him, so he doesn't mention that there won't be such an article. "So here we stand," Elliott goes on after a windy sigh, "the Sultana Survivors' Club, you might call us..." He waves his wad of newspapers. "All the newspapers have our story..." There seems to be a terrible nervousness in the captain when he's between words, so he keeps talking. "We really should have, ah, reunions and all, eh? Why, I've already been invited to give a lecture, telling about..." He starts blinking, seems suddenly to have forgotten what he was saying, and is now gazing down at one of the sidewheelers at the quay. Then he seems to come back, and says, "Well, I don't know your plans, but may I suggest a good breakfast? You could look over these papers. Maybe we could arrange to get you on with us for the, uhm, lecture, Mister Quinn? What a crowd we'd draw with a man of your renown.. . River towns are agog over us, already...They say, 'There goes a *Sultana* man.' They don't say an Antietam man or a Gettysburg man. Or an Andersonville man. Just a *Sultana* man..." He takes a deep breath and, eyes sparkling, resumes, "So we'd tell 'em what they want to hear. Just think, telling them about how we three found each other, just that one minute in the middle of that river before daylight, when you tried to give me a drink from your keg but we got separated again? What a show we could give 'em..."

Now, before Paddy can think up an excuse for not participating in such a dreadful lecture, it's Robbie who speaks up. He hasn't much of a voice or breath to speak with, but seems to be taking charge. "Cap'n Elliott, sir, that's a mighty nice invitation, thankee, but, see, Mister Quinn can't stay around for any such a thing... He's on his way t' New York, has a deadline up there. As it is, I already delayed him something awful. Y'see...he was kind enough t' take me up t' see Mister Abe Lincoln...Still more kind t' come out of his way and bring me down here. Promised t' take me up t' Uncle Alexander's house...go see Grandpa's grave at Saluda Cemetery...But then he's got t' get right back on a train for New York." Paddy is impressed by Robbie's quick invention of this excuse, but thankful for it. For all his qualities, Elliott would be tedious and overweening company at this delicate time. Robbie goes on: "Maybe someday, Cap'n, God willin' I live that long, I'll lecture to the local folks myself, tell how I went t' Mister Lincoln's funeral with a pretty Negress on my arm!"

They all look at him, agape. Even Captain Elliott, who had commanded black troops, seems taken aback. But now Tolbert clears his throat and says, "Robbie, I just figured you'd *know* already, but guess y' don't...Your uncle Alexander he passed away last summer..."

"Y' say *what*?"

"Yeah. Sorry. His Missus and all, they moved back up t' Pennsylvania where th'r kin are..."

Robbie slumps, blinking at Tolbert, gone paler than ever. Paddy lays his hand on a shoulder so bony he feels he's touching the wheelchair instead of the man. He can feel this rack-of- bone breathing fast and shallow.

It's a long time before Robbie says, "Well, is he up in Saluda graveyard too?"

"By what I read," Tolbert says.

"Well, then," says Robbie, "we'll visit 'em *both* there, I reckon." He looks up at Paddy.

"You ready, Son?"

Tolbert says, "I can ride y'up. My buckboard's hitched up on Main Street."

"Got room in it for a wheelchair?"

"Sure do."

"We'd be much obliged."

*

On the valley road about three miles out from the town, Romulus Tolbert pulls the reins and the wagon stops in the middle of a wood-timber bridge. Without the rattling of the wagon, there's just the music of falling water.

"This's what they call Clifty Falls," Romulus tells Paddy, pointing up to the right. "In that prison, I dreamt o' this here waterfall."

"Amen," says Robbie, who sits in his wheelchair in the back of the wagon as if the chair were a back seat.

Paddy gazes up at the cascade, which comes spilling and spraying down the shady, mossy cliff for about a hundred feet, Paddy guesses, and he is almost spellbound by the way the falling water shapes itself over the cliff stones and creates a clean-smelling mist that cools the skin of his face and hands. He steps down onto the bridge and leans with his elbows on the oaken bridge rail, gazing at the cascade for a while. Then he looks down to watch the foamy stream settle to limpid clarity and flow under the bridge, down toward the Ohio. He imagines something that he and Felice never had a chance to do: bathe naked together in a pure, Edenic place like this, on some hot summer day. He can hardly bear to visualize that which could have been but won't be. He breathes deeply and blinks, then blows out a sigh. Such a sigh as Felice would have asked the meaning of, if she'd been here to hear it.

When he turns back to the wagon, he sees that Robbie isn't looking up at the waterfall or down at the stream, but is leaning aside and seems to be studying the bridge itself. It's new wood, apparently just recently rebuilt, the oak not even weathered yet, still with its tannic smell so sharp in this cleansed air. Of course Robbie might well be admiring the hewn and fitted joinery of the bridge timbers. He is, after all, a millwright, or was before the war. A builder of gallows when needed. Soldiers aren't just soldiers, they're also whatever else they are.

"Son, do me a favor," Robbie says . "Go back and fetch me a sprig o' that senna, that shrub we passed at the end of the bridge?"

"What, the ferny-looking thing?"

"That's it. Ma used it for stomach aches."

Paddy walks back, selects a slight branch, gets his pen knife out of his pocket to cut it off.

In the wagon, Robbie leans forward in his wheelchair and says in a low voice, "Rom, in that satchel up there you'll find a bottle. Put it under your seat. It's for your kindness of giving us this ride."

"Oh, you don't need to..."

"We insist."

"Well, thank ye, Robb."

"And don't mention it to Mister Quinn. He's kind of bashful when it comes to the graces. Those Irish Catholics are like that."

When Paddy returns and climbs aboard the wagon, Robbie takes the plant, strips off a few leaflets, rubs them between his thumb and fingers, sniffs them, and says, "Thanks, son." He puts some crushed leaflets in his mouth to chew. "Good job on that bridge," he says.

"Yeah. 'Bout time they fixed it up. I 'member it was about to fall down when we joined the Army."

"My brother Jim Alex and I, bless his soul, we used to take a dip under those falls, before Pa moved us back to Pennsylvania. Sure have missed this place," Robbie says. "Clean. *Clean.*"

*

Paddy's first thought in the Saluda graveyard after Tolbert drives away is that he and Robbie should share a toast, on having got here. That's when Robbie tells him he gave their whiskey to Tolbert. Paddy's heart sinks, and then he has a flash of anger. But this is no time to scold or complain, so he says, "That's fair. I should have thought of it."

His second thought is that Felice should have lived to come here with him and see this place. She would love being here, he feels,

feels with intense certainty. And not just because it is beautiful, though it is. On rolling ground at the top of the bluff, behind a modest white frame church, shaded by giant chestnuts and oaks and by maples lacy with catkins. Lilac bushes along the fence, redbud and dogwood blossoms like wisps of pink and white smoke against the fresh spring verdure. The broad, sun-drenched river valley out beyond; dry, mild breeze stirring the fresh green foliage and grasses, songbirds and squirrels everywhere, butterflies swooping and tumbling, all these active little creature lives seeming to belie the mortality manifest in the rows of headstones. Paddy never got to be in a beautiful high place like this with Felice. On the hospital ship where he met her, in New Orleans where he married her, on the *Sultana* where they voyaged on their fatal honeymoon, they had always been down at water level. And yet, they never got in the water together anyplace. He remembers the bathing fantasy he had at the bridge, but it's more painful than pleasurable to imagine it.

He doesn't yet quite understand why Felice is now all at once so resurgent in his feelings. By will power he has fended off her powerful absence during all these travels and travails with Robbie. All that time conceiving and building the story of the funeral pilgrimage, he had tried not to let her loss come forward and distract him. His story wasn't even going to identify her, except as "Felice Beaulieu, one of the Sisters of Mercy," because to specify her as the bride of the author would have made her death disproportionate in an account of 1,700 soldiers dying.

But being here in this place has brought her absence forward and her loss is again all through him and all around. This place is a *whole* place, surrounding him. In his forming of the story Paddy had been looking forward along narrative lines, like going along a railroad or floating between river banks. Now here he is up high, where the horizon is round. For now, at least, he is out of that story, and he can stop progressing forward, can breathe deeply. There is room up here for her absence to sit beside him and watch Robbie lying between the tombstones of his kinsmen, over in that Macombie part of the cemetery. Paddy stays back here on a stone bench in the shade of a chinquapin oak, respecting Robbie's need for solitude, but watching him, trying to forgive him for giving away the whiskey, aware of the probability of seeing him die. Robbie has gotten out of his wheelchair and has been lying supine in the sunny grass and wildflowers between the simple stone slab of his grandfather Joseph's grave and his Uncle Alexander's new marble obelisk. Joseph had been a Scottish immigrant, a mere Revolutionary militiaman eager to fight King George, a hardscrabble farmer. But his son Alexander had distinguished himself as a cavalry officer in the War of 1812, ridden his reputation to prosperity, and become a member of the Indiana Legislature. Of course Robbie would want to lie on this ground that contains them, rather than sit slumped in that wheelchair.

Paddy has pencil and notebook on his lap, intending to start writing the funeral account to send down to the *Picayune* by a southbound steamboat. Maybe he can write it sober. Also, in the back of his mind is the notion that he could just get on a boat at Madison and go back down to New Orleans where his mother lives, and write the *Picayune* story as he goes.

But that would mean going back past that part of the Mississippi above Memphis where they all died. Where Felice died.

That is just out of the question, as yet.

Besides that, he's all out of money at last, and there's no more chance ever of getting Mr. Guernsey to wire him any.

Rolling the pencil between thumb and fingers, he muses on Robbie over there, on the ways he's changed since the President's funeral. Imagine him having the nerve to give that bottle away without asking! Still doesn't call him "Paddy," but has just started addressing him as "Son," which Paddy likes. Though Robbie's body has grown progressively weaker, he is, sure, more forceful in mind and spirit. Paddy remembers him declaring on the train that he is an elder and should be heard. He remembers that Robbie on his own volition decided to come here instead of staying on the train to Pennsylvania. And it was Robbie today who chose not to waste any of his precious remaining hours with the worthy but vainglorious Captain Elliott -- even though it had required that a private refuse a captain's suggestions. How adroitly Robbie had made up that false but plausible excuse that the *Harper's* deadline must still be met.

Of course maybe Robbie said that because he still *believes* it can be met. Paddy knows better, but maybe Robbie doesn't, being, like most everybody, ignorant of editors and deadlines.

Now, everything that would have been that story is just a profusion of scrawled notes and pencil sketches, on papers stacked in a box. There is so much life and death in all that paper and pencil lead and ink that the portfolio should be vibrating and throbbing, but no, it's just inert. Stillborn. It will remain unknown to the world because it won't be midwifed by an editor and publisher.

That story would have been born into the world, to the attention of multitudes, just a few days from now, if Paddy had just decided to stay on the Eastbound train to New York. That simple.

But for some reason, that doesn't seem as important as it should. It's like one of those fantastic dream ideas that vanish into the waters of Lethe with the morning piss.

After all, he thinks, the real tragedies already exist in the world. Why should a printed version be necessary?

That is not a question a professional writer wants to ponder. Success following such a story would have helped him be a better provider for Felice. More worthy of her, that's how he had thought of it when she was alive. But even then, he remembers, she hadn't been at ease with his story's exploitation of the soldiers' suffering. He remembers that she had thought he was using Robbie. He had been learning that it isn't simple living with a high-minded woman. What would she have felt if she'd made it to Mister Lincoln's funeral, and had stood there with Faith and Robbie?

That, he will never get to know. But he will probably wonder about it for years to come.

He does believe she would love this place. It's so much like the place where she grew up in St. Louis: high on a bluff overlooking a great river plied by steamboats. Big trees shading the grass. Here it's tombstones instead of the Beaulieu mansion, but the setting is the same. He remembers the breeze-stirred oak leaf shadows on her front porch, like these dancing on these grave markers. And even that Upper Mississippi shoreline she loved and knew so well couldn't outdo this Ohio River shoreline, the steep, shady, fern-covered cliffs, and especially that splendid cataract that Tolbert called Clifty Falls.

Now Paddy returns to that daydream he had about being naked in the water with her. The reason why they'll never have a chance to do that wondrous thing together is that he had put her on a boat that he sensed was doomed.

And she died in fire, not water.

If only she had jumped into the water when he called her!

He has to turn away from that, but still thinks of her in the water with him. At those beautiful falls, bathing each other. He lets the daydream go on a while, growing aroused by it, and soon is wondering:

What would she think there in Heaven about me getting stiffed-up from imagining her naked? Is this some sort of sacrilege?

No. Why would she mind? She'd understand even more now than when she was alive.

She should have lived long enough for us to bathe together, though, if only once.

The only picture he has of Felice, she's bathing. And no face, just that beautiful back.

I could draw her face, and then I'd have it.

He remembers that he promised himself he'd do that someday. Someday maybe when he wasn't preoccupied with writing a story.

Like right now.

Opening his desk to put away the notebook and get out the drawing pad, he hardly glances at the bathing sketch. He's envisioning her face now.

Over by the Macombie graves, Robbie lies supine in the grass, actually on the grave, it appears now, hands on his bosom, like someone waiting to give up the ghost.

Paddy closes his eyes and makes Felice's image form behind

his eyelids. All the ways he remembers seeing her. Laughing. Pondering. In passion. Even frozen colorless in the photograph from her parents' mantelpiece. Now and then he opens his eyes and draws a deft stroke or two, puts the pencil down, rubs with his thumb to soften a line, make a shadowing. He works rapidly, as he always did on the battlefields. Work too slowly, it doesn't look alive. If he had colors here with him, paint or pastels, that shadow would be blue, first, then he'd lay down the colors of living skin over it and blend them. This is just the sketch from which he'll do the color portrait sometime soon. He thinks:

This is how I would describe of her beauty if I didn't know how to write words.

He remembers that as a small boy in Army garrisons he always had pencils and paper his mother had scrounged for him, and that he had been drawing pictures even before she gave him the gift of literacy, the gift that made him what he is.

The same gift Felice gave to Faith.

He looks up once in a while and sees Robbie still lying there atop his grandfather's grave, supine and serene, like Father Abraham in his casket.

Nothing I can do about it. He came here to do this.

But, damn!

Only man I ever kissed. Or ever will. *That* can go to the grave with him.

But those whiskey transfusions kept us alive. Kept our fires from going out in that cold river.

We have drunk from the same canteen, my friend.

Even by the same mouth.

*

Robbie couldn't have devised a better way than this to find rest at last, after those three years in Hell. Ever since he came out through that prison gate, this is what he'd seen himself coming to: here he lies, close to Grandpa Joseph in the cemetery on the bluff.

The earth is so soft and rich a bed, and it draws his spirit back down into it, back where he came from:

...for dust thou art, and unto dust shalt thou return.

It well could be Grandpa making him so comfortable. One old soldier saying to another, Come on home. Here's where peace is.

Robbie can feel the little bugs in the grass, a lady bird maybe it is tickling his ankle, a gnat crawling behind his ear. Back in the prison those would have been fleas and lice and they would have tormented him. Now these almost feel good.

What doesn't feel so good is that chewed-up senna eating in his stomach like a poison.

Before long I'll know how it feels to be worm food. How it feels to be earth again.

Robbie feels as if he is himself just one big, long, last sigh. Sunlight and leaf shadows dance on the red-gold behind his eyelids.

Take a last look at Mister Quinn over there. He made this possible, bless his big heart.

Best friend ever.

There Paddy Quinn sits, over there under that big chinquapin oak, hair shining sort of reddish when the sun dapples it. As usual bent over a piece of paper with a pencil in his hand.

Robbie shuts his eyes again and thinks about the one thing that he regrets: that his friend gave up so much to get him here. By God, that story should have been in that magazine! Everybody in America should have read about all that. But he'd reckoned it was more important to bring Robbie here to the burial place. Robbie frowns, thinking:

Wonder if he'd feel it was more worthwhile if he'd got me home living, not dying?

Hell, probably so.

*

Felice's eyes have to be drawn more slowly, more carefully. Paddy hones the pencil point on the limestone bench to sharpen it for the details. He leaves white specks to suggest light glinting on the irises. He wipes tears from his own eyes on his sleeve so he can see to draw the details of her eyes.

That's it. Stop. Don't overwork it or you kill it.

Damned good! Now she is here with me on this high place.

He removes the drawing from the pad. When he looks up, Robbie isn't there. There's just his vacant wheelchair parked between two gravestones.

Like that night when he was there in the water hanging onto the keg and then suddenly he wasn't there.

Had to yell and look for him then because he was keeping me alive. Not so now. I can let him go finally.

Paddy, sitting on the bench in oak shade, sun on the grass on the ground and God all around, birds twittering overhead, lays the new sketch of Felice on the bench, and it almost lifts away in the breeze. He pulls the heavy gold San Patricios medallion out of his pocket and puts it on the sheet to hold it down while he puts pencil and pad away. The drawing of Robbie and Faith at Lincoln's casket also seems to want to rise up and ride away on the breeze, but he soon gets everything into the portfolio and latches the lid shut. He wonders whether Robbie will have resurfaced when he looks over there again, the way he did in the Mississippi.

You can sink in a river, but can you just sink into the ground?

Well, it *is* a grave...

He looks over and Robbie still isn't there.

He shuts his eyes and in the dark he sees fire reflecting off water, hears multitudes screaming and praying, feels cold, feels death fathoms below. He draws a deep breath and opens his eyes and Robbie still isn't over there. Paddy gathers himself, gets up. Stoops to pick up the desk.

When he turns to walk over toward the graves, there's Robbie Macombie. Not rising from the grave, but tottering out from behind a lilac bush, buttoning up his trousers. He waves, grinning.

"Hey! Guess what I finally did, son! What y' bet on me walkin' out of this graveyard alive?"

Paddy whoops, almost utters his usual *Hey, I'll drink to that!*

Instead, he says:

"Hey, now! And what'll you bet on me walking out of this graveyard sober?"

THE END

If you enjoyed *Fire in the Water,* read about young Paddy Quinn in *Saint Patrick's Battalion.*

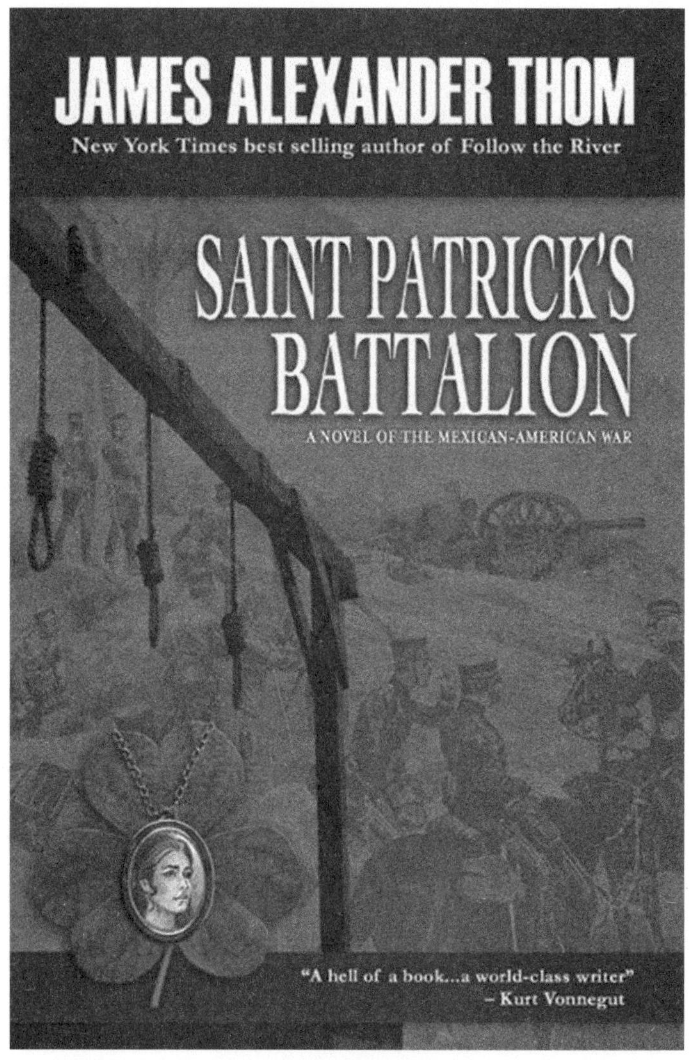

ISBN:978-0-9799240-7-1